Josiah Bull

Memorials of the Rev. William Bull of Newport Pagnel

Josiah Bull

Memorials of the Rev. William Bull of Newport Pagnel

ISBN/EAN: 9783744661348

Printed in Europe, USA, Canada, Australia, Japan

Cover: Foto ©Raphael Reischuk / pixelio.de

More available books at **www.hansebooks.com**

MEMORIALS

OF THE

REV. WILLIAM BULL.

EDINBURGH:
PRINTED BY BALLANTYNE AND COMPANY,
PAUL'S WORK

MEMORIALS

OF THE

REV. WILLIAM 'BULL,'

OF NEWPORT PAGNEL.

COMPILED CHIEFLY FROM HIS OWN LETTERS, AND THOSE
OF HIS FRIENDS,

NEWTON, COWPER, AND THORNTON.

1738—1814.

BY HIS GRANDSON, THE

REV. JOSIAH BULL, M.A.

LONDON:
JAMES NISBET AND CO., 21 BERNERS STREET.
M.DCCC.LXIV.

PREFACE.

It may be right to give some account of the circumstances which have led to the preparation of this volume.

Fifty years have passed since the Rev. William Bull quitted the scenes of earth, and it will perhaps be thought that, however well known and esteemed in his day, the time is gone for any such record as this,—every colour, it may be supposed, has well-nigh faded from the canvas, and almost every link of association with the living must be severed. I trust the volume itself will be the best answer to all such surmises.

The reason, however, for publishing the Memoir at the present time is as follows :— It so happens that the 11th of October of this year (1864) will complete a century since my grandfather, the Rev. William Bull, was ordained Pastor of the Independent Church at Newport Pagnel, and during that long period this church has been presided over by the grandfather, the son, and the grandson in unbroken succession. Under these circumstance, it has been thought right, God willing, to celebrate that approach-

ing day, and to recognise the Divine goodness in connexion with an event so rare in the history of any religious
community.

In the prospect of this service it was necessary to
prepare some fitting memorial, some account of the history of the church and its pastors during that long
period. It soon appeared that, in addition to this, it
would be desirable to publish a distinct life of my grandfather. He was so extraordinary a man, his whole course
full of so many remarkable incidents, and he was so intimately connected with some of the most prominent men
of the religious world in his time, and in addition to all
this, it was found that there existed such ample materials
for a complete history of his life, that I felt a necessity
laid upon me to engage in this work. I knew, also, that
it had been always the purpose of my beloved father to do
something of this kind, and in prosecution of it he had
prepared a number of Memoranda, to which I am indebted
for very many of the incidents of this volume, and entirely
for those of the first chapter. I feel, therefore, that in
undertaking this task, I am acting in accordance with one
of the most cherished wishes of his life. But, in addition
to all this, I cannot help thinking it will be found that
there is so much of vital truth, of originality, and of real
interest in the following pages, that to have repressed
them would have been a positive neglect of duty, and a
great wrong to the many who, I trust, may be benefited
by them.

It will be seen that, during my grandfather's frequent absences from home, he was in the habit of writing daily to Mrs Bull or his son; and when the latter was out, letters were sent to him almost as frequently. All these communications have been preserved, and give the book, to some extent, the character of an autobiography, and so almost the freshness of a recent narrative, while they are rich in interesting facts and valuable sentiment, and all written during a very eventful period of our political and religious history.

There must of necessity be some grave omissions in the history of a life published fifty years after the removal of its subject, yet even this circumstance is not without some peculiar advantages. Many statements which would give interest to a narrative of more recent events must often be kept back from feelings of delicacy, which years after may be mentioned without impropriety; and many names which it might be offensive to parade while those who bore them or their near connexions were living, may be introduced instead of the unsatisfactory blanks which must otherwise supply their place. Even faults and blemishes of character may be spoken of with less reserve, and so one of the great lessons of biography not be lost sight of.

It has, of course, been a work of no small labour to gather together and arrange the materials for this Memoir: to peruse some fifteen hundred letters, many of them in short hand, selecting from them the most appropriate passages; and to collect from various sources what information could be obtained; but I can truly say it has been a labour of love thus to endeavour to embalm the memory of a revered ancestor. I can only hope that the perusal of these remains may prove as pleasant and as profitable to others as it has been to myself. I remember little of my grandfather, or little else than his tall commanding figure, and his tender affection for his grandchildren; but he seems, even to me, to have lived over again in my father's often loving references and deep veneration for his memory, and in the many incidents he would relate of the long and happy intercourse he enjoyed with him.

There are quotations in this book from the published letters of Newton, Rowland Hill, and the poet Cowper; but I think I need no apology for their introduction, inasmuch as they are inserted not so much for their intrinsic value, as because they are essential to the completeness of the narrative. The larger portion of these extracts is moreover from a volume of " Newton's Letters to Mr Bull," published a few years since, and which passed through only one edition, and consequently is but little known. Now, it is obvious that letters thus forming an integral part of a narrative are really a different thing from the same letters following one another in succession, and without any such connecting links. There is all the difference between scattered pearls and those pearls strung together as a graceful ornament, between detached portions of mosaic and that mosaic in its completeness.

There are more things I might say, and almost wish to

say, but I don't suppose there are many who have any great partiality to long prefaces; I will therefore conclude by thanking those friends who, in different ways, have aided me in connexion with this publication; and will only add that, while I have endeavoured to use my best judgment in its compilation, I still fear that it will be found to contain many imperfections. Nevertheless, I venture to hope that it may, in its measure, promote the Divine glory by becoming a source of interest and edification to many.

J. B.

Newport Parsonage, *July* 22, 1864.

CONTENTS.

CHAPTER I.

1738-1761.

CHAPTER II.

1660-1764.

CHAPTER III.

1764-1779.

CHAPTER VIII.

1786-1788.

CHAPTER IX.

1789-1790.

CHAPTER X.

1791-1793.

CHAPTER XI.

1794-1796.

CHAPTER XII.

1797-1800.

CHAPTER XIII.

1801-1802.

CHAPTER XIV.

1803.

CHAPTER XV.

1804-1805.

CHAPTER XVI.

1806-1814.

CHAPTER XVII.

MEMORIALS.

CHAPTER I.

EARLY LIFE OF THE REV. WILLIAM BULL.
1738-64.

His parentage—Anecdotes of the Rev. J. Heywood—Remarkable deliverances
of William Bull in his early life—Residence with his grandfather—Story
of a text—Puritan strictness—The Rev. Mr French—William Bull's extraordinary memory—The Rev. James Hervey—Thirst for knowledge—
Hebrew Bible—Mathematics—Early religious history and experience—
Removal to Bedford—Aided in his studies by the Rev. Messrs Saunderson and Belsham—Admitted a student at Daventry—His tutors and
fellow-students—His orthodoxy—Burying the beer—Illness—First visit
to Newport Pagnel—Invitation to become pastor of the church there
—Mr Whitfield—Ordination.

FOUR miles north-east of the town of Wellingborough, in
Northamptonshire, is the village of Irthlingborough. In
this place there lived early in the last century a godly
Puritan—Francis Bull. He was the son of John Bull of
Rushden, in the same county. He did not belong to the
wealthier class, nor could he boast of an exalted pedigree.
Yet, though but a simple yeoman, living upon his own
little freehold, his strong understanding, his perfect integrity, and, above all, his strict and holy life gave him a position and influence which more showy pretensions alone can

A

never command. Francis Bull was not, however, without some external recommendations, for his personal appearance was very imposing; and all his family, consisting of four sons and one daughter, were more or less remarkable for a like endowment. My father, speaking in his memoranda of the daughter of Francis Bull, and the youngest of the family, says, that on one occasion she came on a visit to Newport, and, though more than seventy years of age, she was the finest old woman he ever saw; tall, well-made, perfectly upright, and with a complexion still retaining much of its youthful freshness.

Like other Puritans of that day, this godly man was a warm friend of the House of Hanover; and in the rebellion of 1745 he furnished a horse, and sent one of his sons, John Bull, to join the army marching against the Pretender.

The eldest son of Francis Bull was Christopher. He lived at Brigstock, and was, like his father, a truly godly man, and zealous in the promotion of the truth. He engaged in a controversy with the Rev. Mr Wildman, a Dissenting minister at Kimbolton, on the question of preaching to sinners. His house was open to Doddridge and other ministers who visited Brigstock to preach the gospel, and whose labours eventually resulted in the formation of an Independent church there.*

Amongst these ministerial guests there was a very remarkable man—the Rev. John Heywood, of Potters Pury, in Northamptonshire, who was always entertained with great gladness and hospitality whenever he came that way

---

* See Coleman's History of the Northamptonshire Churches, p. 314, &c.

in his preaching excursions. Such journeys, performed on horseback, were common in those days, their principal object being to visit the more destitute villages where there were no regular Dissenting congregations, the ministers preaching in houses and other suitable places. Mr Heywood, especially, seems to have made very long tours in the accomplishment of this important work, periodically visiting the spiritually destitute part of the counties of Northampton, Cambridge, and Lincoln.

It may not be uninteresting here to interpose some facts and anecdotes respecting this singular man. I can never forget how well, and with what perfect ease and zest they were often repeated by my father, to whose knowledge they had come through very direct channels.

Mr Heywood was the nephew of the well-known Oliver Heywood, and, as we have stated, he was the pastor of an Independent church at Potters Pury. It may be difficult to say whether Mr Heywood was most remarkable for his eccentricities, his great learning and wit, or his piety and devotedness. He certainly possessed all these characteristics in no common measure. A sister of my grandfather, in her early life, kept the house of her relative, Christopher Bull, who so often entertained Mr Heywood. In her latter years she resided with her brother, and used to speak of Mr Heywood's appearance as very grotesque, as he rode up to the house on his old gray horse, which seemed little more than skin and bone, attired in leather breeches and enormous jack boots, with a large wig and well-worn coat to match.

It is told of him that on one occasion as he was riding into Cambridge he was met by three collegians, who, in their simplicity, thought to make sport of the quaint-looking figure they saw approaching; so, going a little in advance one of another, the first said, as Mr Heywood came up, "Well, Father Abraham;" the second, "Well, Father Isaac;" and the third, "Well, Father Jacob." Upon which, the good man bade them stop, and thus smartly answered their folly:—"Young men, I am neither Father Abraham, nor Father Isaac, nor Father Jacob, but if ye would liken me unto any Scripture character, I think I may be compared to Saul, the son of Kish, who went out to seek his father's asses, and lo! here I have found them." He then rode on, leaving these youths to digest his witty rebuke of their impertinence as best they might.*

Mr Heywood's acquaintance was sought in some instances by those who occupied a very different position from that in which he generally moved. Earl Temple, especially, regularly invited him once a year to his seat at Stow, when he would often surprise his friends by the extent and accuracy of the learning of the humble Dissenting pastor. He used to call him his "Chronological Table."

Mr Heywood was strongly attached to the House of Hanover; and upon the accession of George III. to the throne he was anxious to give expression to his loyalty, and determined to go up with the Dissenting ministers of London when they should present their address. Mr

* This story, I know, has been told of others, but I have reason to think I am correct in attributing it to this remarkable man.

Heywood was told that he could not go with them; it was informal,—country ministers were not admitted on these occasions. But the remonstrance was to no purpose, and the result was amusing enough. While the party were waiting to be presented, Mr Heywood encountered his friend Lord Temple. He was soon in earnest conversation with that nobleman, when the latter observing the ministers coming away from the king, told Mr Heywood that he would lose his opportunity. "No," he said, "I will not;" and just as the king was quitting the place of audience he approached him. The king paused, and very condescendingly received the ardent expressions of loyalty poured forth by his eccentric subject—not a little, it may be supposed, to the astonishment of Mr Heywood's metropolitan brethren.

At a later period this good man was well known to my grandfather, who, when he came to Newport, was within a few miles of Pury. He preached Mr Heywood's funeral sermon in the year 1778.

But to return to our narrative. The fourth son of Francis Bull was John Bull. He unhappily did not tread in the steps of his excellent father. He fell into evil courses, and married a person who had little sympathy with the puritanical predilections and practices of his family. She had five children, of whom the third was William, the subject of our memoir. The father neglected his business, and brought himself and his family into great straits; and so—and it affords a most striking illustration of the wonderful working of God's providence —the children of this family were taken under the roof of their pious grandfather, Francis Bull, and brought up by him.

It was on the 22d of December 1738 that William Bull was born. His early life was eventful, and, from the circumstances just referred to, in a great measure dependant. Three several times, when quite a child, he narrowly escaped a fatal termination of his earthly existence. Once he fell into a well, and was not rescued until animation was suspended; and was with great difficulty restored. On another occasion, one of his father's companions swam with him on his back across a deep part of the river; the child fell in; but his father, standing on the bank, and being a good swimmer, jumped into the water, dived down, and rescued him. And yet again, on a third occasion, he was very dangerously hit by a stone upon the head, and carried the scar to his grave. But God had a work for him to do, and so, preserved like others who have afterwards become useful and distinguished in the Church, that life was spared.

It was probably soon after William Bull went to reside with his grandfather that a circumstance occurred hardly worth putting into print, but as connected with an event of interest in his future history. It appears that a good man, named Twelvetrees, then young, and certainly in some respects but very imperfectly qualified to instruct his neighbours, was to preach to the villagers of Irthlingborough. My grandfather was taken to hear him. The good man's text was that striking passage in the Revelation: "Write, Blessed are the dead that die in the Lord." And he gave the following very original division of the words :—" We shall consider," he said, "who are *right* blessed, and who are *wrong* blessed." This very odd treatment of the passage amazingly tickled the fancy of the shrewd child who was listening to him, and, forgetting where he was, he broke out into a loud laugh ; whereupon the preacher, all unconscious of the cause, bade them turn out the little curly-pated boy who was behaving so irreverently in the house of God.

Living with his grandfather, William Bull was brought up in all Puritan strictness. The family was gathered together early on Sabbath morning, and the day was commenced with reading for a considerable time from Poole's, or the Assembly's, Annotations. They then proceeded to Wellingborough, to attend public worship at the meeting-house in Cheese Lane. The interval between the morning and afternoon services was spent in the vestry in reading the Scriptures and prayer; and then the venerable patriarch and his family returned to their home and passed the evening in religious exercises. On this sacred day no idle words were allowed, and scarcely might a smile play upon the countenance. If these good men erred on the side of strictness, we in more modern times have too surely found our way to the opposite extreme.

The minister at Cheese Lane at that time was the Rev. Mr French. He afterwards removed to Ware, in Hertfordshire.* William Bull was in the habit of writing Mr French's sermons, and a little desk was put up for his

* In Mr French's congregation was a lady equally remarkable for her large bodily proportions and for her loquacity, which latter failing was sometimes a source of annoyance to the good man. She one day said to

use in his grandfather's pew, and for many years it was carefully preserved. He was possessed of a very extraordinary memory; so that when on one occasion he was taken to Weston Flavel, being then about twelve or fourteen years of age, on condition of his remembering Mr Hervey's sermon and repeating it on his return, he without difficulty accomplished the task. He related many years afterwards to my father, that although it was only an ordinary service, the church was crowded to excess, and that the windows were removed that the people outside might hear. Mr Hervey was then in the last stage of a consumption, was pale and thin, and when he stretched out his hand, as the sun shone upon it, it was rendered almost transparent. There was one passage in the sermon to which Mr Bull would sometimes refer. Mr Hervey was speaking of the remains of corruption in a good man while in this world. "You have observed," he said, "the walls on either side the path leading to this church. They are covered, as you know, with ivy. Now you may pluck off the leaves, and break off the branches so that none of them shall be seen on the outside; but the roots of the plant have so worked themselves into the wall, that it would be impossible entirely to eradicate them without taking down the wall, and not leaving one stone upon

him, "If I were to die, and you were to write my epitaph. I wonder what you would say." Mr French immediately returned this smart impromptu reply :—

> " Beneath this stone, full six feet long,
>> And eke as many round,
>> Lies one who never held her tongue,
>> Till silent under ground."

another. And so must this frail body be taken down; and then, and not till then, shall we get rid of the remains of a degenerate nature."

The subject of our memoir at a very early period of life discovered an ardent desire for the acquisition of knowledge. All the money he could possibly spare was spent in the purchase of books; and he submitted to many privations to increase his store. Thus he became possessed of a Hebrew Bible, hoping the time would come when he should be able to read it. He had an elder brother, Francis, who at that time had little sympathy with him in his pursuit of knowledge, though he afterwards became a student and a minister; and on one occasion he turned out all his books into the street. "More than fifty years afterwards," says his son, "I visited Irthlingborough with my father, and he pointed out to me the spot, saying, 'While I live I shall never forget the pang I felt when I saw my beloved books thrown into the road.'" These books were kept in an outbuilding, which was William Bull's study, and his oratory too. Even then it was his desire, and often his fervent prayer, that God would make him a minister of the gospel; influenced possibly at that time, in part at least, by a desire to gratify his thirst for knowledge.

The Hebrew Bible was often looked at, and the earnest desire to read it grew into a resolve to accomplish the task. But how was it to be accomplished? He had no tutor, no grammar, no lexicon. All the help he had was an old Bible, which had the Hebrew letters heading the different sections of the 119th psalm. With this slightest possible aid, he commenced his task. He at once saw that the Hebrew Bible began at what with us is the end. The first word he knew must be either " in " or " in the beginning." He looked in his Concordance (it was a Cambridge Concordance, which I possess to this day) for other places where the word beginning occurred, and finding the same letters, he wrote down the word Berasheeth, (in the beginning;) and thus, with amazing pains, proceeded to make out the text, word by word, till he had formed for himself a rude lexicon, and at length a grammar, and was able to read his Hebrew Bible tolerably well,—a marvellous proof of his thirst for knowledge and of his skill in its acquisition. It is no wonder that the Hebrew was always afterwards a favourite study with him. These particulars were recorded and written down by my father from the lips of my grandfather. William Bull also became possessed of Whiston's Mathematics, and he made such progress in this science as to become a contributor to Martin's *Mathematical Magazine.*

It happened that there was another youth in the same village, named Thomas Smith, who, like William Bull, was bent on the pursuit of knowledge; and as far as they were able they were helpers of each other. A clergyman in the neighbourhood had taken notice of Smith. It was the Rev. Mr Jones, then curate of Finedon. He was afterwards known as " Trinity Jones," and was the author of the Life of Bishop Horne, and of several other works. Smith mentioned the name of his friend to Mr Jones ; but the latter, finding he was a Dissenter, would have nothing to do with him. This young man was afterwards sent to Cambridge through the influence of Mr Jones, and eventually became one of the East India Company's chaplains.

William Bull continued to live with his grandfather, probably assisting him in his business. He appears to have suffered a good deal from ill health, and may have injured himself by his devotion to study. His earnest desire was to give up his secular occupation, and to devote himself to the ministry. At length Providence opened the way. His elder brother John had settled in business at Bedford; and he mentioned to his minister, the Rev. Samuel Saunderson, the circumstances of his younger brother. The result was that he came to Bedford, was introduced to Mr Saunderson, who was struck with his piety and his talents, and determined to aid him in the accomplishment of his wishes.

Before stating the results of this change in his career, it may not be uninteresting to give some account of the religious history and experience of William Bull during the time of his youth and early manhood; and we are enabled to do this from two documents which have happily been preserved—the first being a lengthened statement of his religious experience, presented to the church at Bedford when he was proposed as a candidate for its fellowship; and the other a brief diary or series of meditations, written just before he left Irthlingborough in the year 1758.

In the statement referred to he says,—" In the beginning of my tenth year very much activity of thought discovered itself in me. I began to inquire what I was, by whom created, and for what end I was sent into the world, and what was the wisest method of conducting myself in it.

A dread of the future was before me, and I applied myself to prayer, that I might be saved from sin and the wrath to come. But my convictions wore off, and I satisfied myself with a round of duties, not doubting that in the end I should be brought to heaven by Jesus Christ. Thus I continued till I was about fourteen years of age, when I was deeply moved by a sermon preached by Mr French from Jer. xxxi. 18, 'I have surely heard Ephraim bemoaning himself,' &c. I found that I had been building my hopes upon the sand of a few childish notions, that I had a heart within me full of corruption and apostasy from God—hard as the ground I trod upon—and that I should assuredly have been lost if I had died at that time. Then was I led to cry and pray to God to enlighten and cleanse me. The hearing of the gospel now became quite another thing from what it had been. I perceived that the depths of hell were before me, a world of sin and iniquity within me, the wrath of God just overtaking me. I feared to speak of the unease of my mind to any one but God, and I found God better to me than my doubts and fears. This great work had made but small progress before I fell into temptation, and was frequently questioning my sincerity, the devil and my own deceitful heart seeking to persuade me that none were called by grace at so early a period of life. But just at this time a sermon I heard from the text, 'They that seek me early shall find me,' in God's gracious providence, dissipated these delusions. At another time when I was full of trouble, mingling my prayers with many tears to my heavenly Father, mourning that I had no stronger evidence of his presence, and fearing that I was but an almost Christian, these words came to my mind, 'Fear not, I am with,' &c.; and other passages were applied with great power to my soul. I derived also much benefit from the perusal of 'Doddridge's Rise and Progress.'

"This state of mind continued till I was about sixteen or seventeen years of age; and how shall I with sufficient concern relate the relapses into which I then fell! My mind was filled with the vanity and self-conceit of youth. Again I grew comparatively indifferent to spiritual religion, satisfying myself with its outward form; but in the beginning of my eighteenth year I was visited with a violent attack of fever, and brought so low that my life was despaired of; and while I thus lay upon the brink of eternity I was under the most racking torture of despair. What would I then have given for the presence of God as I had enjoyed it in times past! But, while thus afflicted, it pleased God to give me such a sense of my sinfulness that I was led to humble myself in the dust before Him. At times I had such views of the heavenly state, that I longed to depart and to be with Christ.

"As my affliction was removed I found my affections every day going more and more out after the ever-blessed God; and it now became my great concern how I should walk more uprightly before Him, who was the great object of all my desire and my delight. Still I longed to possess some testimony, some fuller assurance of the reality of my faith in Christ. And one day, walking disconsolately in

the fields, and pouring out my heart before God, these lines
of Young came into my mind,—

> 'Believe, and shew the reason of a man;
> Believe, and taste the pleasures of a God;
> Believe, and look with triumph on the tomb.'

This simple idea led me to cast myself more entirely upon
Christ, and my soul was filled with peace and joy. This
state of mind was confirmed by a sermon I heard from the
words, 'Return, O Shulamite, return, that we may look
upon thee.' I thought that then I had truly tasted that
the Lord was gracious. Christ seemed more than ever the
object of my delight. I could say with Mrs Rowe, 'If I
love Thee not, my blessed God, I know not what I love; if
I am uncertain of this, I am uncertain of my existence.'"

He then speaks of temptations which at this time befell
him. He was tempted to think whether the Roman
Catholic religion might not be as acceptable to God as the
Protestant faith; whether Paganism or Mohammedanism
might not be true; whether or not the Bible was inspired,
and Christian experience a mere delusion; or, if these
things were true, whether his personal hope of an interest
in Christ might not be, after all, false. "These thoughts,"
he says, "led me to fervent prayer, and to inquire with
the utmost diligence into the evidences of the Christian
religion, searching the Scriptures daily if these things were
so; and, blessed be God, I found the sacred writings themselves chiefly instrumental in establishing me in the firm
persuasion that they were the oracles of God, and that if
ever I should be saved from the ruin sin had brought
upon me, it must be wholly and alone by the righteous-

ness of Christ, of which I could have no stronger evidence than in the work of God wrought in the heart by the Holy Ghost. The reading of 'Bennett on the Inspiration of the Scriptures' was at that time of great use to me."

He speaks of his desire to go into the ministry as another source of great anxiety and doubt. "I thought," he says, "that the Lord might permit me to rise to the highest pitch of profession that an almost Christian could arrive at before I fell away; then in the end my fall would be the greater. My earnest prayer was, that the Lord would give me grace and wisdom that I might not bring dishonour on the cause of Christ, the object of my highest veneration and delight. I thought that it would not be a greater trouble to me to perish for ever."

In speaking at the close of this statement of God's providence, he says :—" Permit me to observe that, in a word, it seems to me to have been, from my cradle to this hour, a miracle of mercy, on which I can never reflect without holy admiration and wonder, and sentiments of the most affectionate gratitude and love to the glorious Author of my being; and, at the same time, with inward shame and self-abasement that I have rendered Him such poor returns, and have been altogether so unworthy of the least of the ten thousand mercies He has bestowed upon me."

The exercises of mind through which Mr Bull was called to pass will also appear in the following brief extracts from a diary kept by him for a few months before his residence at Bedford. It was written when he was twenty years of age, and is somewhat after the manner of Mrs Rowe's devout exercises. It is entitled, "Daily instances of the Divine favour and condescension of the Almighty to the most unworthy and meanest of all his creatures, William Bull."

We find him sometimes deeply oppressed with a sense of his sinfulness, and struggling with unbelief:—" Every day brings fresh discoveries of my own unworthiness. I see I am more and more abominable; yet in very death I will trust Thee. My sins are a burden heavier than I can bear; the very ground rises up in judgment against me; the firmament records my wickedness; the brute creation upbraids me; yet will I hope in Thee." At other times he mourns over his coldness and formality:—" How little thankful am I for Thy tender mercies, O Lord. How feeble are my desires after Thee! I am carnal, sold under sin; my vain thoughts are numerous, and I cannot overcome them." He constantly acknowledges his utter helplessness, and his need of Divine influence.

Again, we find him giving utterance to his joy in the Lord:—" Oh, what has the Lord done for my soul! This day Thou hast poured forth Thy Spirit upon me. O that I had words to tell how earnestly I love Thee—what longing to be washed in Thy blood; to be born again of Thy Spirit! Take away all worldly blessings; give me Christ, and I shall be happy. Arise my passions to burn with love equal to my will and my desires, and I shall enjoy a heaven upon earth. Whithersoever Thou goest, I will take up my cross and follow Thee." And once more:—" Lord, I subscribe to Thy faithfulness in the presence of all Thy holy angels; I attest and record the power of Thy grace, in contempt of all my future doubts, and the power of all my enemies. Oh, blessed be Thy name that, being justified by faith, I have peace with God, through my Lord and Saviour Jesus Christ. Oh, I rejoice in Thee, my Jesus, with joy unspeakable and full of glory."

At the close of the diary there are some expressions which seem to have reference to the opening up of his way to enter upon the ministry, when he says:—" Thou hast answered my prayer, O Lord, and dost go before me; therefore, O my God, I will praise Thy holy name." And again, " Thou hast fully granted the thing I have so earnestly sought of Thee."

These extracts will hardly be thought too long by the devout readers of this volume, inasmuch as they not only furnish an insight into the different phases of religious experience through which one individual mind was called to pass, but may afford matter of edification and comfort to the souls of others.

And now we find the subject of our memoir at Bedford, where Mr Saunderson is ready in every way to forward his wishes. His pursuit of knowledge, though ardent and various, had hitherto been desultory. So, to begin at the beginning, though there is evidence that he had some knowledge of Latin, his friend put into his hand " Ruddiman's Rudiments." To Mr Saunderson's astonishment he found that in a *single fortnight* he had made himself perfect master of the entire book. The Rev. J. Belsham was at that time pastor of the church at Newport, but resided at Bedford. He was a profound scholar, and upon Mr Saunderson's mentioning to him the extraordinary talents of his pupil, he at once offered to assist him in the study of the Greek language.

Living with his brother, and without any other demands upon him, William Bull was now able to devote his whole time to study. He attended Mr Saunderson's ministry, of which he speaks as exceedingly useful to him. When he first came to Bedford his mind was greatly depressed; "but it pleased God," he says, " to bless the ministry of this excellent man, and to make it the means of giving me clearer views of the Gospel, and stronger hopes of my interest in its blessings. I seemed to feel the dawnings of the Sun of Righteousness on my soul. I never before experienced so much pleasure or benefit from hearing; and I often thought, if he had been informed of the state of my mind, he could not have expressed my wants and described my various desires before the throne of Almighty grace with greater exactness."

At length, in the year 1759, Mr Bull was admitted a student at the Dissenting Academy at Daventry. It was then under the charge of Dr Ashworth, who had succeeded Doddridge as tutor. It will be readily supposed with what gladness and thankfulness of heart my grandfather thus saw the fulfilment of long years of prayer and of hope; every means for the acquisition of knowledge now within his reach, and the desire of his heart to serve Christ in the ministry of the Gospel likely soon to be realised.

Dr Ashworth, who presided over the Institution, was a man well qualified for his work. He had been a pupil of Dr Doddridge. He was orthodox in sentiment, a rigid disciplinarian, and perhaps not of the most yielding temper. At any rate, he was strongly impressed with the evils which had resulted from the too great laxity of his amiable and excellent predecessor; and it may be that he erred by going to the other extreme. The classical tutor was the Rev. T. Taylor, and after him came, during the time of Mr Bull, the Rev. Noah Hill. Mr Taylor afterwards preached at Carter Lane, in London; and was inclined to Arianism. Mr Hill was thoroughly evangelical. Some of the students at that time had a leaning to Arianism, or even to Socinianism. Dr Priestley had left the Academy just before my grandfather entered it. Mr Bull's opinions, however, were decidedly Calvinistic. He had imbibed them, as he used to say, from his infancy, and was confirmed in them by his beloved friend Mr Saunderson. He had now to pass through a severe ordeal, and was continually exposed to attacks from his companions, many of whom were becoming more and more wide in their opinions.

Priestley was then entering on his career of error, and his writings were read by the students with avidity. He came to Daventry while Mr Bull was there; but such was the displeasure which some of his books had created in the mind of Dr Ashworth, that he would not see him.

Notwithstanding these differences of opinion amongst the students, the good temper, lively imagination, and great talents of William Bull made him a universal favourite. In the college, amongst its members at that time, were several young men of ability, as Enfield, afterwards Dr Enfield, author of the " History of Philosophy " and other works; the Rev. Samuel Palmer, of Hackney. who published the abridgment of the " Nonconformist Memorial;" and Mr Henley, who conformed to the Church, and became President of the East India College at Hertford.

It is matter of little surprise that young men, and even young men preparing for the Christian ministry, should not always act the part of "grave and reverend" seniors, and that fun and frolic did sometimes a little exceed the bounds of propriety. And so it happened, as my grandfather used to tell, that on one occasion when the students had grown somewhat tired of the beer with which they were supplied, they unanimously voted that it was not only very small, but dead; and that being dead, it ought to be buried. Accordingly, it was resolved without delay to perform the ceremony. A large can of the liquor was obtained, and carried at the head of a procession of all the students, wearing the tokens of mourning, preceded by William Bull, arrayed in a surplice formed of sheets of white paper; and when the dead beer was solemnly poured upon the ground, a funeral oration was pronounced by him with all the wit and cleverness for which he was so distinguished.

Nature had bestowed upon him great comic powers, so that at this period of his life he could at any time awaken the laughter of those around him. Possibly his talents in this direction were a snare to him, and the companionship by which he was surrounded was injurious to his religious progress. However this might be, it pleased God to visit him during his residence at Daventry with a very severe affliction. Incessant application to study brought on a brain fever. His life was in great peril, and his reason fled. He gradually recovered, but not without permanent loss of intellectual power and nervous vigour. Before this attack, Mr Bull possessed a memory of extraordinary receptiveness and tenacity. He could repeat the substance of a newspaper after having read it once or twice, and his feat with Ruddiman is another striking instance of this capacity. His memory always continued what is termed "good," but it ceased to be extraordinary. His nervous system, too, suffered greatly; and he was ever afterwards more or less the subject of depression and hypochondriasis. There is no doubt, however, that this chastisement was greatly blessed to him in quickening that religious life which probably had in a measure become deadened by his assiduous studies, and by other circumstances to which reference has been made.

Mr Bull's vacations were chiefly spent at Bedford. On one of these occasions Mr Belsham, who, it will be remembered, preached at Newport Pagnel, but resided at Bedford, was ill, and unable to take his accustomed duty. Difficulty was found in getting any one to supply his place. My grandfather had not at that time entered what was termed at Daventry "the preaching class," to which the students were not admitted till their fourth year. For him, therefore, to supply a regular congregation was a violation of discipline. At length it was agreed that Mr Bull should go to Newport, and after informing the congregation of the illness of their pastor, *read* a printed sermon of Dr Watts. Thus furnished, he went to supply the place of Mr Belsham. He read his sermon with so much propriety and animation, that the attention of the people was aroused to a degree not very common with them; and when, spite of college law, he could not refrain from concluding with an extempore appeal to his audience, his congregation was still more impressed, so striking was the contrast to the heavy and learned discourses to which they were accustomed to listen. And thus Mr Bull most unexpectedly preached his first sermon in a pulpit he was destined of Providence to fill with such benefit to many for fifty years of his life.

When my grandfather entered the preaching class he at once became very popular. Mr Palmer, who left the academy a little before him, says, in a letter written about this time,—"Your preaching was highly acceptable at Bedford, and Mr Saunderson told me he hoped you would shortly be his assistant." This was urged subsequently as a reason to dissuade him from settling at Newport. As his term of study drew towards its close, several congregations, it was said by his friends, would be glad of his services. Dr Ashworth was very desirous he should go to Rotterdam to preach at the English church there, a situation in many respects desirable. In the midst of these deliberations an earnest invitation came from the church at Newport; and though there were at that time but few attractions to the place,—the church being greatly reduced, and there being little scope for a man of Mr Bull's powers,— yet was he strangely drawn to this sphere of labour; and almost in opposition to the wishes of his best friends, he accepted the call. By what motives he was influenced in this choice it is vain now to inquire; possibly his state of nervous depression might lead him to fear at that time entering upon a larger sphere.

During the last week of Mr Bull's residence at Daventry, Mr Whitfield came into the neighbourhood, and preached at Long Buckby. He went to hear him, and was greatly delighted and affected with the sermon, which was addressed to an immense congregation in a field. The distance was considerable, and Mr Bull did not get back to Daventry within canonical hours, when, according to custom, the door was fastened, and the key brought into Dr Ashworth's study. His knock was heard, but unheeded, though the cause of Mr Bull's absence was well known; and it was his last night at college. The key could not be obtained; but the other tutor, Mr Hill, was not quite so inflexible. He opened the library window, and so admitted him into the house. The next day the two principal gentlemen connected with the congregation at Newport arrived at Daventry, and took Mr Bull back with them.

The letters of Mr Saunderson, written to Mr Bull while a student at Daventry, abundantly prove the great esteem and affection in which he held him. He repeatedly urges him to exercise prudence and caution in his studies, especially after the severe illness of which mention has been made. Dr Ashworth, too, had the highest opinion of him, and was very anxious he should remain at Daventry for a fifth year, considering the great natural abilities he possessed.

Arrived at Newport, he became for a time the guest of Mr Beaty; and it is remarkable, that as this was the first house and the first family he visited when he came into the town, so, after an interval of fifty years, it was the last, having dined there just a week before his death. Mr

Bull's preaching at once excited attention, and there were few persons of respectability in Newport who did not occasionally attend his ministry. He soon received a unanimous call to the pastorate, and was ordained 11th October 1764. Some few days before his ordination Mr Saunderson sent him the following letter, shewing his jealous concern that his orthodoxy might not be questioned :—

" DEAR SIR,—I cannot, without great inconvenience, be at Newport before Thursday morning; and as I find that you have ordered matters so that I am neither to see you, nor your confession of faith before it is delivered, you will give me leave to tell you, out of friendship, that as you profess yourself to be a Calvinist in regard to the great doctrinal points of Christianity, you will very much disappoint me, and, I daresay, disgust many of your real friends, if you don't express yourself explicitly and clearly in your confession. It is my most hearty desire, and shall be my prayer to God, that you, and all who are to engage in the solemn work of next Thursday, may acquit themselves well, and that it may be a good day to both ministers and people.—I am, dear Sir, your very faithful affec. friend and brother,   SAMUEL SAUNDERSON.
" BEDFORD, *Oct.* 6, 1764."

The following ministers were engaged in the ordination services :—The Rev. Dr Ashworth of Daventry, and the Rev. Messrs Saunderson of Bedford, Drake of Olney, Benjamin Boice of Kettering, W. Hexhall of Northampton, S. Addington of Harborough, R. Denny of Long Buckby, and T. Strange of Kilsby.

CHAPTER II.

ORIGIN AND EARLY HISTORY OF THE INDEPENDENT CHURCH AT NEWPORT PAGNEL.

1660–1764.

HAVING reached this important period in Mr Bull's history, it will not be out of place to give some account of the church with which he was now so closely connected. To this subject I purpose to devote the present chapter; and for its details I am in great part indebted to a brief narrative of the history of the church at Newport Pagnel published by my father some fifty years since.

There is surely a peculiar interest attaching to such records; for, brief and fragmentary as they too often are, they have to do with the development and progress of the highest forms of truth, and with the earnest and self-denying contendings of its advocates. Our belief is, that there is a volume to be unfolded another day, and to be gazed upon by the wondering eyes of glorified spirits in heaven, in which *all* this history shall be recorded. Now, however, we know but in part, and such fragments of knowledge it is surely our sacred duty to rescue from oblivion.

The history of the Independent church at Newport dates from 1660, two years before the passing of the famous Act of Uniformity.

Fuller, in his Church History, says,—"It is no small praise to Buckinghamshire that, though it is one of the lesser counties of England, it had before the time of Luther more martyrs and confessors than all England beside." In the reign of the good King Edward certain chaplains in ordinary were appointed—four of whom were constantly to itinerate through the country—a measure, it appears, rendered necessary by the extreme ignorance and disguised Papacy of the greater part of the clergy. They were men in every way qualified for their work. Of their number was Bradford, who sealed his testimony with his blood in the fires of Smithfield; Grindal, who, surviving the Marian persecution, became Archbishop of Canterbury in the reign of Queen Elizabeth, and who has gained a worthy name to himself by his noble resistance to the arbitrary will of his imperious mistress; and John Knox, the most illustrious of these godly men, in reference to whom, as shewing the kind of oratory of which he was master, we may quote the words of the English Ambassador to Scotland, who, in a letter to Cecil, says,—"When your Honour exhorts us to strictness, I assure you, the voice of one man is able in an hour to put more life in us than six hundred trumpets continually blustering in our ears."

This good work and these distinguished names we have mentioned here because another of these itinerant preachers of King Edward was John Hartley, (otherwise written Harle or Harley,) who was a native of Newport Pagnel. He was made Bishop of Hereford; but was deprived by Queen Mary, and died almost immediately afterwards. Hartley, while King Edward's preacher, would hardly be unmindful of his native town.

Even before this time, from the testimony of Fuller, already quoted, the good seed of the truth was evidently sown in these parts, and in all likelihood by "the poor priests" of Wyckliffe. Certain it is that Buckinghamshire still maintained its honourable distinction in the time of the Marian persecution.

All this history, now so obscure, another day shall unfold. The first authentic record for us is found in the year 1646, when the Rev. John Gibbs was a candidate for the vicarage of Newport Pagnel, then vacant. Before, however, Mr Gibbs was fully inducted into the living, he was engaged in a controversy with one Richard Carpenter, a native of the town, on the subject of Baptism. Mr Gibbs at this period of his life entertained peculiar views upon this subject. He was, in fact, a Catabaptist, holding that the ordinance of baptism was to be administered only to converted Jews and Pagans. He is thus designated in the church book belonging to the old meeting at Bedford. It is pretty evident that Mr Gibbs afterwards changed his views in reference to this matter, and became an advocate for infant baptism.

It seems that this subject had already occupied the

minds of the serious portion of the inhabitants of the town, and that Captain Paul Hobson had been put into custody by the Governor of Newport for preaching against infant baptism.

Carpenter had received his education at Cambridge. He was a man without settled religious principles, and was Papist and Protestant as it suited him. In a manuscript list of eminent men, natives of Newport Pagnel, he is styled a Jesuit. His pedantry and arrogance were unbounded. He, of course, claimed the victory in his dispute with Mr Gibbs, and published an account of it under the following title : "The Anabaptist* washt, and washt, and shrunk in the washing; or a scholastical discussion of the much-agitated controversie concerning Infant Baptism, occasioned by a public disputation, before a great assembly of ministers and other persons of worth, in the church of Newport Pagnel, between Mr Gibbs, minister there, and the author, Richard Carpenter, Independent. Wherein also the author occasionally declares his judgement concerning the Papists, and afterwards concerning Episcopacy." Carpenter calls Mr Gibbs " a heady enthusiast, a lean-lone Pagnel saint, sometimes a member of the University, and somewhat vexatious to the Protestant ministers in the circle about him . . . the Carry Castle or Behemoth of the

---

* Why Carpenter calls Mr Gibbs an Anabaptist, I know not. He was not very scrupulous in his statements, and might choose to call him such, because, in opposing all baptism, he, of course, denied the right of infants to the ordinance. There is no evidence at all that Mr Gibbs was a Baptist; but, on the contrary, he is spoken of in the trust-deed of the meeting-house at Olney, founded by him, as an Independent ; and, moreover, there was a Baptist interest at Newport during the time of Mr Gibbs.

country." We shall see afterwards at what we may value this wretched abuse.

Mr Gibbs being appointed to the living of Newport Pagnel, formed a church on Congregational principles, and continued his labours till the year 1660, when, according to the "Nonconformist Memorial," he was ejected from the church for refusing to admit the whole parish to the Lord's Table. The exact truth appears to be, that Mr Gibbs refused the ordinance to a man of considerable influence in the parish, who was notoriously immoral, and that this person procured his ejectment from the vicarage. This was early in the year 1660, as in the March of that year the Rev. Robert Marshall, Mr Gibbs's successor, was inducted.

In Whitelock's "Memorials" there is a curious circumstance relating to Mr Gibbs, as having taken place in the previous year. The following is the statement :—" August 24, 1659.—An account given to the House by Mr Gibbs, minister of Newport Pagnel, in Bucks, of the apprehension of Sir Geo. Booth, whither he came, with four servants, and behind one of them himself rode in the habit of a woman, but acting that part not well, he was suspected, and being apprehended and examined, he confessed himself to be Sir Geo. Booth, and was sent up to London, and by the Parliament committed to the Tower." It appears that Sir George Booth had headed an insurrection against the Parliament in Cheshire, and was defeated by General Lambert. After the Restoration, Sir George was created Lord Delamere, and it has been asserted that it was by his influence (and Macaulay says of him that he was a man of very bitter spirit) that Mr Gibbs was ejected from the vicarage. This, though not impossible, is somewhat doubtful.

At this time Mr Gibbs possessed two houses in the High Street of Newport; and at the farther end of a long yard, running by the side of them, was a barn, which, tradition informs us, had been once used as a Quakers' meeting-house. Excluded from his pulpit in the church, this good man retreated with a considerable portion of his congregation to this place, and there administered to them the word of life. In the persecuting times which soon followed, the situation of this barn was such as to afford great facility of escape to the congregation when they were likely to be disturbed by informers; for not only was the barn at some distance from the High Street, but there was also access from it to a back street. Amongst Mr Gibbs's devoted followers was a physician in the town, a Dr Waller. To avoid imprisonment for the crime of obeying his conscience, he concealed himself, it is said, for ten months in some of the out-offices belonging to his house, which being immediately contiguous to the barn in question, at the time of public worship he left his retreat, and availed himself of these religious opportunities, thus, no doubt, rendered very precious to him. It may be added, that so great was the persecution of Nonconformists in the county, that having filled the common jail at Aylesbury, the magistrates were compelled to hire two large houses in the town to receive their prisoners.

The Toleration Act was passed in the year 1689, and it was probably about this time that the meeting-house at

Newport was erected. It joined the barn where the congregation at first worshipped; and eventually the greater part of that humble but hallowed retreat was removed, to increase the accommodation of the more permanent building. The barn subsequently became the property of the Rev. William Bull and what remains of it is still sacredly preserved. Mr Gibbs now preached the Gospel without fear or hindrance; but in the erection of the new place of worship, an opening was left in the wall at the back of the pulpit to afford means of escape, should times of persecution again return. He gladly used the liberty Dissenters now enjoyed to spread the Gospel in the neighbourhood; and we find that he was instrumental in building a place of worship at Olney.

This good man continued his labours till 1699, when he died at the age of seventy-two, having been vicar of the parish for twelve years, and for thirty-eight the pastor of the Independent church. And it is one of the most glorious things to be told of our nonconformity, that in this, as well as in most other churches founded at this eventful period the same great fundamental Gospel truths have been preached in their fulness from that day to this.*

Mr Gibbs was, in all probability, educated at Cambridge, and was universally respected as a man of eminent learning and piety. On his tombstone, which is still to be

* It is true that some of the Nonconformist churches lapsed into Arianism and Socinianism; but the evil was almost entirely confined to those cases in which the choice of a minister was vested in the trustees, and not in the church,—a mode of action in direct contravention of Congregational principles.

seen near the south door of the chancel of the parish church, there is a Latin inscription, now nearly obliterated, which refers to him as a man of well-cultivated mind, wonderful memory, acute judgment, and great learning; as eminent for piety and great integrity, a fervent preacher, both to saints and sinners. "An elegy," written, as it is headed, "on the death of that famous minister of the Gospel Mr John Gibbs, pastor of the Church of Christ in and about Newport Pagnel," also prove that there was much that was remarkable in Mr Gibbs, both as a man and a Christian. And there is one passage in the elegy which shews that he did not escape the persecutions to which the good men of that day were subject. Thus we are told—

> " In persecution he hath often stood,
>   To seal the truths of Jesus with his blood;
>   In dangers great, and perils night and day,
>   Was he engaged amongst the beasts of prey ;
>   By wicked ones he often was misused,
>   His hair pulled off, his person much abused.
>   .   .   .   .   .   .
>   To prison and confinement he did go,
>   With cheerful heart and countenance also."

These few quaint lines tell us all we know of what the good man endured for the truth's sake. Into what straits and suffering he was brought by the infamous Conventicle and Five-mile Acts we can tell no more.

But there is one singular circumstance connected with these sufferings which must not be passed by. In the year 1769 the Rev. William Bull became the owner of the premises once in the occupation of Mr Gibbs. Mr Bull had lived in the house for about fifty years, when, in making some repairs, he accidentally came upon a small room or closet about four feet square. It was between two walls, at the side of a large old chimney, and had evidently been a hiding-place, for the only entrance to it was from a trap-door beneath, which was concealed from view in the old-fashioned "chimney-place." I have now in my possession some buttons of a coat, two tobacco-pipes, the bowls of which are exceedingly small, and some silver coins,—all of which were found there. It is not unlikely that Mr Gibbs might be surprised in this hiding-place, and perhaps dragged from it by the hair of his head,—"His hair pulled off, his person much abused."

A published sermon of Mr Gibbs's, while conveying many important truths, will indicate to some extent what the good man was as a preacher.

A Mr and Mrs Maxwell, relatives of Mr Gibbs, and who are buried in the same tomb with him, lost a son while a student at Harvard College, New England. For this young man Mr Gibbs preached a funeral sermon, which he dedicated to the parents of the deceased.

In that dedication he says, "You have, my friends, no cause to give too much vent unto your sorrow, for upon very good grounds you have reason to hope that he whom you love is with Him that loves him better than you, and is safely arrived at the haven of rest that you are desirous at last to come to. What though his race was short, his rest is the longer; and if he be gone a little before you, you follow after; and if you are prepared, as I doubt not he was, you will meet together, in an unspeakably, inconceivably far better state and place than was to be enjoyed, or can, in this vale of tears. He is wholly free from those evils that you are still exposed to, and is warm in that bosom wherein you hope to be lodged for ever. My love to him (for the relation I stood in) was very great from his childhood, for I don't remember that I ever did see anything in him but what did deserve it. His nature was very lively, and his deportment very obliging, that drew respect unto him from neighbours as well as relatives that had knowledge of him. And since his departure out of his native country you have had a full account from good hands of his pious and gracious behaviour, that should command your silence under this sharp providence, and, methinks, should not make it difficult for you to determine whether you have greater cause of mourning in parting from such a child than of rejoicing that you had so good and hopeful a one. How many, alas! poor parents that beget and bring forth children for the destroyer, when you had one for the Saviour, whom he sought, and now doth, and will for ever, enjoy. It becomes you not, therefore, to mourn as those who have no hope. That the Lord, who hath done it, would sanctify this stroke, and by the manifestation of his love to your souls, sweeten this bitter cup, and fully satisfy you with his will, is, and shall be, the prayer of your sympathising friend and relation.

" J. G."

The discourse is founded on Job ii. 10: " What! shall we receive good at the hand of God, and shall we not receive evil?" Whence the preacher deduces these observations: " 1. That the life of man in this world is made up of good and evil. Not all good, lest we be full and deny God; not all evil, lest we faint under it, and our lives be too bitter. Our life is a chequer-work, which hath white and black lines, or as the cloud in the wilderness, that had a bright side as well as a dark one. Herein it differs from the future life, that is either all good, and that in the superlative degree, without any alloy of evil, as with the spirits of just men made perfect, or all evil, without any mixture of good that is of comfort and refreshment—no, not so much as a drop of water, which is the miserable case of the damned in hell."

"*Obs.* 2. That the good and evil things we receive are from the hand of God, either immediately or mediately. I shall make use of this doctrine in the application."

"*Obs.* 3. That as we receive good, so must we receive evil." Then follows an account of the reasons why, and the manner how, we are to receive these evil things from the hand of God. The sermon concludes with the following remarks in answer to a supposed objection of the parent,—"That the affliction is more than ordinary. The Lord has, as it were, pricked me in the life vein, taking away the desire of my eyes and the delight of my heart. Had it been in some other way, I hope I could have borne it better."

"*Rep.* 1. Shall we direct our sovereign Lord, nay, our Father, what rod He shall scourge us with? He is at liberty to correct how He pleaseth; and if He taketh away, as none can hinder Him, neither may we question Him, or say. What doest Thou? or why doest Thou so? (Job ix. 12.) 2. Thy child was the delight of thine heart; therefore thou wouldst have had him continued with thee. He was also God's delight, who had most right to him; therefore he is not, because the Lord hath taken him to Himself. You did love him, but your love had too much self-love in it, seeing you would have kept him from his Father, and the glory prepared for him; so that your child might say, If you loved me with a cordial, sincere love, free from a mixture of self-love, you would rejoice, and not over-much afflict yourself with sorrow because I am gone to the Father. 3. This you say is a very heavy burden that the Lord hath put upon you; but not so heavy as your sins were that were laid upon Christ, the which He bore. He bore them on his own body on the tree, to bear or carry them away from us. *Ferebat et auferebat.* Did Christ, silently and patiently, bear and bear away our sins? Was He as a lamb before the shearers, and this burden laid upon Him by the Father; and shall not we be silent under the burden of affliction that the hand of the Lord lays upon us? 4. You complain that the trial and affliction is great; but, alas! it might have been greater. He might have been taken from you by the hand of justice inflicting death for horrid wickedness. He might have died and you had no well-grounded hopes of his eternal salvation; but he gave early proofs of his preparedness to meet with the enemy, though he came suddenly upon him. 5. It may be he had taken up too much room in your heart, and was lodged in the bed which the Lord had chosen to lie in, and therefore takes him out of the way, that He might have your hearts more fixed upon Him. It was, as I have read, the saying of a good woman, whose only son was taken away by water, 'That now the Lord had left her none to love but Himself.' Your son, though not your only son, was thus removed from you that your heart might be more at liberty to love the Lord. 6. If the affliction be great, and the burden be heavy, do the best you can to lessen your affliction, and make your burden lighter. This is done by a quiet, silent submission to the will of God in this awful providence, whereas impatience or discontent under it will add more weight to it. 7. Such a carriage and deportment will bespeak our reverence of God, in resigning up our choicest creature comforts to Him patiently. To part with that which we have no affection unto or kindness for is no proof of our reverence and obedience; but if our Isaac be called for, and we quietly give him up, by this we manifest our fear of God, (Gen. xxii. 12.) 8. Patience under sharp afflictions gives us possession of our souls, as saith Luke, (chap. xxi. 19.) The mind being composed, will render us capable of making use of those means whereby we may gain support and relief under it. Hence the Apostle James, (chap. i. 4 :) 'Let patience have her perfect work, that ye may be perfect and entire, wanting nothing' that is needful for your support under present circumstances. 9. The exercise of patience in our trials will bring in experience of the power, mercy, and goodness of God. Then shall we be capable of taking notice of His merciful dealings with us. Hence the exhortation of Moses unto the children of Israel, (Exod. xiv. 13 :) 'Stand still, and see the salvation of the Lord.' The Lord takes it well when we are graciously silent—not sullenly silent —under our troubles, and quarrel not with his rod. He

glories in his servant Job in the face of the devil on this
account, (chap. ii. 3.)   By such a carriage in our afflictions
we imitate the Lord Jesus, who, by his patient bearing all
He underwent from the hand of God and man, did give us
an example.   And certainly it becomes a Christian, and is
no small part of his glory, to be conformable to his Lord
and Master."

Thus it was that Mr Gibbs, amidst many difficulties,
founded and consolidated the church at Newport Pagnel.
He was succeeded in the pastoral charge by the Rev.
Thomas Tingey, who was educated for the ministry under
the Rev. Thomas Goodwin, (son of the well-known Dr
Goodwin,) and came to Newport about 1699.   After
remaining there ten years, Mr Tingey removed to
Northampton, and subsequently to Fetter Lane, in London,
living only a few weeks after his settlement there.   From
the funeral sermon preached for him by Dr Ridgley, he
appears to have been a man of great worth.   After speaking of the many endowments by which he was qualified
for his work, it is added,—" His method of preaching
was such as gave his hearers the greatest reason to conclude that his heart was in his work, and that it was not
a light matter with him whether he did good or no.   You
are all witnesses what a flow of affection he had, with what
earnestness he spake of Divine matters. .   .   .   .   The
doctrine of justification by Christ's imputed righteousness
was what he most insisted on, well knowing that hereby a
person may be enabled to live safely, and die comfortably.
.   .   .   .   Wherever Providence has cast his lot, he has
been very useful, and had many seals to his ministry.   He

laboured beyond measure, and beyond his strength, and seemed not to count his life dear unto him, so that he might finish his course with joy, and the ministry which he had received of the Lord Jesus, to testify the gospel of the grace of God."

After the removal of Mr Tingey, the Rev. John Hunt of Northampton received and accepted a call to the pastoral office. Thus each succeeded to the charge vacated by the other.

At this time, in the year 1707, a brief form of Church covenant was drawn up, which has been retained to the present day.

On the 14th July 1714 a meeting of ministers was held at Newport, when the Rev. Dr Cumming, then of Cambridge, and afterwards minister of the Scotch Church, London Wall, preached a sermon on " The general corruptions and defection of the present times as to matters of religion." It was a period of general alarm to Protestant Dissenters in consequence of the passing of the Schism Bill, the object of which was to prevent their conducting collegiate institutions and schools, and by which they were even restrained from educating their own children. There was every reason to fear that other attacks would be made on their rights. The providential accession of the house of Hanover to the throne happily changed the course of events.

In the year 1725 Mr Hunt removed to Tunstead, in Norfolk, where he died a few years afterwards. He was a man of considerable ability, and published several useful works. Amongst these were the following :—" Dissenters no Schismatics;" " Infants' Faith and Right to Baptism;" "The Doctrine of God's Decrees;" and " *Vindiciæ Veræ Pretatis*," or "Evangelical Sanctification Stated and Vindicated." He engaged also in the Supralapsarian Controversy, and replied to the writings of Mr Hussey of Cambridge.

Mr Hunt was succeeded by his son, the Rev. William Hunt, who was ordained in September 1725, on which occasion Dr Earle, Dr Calamy, and the Rev. John Troughton took part in the services; and their discourses were printed. In the same year two side galleries were erected, and other improvements made in the meeting-house. During this period the congregation appears to have been in a very flourishing state. Mr Hunt, however, removed in August 1738, and became pastor of the church in Mare Street, Hackney.

About the time of Mr Hunt's removal, a circumstance occurred, which, but for the merciful interference of Providence, might have seriously injured the Dissenting cause at Newport. The meeting-house was built upon the ground of one of the principal members of the congregation. It had never been conveyed to trustees, and the owner becoming a bankrupt, the property was seized by the creditors. At this juncture Dr Doddridge, who was intimately connected with Mr Hunt, very generously came forward, purchased the property, and at once conveyed it to trustees; and by his zeal and influence the necessary funds were soon raised.

The next minister was the Rev. Humphry Gainsborough, brother to the celebrated painter of that name. He did not continue long at Newport, but removed to Henley-on-Thames, where he died. There is a memoir of Mr Gainsborough in the *Gentleman's Magazine* for 1785, where he is spoken of in very eulogistic terms. " His genius," it is said, " as a man, his piety as a Christian, and his universal philanthropy were such, that wherever he was known he was universally esteemed. Considerable preferment was offered to him in the Established Church; but nothing could prevail on him to conform, while his conscience disapproved of the terms. Mr Gainsborough was remarkable for his mechanical genius. He invented a curious sun-dial, pointing the time to a second in every part of the globe. It is deposited in the British Museum."

There is an elegant Latin inscription on a tombstone in the church-yard of Newport of which Mr Gainsborough is the author. It was written on a Mr Saunderson of Newcastle, who died suddenly at Newport, on his way to his native place.*

The pulpit was afterwards supplied by the Rev. Mr Affleck, who removed to Holland, and became preacher at the great church at Middleburgh in Zealand. He was followed by the Rev. David Fordyce, Professor of Moral Philosophy in the Marischal College at Aberdeen, and brother to Dr James Fordyce. It does not appear that either of these

* M. S.
JACOBI SAUNDERSON,
NATIVAS TENDENTIS IN ORAS
NOTI INSIGNIS CASTELLI,
AC SVBITO HIC MORTE PEREMPTI
SEP. 13mo, 176 ;
QUO MENSE DIEQUE (MIRANDUM)
NATUS FUIT A.D. 17..

ministers was actually settled at Newport. Their introduction to the place might probably arise from the fact
that the leading men in the congregation were Scotchmen,
who were engaged in the lace trade, the staple manufac-
ture of the neighbourhood.

In 1749, the Rev. James Belsham undertook the pastoral charge of the church at Newport; but his residence
was at Bedford, a distance of thirteen miles from his
people. This circumstance, as might be expected, did not
much tend to the prosperity of the cause; indeed, it led
to so great a decrease in the church and congregation, that
when Mr Belsham resigned, in 1763, the former amounted
to only fourteen persons. Mr Belsham was a man of considerable ability, and an elegant scholar, but seems to have
been very deficient in popular talent. He published
two Latin poems,—"Mars Triumphans," and "Canada;"
the latter occasioned by the taking of Quebec. These
pieces have been much admired for their classic elegance.
He also translated Dr Williams's works into Latin. In the
year 1764, the Rev. William Bull succeeded Mr Belsham.
The particulars of this important event have been already
given.

Such were the circumstances of the church for the first
hundred years of its existence. Permitted, in infinite
wisdom, to pass through affliction and trial, it was destined
ere long to obtain a position of greater importance than
it had ever yet occupied.

One thing, I think, we may justly infer from the above
history,—that the Dissenting ministers of that day were
not simply good men, but men also otherwise qualified for

their work—possessed, for the most part, of considerable
ability and learning; and if men evidently of some mark
were settled in so comparatively small a place as Newport,
it may lead to a reasonable conclusion as to the general
character of the whole body of Independent ministers of
that period.

Another important observation we may make is this,—
that for a hundred years Congregational principles were
tested, and found to be eminently conservative of gospel
truth. The depression of the cause at the close of this
period is readily to be accounted for from the non-
residence and want of adaptedness of Mr Bull's predecessor.

CHAPTER III.

LIFE OF THE REV. WILLIAM BULL,

1764-1779.

AND now to resume the history of the subject of our
memoir:—soon after Mr Bull's settlement at Newport—his
congregation being small, and his income limited—it was
suggested to him that he might occupy himself with advantage in the instruction of youth. His friends used
their influence to obtain pupils for him, and in a short
time a considerable and highly respectable school was
gathered. Amongst his scholars were some who afterwards obtained good positions in the world, as Sir John
Leech, late Master of the Rolls.

A persecuting law was at that time in existence rendering it illegal for a Dissenting minister to keep a school
without a licence from the bishop. Certain parties in the
neighbourhood took advantage of this statute, and threatened Mr Bull with a prosecution. This was a source of
great uneasiness to him for a time; but his friend Mr
Palmer assured him that, through the intervention of Dr

Chandler, the bishop's licence could be obtained if necessary; and I believe no more was heard of the matter. In 1779 this statute was repealed.

In January 1766, Mr Bull's great friend, Mr Saunderson, died. Speaking of this event in a letter to one of his relatives, he says,—" It was to him an unspeakable grief." He was exceedingly susceptible of impressions of this class; and in the same letter utters himself as if that loss had cast a gloom upon all the prospects of his life.

In the month of June 1768, Mr Bull was married to Miss Hannah Palmer, daughter of a most excellent man, Mr Thomas Palmer of Bedford, and deacon of the Old Meeting in that town. Mrs Bull, like her husband, was of Puritan origin; and conspicuous amongst the names of her ancestors were William Benn, one of the ejected ministers, Theophilus Polwheel, Stephen Lobb, and others. This union was not only a source of great happiness to Mr Bull through his whole life, but was of immediate benefit to him in the conduct and arrangements of his household; for he had been at the mercy of servants, and had suffered much by their carelessness and want of principle.

Though thus happy in his outward circumstances, it pleased God again to visit Mr Bull with severe and protracted affliction. Early in the year '69, he was quite laid aside from all his duties, and for a long time there seemed little probability of his recovery. In the midst of his illness, and at the very moment when her husband was supposed to be dying, Mrs Bull gave birth to their firstborn child,—Benjamin King.

As the spring advanced, my grandfather was advised to

spend as much time as possible out of doors, and on horseback. He was so weak that for some time he could only walk his horse, and was obliged always to have an attendant with him. But he could not even then be idle, and was accustomed to take a book with him; and thus on horseback he read through several volumes, and amongst others Baillet's "Jugemens des Savans," in seven quarto volumes. About this time a house was to be sold in close proximity to his place of worship, and which had once been the property of Mr Gibbs. It was in a higher and more healthy situation than the residence then occupied by Mr Bull. This house he purchased, and soon removed to it, but was still in a very weak state. From this time, however, he began to recover, but did not resume his regular duties until the month of June.

It may be truly said of my grandfather that he was in deaths oft, and as often marvellously delivered from them. It must have been a very little time after his recovery from this long affliction that, in returning from Bedford, he had a most narrow escape of his life. While mounting on the road, his horse started; and his foot being caught in the stirrup, he was dragged a considerable distance, and was so seriously injured that he was only recovered by the application of very powerful stimulants.

Mr Bull was early acquainted with that eccentric but highly gifted man the Rev. John Ryland, an acquaintance which, it may be presumed, though there is little record of it, was on either side interesting and profitable. Dr Gregory, in his memoir of Mr Hall, who in early life was placed under the care of Mr Ryland, speaks of the latter as "a very excellent man, whose excellences and eccentricities were strangely balanced." "In him," he adds, "were blended the ardour and vehemence of Whitfield, with the intrepidity of Luther. His pulpit oratory was of the boldest character, and singularly impressive, when he did not overstep the proprieties of the ministerial function." Mr Ryland often visited Olney, and was on intimate terms with the Rev. John Newton. On one occasion, after hearing him preach there, Mr Newton says in his diary,—"His originality and zeal were strongly marked throughout this sermon." I can find only one entire letter of Mr Ryland's to my grandfather. It is very characteristic of the man, and is as follows :—

"Rev. and dear Sir,—I have not forgotten my promise, as you supposed, but was contriving this week how to fulfil it. Do you know that my wife and son have been at London, for near a fortnight, to receive our rents, as we now do every quarter; for my family costs me about £1000 a-year, and there is no doing without money in a family of seventy-five. And although money is dead matter, quite dead, stone dead, and has no power of motion, much less of thought, of one thought to all eternity, yet this same dead matter which is dug out of the earth's bowels is appointed by infinite wisdom to be the instrument of happiness to rational and immortal substances. And there is no evil in money; there never was any evil in it; and there never will be any evil in it. Not only so, but we are told the Almighty likes it so well, that He chooses to pave the streets of the noblest city in the world with it. Conse quently, all the evil must arise from the foolish, idolatrous, and wicked love of it; and thus, indeed, the love of money has damned millions, and is now hurrying multitudes of our poor, wretched Court harpies to the bottom of perdition; yea, the Scripture says, it *drowns* men in *destruction* and *perdition*. *Drowned in destruction and perdition!* What an energetic phrase is this! Would not one word do? But the apostle must use two that seem of the same import. Do tell me the exact difference between ὄλεθρον and ἀπώλειαν when I come? If the weather proves fine in the morning, I come on Tuesday by Wyke's post-coach, if my cold, with which I have been afflicted all this week, gets better. But if the weather proves wet, don't expect me, because, as no precise day is needful, why should we not choose a good day, if possible? The Lord grant you much wisdom to help me to discern the beauties of the original Scriptures, then I will thank you heartily, and bless God for your assistance. Our kind respects wait on Mrs Bull.

"Yours, with great integrity and honour,

"JOHN RYLAND."

"*Oct.* 23, 1768."

The striking character of Mr Ryland's pulpit oratory has been spoken of; and I remember an illustration of this as it was told to my father by his friend the late Mr Foster of Biggleswade. The Rev. Robert Hall and Mr Foster were conversing together; and the name of Mr Ryland being brought up, Mr Hall referred to a sermon he had once heard him preach. It was at an Association of Ministers, I think, in Northamptonshire; and it must have been when Mr Hall was a very young man, yet the impression of it seems to have been most vivid. The text was in Mark (chap. xiv. 33,) "And he began to be sore amazed." The first head,—"Christ was sore amazed at the extent of human depravity." "It was," said Mr Hall, "as if in the illustration of this point Mr Ryland had condensed into a brief half-hour's statement the reading of a life-time. You felt that he had expended his whole power upon this one topic, and that it was impossible to rise higher. But under his second division,—'Christ was sore amazed at the weight of Divine wrath,'—his exposition was still more striking, and the impression was, 'This surely cannot be surpassed.' But the handling of the last particular (I think it had reference to the malignity of Satan) was the climax of all. It was the most wonderful discourse," said Mr Hall, "I ever heard." And then he most beautifully added, "It was, sir, as if a man had brought the cattle of a thousand hills and all the incense of Arabia to one single sacrifice."

It pleased God, in June 1771, to remove by death Mr Bull's only son, Benjamin, when he was about fifteen months old, and he preached a funeral sermon on the occasion from 2 Sam. xii. 23, "I shall go to him, but he shall not return to me."

Soon after this, Mr Bull formed an acquaintance with the Rev. John Newton, who became curate of Olney about the same time my grandfather was settled at Newport. Some little misunderstanding marred the beginning of a friendship, which afterwards grew so intimate, and brought forth such pleasant fruits. While Mr Newton remained at Olney these friends very frequently met, and a long correspondence was commenced, and continued till Mr Newton's death. Mr Newton's papers came eventually into my father's hands, and so most of my grandfather's letters to him; and I think it will add much to the interest of this volume, and best illustrate the history of the life we are attempting to portray, to give as many extracts from the letters of both these correspondents as may serve to accomplish that object. This connexion had, as we shall see, a very important influence on Mr Bull's after life. It made no sort of difference to either party that they did not quite agree in their ecclesiastical views. They were one in Christ, and nothing can be more beautiful than the illustration their friendship affords of the true Evangelical-Alliance principle.

In a diary of Mr Newton's, which was received with the rest of the papers, he says, " I am struck with the wisdom, grace, and impression of Thine image which Thou hast given to thy servant Bull, and I hope Thou wilt teach me to profit thereby. Surely I love him for Thy sake." And again, " He has a living sense of Thy word, and gracious communications from Thee by it." On another occasion, about a year afterwards, on his return from spending a day at Newport, Mr Newton says, " Had some interesting conversation with Mr Bull on Luke xvi. I find few or any with whom I converse with equal advantage, whose manner of thinking is so deep and solid." And once more, " Thou hast given him great abilities and much grace, yet sufferest him to be afflicted with a malady which at present is grievous," &c. &c. These are but specimens of many such entries.

I may here be allowed to add, what abundant evidence there is in this interesting document of the large-hearted Christian charity of this most excellent man.   Not unfrequently was he found a hearer at the Dissenting meeting-house; he was habitually present at the gatherings of the Baptist Association in Olney, at ordination services, and generally living on most friendly terms with his Dissenting brethren.   On those more public occasions to which reference has just been made, the ministers often received hospitality at Mr Newton's house.   In the diary, under date May 1776, we find this entry.   It refers to the meeting of the Baptist Association.   " Yesterday, the ministers remaining in town breakfasted with me.   We seemed all mutually pleased.   I thank Thee, my Lord, Thou hast given me a heart to love Thy people of every name. And I am willing to discover Thine image without respect of parties."   In another passage he expresses his joy in the prosperity of others, though even at his own cost, and prays that he may be delivered from all paltry jealousy.

In one of Mr Newton's early letters to Mr Bull, written Dec. 26, 1777, he says, " I love you.   I love your company, because I believe the Lord speaks by you to my heart, therefore I wish to see you as often as I can."   The friends communicated very often with one another on the subject of their preaching.   Texts and schemes were exchanged.   On occasion of a fast-day, in February 1778, we find Mr Newton writing, " I send you a text and a plan according to order, and if it puts any hints in your way it is at your service."   And then he adds, " The whole system of my politics is summed up in that short sentence, ' The Lord reigneth.' I wish you would send me by the bearer some hints towards a sermon on it. It would be a good text if I knew how to manage it."

In a letter, written in April of the same year, Mr Newton says, in reference to a call at Newport in Mr Bull's absence, " I would have asked you, had you been at home, to come over to-morrow. We would have given you a bit of dinner, provided you would have preached to us at night, and I suppose Mr Whitford [the Independent minister at Olney] would have thanked me for engaging you. We are rather upon the preach, preach here, but we only want to hear those who can tell us about Jesus, and stir us up to live to Him. The bit of dinner is still at your service, if you will come, or whenever you will come. I beg you to pray for me; I am a poor creature, full of wants. I seem to need the wisdom of Solomon, the meekness of Moses, and the zeal of Paul to enable me to make full proof of my ministry. But, alas! you may guess the rest. Send me ' The Way to Christ.'*　I am willing to be a debtor to the wise and the unwise, to doctors and shoemakers, if I can get a hint or *nota bene* from any one, without respect of parties. When a house is on fire, Churchmen and Dissenters, Methodists, Papists, Moravians, and Mystics are all welcome to bring water. At such times nobody asks, ' Pray, friend, whom do you hear?' or, ' What do you think of the five points?'"

Again in June, in reference to his coming to a visitation at Newport :—

* By Jacob Behmen.

"MON CHER MONSIEUR BULL,—Herewith I send my sheep's clothing as an earnest of my purpose to follow it on Tuesday morning, to beg a breakfast with you, if the Lord permit. My friend, Captain Scott, will pass through Newport on his way to Olney on Tuesday. As it is possible I may be then engaged with my betters, and as such persons as you and he must not dine with the '*we preachers*' of the Establishment when we meet *in pontificalibus*, I have invited him to quarter an hour or two at your house, till I am at liberty to call for him and escort him home. . . . .—Your affectionate, JOHN NEWTON."

In the summer of this year, Mrs Wilberforce, aunt to the celebrated statesman and philanthropist, and sister to the benevolent John Thornton, visited Mr Newton at Olney. She had lost her husband some eight months before this time. Mr Bull came to the vicarage while she was there, and so greatly impressed her by his conversation and his prayers, that a friendship was then commenced between them which was only terminated by the death of this excellent woman. Mr Bull was coming to London in the next month, and Mrs Wilberforce begged that he would visit her. During that visit my grandfather received his first invitation from Mr Thornton.

In a letter written to Mr Bull while in London, Mr Newton refers to a project there was at that time to set up in London what was termed a lay academy. Mr Brewer of Stepney having refused to undertake it, it was proposed to offer the presidency to Mr Bull, and this was warmly seconded by Dr Conder, the tutor of Homerton College.

" I have frequently thought," says Mr Newton, " of what you mentioned to me, and it appears to me highly probable that if the purpose is of the Lord, and what He designs to give a blessing to, you will be the person appointed. It seems a service just suited to you, and for which you have been trained and prepared."

In another letter, written a week later, Mr Newton says :—" I do not wish you to live there, for my own sake as well as yours; but if the Lord should so appoint, I believe He can make you easy there, and enable me to make a tolerable shift without you. Yet I certainly should miss you, for, excepting a friend about twelve miles off,* I have no person in this neighbourhood with whom my heart so thoroughly unites in spirituals, though there are many whom I love. But conversation with most Christians is something like going to Court, where, except you are dressed exactly according to a prescribed standard, you will either not be admitted, or must expect to be heartily stared at ; but you and I can meet and converse *sans contrainte*, in our undress, without fear of offending, or being counted offenders for a word out of place, and not exactly in the pink of the mode." And then he goes on to say :— " I know not how it is; I think my sentiments and experience are as orthodox and Calvinistical as need be, and yet I am a sort of *speckled bird* amongst my Calvinistic brethren." . . . .

This allusion to a speckled bird brought the following letter from Mr Bull :—

* John Foster Barham, Esq., of Bedford, also a very intimate friend of Mr Bull's.

" One speckled bird to another speckled bird, whom he lores most dearly, sendeth greeting :

" DEAR BROTHER,—Through the great goodness of the blessed Lord of all the feathery tribes, I yesterday morning took my flight from the great wilderness, and winged my way most safely to this quiet retreat, where I am comfortably seated in my own old nest again. 'Home is home, though ever so homely.' Here I found my dam quite well, and Tommy and Polly chirping, and Billy very indifferent indeed, with the hooping-cough ; but I know that our dear Lord will order it for the best. Oh, help me to bless His holy name! You know, brother, that those of our fraternity which are called birds of passage, before their flight hold a kind of national assembly for several weeks, to consult about the coast to which they shall direct their flight, to try their pinions, and adjust their plumage. Exactly for the same reasons I long to see you; for I think we are not only speckled birds, but birds of passage too, and I long to hear and speak about that glorious shore to which we are bound. It is true we shall not cross a briny deep, but our singular circumstances require us to pass (not over, but through) a sea of *precious blood*, and our only strength will be not a pine plank, but a *glorious cross.* You know, brother, it belongs to our nation to chirp, to whistle, to sing; and though I cannot (like you) sing the songs of Zion, yet I can brokenly chirp the short sweet note, 'Precious Jesus! precious Jesus! He is my Lord and my God.' . . . . . The academy scheme we will speak of when we meet. I cannot think of leaving Newport at present; otherwise there is an opening at the Weigh

House. Give my love to the dear mistress of your nest.
I long to see you. . . . .—Your affectionate brother,
and obliged servant,   W. BULL."

August 4, Mr Newton writes :—

" DEAR MR BULL,—What a calf am I ! You mentioned
preaching here to-morrow, and I had not wit enough to say,
Be sure you dine with us. My heart positively meant it,
though my head (which is often wool-gathering) missed
the nick of telling you so. I committed the fault, and
you must pay the penny!" Then follows this beautiful
passage :—" When you are with the King, and getting
good for yourself, speak a word for me and mine. I have
reason to think you see Him oftener, and have nearer
access to Him than myself. Indeed, I am unworthy to
look at Him, or speak to Him at all, much more that He
should speak tenderly to me. Yet I am not wholly without His notice. He supplies all my wants, and I live
under His protection. My enemies see His Royal Arms
over my door, and dare not enter. Were I detached from
Him for a moment, in that moment they would make an
end of me."

In September of this year, " Billy," referred to in a
previous letter as suffering from the hooping-cough, was
removed by death, and Mr Newton expresses his condol-
ence in a beautiful letter, rejoicing with his friend in the
Lord's goodness, " enabling him to be resigned and satisfied with His will, maugre all the feelings and pinchings
of flesh and blood."

Mr Bull's health was never vigorous, and his spirits were now more than usually depressed by threatening symptoms of nephritis; and Mr Newton says, " The gloomy tinge of your weak spirits leads you to consider yourself much worse in point of health than you appear to me to be. I heartily sympathize with you in your complaints, but I see you in safe hands. The Lord loves you, and will take care of you."

Mr Palmer, the father-in-law of Mr Bull, died in November, which added to his depression, and led his friend again to address him in a similar strain :—" I shall expect you, with earnestness, on Tuesday, and I hope the weather, and especially illness, will not prevent you. And I beg you not to listen too much to that lowness of spirits which would persuade you, I suppose, to remain always at home; because I am satisfied, that when you can muster strength to withstand this depressing, discouraging solicitation, and force yourself to ride and chat with some friend, you take the best course for relief; and among all the friends you treat with your company on such occasions, be sure none will be more glad to receive you than your friend at the Vicarage, Olney.

" I understand something of your complaint, and know how to pity you; but since you say, ' All is well, and shall be well,'—since you are in the wise and merciful hands of One who prescribes for you with unerring wisdom, and has unspeakably more tenderness than can be found in all human hearts taken together,—I shall sorrow for you as though I sorrowed not; and I hope you will do the same for yourself. I am running on as if you were on the other side of the Atlantic, or as if I had given up the hope of seeing you so soon as Tuesday. Come, if possible. I will endeavour to be alone, and will no more blab my expectation of your company than I would if I had found a pot of honey, and was afraid of my neighbours breaking in upon me for a share."

In the spring or early summer of this year occurred the circumstance I am about to relate. Mr Newton had been dining with Mr Bull, and they were quietly sitting together, following after " the things whereby they might edify one another," and that search, aided by " interposing puffs" of the fragrant weed. It was in that old study I so well remember, ere it was renovated to meet the demands of modern taste. A room some eighteen feet square, with an arched roof, entirely surrounded with many a precious volume, with large old casement windows, and immense square chairs of fine Spanish mahogany. There these good men were quietly enjoying their *tête-à-tête* when they were startled by a thundering knock at the door; and in came Mr Ryland of Northampton, abruptly exclaiming, " If you wish to see Mr Toplady, you must go immediately with me to the Swan. He is on his way to London, and will not live long." They all proceeded to the inn, and there found the good man emaciated with disease, and evidently fast hastening to the grave. As they were talking together they were attracted by a great noise in the street, occasioned, as they found on looking out, by a bull-baiting which was going on before the house. Mr Toplady was touched by the cruelty of the scene, and exclaimed, " Who could bear to see that sight if there were not to be some compensation for these poor suffering animals in a future state?"　"I certainly hope," said my grandfather, " that all the Bulls will go to heaven; but do you think this will be the case with all the animal creation?"　" Yes, certainly," replied Mr Toplady, with great emphasis, " all, all."　" What!" rejoined Mr Newton, with some sarcasm in his tone; " do you suppose, sir, there will be fleas in heaven? for I have a special aversion to them."　Mr Toplady said nothing, but was evidently hurt; and as they separated, Mr Newton said, " How happy he should be to see him at Olney, if God spared his life, and he were to come that way again.'　The reply Mr Toplady made was not very courteous; but the good man was perhaps suffering from the irritation of disease, and possibly annoyed by the ridicule cast upon a favourite theory.　And, after all, is it not a view upon which it may be easy to cast ridicule, but not so easy to confute?　At any rate, it is a notion which has the support of some great names, and which is a relief to some great difficulties; while there is a very simple answer to all such objections as those of Mr Newton, for whatever be the conditions of another state of being, we are quite sure there will be nothing either noxious or imperfect there.

The year 1779 was a very chequered season to the subject of our memoir.　It was a year of joy and of sorrow, and a time of much personal and relative suffering, and yet of quiet resignation and submission to the will of his Heavenly Father.

At the commencement of the year Mr Newton writes, expressing his sympathy with Mr Bull in his personal afflictions, and regrets that he had neglected to confer with him about the business of the fast-day. He mentions his texts, and says he shall be glad to know those of his friend. In the same letter he speaks of having finished the hymn-book, meaning " The Olney Hymns."

In his diary, under date May 25, Mr Newton writes,— " Mr Bull spoke excellently on the words, 'Thou wilt have compassion,' at the *Great House*. It was the first time of his appearance there, but I hope it will not be the last."

A word or two about the "Great House" may not be uninteresting. It was an old mansion at Olney, not far from the vicarage, at that time unoccupied, in which Mr Newton rented a room, and where he held meetings for prayer and exposition of the Scriptures. It was also the place of the good man's frequent resort for private meditation and prayer. There is a list still in existence of the persons who engaged in prayer on the occasions above referred to, in the handwriting of Mr Newton, in which the name of the poet Cowper frequently occurs previous to the sad year of 1773, when his painful malady returned upon him. One who was frequently present on these occasions has said, " Of all the men I ever heard pray, no one equalled Mr Cowper." We shall have much to say of this interesting man hereafter.

Two of the Olney hymns, " On opening a place for social prayer," one composed by Mr Newton and the other by Mr Cowper, were (I believe) used when this room was first set apart for this purpose. They are the 43d and 44th of the Second Book, the first beginning, " O Lord, our languid souls inspire," and the second, "Jesus, where'er Thy people meet."

In July we find Mr Newton writing to Mr Bull :—" . . . Can you provide a breakfast on Wednesday morning between seven and eight o'clock for two hungry parsons? Mr Scott * and I think to call upon you about that time, on our way to the visitation at Stratford. Perhaps you will get your gray horse ready from Bury Field, and take a ride with us."

In September Mr Newton informs Mr Bull of the very important circumstance of his probable removal from Olney. "I wish," he says, "that you may be able to send us word by the bearer that your complaint is removed, or at least abated. If not, still I hope the Lord favours you with soul-peace and resignation to His will.

"Had you removed to the Weigh House we should soon have been neighbours again. My race at Olney is nearly finished. I am about to form a connexion for life with one Mary Woolnoth, a reputed London saint, in Lombard Street. I hope you will not blame me. I think you would not, if you knew all the circumstances. I hope and beg you will pray for me. On Tuesday we purpose going to Northampton, and to return by Newport on Thursday, take a bit of dinner, and change a few expressions of love with you and Mrs Bull, and home early in the afternoon. . . ."

Three weeks later Mr Newton writes from London :—

"MY DEAR FRIEND,—Do not say, do not think, I have

* The Rev. Thomas Scott, the Commentator.

forgotten you. I have waited to tell you some news till I can wait no longer. I delivered my presentation to the bishop's secretary on Friday last, and on Sunday received notice that a caveat was lodged against my institution by some person or persons who pretend to dispute Mr Thornton's right of presenting. The counter claim causes a delay or suspense, but it is thought will soon appear to be groundless. However, through mercy, your poor friend feels himself very easy about the event. The affair is where I would have it—in the Lord's hands. If He fixes me here, I humbly hope and believe He will support me, and it shall be for good. If He appoint otherwise, I trust it will be no grief of heart to me to return to Olney, where I shall be within a few miles of dear Mr Bull. . . .

" While we can meet daily at a throne of grace, and exchange a letter when we please, let us not think ourselves far asunder. Your company has been pleasing and edifying to me, and I shall sensibly miss it. But our friendship will be inviolable. You have a near and warm place in my heart, and will retain it as long as life continues. I confidently expect the same on your part. I long to hear how you do; shall be thankful to know you are getting better, and especially to be told that all your dispensations are evidently sanctified, and that you have that peace which can subsist and flourish in affliction. My dear joins in love to you and Mrs Bull and your two young plants ! May the Lord make them plants of renown ! may they increase in wisdom as in years, and grow up to His praise and your comfort ! Adieu. Send me a letter soon, and believe me to be, most affectionately, your faithful friend and brother,

"JOHN NEWTON.

"*October* 14, 1779."

To this letter Mr Bull replied two days after :—". . . . It refreshes me to feel how warm a place I have in your heart. Sometimes I think nobody loves me, and it makes me very low. But I know you do, and I am sure Jonathan did not love David more than I do you. You speak as a child of God should do about your present situation, and I doubt not it will be just as it should be as to the demurrer about the presentation. What think you? my poor, weak, silly self perks up its head and softly whispers, There is yet a glimpse of hope. I am ashamed to say the rest, for you must be where you should be. The will of the Lord be done. I need no incentive to pray for you, and as to letters I will keep you in my debt.

" My nephritic pain continues much as usual. Though constant, it is tolerable ; and though it is uncomfortable, it does not make me miserable. The Lord has shewn me daily that I may be ashamed to complain, my pain is so little in comparison with what I deserve. O Sir, in this view the stone is nothing, nothing at all; I should be in hell-fire but for the sovereign rich free grace of Father, Son, and Spirit, sweetly flowing down upon me through the wounded side of Jesus. . . . . I wish my few faithful friends may forgive me, that I have been so often complaining about health when I ought to have been mourning about sin. And now, dear brother, as I am a little better, will you pray that I may get quite well? It would be very acceptable, if the Lord sees fit, though I find it good to be afflicted; so that I am not at all sorry that it is as it is."

Mr Newton hoped that Mr Scott would have succeeded him at Olney, but the people were unwilling to accept of him. Mr Bull says in reference to this matter, "I am grieved for Olney, and, although they have done wrong, very wrong, they meant right, and I believe they are sorry. Pray for them, and endeavour, if you can, to bring Mr Scott amongst them, though against their will. Don't let them fall into the hands of a wolf in sheep's clothing. You know you love them; and you know that love let loose can do great things. In one Person it was omnipotent, and in many of His followers it has wrought great wonders. Find out the obstacle, and try to remove it,—I mean to Mr Scott's coming to Olney. I will throw in my mite of prayer into heaven's huge box about it. But in all this I mean only if the thing be suitable to the will of Jesus. You know He has said, 'I will be sought unto,' &c., and, although He will do everything right, yet He likes to have our earnest prayers harmonizing with his purposes . . . My dear Polly [one of the "two young plants" Mr Newton mentions in his previous letter] is very ill of a fever; a few days will, I think, determine the event one way or other. I dare say nothing on this head, but I feel much. . . . — Your affectionate brother and obliged servant,

"WM. BULL."

Mr Bull's sad anticipation was verified, and a few days

afterwards the dear child was taken to the Paradise above. It had pleased God already to remove four of Mr Bull's children; two only were now left, a boy and a girl. The latter was a peculiarly interesting child. Though only five years of age, she discovered a great precocity of talent, and a disposition remarkably amiable. My father says, "Though myself then but a child, (he was about two years older than his sister,) I well remember how deeply my parents felt this stroke." The sad event was communicated to Mr Newton in the following letter, I think I may venture to say, hardly to be equalled for its tenderness, its pathos, and its sweet spirit of submission to the Divine will :—

". . . My very, very dear young lamb got comfortably through her fever last week, but the night before last she was worse. Yesterday again better; but at night her throat again became worse; in an hour or two quite ulcerated, and this morning, at four o'clock, the Lord Jesus put an end to all my anxiety by taking her to Himself. She died very easily indeed.

"Oh, how glad, and yet how sorrowful I feel! I tremble and rejoice. Dear sir, pray for me. My bodily pain is great, the sorrow in my heart is real, but the love of my Lord is the same. Oh, how I rejoice in Him this day; while I grieve in self, I seem to long to be where Polly is, and, blessed be my God, I shall go there some day, perhaps soon. My dear lamb has discovered a peculiar sweetness of temper these three or four months, and a fondness for reading quite remarkable. For five or six weeks past she has got up before me in the morning to read a chapter to me while I was dressing, and one day she cried very much because I put her by, getting up before her. She gave me great delight by this practice, and it was her own. This is a pleasant tale to me, and you can excuse it. The lamb looks exceedingly beautiful, now she is laid out; but, oh, my faith sees her spirit in the hands and heart of God my Saviour; and that delights me. My dear wife is very poorly; and poor, lonely Tommy is tolerable, and is kept for some future trial.

" Since I have been writing, a letter has come from Mrs Wilberforce. Do thank her for it, and tell her my great trial. I know she respects me, and will pray for me, and her prayers will do me good. Ask her to pray that I may behave well, that I may be still; and if any ask, ' Is it well with the child ? ' I may say, ' It is well.'

"You know I sometimes speak as if I loved the Lord, and I think I do, but you know, too, that words and actions should hang together, and, therefore, I wish that I may silently rejoice in my Saviour for cutting off all sources of comfort but Himself. Indeed, it does look as if He would have my whole heart, and would make everything else taste bitter, that He may taste the sweeter. So lately as yesterday, dear Polly read me the 23d Psalm before I was up. Oh, how little did I think affliction and death were so near! This evening one of my poor orphan nieces complains of her throat. Where will this putrid sore-throat end ? and how shall I behave ? Pray for me. I hope you will write soon. I am a poor sinner ; but, at the same time, your sincere and affectionate brother and obliged servant,
W. BULL."

The above was written on Saturday. He adds :—

"*Lord's-Day Evening.*—I have been preaching in my poor way on Heb. xii. 6, 'Whom the Lord loveth he chasteneth,' &c. The Lord was with me. I never before experienced more sensible delight in Him, and I am just now come home exceedingly refreshed and comforted."

A Mr Whitehouse, who afterwards became a clergyman in the Church of England, was residing with Mr Bull at this time. He wrote an elegy on the death of this interesting child, in which occurs the following stanza :—

> " How oft with undesigning art.
> And every soft, endearing wile,
> She won the fond beholder's heart,
> And held it tangled in a smile."

This elegy was published at the time in the *Gentleman's Magazine*, and afterwards in a volume of poems by the author.

I distinctly remember seeing, and it must have been more than fifty years after her death, some of this little girl's toys,—a doll, I think, and doll's house,—which were preserved as precious memorials. The orphan nieces referred to in Mr Bull's letter were three young people left without a home, who were taken into his house, and brought up by him.

In a letter from Mr Newton, in reply to Mr Bull's, the former says, " I feel for you a little in the same way as you feel for yourself. I bear a friendly sympathy in your late sharp and sudden trial. I mourn with that part of you which mourns, but, at the same time, I rejoice in the proof you have, and which you give, that the Lord is with you of a truth." And, again, in November :—" . . . . Tell Mrs Bull we love you both, have felt for you both, and shall be glad to hear that you are both pretty well. The Lord loves you likewise, and therefore He afflicts you. He has given you grace, and therefore He appoints you trials, that the grace He has given you may be preserved and manifested to his praise. He has made you a good soldier, and therefore He appoints you to a post of honour. You are not a beef-eater, to walk about in a soldier's coat, at a distance from the noise and clangour of war, and to brandish your firelock without any danger of meeting an enemy, but He sends you down to the field of battle. You feel as well as hear that our profession is a warfare, and you feel as well as hear likewise that the Lord is with you, fights for you, and supports you with strength, and covers your head in the day of conflict." . . . . . .

Mr Bull received many other letters of sympathy on this sad occasion. The loss of his children, one after another, will readily account for the special manner in which the affections of my grandfather clung to his only remaining child. All the love of his bereaved heart, which could no longer be with them, seems to have gone out and centered there.

Mr Bull's intercourse with Mr Newton, while the latter resided at Olney, was not confined to their meeting at each other's houses. They were accustomed, not unfrequently, to enjoy each other's society in the dwellings of some of the godly people in the neighbourhood. Lavendon Mill, the residence of Mr Perry, was one of these favoured spots; and there, it is evident, all the parties enjoyed the most delightful spiritual communion,—times of refreshing often mentioned by Mr Newton in his diary. This will not be wondered at, when we read such references as the following to this godly miller. Mr Cowper, in writing to Mr Newton, when Mr Perry was dangerously ill, says, " He will leave none such behind him. He is dying, as I suppose you have heard." It pleased God, however, to restore the good man; and in another letter, Mr Cowper says, " The only consequence of his illness seems to me, that he looks a little paler; and though always a most excellent man, he is still more angelic than he was." At the house of this good man Mr Newton and my grandfather always met on the Friday in Whitsun-week, and, after spending the day there, Mr Bull preached in a barn at Lavendon. This service was commenced in 1776, and continued after my grandfather's death by my father till 1843, when circumstances led to its being abandoned. This was only one out of three such services held at different places in Whitsun-week, and continued by Mr Bull as long as he lived.

CHAPTER IV.

LIFE OF THE REV. WILLIAM BULL,

1780–82.

IN the beginning of the year 1780, the disease from which Mr Bull had been so long suffering began to assume a more serious form, and it was judged necessary that he should undergo a surgical examination. For that purpose he went to London; but the fears of himself and his friends were happily, in a measure, disappointed; for the evil was not found to exist in its worst form, and no operation was necessary. Still, my grandfather suffered, more or less, through life from this complaint, and it was at last the immediate cause of his death. I believe it was at the house of Mrs Wilberforce that my grandfather met with a Miss Myers, a converted Jewess, who was thenceforth greatly indebted to him for instructing her in the way of Christ more fully. She suffered great persecution from her friends, and passed through much spiritual conflict. Mr Bull kept up a correspondence with her, and invited her more than once to his house; and it is evident how greatly she valued his friendship.

Mr Bull continued much enfeebled, and writes to his friend, Mr Newton, under date March 13 :—

" DEAR SIR.—Here are the names of seven friends to whom I owe letters, and all common decency insists that I should write to each of them directly; but I have neither head nor heart to write three lines worth reading. I am dull to-day, and good for nothing. To write is, therefore, imposing a tax on my friends; but why should not friendship be taxed as well as everything else? Then I will begin with you, because you lie very near my heart. I can tell you that, through the blessing of my great and dear Master, I am tolerably easy, but whether I shall ever be able to go out again from home is very doubtful. Dr Benamore's medicines certainly do me good, but I fear my complaint will not be so far removed as to enable me to ride out above a mile or two at a time; but that matter is at present with the Lord, and I am very easy about it. Mrs Bull is tolerable, and poor little Tommy. And now I must ask you a question or two :—Are you well? Are you comfortable? Does the Lord keep you humble, and near to Himself? Your situation has its snares, and my earnest prayer is, that you may be kept from their influence, and that the Lord may greatly bless you. I think I never felt much more easy in my soul than I do now; and, as a minister, my obscurity and little usefulness admirably suit with my own proper nothingness. I bless the Lord that He keeps me out of those snares to which I see you are exposed. You, I hope, may have grace to withstand them, and, therefore, are where you should be.

I pray the Lord to own and bless you, and shall rejoice to hear of your welfare. . . . . Pray for me, that I may be kept from pride and despair, for I fear and tremble. When I am comfortable, I dread the former; when humble, the latter. Indeed, they are to me a Scylla and Charybdis, but hitherto the Lord hath helped me. . . . . . . I commit you to the tender love of Jesus Christ.—Your affectionate brother and servant,   W. BULL."

" You are inquired of," says Mrs Wilberforce, writing the same month, " by very many. My dear brother, [Mr Thornton,] who dined with me yesterday, favoured me with the perusal of your letter. I think you bless when you break the bread that perishes; it seems to multiply under your hand." And, again, in the month following :— " I never receive a letter from you but it affords me pleasure and profit. Many wise things you said here."

Mr Bull writes to Mr Newton, April 20, and after thanking him for the present of Kennicott's Bible, he proceeds :— " I can truly say that, whether I am well or ill, low or lifted up, I am firmly persuaded I am as the Lord would have me to be. I am well satisfied with all his conduct. My weakness answers a good end, for it shews me more plainly and effectually the strength and power of Divine grace, which can support and comfort a poor sinner under so great a natural and constitutional drawback on all comfort. My excessive propensity to dejection does make Jesus Christ look very bright, and beautiful, and lovely in my eyes; and it makes me exceedingly rejoice in Him, that He will and does condescend to give a lively hope of salvation to one who, otherwise, would be quite melancholy. . . . I have no cause to complain of the Lord, though much of myself; but I cannot help an infirm constitution that must and will decay. But I can do more than help it—*through special grace*, I can be thankful for it. Paul's thorn might not be taken away; but that sweet word, 'My grace is sufficient for thee,' was better to him than if it had been removed."

He concludes the letter thus :—" I pray for the Divine blessing on your labours, and commit you both to the tender love of my dear, though great and glorious Master, who, I hope, condescends to know poor me, and know me in a covenant way, as He does his dear children. The contrast between Him and me is so great that it astonishes me and makes me tremble; and yet I half believe the fact. The Lord help me, not only half or almost, but altogether to believe in Him, and you too.—I am, dear Sir, your affectionate brother and servant,

"W. BULL."

It was in the summer of this year that the "No-Popery Riots" occurred in London—

> " When the rude rabble's watch-word was ' Destroy,'
> And blazing London seem'd a second Troy."

In reply to Mr Bull's anxious inquiries, Mr Newton gives the following account of these disturbances :—

"Charles Square [Hoxton, Mr Newton's place of residence] was full of people on Monday the 5th; but they behaved peaceably, made a few inquiries and soon went away.

The devastations on Tuesday and Wednesday nights were horrible. We could count from our back windows six or seven terrible fires each night, which, though at a distance, were very affecting. On Wednesday night and Thursday the military arrived, and saved the city, which otherwise, I think, would before this time have been in ashes from end to end. So soon, so suddenly, can danger arise. So easily, so certainly, can the Lord set bounds to the wickedness of man, in the height of its rage, and say, ‘Hitherto shalt thou come, and no farther.’ . . . I preached on Wednesday, and had a tolerable audience; but I cannot describe the consternation and anxiety which were marked on the countenance of almost every person I met in the streets on that day.”

It so happened that the brother of a young man living at Newport, and to whom Mr Bull was much attached, was unfortunately implicated with the rioters. He was accidentally passing down Snow Hill at the moment the mob were in the act of destroying a distillery belonging to a Roman Catholic; and, being prevailed upon to taste some spirits offered to him by one of the rioters, he was seen and immediately taken into custody.

Mr Bull writes to Mr Newton respecting him :—“ I don’t know his parents, but have reason to believe them the children of your Father and my Father. . . . I beseech you, assist me with your prayers daily and earnestly, that the Lord may by His good Spirit comfort and strengthen this very afflicted family, most of whom are children of God, and that He will prepare for death him who expects it, and who seems much more earnest for the pardon of his sins than for the preservation of his life. If I had any interest by which I could promote a petition for his life, my heart, afflicted for his parents, would insure the exertion of it to the uttermost; but I have not, and must therefore be silent on this head. If you have neither opportunity nor interest to serve me outwardly in this affair, I know you have inwardly and spiritually; and I doubt not you will use it at a throne of grace. I could wish you to call on and converse with the criminal, if convenient. His afflicted parents exist in King John's Court, Bermondsey."

Mr Newton attended to both these requests. He saw the young man repeatedly. Mr Thornton exerted his influence on his behalf, and he was eventually pardoned, became a truly pious man, and to the end of his life, maintained a consistent character, discovering to the last his deep sense of obligation to those who had befriended him in the day of his calamity.

In the same letter, my grandfather speaks of the loss he sustained in Mr Newton's leaving Olney, "as one of the greatest trials I ever met with. I rode to Olney this week. I believe it is only the second time since you left it. The name of the place seems to have quite altered its signification, and the once dear Mr Newton is (in a great measure) to me no more. . . . Whatever be the general complexion of my experience, I know it is from the Lord, and is intended for His glory in my salvation. Every trial is a part of that cross which every believer must feel who is really following Christ into his kingdom; and truly my greatest trials are my greatest comforts. This paradox you can easily understand. I do not wish to be without them. I do not wish any departure in my experience from the will of my dear Redeemer. All this week I have been enduring a sort of crucifixion from my old complaint. What a blessing the pain is not constant! What a blessing to have it sanctified when it is upon me! It helps to make me humble; it renders Jesus Christ exceedingly dear to me; it makes me think, and think again, with a sweet, heartfelt, unutterable joy, of what He has done for me on Calvary, and what He will be to me on Mount Zion by and by."

About this time Mr Newton determined on publishing his "Cardiphonia," and requested Mr Bull to send him some of the letters he had written to him for insertion in that work. The last fourteen in the second volume are addressed to Mr Bull.*

With respect to the letters written to himself, Mr Bull playfully says Mr Newton might introduce them as, "addressed to a person I always thought eaten up with the

---

* It may not be uninteresting to give the names in full of the parties to whom these letters were addressed. Those of the first volume were written to the Earl of Dartmouth, the Rev. Thomas Scott, J. F. Barham, Esq., the Rev. Mr Rose, (a clergyman, son-in-law to Mr Barham,) the Rev. F. Okeley, (a Moravian minister at Northampton,) the Rev. Mr Powley, (son-in-law to Mrs Unwin, and vicar of Dewsbury, Yorkshire,) Mrs Gardiner, Miss Foster, Mr A. B., (who is designated by these initials I am not aware.) The letters of vol. ii. are addressed to Mrs Thornton, Mrs Talbot, the Rev. Mr Jones, (curate of Clifton,) the Rev. Mr Whitford, (Independent minister at Olney,) Mrs Place, (a Moravian,) the Rev. Mr Bowman, (a clergyman in Norfolk,) the Rev. John Ryland, jun., (afterwards Dr Ryland of Bristol,) the Rev. Dr Ford, Miss Thorpe, Sally Johnson, (Mr Newton's servant,) the Rev. Mr Collins, Mrs Wilberforce, Miss Delafield, (afterwards Mrs Cardale,) Mrs Harvey, Miss Perry, and the Rev. William Bull.

vapours." Another circumstance of interest occurred this year in the correspondence of these friends, in reference to a publication probably now (and justly) forgotten, but which at the time awakened considerable interest in some quarters—a book entitled "Thelyphthora; or, A Treatise on Female Ruin," by the Rev. Martin Madan. He was chaplain to the Lock Hospital, and was for some years a very popular preacher. He was the intimate friend of Mr Newton, and related to Mr Cowper. Hence the interest taken in the book by both these individuals, and the frequent reference to it in their letters.

Addressing Mr Bull just before its publication, Mr Newton says, "I feel a sort of trembling for its appearance. Much has been attempted to prevent its coming abroad, but in vain. The world are expecting it with an air of triumph; and in a few weeks more, I suppose, it will require some grace not to be ashamed of the name of Methodist. Let us pity and pray for the author. He ran well in time past, though now, alas! hindered and turned aside. Let us fear and pray for ourselves."

In a letter to Mr Cowper, Mr Newton says, "I have now read the first volume. It is specious certainly, and well calculated to convince those who have hitherto felt a conflict between their passions and their consciences. The violations of the seventh commandment, according to this writer, are few indeed. A man may leave his wife, or put her away,—if she is cross or ill-tempered to a certain degree, of which he is the proper judge,—without harm."

Mr Bull says of this work, in a letter to Mr Newton,

"I have just read with the utmost attention the first volume of 'Thelyphthora,' viewed and reviewed it with all the candour, generosity, and penetration I can possibly exert. It is an amazing compound of sound learning and abominable sophistry, evident truth and disguised falsehood, fine criticisms and foul applications of them, good talents greatly abused, a clear head, and a most corrupt heart. In short, it seems to me as deep-laid a scheme of Satanical device as anything I have read from the Koran of Mohammed down to the book called 'Christianity not Founded on Argument.' The memoirs of a woman of pleasure could not more promote the ruin of souls than this pretended defence of Divine truth bids fair to do."

Mr Cowper, in writing to Mr Newton, says of the publication, "I have read the second volume, and had some hopes that I should prevail on myself to read the first; but endless repetitions, unwarranted conclusions, and wearisome declamation conquered my perseverance, and obliged me to leave the task unfinished. I began his book at the latter end, because the first part of it was engaged when I received the second; but I had not so good an appetite as the soldier of the Guards, who, I was informed, would for a small matter eat up a cat alive, beginning at her tail and ending with her whiskers."

This work was satirised by Mr Cowper, in a poem called "Anti-Thelyphthora," and Mr Newton, in a faithful letter, declined all further communication with the author.

While there was a great talk about this dangerous book Mr Bull visited Potter's Pury, (once the scene of Mr Heywood's labours,) on occasion of the erection of a new meeting-house there. Some one present intimated that Mr Newton had said that the arguments of Mr Madan were unanswerable. Mr Bull at once, and with all the warmth of friendship, repelled this unjust attack. He wrote an account of the circumstance to Mr Newton, and says, " If I had health and strength I would publish a short argument against polygamy; but as it is, I cannot trouble myself about it." Mr Newton's reply is worth quoting :— " Though in haste to satisfy you, I am in no haste for rectifying the minister's mistake in what he thought proper to assert. I remember when I should have flown like a lapwing from house to house, from town to town, to justify my own dear self's own dear character. But of late I have in some measure learned one may be tolerably at ease though other people may say more than they ought. And if conscience is on my side, if the matter affirmed be not true, I sit quiet, and do not feel myself bound to make everybody as wise as myself."

September 8, Mr Bull writes to Mr Newton :—" I have this week had again to lament your absence from Olney. On Wednesday night I preached there. I believe almost every one of your serious friends came to the meeting, and indeed I may say I think that they seemed to love you in me. . . . My complaint has been easier of late, and the hot weather is going away. I long to see you, and hope the time is not far off. But let me ask, have *you* no thoughts of seeing the country before the winter? How glad should I be to see you both at Newport, and what a cordial would it be to some hundreds in and about Olney. If your empty-headed successor should have the rudeness to refuse you Olney Church, you know the doors of Weston and Clifton would be wide open to you, and I think, if need be, I could procure Newport Church for a day. On your part such a visit may not be desirable, but on the part of many that love you dearly it would, and highly pleasing to our dear Lord, and very useful to his dear children. I love you in yourself, and I love you in your own spiritual children at Olney; therefore I use this free-dom, and mention these things."

He writes again September 29, and, after speaking of an attack of fever, he proceeds:—"My dear friend, let us talk about London. My dear wife thinks I cannot come, that I am unable to undertake so long a journey; but I sadly long to come, and shall not be easy at all if I don't. I long to see you, to look at you; and if either you or Mrs Newton or I can say anything profitable, it will be very well; but if not, it will do me good to see you. It would be a great treat to shew Tommy London, and especially to shew him Mr Newton and family there; besides this, I think it would greatly relieve my own spirits, if I should be lonely and dejected in the night as I often am. The best scheme would be for Mrs Bull to go with me, but we cannot think of leaving home together at this time. One thing more, and I have done. I seem to myself as if I were wearing out, and another year or two would send me home; but I don't feel any anxiety about that. I think, through rich sovereign grace, when I am absent from the body I shall be present with the Lord, and I often long to enter on that glorious state where there is perfect holiness; for of all things sin is my greatest sorrow, and Jesus is the sweetest sound that ever catches my ears. Oh that it could once catch my heart, and be for ever fixed there!"

A few days after, again speaking of coming to London, he says, at the close of his letter,—"I shall only add, that if I come I hope the Lord (not self) will bring me there; and if *He* brings me, He must needs come with me; and if He comes with me, it will be for your good, and my good, and Mrs Newton's good, and then we shall all be glad together."

Mr Newton replies :—

"My dear Friend,—I am glad of the good news your letter contained. You will find a hearty welcome; but I charge you, upon your allegiance, to bring Tommy with you, and not venture into my presence without him. *Quam multa quam caria* shall we have to talk about! I shall think of you hourly till I see you, as children count the hours for days before the fair. Then the journey, the prospects, and the new objects will, I expect, so exhilarate your spirits, that when you come to us you will put us in mind of a bottle of well-corked cider when the cork is newly drawn. Oh, methinks I see, or rather foresee, how you will sparkle! . . . The week before I was at Ramsgate; but I was then a turtle without my mate, which was a little abatement. But why should *you* be without your mate? I wish Mrs Bull could come with you. Tell her I say so, and that we both send our love to her. But Tommy must come positively.

"Farewell. May the Lord be with you on the way, and at your journey's end! I hope He does favour us with his blessing. You will come to a house of peace, where every face will smile upon you.—I am, your affectionate poor brother, JOHN NEWTON."

The love of Christ was ever the theme on which Mr Bull delighted to dwell; and he thus expresses himself on that subject in a letter to Mr Newton soon after his return home,—" Yesterday, I spoke from John xv. 1-7 about one of the greatest, best, and most dear Masters that ever any servant has had the honour to be employed by. It is impossible to express with too great ardour how pure, holy, wise, powerful, and glorious He is. Nothing in the world can equal my admiration of his glory, on the one hand, nor, on the other, nothing can exceed my contempt for my old carnal self. And yet, I have no new views of Jesus Christ, or particular discoveries of his glory, which I have not had these twenty years; but, somehow or other, the older I grow the more my heart is affected with that little knowledge I have of Him. I tell you freely, my friend, (*inter nos*,) that I think myself one of the happiest men alive in this matter—viz., that I do know a little about Jesus Christ. I know there is such a Person. I know a little what kind of person He is in respect of poor lost sinners such as I am; and though I do not know certainly that I am interested in Him, yet I hope, and in general believe I am, if my heart does not cheat and deceive me. There are many things I say and do that don't look as though I really did love Christ, though I may think I do. Be that as it may, by the grace of God I am what I am; and all the rest our dear Master will settle for us very soon, and clear up everything

" In the meantime, next to the Lord, let us love each other, think of each other, and pray for each other daily; and let us rejoice in the Lord's goodness to each other in things outward and things inward. My heart blesses the Lord for his dealings with you; and I love to meet you at the throne of grace, and I long to see you and be with you before the throne of glory. Don't be lifted up by the world, and so forget to love and pray for me. I am not afraid that you will, but the temptation lies around you. Wishing you both health and comfort, we all three join in love, and I am your brother and servant.

"W. BULL."

In another letter, as Christmas was approaching, Mr Bull writes,—" The birthday of our dear Master is at hand. Blessed be his glorious and lovely name. May you and I keep it with pleasure and delight 365 days every year. But what shall we say to others to induce or allure them to love Him? I can't think of a text as yet. I wish Sunday's post may bring a line from you with a text or two for the day. I feel as if I should like to speak on a text of your pointing out, and especially if you are preaching from the same. Whatever the text, if our hearts are warmed with a sense of redeeming love, we shall be comfortable, and those that hear us comfortable too."

In the same letter,—" I see by the papers the second volume of Kennicott's Bible is out. I would not send for it, as I thought you might like to see it first. I expect the Prolegomena will be very curious and entertaining. especially his answers to the several objections which have been

started by a French abbé and other writers, since he has
been about the work. If you should be curious to search
the controversy *ad fundum*, I can send you an octavo
volume of letters on the subject in French; but if you
don't wish to keep it any time, you may send it down by
Mr Perry," &c. &c.

To this letter Mr Newton replies :—

" MY DEAR FRIEND,—Two letters for one,—how kind !
I would send you one every week if I had time. This
you know, and therefore accept the will for the deed.
I have not leisure—nay, I have hardly curiosity, to read
Dr Kennicott's curious Prolegomena. I thank you for
your offer; but if the book come hither, I must either
forward it unread, or keep it a whole year; therefore I
will desire Buckland to send you the book at once.

" I have not yet fixed on my texts for Christmas-day.
The two candidates that seem at present disposed to offer
are Gen. xlix. 10-12, for the morning, and John ix. 39
for the evening. . . . . We are glad to hear Mrs Bull
and T. are well, and you so-so. I hope your cough will
mend. We are past the solstice, and shall soon perceive
the peep, at least the forerunners of spring. Come May !
come June ! that we may trot down to Olney, Weston,
Newport, Bedford. Ah, wretched creature ! will you dare
to wish the time away ? Rather wish every minute was
an hour, while you have so much to do, and can so poorly
improve the little space allotted to do it in. Well, I wish
to wait patiently. May I improve the interval ! June
will arrive. Then, if we shall be spared, be alive, well,

and have money in our pockets, and the Lord's good leave
away for Bucks; and then I shall hope to share

A Theosophic pipe with Brother B.
Beneath the shadow of his fav'rite tree;
And then how happy I! how cheerful he!

Adieu.—Your very true friend,   JOHN NEWTON.
    "*December* 24, 1780."

These letters, with others which follow—and we are
happy in the possession of the letters on both sides—will
better than anything else illustrate the real history of Mr
Bull's life at this period, and the character of that happy
intercourse which still subsisted between himself and his
friend. The many beautiful sentiments, and the expression of devout and holy feelings thus exhibited, must
render their perusal interesting and instructive to every
pious mind.

Many letters were also received by Mr Bull from Mrs
Wilberforce, Mr Barham, and others, full of the warmest
expressions of esteem and affection, as well as rich in the
utterance of religious sentiment. The replies to them are,
alas! not within our reach—probably not in being.

In February 1781, Mr Newton writes,—"I do not envy
you your pleasure with Dr Kennicott. One hundred and
fifty folio pages in Latin, and upon a critical subject, would
have taken me a year instead of a month to wade through.
I have lost my acumen for such disquisitions, and perhaps
I am as well without it.

"While I was writing enter Mr Barton. We never
meet, I believe, but we talk more or less of a friend at

Newport. He tells me that he has prescribed something to good effect, and that your pains have retreated before his medicines. If it be for your good I wish them never to return; but if the Lord makes them messengers of grace and blessing to you, I dare not shut the door against them were I able."

The Mr Barton referred to in the above paragraph was a medical gentleman in London, a most excellent man, and a member of Dr Gifford's church, where Mr Bull had become acquainted with him.

The times were serious, and frequent reference is made to the subject in the letters of Mr Bull and his correspondents. Mr Newton sent his Fast sermon; and after thanking him for it, his friend adds,—" It is a mercy any one will step forth to bear a testimony to these awful and very questionable times we live in. I tremble at the blackening cloud that gathers around us, and must, and will, burst over us. It may perhaps be yet suspended in the atmosphere of God's long-suffering some twenty or thirty years longer, and it may not; but I feel sure that our destruction as a nation draweth nigh." .... In a subsequent part of the letter, Mr Bull thus proceeds,—" But now, dear sir, you shall have the best part of my story. I have lived almost three weeks in greater freedom from bodily pain than I have done for eighteen months past; and although I feel a little every day, it is but little to what I used to feel, excepting on the Sabbath-day, after preaching, and then the pain is pretty smart for twelve or fourteen hours; but what is better than all,—that I verily believe, when I have finished the ups and downs of my pilgrimage, the Lord Jesus Christ

will (through the infinite merits of his blood and righteousness) receive me into his everlasting kingdom and
glory. And what a mercy that will be! What a display
of rich, free, sovereign and distinguishing grace, to be brought
safely to glory, notwithstanding all my weakness, folly, unbelief, and at times, I may say, despair, which I suppose
is a great sin, and which I am too much guilty of! But
whether the barometer of my spirits is high or low, I can
think of a crucified Saviour with reverence, with strong
desire, and at times with real pleasure. And even when I
have no sensible delight in thinking of Him, I can truly
say I have no desire to think of anything else; and that's
a mercy.

"When you see Mr Barton, thank him for his medicine.
I ought to thank him myself, and perhaps I shall do so
some time. Miss Myers is here, and wishes to be remembered to you both. Her visit is pleasant to us, and I hope
not unprofitable to herself. We shall be very glad to see
you at Newport when it suits you. I hope you go on
comfortably, and keep near to the Lord, and as much out
of the world as your much-in-the-world situation will possibly admit of. I often pity you, and do not envy your
situation in the least; but you will say, and say truly, that
you are where the Lord would have you to be; and so say
I, and pray daily that you may have strength given to
meet the peculiar snares which surround you. . . . . . .
—Yours affectionately,   W. BULL."

Mr Barham, just at this time greatly occupied by family
business in consequence of the death of his brother-in-law,

late governor of one of the West Indian islands, says to Mr Bull,—" My pen has long been silent, but my heart is alive towards you;" and again, "Don't deny me your letters, they help to lighten my burden." In the same communication, he adds, " Mr Ryland, an awakened minister of the Establishment, comes to Newport to make your acquaintance."

In April of this year, Mrs Wilberforce came to visit Mr Bull; and in June Mr Newton was with him, and afterwards thus speaks of his visit,—" . . . My late visit to Bedford, Newport, and Olney left a pleasant savour upon my mind; and the recollection of incidents, which by the Lord's blessing may be profitable, remains with me. I was glad to find and leave you so well, for you seemed to me better than at any time since I have known you. I hope you will continue mending, till you are as sound and hearty as an oak—I mean, if so much health be good for you. But if indispositions, &c. are means by which the Lord designs good for your soul, then I must consent that you be afflicted. It is better to be sick or low-spirited than to be proud or careless, or to write foolish books, or to do foolish things, to make the Church weep, and the world laugh.

" Public affairs look darker still. Expectation is on tip-toe waiting for hourly news from all parts of the world, but foreboding that the news, whenever it comes, or from whatever quarter, will be distressing. I am afraid what we next hear from America will not be pleasing. That unhappy country is still likely to be a scene of desolation, and our people there to sink under the weight of pretended successes. In the West Indies, Tobago is gone, and perhaps by this time some other of our islands. And the cry of oppression in the East Indies seems at length to have awakened judgment there. Yet the spirit of the nation seems like that of the thoughtless mariner, asleep on the top of the mast, regardless of the danger every moment increasing. Yet still I hope there is mercy. The gospel spreads; grace reigns; the number of praying souls is on the increase, and their prayers I trust will be heard. We are sure that the Lord reigns; that the storm is guided by the hands which were nailed to the cross, and that as He loves his own, He will take care of them. But they who have not an ark to hide themselves in will probably weep and wail before the indignation be over-past. Blessed be God for a land of peace, where sin and every sorrow will be excluded."

In reply to this letter, Mr Bull says,—" Your views of our situation as a nation are just my own. I think we are ripe for ruin. Oh, what a mercy in all this to know Jesus Christ, and to love Him, and to fly to Him! I often think of those words, ' Enter thou into thy chambers,' &c. They that walk with God, and have their conversation in heaven, will either be taken out of danger or else be kept in safety through it.

" Last Monday, before I was aware, I got into a return chaise, and soon found myself at Northampton. On Tuesday night, I preached at Mr Horsey's meeting; Wednesday, at Mr Ryland's; Thursday morning, in Mrs Trinder's school; and in the evening, at Mr Ryland's again. On Friday morning I got into the coach and came home, and in the afternoon rode to Sherington to visit the sick; and to-day am dull and stupid, and good for little. But you see this has been a very busy week, and my spirits are all the better for it. I am very glad to find hard labour agrees so well with you; if I had more of it, it might be better with me. I feel thankful for the measure of health I do enjoy; 'tis all of it more than I deserve. But as for my soul, I think that is in a very sickly state. I long to see it more deeply humbled, and at the same time actuated by the warmest and most lively zeal for our great and dear Lord. I would have my soul live in the habit of prayer. I long to be cleansed from sin by the precious blood of a crucified Saviour, and to be adorned with his most glorious righteousness. These things I long for, but do not obtain; I pant after, but do not enjoy them. I would fain live in the Lord's will, and not in my own, in everything; and then I should think my soul more healthful than I do my body. But, after all, I would not complain. The Lord has done great things for me, and I rejoice in Him." . . . .

In the month of September Mr Bull was in London, and Mrs Wilberforce, speaking of his visit, says,—" I know it will greatly rejoice your heart to hear that many say they had great revivals while you were at Greenwich. I bless the Lord I can say it was a useful season to my poor soul. The views of Jesus, which seemed to absorb you in speaking of Him, both in John Street and St James's Place, kindled some sweet fire of love towards his glorious person, which I bless God for."

October 1st, Mr Bull addressed the following letter to Mr Newton:—

" MY VERY DEAR SIR,—You can easily form an idea of

a person who has just knowledge enough of himself to know that in general his company is more burdensome than pleasing, and who knows enough of the world to think that its smiles are not worth seeking, and who has constitutional pensiveness enough to prefer solitude to society : think of such a person seated in one corner of a little garden quaffing an Indian weed, warmed by a gentle tide of sunshine full on his face, and that pleasantly intersected by the intervening shade of a friendly lilac, whose gently waving leaves pleasingly variegate the solar influence,— think of such a one, free from bodily pain and mental dejection, serenely occupied in communion with his Saviour and his God, and you will then see and know how I do this morning. Blessed be the Lord Jesus for it.

"Last week I wished to write to you, but was too much indisposed, and I was glad to avoid wearying you with a string of gloomy complaints.

"I have just seen by the paper that our dear friend Mrs Barham is dead; in one view a very desirable event, but in another very affecting. What a world is this, and what a mercy to be taught by Divine grace justly to estimate its value, and treat it accordingly! 'Tis a great mercy while we are here to have health and outward comfort; but how much greater to have that health sanctified and laid out for eternity! I long exceedingly to be living daily to the honour of our great and dear Redeemer; but, alas, what constant cause do I see and feel for humiliation that so many things are said and done daily that fall short of this great aim!

"On Monday, a Mr Bridges from Oxford called, and stayed all night. Do you know him? He seemed to know something of the gospel, and a great deal of the world—a very accomplished man. What a mercy if he is equally humble and holy!" . . .

Shortly after, Mr Newton writes:—" . . . I believe you are indebted to me for Mr Bridges' visit. I met him at Mr Wilkinson's, and we happened to talk, amongst other things, of my Newport ale.* It seems he had a mind to taste it, which I barely expected, for he is a prodigious High Churchman, and rather disposed to stand aloof from Dissenters and Methodists. He is, however, a good man, and a faithful preacher. Indeed, you were not a little honoured (if you could think so) by his calling on you."

In the same letter Mr Newton says:—" I think Mr Scott has a crook in his lot. It will be good and charitable in you to see him often, to clap him on the back, and to say, Be of good courage. The ride will be useful to you; and while you attempt to water others, you will be watered yourself. Do not burn out in waste, like a candle in an empty room, but ride about for the consolation and edification of your fellow-creatures. But allow yourself time to write to your poor friend, JOHN NEWTON."

The following extract from a letter, written by Mr Cowper to Mr Newton, will explain the allusion to Mr Scott:—" Mr Bull is an honest man. We have seen him twice since he received your orders to march hither, and faithfully told us that it was in consequence of those orders that he came. He dined with us yesterday. We were all

---

* Evidently a covert allusion to something a little more intellectual. The reference is found elsewhere.

in pretty good spirits, and the day passed very agreeably. It is not long since he called on Mr Scott. Mr Raban came in. Mr Bull began addressing the former,—'My friend, you are in trouble; you are unhappy—I read it in your countenance.' Mr Scott replied he had been so, but he was better. 'Come, then,' says Mr Bull, 'I will expound to you the cause of all your anxiety. You are too common; you make yourself too cheap. Visit your people less; converse more with your own heart. How often do you speak to them in the week?' 'Thrice.' 'Ay, there it is. Your sermons are an old ballad, your prayers are an old ballad, and you are an old ballad too.' 'I would wish to tread in the steps of Mr Newton.' 'You do well to follow his steps in all other instances; but in this instance you are wrong, and so was he. Mr Newton trod a path which no man but he could have used so long as he did, and he wore it out long before he went from Olney. Too much familiarity and condescension cost him the estimation of his people. He thought he should insure their love, to which he had the best possible title, and by these means he lost it. Be wise, my friend; take warning, and make yourself scarce if you wish that persons of little understanding should know how to prize you.' When he related to us this harangue, so nicely adjusted to the case of the third person present, it did us both good; and as Jacques says—

'It made my lungs to crow like chanticleer.' "

The following letter refers to this and some other matters of importance :—

"My dear Sir,—Not a word have I got to say; but
the almanac says, and my conscience says, I ought to
write to you; and my heart says, Do, do thank your dear
friend for his last letter. Tell him how acceptable it was,
tell him how much it always cheers you to receive a letter
from him, and tell him briefly how the winter approaches,
and it much affects your health and spirits, and that you
begin to feel low and dejected, and unfit for everything
that is amiable or useful; that most things are a burden to
you, and that you are greatly, if not wholly, unworthy of
his favour and esteem. Tell him that you have visited Mr
Scott, and was grieved for him, but that you think there is
something in that dear and precious man which his present experience is the only proper cure for; and if Infinite
wisdom could have discovered a better remedy, this would
not have been made use of. Tell (says my heart) your
affectionate friend that you obeyed his orders, and improved the kind commission he indulged you with for
calling on Mr Cowper, and that you went again last week
and spent a day with him; and that if Mr Cowper and his
most amiable hostess were not weary of your company it
was well, for you were much pleased with them, and that
you quite forgive the idea of being an old square-toes.
Tell him also that you love Jesus Christ, and that your
whole soul is devoted to his service, and that you would
not leave one stone unturned for this end. Tell him that
your heart is impressed with earnest desire to devote your
relative to the ministry, because you believe the Lord
Jesus intends him for it, and will bless him in it; and that
you, with this view, purpose on Monday se'nnight, or

thereabout, to go with him to Oxford, to settle him in Edmund Hall, or some other college. Tell him your expense will be a great burden, but that your Master is omnipotent, and will bear you through.

"My heart bids me write to you, my dear Sir, about all these things, *cum multis aliis*. When you are not better employed, do write to me on this weighty affair. God knows the sincerity of my heart, and the liberality of my principles. Men will blame me; but my whole soul says, Go on. He that inclines you to it will carry you honourably through, and bring something out of this design for his glory, and the good of souls. . . . May the Lord bless you in all ways, and fit you and me for his glory!—Your affectionate servant, W. BULL."

Mr Newton replies:—

"DEAR SIR,—your trusty paper messenger told me everything you bid it. I am not surprised that a little of the gloom of November should tinge your spirits; but I hope, as the weather is bright again, your barometer will stand higher when you read my letter than when you wrote your own. . . . I am glad you have a pupil to send to Oxford, and I have no doubt the Lord will support and own you for what you do for *his* sake. I am glad also that you have been to see Mrs Unwin and Mr Cowper. He sent me an account of what you said to Mr Scott *coram* Mr Raban. I think it was well said. The truth is, the next time I am young, and begin to preach in a country place, I intend not to do just as I did at Olney.

"Commend me to your Lord and mine, when you are

with Him. I hope I long to know, and love, and trust and serve Him better than I have yet done." . . .

About a fortnight after, Mr Bull gives Mr Newton an account of his journey to Oxford. His strength was unequal to the fatigue :—" I neither felt nor tasted any Attic salt at Oxford that could in the least degree rouse my torpid spirits, or give vivacity to my imagination, Neither Mr Woodd (Basil Woodd) nor Mr Goode were at Oxford, but Mr Bridges carried me safely through every little difficulty. . . . I will trouble no one with even a distant hint that any help will be acceptable, only yourself— nor you either, if I did not love and honour you above all men; but as there is an exhibition from the Fishmongers' Company vacant at Christmas, and another next Midsummer, I wish you would engage Mr Foster, or some other friend, to apply for it. . . . I have this week taken a young lad into my house from North Crawley, with a design to give him his board and education for two or three years, hoping it may promote His glory whose I am, and whom I serve. I would imitate his example."

CHAPTER V.

Mr Thornton—Mr Cowper—Mr Bull a smoker—Evangelical Institution at Newport—Madame Guyon—Mysticism—Visit to Hastings—Letters from Mr Cowper.

THE year 1782 was a very important one in Mr Bull's history. From its commencement Mr Thornton became a very frequent correspondent of Mr Bull's; and that most excellent and large-hearted man gave him his warmest friendship. His acquaintance also with Mr Cowper speedily grew into a friendship, which was confirmed by frequent interviews; and about the same time the Evangelical Institution, as it was designated, was established at Newport, under the presidency of Mr Bull, and continued for many years to be a source of great blessing to the Church.

Writing early in the year, Mr Thornton says,—" You have been often in my thoughts, though I am become a bad correspondent; but I trust I shall be always thankful to hear of your welfare, and that the Lord prospers your work. I trust I am with you in joining heartily in wishing well to all that love the Lord Jesus Christ in sincerity, by whatever name distinguished. The misfortune is, we are all impeded, and ruined nearly, by being of one prevailing

G

sect,—*Selfists*, under various disguises; and all men think all men wrong except themselves. The devil's endeavour is to turn our work to others, and to make us unmindful that our business lies chiefly at home." Mr Thornton congratulates Mr Bull on his success in preaching at the neighbouring villages; and in reference to his placing his relative at Oxford, he says,—" I should not have suspected your business at Oxford, but it is a blessed one; and when the wheels stick, I hope to be able to supply you with somewhat that will keep them going. I think the expense is heavier than you are aware of." Sometime afterwards Mr Thornton thanks Mr Bull for his many comfortable and refreshing letters.

Mr Newton was very anxious, before he left Olney, that Mr Bull should be acquainted with the poet Cowper, in the hope that, while it would be mutually interesting, it might at the same time be a source of comfort to his much-gifted, but afflicted friend; and so it proved. A preceding letter of Mr Cowper's makes reference to Mr Bull's first visit. These visits very soon became a stated custom; and as Mr Cowper seldom went far from home, my grandfather dined with him regularly once a fortnight, or oftener, on which occasions my father generally accompanied him. Mr Cowper addressed the following letter to Mr Bull, dated March 24 :—

" My dear Sir,—If you had only commended me as a poet, I should have swallowed your praises whole, smacked my lips, and made no reply; but as you offer me your friendship, and account me worthy of your affection—which

I esteem a much greater honour than that of being a poet, even though approved by you—it seems necessary that I should not be quite dumb upon so interesting an occasion. Your letter gave me great pleasure, both as a testimony of your approbation and your regard. I write in hopes of pleasing you, and such as you; and though I must confess that at the same time I cast a sidelong glance at the good liking of the world at large, I believe I can say it was more for the sake of their advantage and instruction than their praises. They are children; if we give them physic, we must sweeten the rim of the cup with honey. If my book is so far honoured as to be made a vehicle of true knowledge to any that are ignorant, I shall rejoice; and do already rejoice that it has procured me a proof of your esteem, whom I had rather please than all the writers of both reviews.

"When your leisure and your health will allow you to trot over to Olney, you will most assuredly be welcome to us both, and even welcome if you please to light your pipe with the page in question.—Yours, my dear friend, affectionately, WM. COWPER.

" *March* 24. 1782."

In speaking of Mr Bull, in a letter to Mr Unwin, Mr Cowper says,—" You are not acquainted with him; perhaps it is as well for you that you are not. You would regret still more than you do that there are so many miles interposed between us. He spends part of the day with us to-morrow. A Dissenter, but a liberal one; a man of letters and of genius; a master of a fine imagination, or rather not master of it—an imagination which, when he finds himself in the company he loves and can confide in, runs away with him into such fields of speculation as amuse and enliven every other imagination that has the happiness to be of the party. At other times he has a tender and delicate sort of melancholy in his disposition, not less agreeable in its way. No men are better qualified for companions in such a world as this than men of such a temperament. Every scene of life has two sides,—a dark and a bright one; and the mind that has an equal mixture of melancholy and vivacity is best of all qualified for the contemplation of either. He can be lively without levity, and pensive without dejection. Such a man is Mr Bull. But he smokes tobacco! Nothing is perfect. '*Nihil est ab omni parte beatum.*'"

Many of his friends felt the charm of Mr Bull's society, and so it was eagerly sought by those who really knew him; but none could perhaps have drawn so true and beautiful a picture of the sources of its attractiveness as he whose genius could appreciate another's excellences, and whose pen could so exquisitely depict them. One element, however, of his character and converse must be added even to this high panegyric of the poet—one upon which he perhaps had a morbid dread of touching,—the deep religious tone of thought and feeling, that could not fail at all times to find utterance, or indirectly to manifest its existence. Still, possibly, under the very peculiar circumstances of this intercourse, the more solemn phase of experimental religion could seldom be brought forward; and it would appear that it was rather by letter than otherwise that attempts were made to remove, if possible, that unhappy perversion of sentiment that ever hovered like a dark cloud over the mind of this gifted but unhappy man.

Yes, Mr Bull smoked tobacco! Three pipes a day: but he was always a dry smoker. I don't know how the habit was formed; but it is very likely he found it an anodyne to his frequent pains of body, and that it soothed his nervous irritability. Perchance it might be supposed to give a gentle stimulus to thought. But of these things I am a very incompetent judge, for I have no experience to guide me. I only know that my grandfather regretted a habit which he often found inconvenient, and that he wished his son never to copy his example in this respect. His friends, however, were all very kindly considerate of him in this matter. Mrs Wilberforce, in making some alterations in her garden at Blackheath, told Mr Bull she had fitted up an arbour for him, where he might quietly enjoy his pipe. "I have visited," says Mr Thornton, "the lady at the Hill, and penetrated as far as your bower; but as there were no refreshing quaffs, my visit was short." So Mr Whitbread, in a poetical epistle (which is given in a future page) inviting Mr Bull to his seat at Southhill, says,—

> "I 'll fetch you here, if you will come;
> Pipe and tobacco-box are welcome.
> Your friends must always bless the art
> That mends your health and cheers your heart."

Mr Bull always smoked a particular kind of tobacco, and so was accustomed to take his box with him. On one occasion he left it at Mr Cowper's, who returned it to him with the well-known lines,—

> " If reading verse be your delight," &c.

where, it may be remembered, he says,—

> " Forgive the bard, if bard he be,
> Who once too wantonly made free
> To touch with a satiric wipe
> That symbol of thy power, the pipe."

The tobacco was Orinoco; and addressing the supposed nymph of that river on whose banks it grew, he concludes his poetical epistle,—

> " So may thy votaries increase,
> And fumigation never cease.
> May Newton with renew'd delights
> Perform thine odoriferous rites,
> While clouds of incense half divine
> Involve thy disappearing shrine,
> And so may smoke-inhaling Bull
> Be always filling, never full."

In April of this year, Mr Newton addressed Mr Bull on the subject of the academy. From his letter we give the following extract :—

" Mr Clayton [the Rev. John Clayton of the Weigh-house] lately called on me to tell me that many persons are seriously thinking of establishing a new academy, on liberal grounds, for preparing young men for the ministry, in which the greatest stress might be laid upon truth, life, spirituality, and the least stress possible upon modes, forms, and non-essentials; that it must be at a moderate distance from London; that, in fact, Newport was the place fixed upon, for the sake of one Mr Bull, who lives there, and who, it is hoped, would accept the superintendency. He said it was his request, and the desire of many of his friends, that I would draw up a plan for the forming such an academy; and, likewise, that I would write to you on the subject. The design met my hearty approbation, as it stood connected with Mr Bull, who, I said, appeared to me the most proper person I could think of to undertake it. As to my drawing up a plan, I half promised to write my thoughts upon it; that is—as I mean to tell Mr Clayton— how I should sketch out such an institution if I lived in Utopia, or Otaheite, and could have the management of things my own way. If they can pick any hints worthy of notice from such an attempt, they shall be welcome to them; but to draw a formal plan how an academy should be regulated in this enlightened age and country, and to hit such a medium as might unite and coalesce the respect-able Dissenters and Methodists,* who seem willing to pro-mote this business, might savour too much of presump-tion in one who was never either at university or academy himself, but rather spent the time which other young men employ in study in the wilds of Africa.

"However, feeling rather awkward at the service as-signed me, I told Mr Clayton I should wait to hear from you first, expecting that a sketch from you would in a measure illuminate me, and qualify me for the undertaking. I write, therefore, to know something of your mind. It is a service I have long wished to see you more fully engaged in."

Mr Newton having finished his task, writes again in May:

* A term then employed to designate Evangelical Churchmen.

—"... The most flattering sentiment I form of my work is, that though I have filled seven sheets of post paper with very close writing, I have a good hope there will hardly be found a single period which will meet your disapprobation. Your good opinion is of more consequence to me than that of others, because you are a nearer neighbour to me; for you live, or frequently reside, in Utopia, as well as myself. Though you and I are both originals in our way, have our separate and distinct peculiarities, and consequently cannot be exactly alike, yet, it appears to me (*absit invidia*) that I have the honour to think more with you upon the whole circle of our professional subjects than any minister I know; accordingly, I expect that you will approve in a manner of the whole and every part of my plan; whereas, I can hardly think of any other friend of mine who may not find something to object to here and there. But if I should be disappointed in this my sanguine expectation, and have not come so near your views as I think, you must let me down as softly as you can, for fear the mortification should hurt me, and I should feel too much when constrained to say, '*Ah, miser quanta spe decidi.*' The scene of my play is laid in Utopia. The acts, or heads, are four :—

"1. *The situation*—Why, not too near the metropolis, nor too far from it, but about a moderate day's journey of fifty or fifty-one miles.

"2. *The choice of the tutor.*—I will not tell you that it is your picture drawn from the life. It is sufficient if I have hit off a general idea of what you wish to be.

"3. *The choice of pupils.*—Why, they must be serious,

capable, and having desires already toward the ministry upon just and solid grounds.

"4. *Their studies and line of conduct. What they are to learn and do, and what they are not to learn nor do.*—If this should be thought a satire upon some academies, I can honestly say I did not intend it as such." . . .

In a subsequent communication, Mr Newton says,—" Mr Clayton and Mr John Wilson are both out of town. The latter is expected home to-morrow. I understand the present tutors of the Evangelical Academy (afterwards Highbury College) have proposed to resign their charge. I believe some of the supporters of that institution thought of you as the properest person to undertake it. But my plan will not suit with their design, which seems to be to give a little assistance to persons who have already begun to preach. But Mr Wilson told me that he did not doubt but there were people enough both willing and able to carry my scheme into execution."

Mr Cowper took a lively interest in this matter, and writes in June :—

" MY DEAR SIR,—Behold the plan of your future operations ! [The paper had come under cover to Mr Cowper] which, as I have told Mr Newton, the man being found who is able to carry it into practice ought not to be called Utopian." And again,—" I am glad you have read the plan three times with great pleasure. It is a sign that you have pretty well overcome your fears about the execution of it ; for fear hath torment, and is therefore incompatible with pleasure."

While the academy scheme is quietly advancing to its fulfilment, we may take note of some incidents that occurred in the interval.

In the letter of Mr Cowper, from which an extract has just been given, he says,—"I would willingly send you the lines that proceeded from the lips of my snuff-box, but, alas! they are no longer in being. I am a severer critic upon myself than you would imagine, and have the singular knack of being out of humour with everything, or almost everything, I write when it is about nine days' old. Accordingly, I have used them, no matter how; but Bentley himself could not have treated them with more indignity."

The knowledge of this fact led Mr Bull earnestly to request his friend not to judge his performances so harshly, and ere the fatal day of destruction arrived to send them to him, out of harm's way; and thus happily was preserved that exquisite piece,—

"The Rose had been wash'd, just wash'd in a shower," &c. ;

concerning which Mr Cowper says,—"I send you the *petite pièce* I promised—not quite so worthy of your notice; but it is yours by engagement, otherwise I believe you would never have seen it." So also was preserved the "Ode on Peace," composed at the request of Lady Austen,—

"No longer I follow a sound," &c.

Mr Bull's intimacy with Mr Barham of Bedford, and with the Rev. F. Okely, a Moravian minister at Northampton, induced him to take a great interest in the history of the Moravians, and also led to his acquaintance with the writings of the Mystics. He was greatly delighted with the poems of Madame Guyon. It seemed to him that it would be doing a good service to Mr Cowper in occupying his mind indirectly on the subject of religion, and perhaps eventually a benefit to the public, if he were induced to put some of these beautiful productions into an English dress.

In a letter dated August 14 of this year, the poet says, —"I thank you for Madame Guyon. I often spend a morning in translating some select pieces, such as I think may be successfully rendered in English. When time shall serve, you shall have the fruit of my labours."

Writing to Mr Unwin some little time before this, Mr Cowper says,—" Mr Bull, a Dissenting minister of Newport—a learned, ingenious, good-natured, pious friend of ours—has put into my hands three volumes of French poetry, composed by Madame Guyon. A Quietist, say you, and fanatic—I will have nothing to do with her. It is very well—you are welcome to have nothing to do with her; but in the meantime her verse is the only French verse I can read that I find agreeable. There is a neatness in it equal to that which we applaud with so much reason in the compositions of Prior. I have translated several of them, and shall proceed in my translations till I have filled a Lilliputian paper-book I happen to have by me; and when filled I shall present it to Mr Bull. He is her passionate admirer, rode twenty miles to see her picture in the house of a stranger, which stranger politely insisted on his acceptance of it, and it now hangs over his parlour chimney. It is a striking portrait, too characteristic not to be a strong resemblance; and were it encompassed with a glory, instead of being dressed in a nun's hood, might pass for the face of an angel."

The little book and the likeness are still in being; the latter is a well-executed drawing in crayons. None who are acquainted with these poems will wonder that they so much interested Mr Bull. There is a beauty, a tenderness, and a devoutness about them which rendered them peculiarly attractive to a man of his temperament, and a breathing of ardent love to the Saviour which would awaken his most hallowed sympathies.

Mr Cowper writes to Mr Bull at a subsequent date, when he was absent from home for some weeks :—" I have little leisure, strange as it may seem. That little I devoted for a month after your departure to the translation of Madame Guyon. I have made fair copies of all the pieces I have produced on this last occasion, and will put them into your hands when we meet. They are yours, to serve as you please; you may take or leave them as you like, for my purpose is already served. They have amused me, and I have no further demand on them." On Mr Bull's return Mr Cowper presented him with these translations; to which he added the Letter to a Protestant lady in France, and the poem on Friendship.

It may excite some surprise that Mr Cowper could write, or even translate, on subjects in verse which he trembled to approach in prose. "There is," he says, in a letter to Mr Newton, " a difference; the search after poetical expressions, the rhyme, the numbers, are all affairs of some difficulty. They arrive, indeed, but are not to be attained without study, and engross perhaps a larger share of the attention than the subject itself. Persons fond of music will sometimes find pleasure in the tune, when the words afford them none."

The idea of printing the poems was afterwards suggested to Mr Cowper, to which he gave his full consent. For this purpose, he intended to revise them; but circumstances prevented it, and therefore they were published in the form in which they now appear. "Nor can I imagine," says my grandfather, in his brief preface, "that even in their present form they will on the whole tend to diminish the well-deserved reputation of their excellent author."

One paragraph in that preface must be quoted. "To infer," says Mr Bull, "that the peculiarities of Madame Guyon's theological sentiments were adopted either by Mr Cowper or by the editor would be almost as absurd as to suppose the inimitable translator of Homer to have been a Pagan. He reverenced her piety, admired her genius, and judged that several of her poems would be read with pleasure and edification by serious and candid persons."

I have quoted this passage because Mr Bull was foolishly charged with being a Mystic. It is true enough that he studied Jacob Behmen, and other books of the same kind; but it might be said of him as Archbishop Secker said in refutation of a similar groundless charge made against Bishop Butler, "that the Bishop read books of all sorts, and knew how to pick the good in them out of the bad." The popularity of this translation of Madame Guyon's poems was very great, so soon as the book became known.

In September of this year, Mr Bull visited Mrs Wilberforce and Mr Thornton, at Hastings. "I long to have you added to my family," says Mrs Wilberforce, "as do the rest of us. I have found out a snug place for you to smoke a pipe in, and talk and think on Him who stilleth the waves." Mr Bull went down in company with Mr Newton. Mr Thornton took three houses, and one of them for his ministerial friends to preach in.

My grandfather was greatly pleased with Hastings. "If," he says, "it were in my power to live where I please, I should like above all places the sea coast; but it is best to be where the Lord would have us, and that is surely where we can do the most good. There is no meeting-house here, and the church people are as ignorant as possible. We had a delightful meeting last night. Mr Newton preached in Mr Thornton's house to about thirty." Dr Conyers was of the party. Services were held night and morning, in which one or other of the ministers were engaged; and in a letter afterwards written by Mrs Wilberforce to Mr Bull, she says :—"Your visit was a refreshing time to all of us. You feasted us with such dainty food. I hope it will be always remembered with gratitude."

On their return through Tunbridge, where they stayed a few days, "Tommy" had the measles, which was a source of much anxiety to his father. He was obliged to leave him for a few days, while he went to London; his son, of course, received every attention. Mrs Wilberforce speaks of him "as a very desirable child, and much to be loved by all who know him"—a promise which the future did not belie.

Some little time after his return, Mr Cowper wrote his friend the following beautiful and touching letter :—

"Mon aimable et très cher Ami,—It is not in the power of chaises or chariots to carry you where my affections will not follow you. If I had heard that you were gone to finish your days in the moon, I should not love you the less, but should contemplate the place of your abode as often as it appeared in the heavens, and say, Farewell, my friend; lost, but not forgotten. Live happily in thy lantern, and smoke the remainder of thy pipe in peace. Thou art rid of the earth at least, and all its cares. So far, I can rejoice in thy removal; and as to the cares that are to be found in the moon, I am resolved to suppose them lighter than ours below—heavier they can hardly be.

"I have never, since I saw you, failed to inquire of all the few that were likely to inform me whether you were sick or abroad, for I have long wondered at your long silence and your long absence. I believe it was Mr Jones who told me that you were gone from home. I suppose, therefore, that you have been at Ramsgate; and upon that condition I excuse you. But you should have remembered, my friend, that people do not go to the sea-side to bring back with them pains in the bowels, and such weakness and lassitude as you complain of. You ought to have returned ten years younger, with your nerves well-braced, and your spirits at the top of the weather-glass. Come to us, however, and Mrs Unwin shall add her attentions and her skill to those of Mrs Bull; and we will give you broth to heal your bowels, and toasted rhubarb to strengthen them, and send you back as brisk and cheerful as we wish you to be always.

" Both your advice and your manner of giving it are gentle and friendly, and like yourself. I thank you for them, and do not refuse your counsel because it is not good, or because I dislike it, but because it is not for me. There is not a man upon earth that might not be the better for it, myself only excepted. Prove to me that I have a right to pray, and I will pray without ceasing; yes, and praise, too, even in the belly of this hell, compared with which Jonah's was a palace, a temple of the living God. But, let me add, there is no encouragement in the Scriptures so comprehensive as to include my case, nor any consolation so effectual as to reach it. I do not relate it to you, because you could not believe it; you would agree with me if you could. And yet, the sin by which I am excluded from the privileges I once enjoyed you would account no sin; you would even tell me it was a duty. This is strange. You will think me mad; but I am not mad, most noble Festus—I am only in despair; and those powers of mind which I possess are only permitted to me for my amusement at some times, and to acuminate and enhance my misery at others. I have not even asked a blessing on my food these ten years,* nor do I expect that I shall ask it again. Yet I love you, and such as you, and determine to enjoy your friendship while I can. It will not be long. We must soon part for ever. Madame Guyon is finished, but not quite transcribed. Mrs Unwin, who has been lately much indisposed, unites her love to

---

* On such occasions he would sit down and take his knife and fork in his hand, to signify that he had no part in the exercise. My father has often witnessed this.

you with mine; and we both wish to be affectionately
remembered to Mrs Bull and the young gentleman.—
Yours, my friend,   WM. COWPER.

 "*October* 27, 1782."

Again, Mr Cowper writes in a somewhat more cheerful
strain :—

"CHARISSIME TAURORUM,—*Quot sunt, vel fuerunt, vel post-
hac aliis erunt in annis.* We shall rejoice to see you, and
I just write to tell you so. Whatever else I want, I have
at least this quality in common with publicans and sinners,
that I love those that love me, and for that reason you
in particular. Your warm and affectionate manner demands it of me; and though I consider your love as
growing out of a mistaken expectation that you shall see
me a spiritual man hereafter, I do not love you much the
less for it. I only regret that I did not know you intimately in those happier days when the frame of my heart
and mind was such as might have made a connexion with
me not altogether unworthy of you.

"If Mrs Bull will accept of a bed at our house, we have
one most heartily at her service. We hope that Master
Bull will accompany you; we can accommodate him too.
I add only Mrs Unwin's remembrances to yourself and
them, and that I am glad you believe me to be what I
truly am, your faithful and affectionate

                        " WM. COWPER.

 "*November* 5, 1782."

CHAPTER VI.

In the beginning of 1783 Mr Bull was in London. In reference to which visit Mr Newton says,—" My house will be at your service for the whole time, if you please. We love your company, and shall not be weary; but I do not mean to chain you. You shall be quite at liberty to please yourself if you can, and I will do my best to please you likewise.

"It would be strange if the men of the world were to have no fling at Utopians. But you know the fable of the dog and the moon. Let them bark; let us shine. Let them scold us, and let us pray for them. If we are in the Lord's way, in the path of duty, a bushel of our fellow-worms' opinions, either *pro* or *con*, can do us neither good nor harm."

During this visit Mr Bull preached his first sermon at the Tabernacle, Moorfields; and it came about thus:—Mr Berridge, writing to Mr Thornton, says,—" I have been laid up with a fever and sore throat since Sunday, and was not able to preach at the Tabernacle last night. My place was supplied by Mr Bull, an able minister. The chapel was full. His sermon was noble and bold; and the people were so agreeably disappointed, they thought no more of old Everton, but begged he might preach again next Wednesday, which was granted!"

"This circumstance," Mr Bull says in a letter written home, "many think will be of great use to the business of Utopia." He adds,—"Yesterday I left Mr Newton's; preached for Mr Crowle in the morning. Mr Frost carried me, after dinner, to Dr Gifford's meeting, where Mr Ryland preached in the morning on the words, (Luke ii. 14,) 'On earth, peace.' In the afternoon he sat by and heard me on the next words, 'Good will toward men.' An amazingly large congregation. Then I came to Mrs Wilberforce's, where I preached on Jer. viii. 22, 'The balm of Gilead,' and afterwards administered the Lord's Supper. Lady Smythe was present, and insists on my dining with her next Monday or Tuesday, so that I must stay here another week. This grieves me much, but I cannot get off. On Friday next I am engaged to preach at the Pantheon for Lady Huntingdon. The Lord makes my preaching here wonderfully acceptable."

Some little time after his return home Mr Bull endeavoured, amidst some opposition, to introduce the gospel at Woburn, in Bedfordshire, about nine miles from Newport. For this purpose he obtained a barn, which was fitted up as a place of worship. In connexion with this effort, Mr Thornton writes,—" I am glad to hear from you at all times, and congratulate you on Old Nick's ill success, that neither man nor cats could silence you from delivering your message faithfully; and as you are rewarded with an old barn, I cheerfully send you my contribution towards getting it wind and water tight; and may that Lord who once took up his abode in a stable be at your right hand in the barn, and grant you a good thrashing season!"

Mr Bull visited Woburn once a fortnight, and this effort resulted in the establishment of an Independent interest in that town. In writing to Mr Newton, Mr Bull speaks of this success at Woburn, and adds,—"The Sherington meeting (a village not two miles from Newport) goes on well; I hope the Lord is with us there dispensing the blessing of his grace and love. I know several persons who, I hope, are savingly awakened. 'Tis a comfort to be owned and blessed anywhere, and we ought to leave it to the Lord to determine where and when He will make us useful."

An amusing circumstance happened on one occasion in connexion with the preaching at Sherington. As Mr Bull was one evening riding into the village to conduct the service, he was met by the rector of the parish, also on horseback. They were on terms of civility, and Mr Bull said to him,—"I am going to attempt to do good to some of your parishioners." "Well, I wish you success," was the reply; "but I thank God I am not afflicted with the *cacoethes prædicandi.*"

It seems that Mr Bull was not favoured with much success at that time at Newport. He often speaks in his letters of his great discouragements; and but for his feeble health he would not have remained in what seemed so unsuitable a position; but it was the will of God, and better days were to come.

About this time my grandfather addressed the following consolatory letter to Mrs Newton, who was greatly affected by the death of her sister, Mrs Cunningham :—

"MY DEAR MADAM,—I am much affected by the afflicted state of your sister's family. We ought to bear each other's burdens, and thereby fulfil the law of Christ, which I am sure is a law of love. I could not withhold a few lines from you at this time, to remind you that I feel for you and pray for you, and do much wish you Divine support under your afflictions, and that they may be blessed and sanctified to you, and, in the hands of a wise and merciful Saviour, may be the means of weaning your heart more and more from the world, and of drawing you nearer to the throne of grace, where I could wish to live and die. Our afflictions are said to be but for a moment. And such they are, compared with eternity. But we who live in time, and are so little acquainted with eternal duration, are very apt to think them long and heavy, and should surely sink under them but for the special and peculiar support of Divine grace, which a dear and blessed Saviour is pleased to indulge us with. Our past experience of His kind support under trouble should operate upon our spirits to quicken and confirm our cheerful trust in Him. He has said, 'I will never leave thee,' and we have not the least reason to doubt His veracity.

"It is certain we have not long to continue in the present state. Happy will it be for us if it should prove the prelude to a better, which it indeed will if we are following the Lord, and those his servants who through faith and patience are now inheriting the promises. The ways of God are better to us than we suspect. All his dealings are founded on his covenant love, and are conducted with Infinite wisdom,—a wisdom so deep, so fine, so pure, so spiritual, that we cannot perceive it. Our shallow optics cannot penetrate it, and therefore we often misconstrue his light for darkness, his love for anger, and his very smiles for frowns; and yet after a time the Lord is pleased to rectify our misconceptions by pointing out to us the real benefit we received from this and that other trial which we have experienced in life. Indeed I do esteem afflictions a most important part of the spiritual life; not that there is anything good in afflictions themselves, but the Lord does use them so frequently and so effectually, that we cannot conceive how it is possible to go to heaven without them. I pray the Lord to render you serene, and silent, and comfortable under those you meet with, and thankful that they are seasoned with such plenty of the richest and most solid comforts. We all unite in praying for you, and commit you to the grace and love of the Lord our God." . . .

In another letter to Mr Newton he speaks with pleasure of his relative, Mr Thomas Bull, at Oxford, and after quoting some passages from a letter received from him, he adds :—" Thus you see, dear sir, how one of my chickens begins to chirp in Utopia. It fills my heart with joy to read his letter. Oh, blessed be God for his great mercy in so far answering my prayers; and I must add, that I have growing hopes of George Marshall, another little chicken that I much delight in. How wondrously has the Lord guided my poor vows and resolves to serve Him in the gospel of his dear Son. As soon as we have two pupils on the Society's foundation, we turn the school out of doors; but till then we cannot, for these two great chickens of mine need a great deal of corn to feed them. Next week the masons and carpenters come to make the necessary alterations for the accommodation of the students. May the Lord bless and support you both under all your trials! Accept our threefold love.—Your own

"W. BULL."

At the close of a letter from Mr Newton, written April 25, he says,—"I have found your letter of the 9th, and congratulate you on the chirping of your Oxford chicken. I hope (as old Honest says) he may prove a cock of the right kind, and crow to some purpose."

Mr Hill was anxious that Mr Bull should be present at the opening of Surrey Chapel, which was expected to take place in April. "It will rejoice the hearts of many that sincerely love you if you can make a little elopement for the Easter week, to help us in our gospel jubilee. If you could come and preach the afternoon or evening sermon, it would be very acceptable." The chapel, however, was not opened till the 8th of June, and Mr Bull did not preach there till the month of August.

The academy commenced with two students. "I have only time," says Mr Newton, "and room to wish you good success, in the name of the Lord, that his blessing may rest upon tutor and pupils, upon Mrs Bull and Tommy,—your heart, your house, and congregation,—upon all you preach to at Newport, Sherrington, Woburn, and everywhere else."

Writing on Jan. 10 to Mr Newton, Mr Bull, after speaking of his labours in teaching, says :—" Last Wednesday (the king's birthday) I opened our meeting-house at Woburn, with a long talk about the King of kings, from Zech. vi. 13. I have not been at Olney this summer, but I will smoke one pipe this afternoon with Mr Cowper, if I can, though I am exceedingly hurried." This expression was probably suggested by the following beautiful passage from a letter of Mr Cowper's a few days before :—

"My dear Friend,—My greenhouse, fronted with myrtles, and where I hear nothing but the pattering of a fine shower, and the sound of distant thunder, wants only the fumes of your pipe to make it perfectly delightful. Tobacco was not known in the golden age,—so much the worse for the golden age! This age of iron or lead would be insupportable without it, and therefore we may reasonably suppose that the happiness of those better days would have been much improved by the use of it. We hope that you and your son are perfectly recovered. The season has been most unfavourable to animal life, and I, who am merely animal, have suffered much by it."

On June 29, Mr Bull writes to Mr Newton :—

" My dear Sir,—. . . I hope Mrs Newton is reconciled,

at least still and quiet, under the Lord's hand in the removal of Mrs Cunningham, and that the child may yet be spared to be a great and real comfort to you both. Through mercy, I am tolerable, but not quite so well as I have been; but the vacation begins soon, and I shall get rest. Mrs Wilberforce has kindly invited me to visit the sea coast, which, I think, may do me a great deal of good, if my call is clear.

"The Utopian College is open, and I bless the Lord for it. I never felt more easy and happy in all my life than I do now. Mr Armstrong and Thomas Bull read Greek to me in the morning, and Mr Inglis, Church History in Latin; and then Mr Armstrong and Thomas read Latin together. George Marshall reads Latin to Thomas, and so does my dear Tommy.

" The Society meet on the 30th. I wish, as Paul said to Philemon, you could provide me a lodging with some friend or other for four or five nights, on purpose to spend an hour or two with the Society. It will not be in my power to serve them by procuring subscriptions or students. My duty seems to be chiefly in two things : first, to teach the students with care and diligence; and, secondly, to bear with patience a number of unkind things which one and another are severely, if not unjustly, saying of me. Last Tuesday I ordained a minister at Buckingham, where Mr Palmer of Hackney was, and who gave me a smart drubbing about the sermons I preached at the Tabernacle, when in town. The remarks were severe, but they did not hurt me. I thanked him, but did not promise to mend in future. I am not at all formed for a time-serving, man-pleasing preacher; but I am in all things to obey Him, whose I am, and whom I serve. I seek to please God, but not man; and sometimes it will happen that these two things are incompatible. Last week I concurred with Mr Horsey and Mr Carver in the ordination of Mr Raban. He has been much owned at Yardley, and I think verily the Lord will do much good there by his means. I hope and pray that in all things he will behave as becomes his profession. Mr Scott was with us there, and the next day dined with us at Mr Perry's [Lavendon Mill.] His conversation is very warm, lively, and zealous, on the best of subjects. Self, naughty self, is fully as troublesome at my house as at yours; but whether I take so much pains as you do to keep it at a distance may justly be questioned. I hope the Lord will overcome it in due time, but I never shall.

"Will you come down this summer? Come, and give us as much time as you can. We shall have two beds at your service, and three hearts that will rejoice to see you. We write in love to you both, and your two dear orphans. I pray the Lord Jesus Christ to be a Father and Saviour to them both; and am, very dear Sir, your most affectionate humble servant,   W. BULL."

The allusion in this letter to "naughty self" arose from a striking paragraph in a previous communication of Mr Newton's. He had said,—"I have many pleasant and kind connexions; but I have a troublesome inmate—a lodger—who assumes as if the house were his own, and is a perpetual incumbrance, and spoils all. He has long been noted for his evil ways, but though generally known, is not easily avoided. He lodged with one Saul of Tarsus, long before I was born, and made him groan and cry out lustily. Time was when I thought I would shut the door to keep him out of my house; but my precaution came too late. He was already within; and to turn him out by head and shoulders is beyond my power. Nay, I cannot interdict him from any one single apartment. If I think of retiring into the closest corner, he is there before me. We often meet, and jostle, and snarl at each other; but sometimes (would you believe it?) I lose all my suspicion, and am disposed to treat him as an intimate friend. This inconsistency of mine, I believe, greatly encourages him, for I verily believe he would be ashamed and afraid to be seen by me if I always kept him at a proper distance. However, we both lay such a strong claim to the same dwelling, that I believe the only way of settling the dispute will be (which the landlord himself has spoken of) to pull down the house over our heads. There seems something disagreeable in this mode of proceeding; but from what I have read in an old book, I form a hope that when things come to this crisis I shall escape, and my enemy will be crushed in the ruins!"

Writing to Mr Newton on the 25th of June, Mr Bull says,—" I have just been reading a letter of Mrs Powley's to Mrs Unwin, which gives a very pleasing account of some very promising young men lately ordained in the Church of England. 'Tis good news, and calls for the thankfulness of all who wish well to Zion. Surely the Lord will bring some great good out of these pleasing appearances. And if the Lord's own work is but going on, and the gospel prospering, it is matter of little consequence with me among what party it is, or by what instruments. My duty is to rejoice in its success; and I do rejoice. The time is short with me in this world, and it is little I can do, however faithful, or however diligent and active; but at least I can say that my heart earnestly wishes well to the cause of Christ and the salvation of souls.

"The hints you drop of the state of your own congregation shew that the Lord is with you; and I doubt not that you are thankful to Him, and rejoice in his work. Nor am I utterly forsaken. I preached at Bedford three times last Sabbath, and on Monday at Stagsden, in John Goodman's barn. I think there were near 200 hearers, in doors and out. Most of them seemed much affected, though my preaching talents (if I have any) are certainly much on the decline; indeed, I do not think by this time that I am fit to preach anywhere but in barns or chimney-corners; yet surely, in some small degree, the Lord is with me."

In August, Mr Bull visited Mrs Wilberforce at Brighton and Rottingdean. He writes to Mr Newton, and tells him "that he had not been altogether idle, but had been preaching, being earnestly desirous (if it might please the Lord) of promoting the knowledge of his great and dear name. Rottingdean," he adds, "is a place where the gospel is exceedingly hated, yet it has so happened that I have had from 130 to 300 hearers each time I have spoken. Their prejudices are abated. Many seem affected; and I hope I may say the blessing of the Lord has been amongst us. . . .

" I long to be at home again. 'Tis a wearisome pilgrimage: if it is but a useful one, all will be well; and when my poor day's work is done, I shall be glad that I may fall asleep in the Lord, and I hope be *for ever* with Him, notwithstanding the late Bishop of Bristol (your namesake) says, that the saints in glory may fall from heaven, and will, if they don't behave well."

Rottingdean was at this period a place of little religion: it was chiefly inhabited by smugglers. Here Mrs Wilberforce hired a house, I have heard, the only large and suitable house in the place; and Mr Bull preached daily in it, standing sometimes at the window, and at other times upon the lawn in front of it. This excited the anger of the clergyman, who resided at a neighbouring village, but performed duty at Rottingdean. Mrs Wilberforce and her family attended church on Sunday morning, the only time of parochial service; and on one of these occasions they were treated to a discourse on 2 Tim. i. 13, " Hold fast the form of sound words," &c., in which no doubtful or gentle allusion was made to the irregular proceedings which had recently taken place in the parish. This, however, only served to increase Mr Bull's popularity.

Before he left home Mr Cowper had written thus to Mr Bull:—" I wish you and yours a pleasant excursion, [Mrs Bull and his son accompanied him,] as pleasant as the season and the scene to which you are going can possibly make it. I shall be rejoiced to hear from you; and am sufficiently flattered by the recollection, that just after hearing your protest against all letter-writing, I heard you almost promise to write a letter to me. The journeys of a

man like you must all be sentimental journeys, and better
worth the recital than Sterne's would have been had he
travelled to this moment."

Mr Bull redeemed his promise, and, amongst other things,
gave Mr Cowper an account of the clergyman's tirade
against his methodistical doings, and received in reply the
following letter :—

" My dear Bull,—I began to despair of you as a
correspondent, yet not to blame you for being silent.   I
am acquainted with Rottingdean and all its charms—the
downs, the cliff, and the agreeable opportunities of saun-
tering that the sea-side affords.   I knew, besides, that
your preachings would be frequent, and allowed a special
force above all to the consideration of your natural indolence; for, though diligent and active in your business,
you know in your heart that you love your ease, as all
parsons do.   These weighty causes all concurring to justify
your silence, I should have been very unreasonable had I
condemned it.

" I laughed, as you did, at the alarm taken by your
reverend brother of the Establishment, and at his choice
of a text by way of antidote to the noxious tendency of
your discourses.   The text, with a little transposition and
variation of the words, would perhaps have come nearer to
the truth, and have suited the occasion better.   Instead of
exhorting his hearers to hold fast the form of sound words,
he should have said the sound of a form, which I take to be
a just description of the sermons he makes himself, which
have nothing but a sound and a form to recommend them.

" I rejoice that the bathing has been of use to you. The more you wash, the filthier may you be, that your days may be prolonged, and your health established. Scratching is good exercise, promotes the circulation, elicits the humours, and if you will take the word of a certain monarch of itching memory, is too great a pleasure for a subject. . . . .

" Mrs Unwin is well, and begs to be affectionately remembered to you and yours. I wish you many smugglers to shine in your crown of rejoicing at a certain day that approaches, and would take up the trade myself, if I could suppose it might be a means of introducing me to a place among them; but I must neither wear a crown, nor help to adorn one." . . . .

It appears, from a list of sermons kept by Mr Bull, that he preached in less than four weeks between thirty and forty times in Rottingdean and Brighton; and, as it was afterwards found, not without some blessed fruits.

In November, Mr Hill wrote to Mr Bull, requesting his services at Surrey Chapel about Christmas. He says,— " I trust the Lord will incline your heart to come, nothing doubting but that it is his will that you should come. I write to you thus early, that I may have timely notice when you can favour us with a visit, and how long that visit is to last. Short visits from some people, I confess, I like better than long ones; but from you, I not only can say in regard to myself, but for many others, the longer your visit is made the more thankfully will it be acknowledged.

"It is somewhat pleasant now and then to graze in a fresh pasture, especially when people seem hungering for the word. Such, I trust, you will find the congregation in this place. The Lord constrain you to come and see; to come soon, and stay long.—So prays your affectionate, though unworthy brother,　　　　　　　R. HILL."

To this request Mr Bull acceded, and preached at Surrey several times in January of the year 1784. He preached also at Jewin Street, Pinner's Hall, and Tottenham Court, and at private houses as well.

In February Mr Cowper writes :—

". . . Are you not afraid, Tory as you are, to own your principles to me, who am a Whig? Know that I am in the opposition; that, though I pity the king, I do not wish him success in the present contest; but this is too long a battle to fight upon paper. Make haste, that we may decide it face to face. We shall be happy to see you, but beg that, if possible, we may have notice of your coming to take a dinner with us, that we may take care to be at home. Our respects wait upon Mrs Bull, and our love upon the young Hebraean. I wish you joy of his proficiency, and am glad that you can say with the old man in Terence—

'Omnes continuo laudâre fortunas meas,
Qui natum habeam tali ingenio praeditum.'

—Yours,　　　　　　　　　　　　　　　W. C."

In April there occurred some little unpleasantness among the students, fomented by a self-willed Scotchman who was of their number. It issued in his expulsion, and afterwards all went on smoothly. It was, however, a very great trial to Mr Bull. His habitual tendency to look at matters of this kind in the most unfavourable aspect perhaps prevented the exercise of that courage and decision so necessary in such cases. He says, in reference to it, " The academy was exceedingly pleasant to me on many accounts; but its duration will be short, very short indeed."

" I am still willing to hope," says Mr Newton, in reference to this matter, " that the Lord was favourable to the setting up of the Newport Academy, and that He will not forsake it. It is not the first time Satan has attempted to interrupt good beginnings. We have likewise often heard of his disappointment. This shake may prepare the way for an establishment, for clearing up and settling things more firmly."

In July, Mr Bull visited Lymington, in company with Mrs Wilberforce and Mr Thornton. He writes to Mrs Bull from the Isle of Wight; and, after speaking of the beauty of the scenes by which he was surrounded, he adds,—" But how infinitely short does it fall of my faintest views of the Kingdom of Heaven, that blessed world of spirits, where I hope and pray that you and I shall spend an eternity together!" And again, referring to the ease with which they can correspond with one another, and observing how pleasant it would be if friends beyond the sea of human life could as easily carry information to us and we to them, he says,—" But one thing is certain, that

we may correspond with One in the invisible world, even
Jesus Christ, who always receives our information safely
and speedily, and we receive his gracious answers without
any failure or miscarriage.   In this view, a correspondence
in heaven is more easily carried on by far than one on
earth!"

Coming home by Portsmouth, Mr Bull preached there
twice on the Sabbath.   At night he addressed a very
crowded congregation.   "The sermon," he says, "was all
about the *Royal George*."*   A great anchor had been got
up from the wreck the previous week, and his text was (as
I find from the sermon index) Heb. vi. 19, "Which hope
we have as an anchor of the soul," &c.   My grandfather's
services at Lymington were frequent; and on his way home
through London he preached at Surrey Chapel, the Tabernacle, and elsewhere.

On his return to Newport, Mr Cowper writes the following letter :—

"MY DEAR FRIEND,— . . . We are both indebted and
obliged to you for your journal of occurrences, and are glad
that there is not one among them for which *you* have
reason to be sorry.   Your sea-side situation, your beautiful
prospects, your fine rides, and the sight of the palaces
which you have seen, we have not envied you; but are
glad that you have enjoyed them.   Why should we envy
any man?   Is not our greenhouse a cabinet of perfumes?

---

* The *Royal George*, sunk at Spithead, August 1782—
"When Kempenfelt went down,
With twice four hundred men."

Is it not at this moment fronted with carnations and balsams, with mignonette and roses, with jasmine and woodbine, and wants nothing but your pipe to make it truly Arabian,—a wilderness of sweets?

"The 'Sofa' is ended, but not finished—a paradox which your natural acumen, sharpened by habits of logical attention, will enable you to reconcile in a moment. Do not imagine, however, that I lounge over it; on the contrary, I find it severe exercise to mould and fashion it to my mind.

"Let us see you as soon as possible. Present our affectionate respects to your family; and tell the Welshman and his chum that if they do not behave themselves well I will lash them soundly. They will not be the first academies to whom I have shewn no mercy.—Yours, with Mrs Unwin's love, WILLIAM COWPER."

*   *   *   *   *

When Mr Bull was at Lymington he preached at the Independent chapel. The people were without a minister, and were exceedingly anxious that he should settle amongst them; and though he had said in one of his letters from that very place that he thought he was buried alive at Newport, and had other reasons for not being altogether happy there, he did not feel at liberty to accept the invitation.

Mr Thornton, still at Lymington, writes to Mr Bull:—"Your company was, I trust, much blessed to my sister Bewicke, and when you visit town you must call on her." Another passage in the same letter may be quoted:—"I have so much to deaden me, that I want a pair of bellows to be blowing continually to keep up the Divine flame blazing in my polluted heart. The cares of this world and the hurry of life are sad dampers. Through mercy, I have been hitherto kept in the midst of the fire, and can rejoice with trembling when I look back at past scenes. I trust I shall have your prayers."

In the latter part of this year Mr Cowper was about publishing his "Tirocinium," and he wrote the following letter to Mr Bull in reference to it :—

" MY GOOD FRIEND,—The 'Task,' as you know, is gone to the press. Since it went I have been employed in writing another poem, which I am now transcribing, and which I design in a short time shall follow. It is called 'Tirocinium; or, A Review of Schools.' The business and purpose of it are to censure the want of discipline and the scandalous inattention to morals that obtain in them, especially in the largest, and to recommend private tuition as a mode of education preferable on all accounts; to call upon fathers to become tutors of their own sons, where that is practicable; to take home to them a domestic tutor, where it is not; and if neither can be done, to place them under the care of such a man as he to whom I am writing, —some rural parson, whose attention is limited to a few. Now, what want I? A motto! I have taken mottoes from Virgil and Horace, till I begin to fear lest the world should discover (what is indeed the case) that I have no other authors of the Roman class. Find me one, therefore, in one of your multitudinous volumes. No matter whether it be taken from Burgersdicius, Bogtrottius, or Puddengulpius—the more recondite the better. The world will suppose that at least I am familiar with the author I quote; and though the supposition will be an erroneous one, it will do them no harm, and me some good.

"When you have found it, bring it with you, either to-morrow, Saturday, or Monday. One of these three days you and your son must dine with us. Choose, and let us know which you choose in answer by the bearer.—Yours, with our joint love to Mrs Bull and Tommy,

" WILLIAM COWPER.

"*November* 8, 1781."

In accordance with this request, my grandfather sent his friend two mottoes in Greek—one from Plato, and another from Diogenes Laertius.

CHAPTER VII.

Mr Greatheed—Mr Bull's Letter on his Son's Birthday—Visit to Ireland—
Preaching at Cork—Peril in Cork Harbour - Story of Mr Thornton—
Letter to Mr Newton on the Death of his Niece—Mr Storry—Mr Bar-
ham—Letters to and from Mr Newton—Comment on the Psalms—Mr
Wilberforce—Visit to Yarmouth—Accident at Norwich—Mr Newton's
Letter on the occasion—Person taken up for Forgery—Letter to Mr
Newton.

In the early part of 1785, Mr Bull was in London, his
friends almost contending for his society.

About this time Mr Greatheed became one of Mr Bull's
pupils. He was a man of considerable ability, and for a
long time was more or less connected with Newport and
its neighbourhood. Mr Greatheed was originally in the
army, and attached to the corps of Engineers. While
engaged in service in British North America he became
sensible of the importance of personal religion, chiefly
through the instrumentality of a brother officer (afterwards
Lieutenant-General Mackelcan.) Before this he led a
dissipated life. In a letter to my father, he says,—" I
feel more than you what I owe to the grace of God, through
Christ Jesus, in extricating me from the way of trans-
gressors ; for I don't suppose there was a greater profligate
than I was at eighteen."

Having tasted of the grace of God, he was anxious to bring others to the Saviour, and resolved to devote himself to the work of the ministry. For this purpose he gave up his prospects of promotion in the army, and entered the Institution under the direction of Mr Bull. In some departments of study he was already qualified to give aid to his tutor, and before long took a portion of the labour off his hands. Mr Greatheed subsequently married a lady of Newport; and there he resided nineteen years, being during part of that time pastor of the Independent church which Mr Bull had raised at Woburn.

Mr Greatheed was a man of considerable ability and very extensive reading, one of the most active founders of the London Missionary Society, and the first Editor of the *Eclectic Review*. He was also a fellow of the Antiquarian Society, amongst whose "Transactions" is a learned and curious dissertation "On the Origin of Nations" written by him. During the latter years of his life Mr Greatheed was the subject of considerable infirmity. He died in Somersetshire in 1823.

Being in London in July on a visit to Mrs Wilberforce, at Blackheath, Mr Bull wrote to his wife on the birthday of their dear son, who was with his father. "This," he says, " is a memorial day, (as the Brethren say,) and I write to remind you that I do not pass over it without notice. This day thirteen years the Lord gave us a son, and he is now alive and well, and the only child we have alive. All these things loudly call for humble and hearty thanks to a dear Saviour, who has been so good to us, and dealt so bountifully with us. We have great reason to rejoice that the Lord has indulged us with thirteen years' enjoyment of the presence of our child; but we ought to rejoice with trembling, and not forget that life is uncertain. He may be removed from us, or, if spared, may be a sorrow to us; still we have to be thankful that at present we have no great cause of uneasiness from Tommy, nor any very strong symptoms of future sorrow. . . . I do bless God for him, and he is my great comfort; but I remember a Benny, a Billy, a Polly, and Sally; but, blessed be God, I can rejoice on their account, and I do rejoice. I hope this dear child will many years hence support and comfort us when we are on a death-bed, and that he may grow up to know and love the Lord Jesus Christ, and to serve Him in his vineyard; and I pray God that your life may be spared to see many returns of this day."

Mr Bull left Blackheath in company with Mr Thornton on a journey to Ireland. The Rev. R. Storry, an excellent clergyman, from Colchester, and my father were of the party. They passed through Stratford-on-Avon and Birmingham, and reached Shrewsbury on Saturday. There Mr Bull preached on Sunday, and also heard Mr De Courcy. On Monday they breakfasted with the devout Fletcher of Madeley, entered Wales, passed through the magnificent Vale of Llangollen to Bangor and Anglesea, and reaching Holyhead, crossed to Dublin. Mr Bull preached there four times, and again they were on the move. Mr Thornton was always active, and full of energy. My grandfather says in one of his letters home, " I fear Mr Thornton finds me troublesome. He is always in motion; I am always wanting to sit still."

From Waterford Mr Bull writes,—" The Irish, I think,

are nearly all of them rebels to their king, tyrants or beggars to each other, and awfully ignorant of their God. The country is very pleasant to travel through, as far as regards the prospects; but their inns are dirty and miserable; provisions very so so, excepting the fish, which is plentiful and excellent.

"I bless our dear Lord that I have to add, that I hope through rich mercy we have his gracious presence in our devotional exercises; and Mr Thornton's kindness and love keep us all in good spirits, while his generous heart and good purse procure us the best of everything the place will afford, wherever we come. His company would make a journey through the deserts of Arabia cheerful and pleasant. Mr Storry is very pleasing to me, especially when he prays or converses. To be sure he loves to run about, and so does your son, but you know I love ease. We often think of our wives, speak of our wives, and would write if we could more readily send to you; however, we pray for you, and drink your health; and whenever we come near you, certainly will do ourselves the pleasure to wait upon you. But if we never come, be assured we dearly love you, and you live very near our hearts, especially when we are near the throne of grace, and are speaking to our best and dearest friend, the Lord Jesus Christ, to whose grace and love I tenderly commit you." . . . .

On the 11th August they reached Cork. Writing from thence, Mr Bull says,—"I fear you will not receive this in less than a fortnight; but I wish to write that you may know that we are alive and well, and do by no means forget you. If wishing would bring it to you, it should be

with you to-morrow morning.   We are all well, and in
good spirits; but I confess I begin to wish myself in England again.   This morning we had a very fine voyage of
nine miles to Cove, in Cork harbour; but in coming back
it was stormy and dangerous; we were, however, through
God's mercy, brought home in safety at last."   The fact
was, that a tremendous storm overtook them, one of the
sails was torn to rags, the mast broken, and a wave washed
away the rudder; but that was happily regained.   To add
to their trouble, one of the two sailors was intoxicated.
The party were obliged to lie down in the bottom of the
boat, and, after two or three hours' tossing about, they
reached a landing-place, and walked to Cork.

Being at Cork on the Sabbath, Mr Bull preached in the
Presbyterian chapel.   This was in the morning; and
before the service the assistant minister, who was the
evening preacher, asked Mr Bull to take his duty also;
telling him, however, that the congregation would be very
small, as the people were not in the habit of coming out
more than once a day.   And no wonder, for they were
reputed to be Arians.   The morning service was probably
not much to the taste of the regular congregation, but, to
the surprise of every one, the chapel was filled in the
evening by Wesleyans, Catholics, and persons of all classes.
The Wesleyan minister came up to the pulpit to Mr Bull,
and asked him to preach for him on the Monday, to which
he consented, when the interest of the people was so much
engaged that he addressed them again the next evening;
and then there was so great a crowd it was with difficulty
my grandfather could get to the pulpit.

At Mr Thornton's suggestion, Mr Bull wrote a tract, entitled "The Seasonable Hint." This was printed at Dublin, and hundreds of copies of it were distributed in the journey.

I remember my father often relating a circumstance in connexion with this visit to Cork, strikingly illustrating Mr Thornton's generosity, and his tact in business. He walked out early one morning, and took my father with him. They went down to the harbour, where a number of vessels, laden with tallow, had just arrived. Mr Thornton made some inquiries, not of any interest or apparent importance to his little companion. They then went to a nursery ground, and got into conversation with the man who occupied it. He appeared to be a worthy man, but was in great trouble, as Mr Thornton found out, for the want of £10 to lay out upon his ground, without which it was of little profit to him. On their return to the inn, Mr Thornton made full inquiries about this person, and, finding that he was all that he appeared to be, he enclosed a £10 note in a paper, and sent it to him by my father. The inquiries in the harbour had also an important result. Some months after, Mr Thornton asked my father if he remembered their morning walk on that day; and he told him that he then bought up all the tallow in Cork, and that the purchase had more than paid the expenses of their journey.

The party left Ireland on 23d August, and arrived at Bristol; and in a letter written thence Mr Bull says,—"Through the blessing of that Jesus who is ever faithful to those that fear Him, we safely landed this morning from a four weeks' tour through Ireland—a land overflowing with pride, rebellion, beggary, and dirt. But we have many things to be thankful for on this occasion. It has made me think of England, of Newport, of you, with more pleasure and delight than ever, if possible. The best thing in Ireland was, that we preached the gospel with acceptance, and that we had but a little time to stay there. We have been wonderfully favoured with health, and with a safe voyage back again. I shall exceedingly rejoice to see you once more, and to find you well; and certainly I may add, that the older I grow the more dear you are to me, and the more necessary for my comfort. I think of you, speak of you, and pray for you daily.

"I could make a hundred remarks on what we have seen, but must refer you to Tommy's journal; and shall only say that, whether at home or abroad, I find the Lord Jesus ever faithful, and ever tender and affectionate and good to me; and therefore I cannot but love Him and delight myself in Him. 'He is mine, and I am his.'"

On his homeward journey Mr Bull preached at Bristol, Bath, Reading, and in London at Surrey Chapel, and elsewhere, reaching Newport on 8th September.

In the month of October, Mr Newton lost his niece, Miss Cunningham. Mr Bull thus expresses his sympathy with him on the occasion :—

". . . There is great reason to be thankful for the easy and happy manner of her departure, and I bless God on that account, and rejoice in this instance of his condescending grace and love, both to yourself and the child. It greatly pleased me to see with what serenity and piety you talk about this event, but much more to mark the divine resignation that discovered itself in your niece. Behold and wonder at what God can do, and does do, to manifest the glorious power of his grace and love. Such evidences of the spiritual presence of the Lord Jesus do me more good than a thousand sermons, even of the best. It cheers one's spirit, confirms one's faith, disarms one of the fear of death, and makes futurity look cheerful. Though you seem very comfortable, and I bless God for it, yet no doubt you both feel something for the loss of one whom you considered as your own, and the more for her being so graciously formed to engage your best affections. I feel for you, and know something of the conflict between grace and nature on such occasions. Each puts in its claim; each has a just demand; each will be heard; each must be felt. To reason on the matter is impertinence; to feel is a duty; to be silent is divine.

"Your sympathy with me on a like occasion, and your pity, was a cordial; but God's voice is peremptory, and duty is painful. What a mercy it is Mrs Newton is so comfortably supported! I ought to bless the Lord for his goodness to her, and I do it; but the time makes haste when sighing and sorrowing shall be for ever done away. Yes, we are going; and though they cannot come back to us, we shall go to them. And how delightful that interview! How sweet the converse we shall then have with them! Those who on earth could charm us in a mortal frame, how shall they delight us amongst the spirits of the just made perfect, when dressed in all the glory of eternal life, brightened by all the joys of salvation!

" If one can do a little good by staying longer in the world, to be sure we ought to stay. 'Tis no great thing to let them that are most dear to us go a little before us, or for us to be willing to stay a little after them for the benefit of others. And yet, were it not for that benefit, we would wish to depart and to be with Christ, which is certainly much better than to be here. I would rather wish on a deathbed to believe my children are safe in glory before me, than to see them about me, and to be doubtful whether they will ever follow after." . . . .

How much Mr Bull won upon all with whom he became acquainted, and how edifying his intercourse was, we have already seen. This is further confirmed by the following extract from a letter of the Rev. R. Storry, his travelling companion in Ireland :—" I have reason to love and to esteem you on a higher and better account than your attention to me. I love you for what you have so often told me about your Lord and Master, and for your brotherly endeavours to stir me up to use all diligence in his blessed work. If it had pleased God that my lot had been cast near you, I think I should have been able to profit much from your friendly hints and conversation ; but I should be thankful for the opportunities I have enjoyed, and desire to retain many things that I have seen and heard." He then requests that Mr Bull would give him in a more permanent form some of those hints made during their " happy excursion," and begs he will not fail to write when he could steal half an hour.

In January of the following year, Mr Bull visited Mr Storry at Colchester; and on the night of his arrival preached in the good man's kitchen, and the next night at the Independent chapel. With all Mr Bull's liberality of sentiment, he was never ashamed of his Dissent; and the Church party of that day, with many of whom he was so intimately associated, never seem to have respected him the less because he did not in all things see with them. Gospel truth was the one cherished object of their thoughts, and concern for its promotion the work for which they lived and laboured.

In November, Mr Thornton paid a short visit to Mr Bull at Newport. He spent the Sabbath with him, and wrote back,—"I was thankful for all I saw and heard at Woburn, Newport, Sherington."

At the end of the year my grandfather went to London, and was welcomed, with his son, at Clapham, Blackheath, and elsewhere. He supplied, during the same visit, the pulpits he was accustomed to occupy.

Many were the affectionate and christian letters Mr Bull received from his friend Mr Barham. In one of them, dated February 18, 1786, he writes,—" If you could know my heart, you would find it echoed back the sentiments of your letter. I am, or seem to myself, tired, very tired, of the world, carnal and religious; tired of myself, and sighing out in secret places, Oh that He would come and rest in his love! But, alas! this heart of mine, when shall it be emptied of all other love, to give Him alone entrance and possession! My dear Lady Hill [Mr Barham had married the widow of Sir Rowland Hill] pleases herself, as I do myself, that the time will come when Hardwicke shall see you." In a subsequent letter, Mr Barham writes,

—"My dear friend whom the Lord has given me as my companion in my pilgrimage loves you, salutes you, and bids me say—which I do with all my heart—Come to see us, when you can, in Shropshire. Whether you come or not, we shall believe that you love us."

In the same month Mr Bull addressed the following letter to Mr Newton :—

"My dear Sir,—You and I are both hastening to the grave, but in very different circumstances. You at your leisure may sit all day and contemplate the coming foe, till you grow quite familiar. You can look beyond the grave, and in the prospect of eternal rest and joy can find time to say, 'Come, Lord Jesus, come quickly.' I congratulate you, and feel the pleasing prospect that is before you. How different is my situation! On the pillow I have the necessary business of the day to contemplate, under the gloomy pressure of my own inability to get through it; and when up, either the pen or the tongue must be active till I return to that pillow, not to prepare myself for death, but others for life and usefulness.

" But, through the wonderful goodness of God, I run through the daily task with ease, with pleasure, and with enjoyment. What was a great fatigue two or three years ago is now a constant pleasure. Habit makes things easy, and Divine assistance makes duty a delight. I think the Lord is with me, and his blessing on the Utopian Academy, notwithstanding it enjoys so little popular applause, or may prove so little acceptable to many. God helps me to be faithful and diligent; and if I can't meet the smiles of many, but must work under the weight of their contempt, yet I can remember a line in Addison,—

> ‘ We can't command success, Sempronius;
> But we 'll do more, we 'll deserve it.’

“ And now, sir, what shall I tell you, to make this sheet of paper worth half the postage? What shall I tell you that you do not know already better than I do, or that can be worth your reading? I will remind you that I am under the greatest obligations to you, and I feel them; that I count upon staying in Charles Square a few nights in Easter-week, but Mr Thornton says you are going to leave the Square, and have taken a house somewhere else. Jesus Christ is preparing for us both a house in heaven—a house so high, so broad, so bright, so beautiful, that the most capacious mind cannot conceive its grandeur, nor the most enlarged understanding comprehend its glory. Now and then, amidst a crowd of pleasing toils, I catch a peep at the all-important prospect, and feel as if I should be glad, mighty glad, when the time comes, to have the weighty question solved, Is that house for me, or is it not? But why make a question of the most delightful subject that can furnish the human understanding or warm the heart of man. Is not Jesus faithful? And surely his promise belongs to me. I do not like the grave, though *it* is a house, and a house appointed for all living; but our time there will be short; and though a small house, 'tis a quiet one, a peaceable one, and there nothing is to be feared from the ignorance, pride, or ill-temper of mankind. In that little house we shall be quite still and easy, shall have

K

something to hope for, and nothing to fear. Well, then, I'll bless the sacred turf, call it my freehold, and rejoice in the prospect of my removal to it. But if a little thinking can make that house look so friendly, what shall we think of another house, 'not made with hands, eternal in the heavens!'

"Sometimes I get a little ride to Woburn or to Olney, and then I think (being alone) of things above. What wisdom, what perfect holiness, what divine joy shall we possess! While our bodies—our weakest, meanest, and vilest part—shall lie easy in the grave, every thinking power will be infinitely enlarged, and delightfully occupied in contemplating the joys and the glories of God and his saving love,—of Jesus and his wonderful grace,—the Spirit, and his divine and most astonishing operations on the soul of man; and we shall be quite above the noise and nonsense, the folly and wickedness, that fills this world. I do rejoice in the prospect, and will rejoice, God helping me, and endeavour to treat everything under the sun as one who has almost done with this world. But yet, you know, while we are here we must go through our duties; and this reflection shall lead me through them with cheerfulness.

"But now I must go and study my lectures for to-morrow. May God bless me in studying, and others in hearing them delivered.

"Is Mrs Newton well? are you well? and my good-natured young friend, Miss Catlett? My love to them both. A few lines from you would be very acceptable. My dam and little calf are well, and unite in love to you and all yours. I want to know how you do, and how the

Messiah' goes on. I commit you to the grace and love of Jesus; and am, dear sir, your most affectionate and obliged servant,

"W. BULL.

"*P.S.*—Mr Postlethwaite, or some such name, lives at Olney, [he was curate there.] He dines with me to-morrow. I hope he will prove very clever, and do good. I cannot possibly find time to visit him, but I believe he will me, and if I can neither get good nor communicate it, I shall be sorry indeed. My breath is very short; I can scarcely walk out at all; but no wonder—I weigh 14 stone 11 lbs."

Mr Thornton tells Mr Bull subsequently, " P—— thinks highly of his tutor, and is thankful for your friendship."

Here follows a part of Mr Newton's reply :—

" MON CHER TAUREAU,—Your letter was very welcome, and I thank you for it. We are both travelling towards that land from whose bourne no traveller returns; but I am so many miles before you on the road, that it is probable I may finish my journey first. Be that as it may, our times are in the Lord's hand. I trust we shall meet there at last. In the meantime, may we be enabled to live while we do live. . . .

" Did you possess the gift of foresight, and think to save your credit upon easy terms, when you promised to lodge in Charles Square next time you came to town, if we could receive you? I no more thought of removing into the city when I saw you last than of going to Bengal. But sure enough I have taken a house in Coleman Street

Buildings, and it will be mine at Lady-day. But I fear if you come up in Easter-week you will find us either in the hurry of removing, or so entirely unsettled that we shall not be able to take you in. If it should prove so, I shall be very sorry; but I must be patient, for I cannot help it. If we are in town at your vacation, there is a prophet's chamber; but it is possible that much about that time we may be at Southampton, or somewhere else. We must then wait till Christmas, if we are spared so long. I can only say, that whenever it suits you, and we are upon the spot, you may be assured of a hearty welcome. I trust you will pray that the Lord, who has shewn us so much goodness in Charles Square, will afford us his gracious presence in Coleman Street likewise; for without Him a palace would be a dungeon.

"P—— is a good man, but young and warm. He knows little more of the world than if he had lived all his days in a wood. Help him with your advice. I hear he intends setting up Wednesday and Friday prayers in Olney Church. Poor man! he is little aware that such an attempt will be sufficient in such a place as Olney to set up his name as a heretic and a pharisee. If you can dissuade him from being over-churchish, at least while he stays there, you will do him a kindness.

"You have the love and good wishes of our whole family. Love to Mrs Bull and to Tommy the Grecian. Be assured that I am sincerely and always, your affectionate friend and brother,

"JOHN NEWTON.

"HOXTON, 13th March 1786."

The Book of Psalms was always a part of the Scriptures in which Mr Bull was especially interested. He often made it a subject of comment in public and private. Mr Thornton suggested to his friend the desirableness of his writing an entire exposition of this important book. It was a work very congenial to Mr Bull's taste, and he betook himself to it with a willing mind. It occupied him some three or four years, and is a very scholarly and interesting production, shewing an accurate acquaintance with the original language, diligent research into all the available helps to its exposition, with that real sympathy with the spiritual tone of the Psalter which must ever be a necessary qualification for its right interpretation. It was arranged that Mr Bull should send Mr Thornton copies of his observations on each psalm as he proceeded with the work. These were transcribed by Mr Thornton, and before his death he had written up to the 138th Psalm. In return, Mr Bull was supplied with every comment which could be obtained on the book, and no expense or pains were spared to accomplish this object. Many are the allusions to this subject in Mr Thornton's letters. In one of them he says,—"I trust the Psalms will be a blessing to us both. I am sure they do me good, and I hope we shall find abiding and increasing life and light therefrom." Mr Bull entertained the views of Bishop Horne and others, that the Psalms referred principally to the Messiah; and he also thought with Bishop Lowth, that many of them had a dramatic form. Some portions of the MS. were seen by Mr Romaine, who, in a letter to Mr Bull, expresses his entire concurrence in the views of the latter. Mr

Cecil also, on another occasion, gave utterance to a similar opinion.

Not only did Mr Thornton furnish Mr Bull with every work needful for the illustration of the Psalms, but with many other books as well. "Any book or books you want," he says, "or that can shorten your labour, I shall with great pleasure send to you, and not regard the cost. I paid," he adds, "£2, 5s. for Blair, (his Chronological Tables,) and had it been £25, should have deemed it a privilege to have furnished it."

In the spring of this year Mr Bull visited London. "I hope," says Mrs Wilberforce, "to get a little bit of you when you are at Mr Newton's, at Easter. The Lord long preserve you, dear sir. Many will never grow tired of you, I dare believe." In the same letter, Mrs Wilberforce speaks with deep feeling of the religious change that had taken place in the views of her nephew, Mr Wilberforce, and begs the prayers of Mr Bull that he may be kept. In early life he had received strong impressions of religion under her pious training. There is a similar allusion to this subject in a letter written about the same time by Mr Thornton, and affording a curious illustration of the almost utter absence of religion in certain classes of society at this period. "Mr Wilberforce told me the Speaker invited him to dine on Sunday, and he wrote him a handsome apology, that he kept with his family that day. He called him to him when next he saw him in the House, and said, 'he had received his note, and would hope to see him some Saturday; and that he did not think any member of that House had been so strict.'"

While Mr Bull was in London he heard Dr Conyers (Mr Thornton's brother-in-law) at Deptford; and the following Sunday he was struck with apoplexy, just as he was concluding his sermon, and died in a few hours.

In August of this year Mr Bull visited Yarmouth, as Mr Thornton's guest. He went with Mrs Wilberforce, about a week after Mr Thornton's arrival. This made the latter a little impatient. He speaks of Mr Bull as his "dear chaplain, and will not part with him to please any lady in the world!" The party at Yarmouth was large, consisting, in addition to Mr Thornton, Mrs Wilberforce, and Mr Bull, of Mr Storry, Mr Foster, and Mr Venn the younger.

While at this place Mr Bull was most abundant in his ministrations in the Wesleyan, Free-will and Strict Baptist, and Independent chapels. "Yesterday morning," he says, writing home, "I preached at seven o'clock at Mr Wesley's place; at ten I went to church, and heard Mr Foster; at two I preached in the meeting, which was exceedingly crowded. At night I preached in a smaller meeting, and the place so full that I was almost killed with the heat; but I am very well to-day. Mr Foster's name and mine are both up, and we are followed by everybody; but the clergy here don't like it at all. I was never so popular before, and I should be quite as well pleased if I was not so now." And he preached thus on the Sabbath and during the week while he continued at Yarmouth. One Sabbath was spent at Norwich, Mr Foster accompanying him. They proceeded to Cawson, a village about twelve miles from Norwich; and there Mr Bull preached in a room, fitted up as a chapel by the clergyman of the place,—the Rev. Mr Bowman. There were four clergymen and four Dissenting ministers present. In a letter to Mr Newton, Mr Bull speaks of his preaching at Yarmouth, Norwich, and Cawson, and then goes on to say :—" The next day we breakfasted with Mr Baker, the parish minister, who talks like an awakened man, and one who knows something of the gospel. His conversation gave pleasure to the whole party. We returned to Norwich on Tuesday. Mr Foster drove me in a one-horse chaise; and in coming through the streets he managed to overturn the chaise as completely as ever you were overset in your life. He laid himself in the channel, me upon him, and the chaise on us both. But He who manages all things for the best so ordered it that we neither of us received any hurt. We ought to be very thankful; and so the people told us who stood by."

To this letter Mr Newton thus replies :—

" MY DEAR FRIEND,—Methought I saw them fall! Poor Mr Foster first, then Mr Bull upon him—he had the best of it. How soft he fell! Like downy doctor upon a downy bed! Then the chaise upon both! So they were well packed—

> ' Like two round nuts close squeezed in one strait shell.'

When I found that these two valuable bodies of divinity had only a little dirt upon their binding, and had received no harm, I could not help smiling, to observe how they looked upon themselves, upon each other, and upon the chaise, when they were safely upon their legs again. I was reminded of the old adage, '*Ne sutor ultra crepidam.*' To preach the gospel acceptably to thousands is one thing; to drive a one-horse chaise through the streets evenly, so as not to spill the contents, is quite another thing, and requires very different gifts and talents.

" But, seriously, I would be very thankful that neither of you are hurt. Such catastrophes, as these may properly be called, have often been attended with dislocated or broken bones, a fractured skull, or instant death—so frail is man. Often, when he thinks himself safe, and is dreaming of his own importance, and as if he were a necessary part in the complicated movements of Divine Providence, he falls like grass before the scythe, not by the hand of a giant or the fangs of a tiger—the veriest trifle is sufficient to destroy him. How many loose stones do we see in the road?—it seems no great matter where they lie; yet any one of them, by changing the direction of a wheel, is sufficient to confound all the plans of this mighty creature. One throws him down—he falls with his head upon another; in that very moment all his thoughts perish. But the Lord gave his angels charge over you and brother Foster; therefore you fell unhurt, and are still alive to praise and serve Him." . . .

Mr Bull, writing home, gives the following account of the way in which the time was spent at Yarmouth :—" We rise at six, walk to the sea at seven, return at eight, breakfast and speak till half-past nine, write letters till eleven when the post goes out, ride at twelve, and return to dinner at three, smoke a pipe, and then walk out an hour, return at half-past five to tea, and most evenings go out to preach. I believe," he adds, " Wesley's folks have done with me; but the two Baptists and the Independents seek after me. I have plenty of preaching, and my health begins to improve. Mr Thornton lets me have his chaise whenever I please, to go an airing in. The people of Norwich have sent to me to preach at the Tabernacle again, and express great thankfulness for our having been there."

Referring in the same letter to the Academy, he says,— " We had no meeting of the Society when I was in town, and there certainly is a spirit of indifference in those who support the Academy. I do not think they will be able to keep it up long. . . . I daily pray for you, and beg of the Lord that you may enjoy every blessing of his grace and love. I hope He is with me, and blesses my poor labours in all my feeble attempts to serve Him; at least He gives me frequent occasions of preaching his most blessed word."

In a subsequent letter he says, after speaking of the comfort he had enjoyed in preaching,—" My preaching seems rather more popular at Yarmouth than at Newport. Oh, what a contrast! What am I doing by spending my days at Newport? This I owe to weak natural spirits. May the Lord pity and pardon me if I am doing wrong. But I know that his grace is sufficient for me. I leave myself with Him, and you too. May we come together again under his blessing, live in his love, and meet in his kingdom, to part no more. His door stands wide open to all who have a will to enter in. May you and I have grace to be daily entering in, and find pasture to our souls."

The next day he says,—"I hope I shall not weary you with letters. I write with pleasure, and I hope you read with pleasure. I have not missed one day writing to you. The old post-woman must think you highly favoured, and perhaps may envy you. I suppose the people begin to grow crusty at my absence; but I am more useful as a preacher here than when at home, and I want Tommy to have as much sea-bathing as possible. Give my love to Mrs A. I hope she is well, and specially good-tempered."

He writes again September 14:—"The night before last, a gentleman danced at the Assembly, and yesterday was taken up for forgery; but it was none of our party." Mr Bull repeatedly visited this young man, whose name was Gregson; talked and prayed with him, and lent him suitable books; and at first had some hope that his intercourse was not altogether in vain. He managed to escape from the jail at Yarmouth, and wrote to Mr Bull from Holland, addressing him as his "Dear Father in God." It was the letter of a man quite ignorant of religion, though expressing much gratitude to my grandfather for his kindness. This unhappy man was retaken and confined in Newgate, from whence also he escaped, under circumstances which shewed singular cleverness. I have a curious newspaper account of that escape before me, which was sent by Mr Thornton to Mr Bull. I believe he was again discovered, and at last executed.

In a letter written to Mr Newton, September 15, in reply to his of the 5th, his friend says:—" . . . . Our vacation draws to a close, and I long much to see Newport again; but Mr Thornton says he and his sons are members of the Newport Society; and if they have not a majority of votes, he thinks that he should be indulged with a week's grace. I rejoice in the prospect of returning to my favourite employment, if possible to serve the Lord by training up others to serve him, who, I hope, will be more faithful and active than I have been.

" I have but ten minutes before the post goes out. How shall I fill them up? Let me just remind you of our great and dear Lord, of his grace over us, his love to us, his wisdom to direct us, his power to protect and bring us safe to glory, and that He has the will as well as the power to do it." . . . .

Again he writes to Mr Newton, September 21, just before leaving Yarmouth :—" . . . . . If much preaching and hearing are signs of usefulness, my visit here is very useful indeed. We have met with many people here who seem to know the truth, and to feel its power,—who are really walking with God, and have their conversation in heaven. Yarmouth has proved, (rather contrary to our expectations,) in a spiritual sense, a very pleasant place to us, as well as in many other respects. However, I am glad we are on the move; otherwise, between Mr Thornton and the people, I shall preach all the flesh off my bones. I want to go to Newport and study humility. The Lord does all things well. He has blessed this vacation to the health of my dear child, and to the good of many souls. I have been much affected by several, I fear fruitless, visits to a person in the jail here for forgery." . . . . .

CHAPTER VIII.

LIFE OF THE REV. WILLIAM BULL.
1786-1788.

Newton's "Messiah"—Rev. Mr Johnson and Botany Bay—Spiritualizing Gospel in the South Seas—Death of good Men—Lessons of Divine Providence—Letter from Lady Hesketh—Journey to the South—Letter on the Death of Mrs Bull's Sister—Mr Thornton undertakes the support of the Academy—Rev. Thomas Bull—Rev. Samuel Furly—Story of the Rev. R. Robinson—Glories of Heaven—Visit to France—Letter to Mr Newton—Mrs Wilberforce's last Letter.

SOME time after Mr Bull's return home he addressed a letter to Mr Newton, under date October 25, from which we give the following passages :—

"I always expected more from your 'Messiah' than from your other works, and am not at all disappointed ; but I am not willing to gallop through it. It is read three times a-week by the students in turn. We have finished the second sermon of the second volume. There was one sentiment in the first sermon I did not like, about not applying passages in the Old Testament to Jesus, unless they are expressly quoted in so many words in the New. I think I could advance a solid and scriptural argument against it ; but I love the author, and I love the book—indeed, am highly delighted with it ; and I think you said more than you intended. I pray God to bless and reward you for this publication. I doubt not but it will be highly pleasant to many readers as well as to myself.

"How is Mr Johnson's Botany Bay scheme likely to end? I have seen a copy of his feelings on the occasion, and seemed to feel them all myself. It filled me with a thousand thanks that the Lord did not call me to that cross. A call to be bound to the stake does not seem to me more painful; but I bless the dear Fountain of all comfort that I am not bid to try the experiment. It seems a call only fit for a hardened profligate, or a saint panting for the crown of martyrdom. However, I can easily believe it possible his call may be from God; and if it is, I have no doubt but He will fit him for it, and support him under it. I am glad it was not in my way to tell him what I thought of it, and you have too much humanity to let him know. It almost makes me tremble when I think of it; but what the Lord actually calls us to be He gives us strength for. I have just read Cook's account of the country, and the temper of the natives. If Johnson goes, I pray the Lord to go with him, and fit his mind for everything that lies before him.

"We are tolerably well crowded at the evening lectures.

"I hope the Lord is with us. In the family we have peace and comfort, and things go on well." . . .

Mr Newton replies:—

"MON CHER TAUREAU,—I believe what you disapprove about not applying passages in the Old Testament to the Messiah, without express authority from the New, is in the 23d sermon of vol. ii. I have met with such trash from some who pretend to *spiritualize*, and obtruded with so much confidence, that I thought it right to enter my protest against the practice, especially as I think it obtains most amongst rash and injudicious preachers. And though sometimes wise and good men give a little into it, I think it is rather countenanced than justified by their example. For instance, I remember to have heard Mr Bull preach a sermon, and a very good one, from Exodus iv. 14; but though the sermon was a good one, I thought the points enlarged upon were no more deducible from the text than from the first verse in Genesis. Mr Bull, however, knew what he was about; but when such men as Mr Page [the curate at Olney] attempt to preach from Genesis xxxv. 8 that Deborah is the law, the oak under which she was buried the cross, &c. &c, they make wild work of it. I have allowed the propriety of preaching by way of accommodation, and *I think I have not said that we should apply no passages to Jesus, unless quoted in so many words in the New Testament;* but that when we propose our own sentiments, which are not so supported, we should do it under great modesty, (p. 406,) which perhaps you will readily allow. After all, if in this point the observation that doctors differ should apply to you and me, I have still the comfort of thinking that there are not many doctors who differ less, or in fewer particulars, than we do. *I* like to have the proofs of the subject lie plainly in the text; but if another preaches solid scriptural truth from 'Higgaion, Selah,' I am content. My censure is only intended against those who affect to please, and to shew their superior sagacity by the singularity, quaintness, and novelty of their conceits; and who think they can discover mysteries in a text, when, perhaps, they do not understand even the literal sense of it.

"A minister who should go to Botany Bay without a call from the Lord, and without receiving from Him an apostolical spirit, the spirit of a missionary, enabling him to forsake all, to give up all, to venture all, to put himself into the Lord's hands without reserve, to sink or swim, had better run his head against a stone wall. I am strongly inclined to hope Mr Johnson is thus called, and will be thus qualified. I should not advise him to consult with you upon this point. Your appointment is to smoke your pipe quietly at home, to preach, and to lecture to your pupils. You are not cut out for a missionary; and nothing, perhaps, would have been done either in the Danish West Indian Islands, or in Greenland, if the attachments and feelings of all men had been like yours and mine. I must have my tea, my regular hours, and twenty little things which I can have when my post is fixed. I should shrink at the thought of living upon seals and train oil. I have not zeal to sell myself to be a slave for the opportunity of preaching to the slaves while I was working with them; but the Lord inspired the Moravian missionaries with the resolution to court hardships like these, so that they might win souls, and He gave them success. Oh, if Johnson is the man whom the Lord appoints to the honour of being the first to carry the glad tidings into the southern hemisphere, he will be a great and honoured man indeed! Let the world admire Columbus, Drake, and Cook, Johnson in my view will be unspeakably superior to them all. I be-

lieve, with his simple views, the Lord will not permit him
to mistake his will in an affair of such vast importance;
therefore, if he does go, I shall hope for a happy event.
If I am not mistaken, sooner or later the gospel must be
preached in the South Seas; if so, there must be a beginning. We hope this is the time. Perhaps this is the final
cause of our attempting a settlement in New Holland.
Often when politicians have one thing in view, the Lord
has another; and their plans succeed in order to the
accomplishment of his. With love to Mrs Bull, Tommy,
and the Utopians, I remain, your affectionate brother and
servant,   "JOHN OMICRON.

"27th Oct. 1786."

In December, Mr Bull writes again to his friend, from
which the following paragraphs may be quoted :—

"We have just finished your 'Messiah,' and I hope have
been edified and benefited by it; at least, I have heard it
read with real pleasure, and many parts of it with great
improvement. I pray the Lord to give it general acceptance and usefulness. I never yet got harm from you.

"How awful the providence! Mr Latrobe dead—a truly
great man, and consequently a great loss; and Mr Unwin.
Poor Mrs Unwin, and Mr Cowper! I rode over to smoke
a pipe yesterday, and sympathize a little with them, and
saw your pretty letter to him. They bore it better than I
expected, but I had fully prepared them for it by a visit
the night before last. Mr Smalling is just dead at Bath.
I think you knew him. He belonged to the Brethren, and
I much esteemed him.

"So at last you have given the good Bishop of Botany Bay a wife to take with him—a very good thing, if she be a good wife. I pity and rejoice, pray for, and congratulate them both. I have just got a letter from him, and indeed am affected by his feelings. Poor man! it is surely of the Lord; and I think, from the face of the thing, it is certainly intended for the good of souls. How anxious shall I feel, if life is spared, to hear of somebody who has heard from him at Botany Bay, and how it goes with him!

"Through great mercy we are going on in the Academy with a high spirit of diligence in study, and in much peace and comfort. I lament that I cannot get a title for poor Sparks. He preached us an excellent sermon last Saturday; and I have ordered him to translate and preach it again in Latin next Saturday. Thomas Bull has just got a title for priest's orders from his crusty rector, who refused it but lately. What! has the evil genius of scepticism got hold of good Mr R——d at Birmingham? Alas! poor man, I can only say they are well kept whom the Lord keeps. But the truths of the gospel seem to be a bugbear even to those that know the Lord. What has Jesus done, that his truths are looked at with so questionable a countenance in the house of his friends? I expect the time will come when they will not dare to say anything but what may be proved by '*Cicero de Officiis*' or '*Woolston's Religion of Nature.*' I wish amongst the various parties there may be some for Christ, as well as for Paul and Cephas. Surely there will remain a few for Christ, though in some it may be envy, and in others love." . . . . . .

Mr Newton thus writes in reply:—"When once we

consider a man as great and useful, as one who cannot be spared, and whose loss cannot be easily replaced, we may look at him as standing upon dangerous ground. Do we not provoke the Lord to jealousy by holding an instrument so high? Do we not sometimes render it proper and fit for Him to shew us that He standeth not in need of a sinful worm? One such instance may do more to wean the rest of his servants from that idea of self-importance, to which we are all liable, than a thousand sermons on the subject. And, so far as it has this effect, the death of a Latrobe may be more useful than his life.

"Dear Mr Unwin moved in a less extensive sphere, yet the loss of him will likewise be felt in his connexions. Mr R. of Birmingham has indeed had some sceptical qualms about his situation in the Church, and some thoughts of seceding or dissenting from us, but I hope they are blown over. I shall be sorry if he scruples himself out of a sphere of usefulness; but I have never heard that he wavered as to the doctrines of the gospel. I hope it is no more than I have mentioned, misrepresented or misunderstood. But I cannot answer for him, or even for myself, unless I am upheld. We are all poor weathercocks if left to ourselves. I have always thought him an upright, good man, though not the most judicious." . . . . . .

At the beginning of the year 1787, Mr B. was in very poor health. He was urged by Mr Thornton, in a most affectionate letter, to relax his efforts. Others thought that the Academy was too much for him; and he himself was a little discouraged at the slackening zeal of some of its early friends. He says, in a letter from London to Mrs

Bull, "We have had no meeting of the Society, and I think it looks like an old house that must soon tumble down." Still, all this might be just the result of his naturally desponding views. In March he is in London, and meets Mr Berridge, Mr Newton, Mr Basil Woodd, and others.

It is curious to note the history of bypast events, which are now old stories. Mr Greatheed writes from London about this time: "You know that the repeal of the Test Act is rejected in the Commons by a considerable majority. Mr Pitt spoke against it—Mr Fox for it. That old scoundrel Lord North came to town on purpose to oppose it. Mr Hastings is to be impeached on Monday."

In the early part of this year, Mr Cowper's malady returned upon him in its full force,—happily, however, after some months, it passed away. Lady Hesketh, in a letter to Mr Bull, thus refers to this painful circumstance: ". . . . . I am truly thankful that the ice is at last broken, and that he was prevailed upon to see you. I do sincerely hope that, having once experienced the comfort of your society, he will himself be desirous of renewing it whenever you can indulge him with it. . . . . . . I have often heard from Mrs Unwin of your persevering friendship to this dear and valuable sufferer; and she lamented, in the strongest terms, his determined resolution to see nobody but herself, not even his friend Mr Bull."

This letter is dated July 5, 1787.

Mr Bull's ill-health and depression still continued. He was, however, much revived by a journey to the south, in company with Mr Thornton. They went by Reading and Bath to Minehead, of which Mr Bull speaks as a poor place, with many of the houses unoccupied, and an old meeting-house tumbling down, and used as a school. " I sighed at the departed glory, and wished myself away." Thence they proceeded to Ilfracombe. " On Sabbath morning," Mr Bull says, " I went to church. It was about half a mile from the inn, up a hill as steep as the roof of our house. We heard the people play the Ten Commandments on the organ. The whole was a very merry piece of business ; and concluded with a silly, ridiculous sermon, fifteen minutes long. In the evening I preached in a house to three or four hundred people."

On the following Sunday he preached at Truro. Thence they travelled to Penzance and the Land's End—seeing the Logging Rock—and back to Truro again. " About Redruth," he says, " the country is full of copper mines, and the world is literally turned inside out. But the most curious wonder of all was a rocky mountain, upon one of the projections of which they gravely told us the fatted calf was killed when the prodigal returned to his father. There the stain of the blood is to be seen to this day, and the rock itself is turned into the form of a calf. And it is all as true as you please."

The party settled down for a little time in very pleasant quarters at Exmouth. The rest was very agreeable to Mr Bull. Here he preached. He had officiated at Exeter on the Sabbaths; and on Tuesday he writes, "To-morrow I must preach here. I am told many are coming from Exeter on Sabbath-day to hear me. Alas! alas! if they knew me as much as I know myself, I think they would keep at home. We have a great deal of pleasure in our journey, and a great deal of fatigue; but Jesus is with us, and He is my supreme delight. I love to read, and speak, and pray, because these things lead my attention to Him, and awaken my delight in Him."

Mr Greatheed wrote to Mr Bull from Newport as follows:—" Soon after your departure some intelligent people of the town discovered that you did not intend to return. And since then they have found out the reason—to wit, that the late Mr Woodgate's congregation had given you an invitation, which you thought proper to accept. On which Mrs A. declared, if you went away she would go too; so that if others are of the same mind your return had need be speedy, lest when you come you should find that your congregation had removed into the neighbourhood of Jewin Street, to welcome you thither upon your arrival."

" I have no idea," Mr Bull replies, in a letter to Mrs Bull, " about Jewin Street; and if an invitation were to come you could answer it as well as I could. I have seen and felt enough of the world not to plunge myself into any more care than I can handsomely avoid. We must think and act about all these things just as Providence leads the way. Yesterday I preached three times; and, through the assistance and blessing of the Lord, got through the whole with tolerable ease and comfort."

While he was in Exmouth Mr Bull heard of the death of his sister-in-law, and writes thus to Mrs Bull:—" I doubt not but you feel the death of your sister; and my earnest prayer is that it may be sanctified to us both, and that we may be daily ripening for our change. It is the greatest beauty of a Christian to meet death with perfect calmness and serenity—neither to be hasty for its approach nor in the least fearful of it, but to consider it as the crowning blessing of our lives, when sin and sorrow shall thereby be for ever done away, and Jesus be all in all. The cares of the world and of life are unpleasant things, and the infirmities of age are what we must expect; but the less our minds are affected by these the better it will be for us. In this life it is in vain to seek for perfect ease and comfort; that must come only from the Spirit of Jesus dwelling in us. But of everything outward it may be truly said, 'This is not your rest.' Oh that we may be daily departing out of our own wills into the will of Jesus, in little things as well as in great things! This, and this alone, can constitute solid peace and comfort; but this, when really done, makes a heaven upon earth, and is glory begun below."

Two days afterwards he writes,—" We are very agreeably situated in this still quiet place, and I suppose shall stay a little longer. I hope this journey will enable me to pass more comfortably through the approaching winter; and this will, I know, add to your comfort. It is the warmest wish of my heart that your life may be prolonged many years, your health preserved, and your heart daily enabled to rejoice in Christ Jesus as your portion and your supreme delight. Whether I am near you or far off, remember I am always at your command. I bless the Lord that you continue well, and all about you well!

" Mrs Wilberforce cannot continue long. You know the sincere and hearty love I have always felt for her, and

now I feel not a little pain for her present situation.   It is
a mercy I am so far off.   It would greatly affect me to see
her.   My heart is formed for gratitude, and my head for
vapours.   However, I do and can rejoice in my dear and
precious Lord and Master.   The wish of my heart is to
live and die in the humble, faithful, and most active pursuit of his glory, and in promoting the knowledge and love
of his most precious name.   I long to have my heart more
closely united to Him, and to live in his Spirit and not my
own.   Oh, may this be more and more the case with
me, and with you, my dear love ; then, whether together
or asunder, we shall meet in Jesus, and have union and
communion with Him, and with each other in the Spirit."

Mr Bull returned home about the middle of September,
much invigorated.   Mrs Wilberforce's life was still prolonged ; and Mr Thornton writes to him in October,—" I
have just returned from visiting my sister, to whom your
letters are a great comfort ;" and again, " You cannot write
too often to Hannah."   Mrs W. wrote some very touching
and affectionate letters to Mr Bull from her sick-bed, indi-
cating a very resigned and happy state of mind.

Too soon the effects of over-exertion were felt again ;
and Mr Thornton writes to his friend,—" I am sorry your
nerves are so shattered.   You must not incapacitate yourself for future service.   You might as well eat the week's
provision in one day, to save time.   It is allowable in a
Roman Catholic, but not sound divinity.   This is not the
way to heaven, but a bypath of your own, and what the
blessed Jesus will give you no thanks for.   Again, in a
subsequent letter, he says,—" I am sorry to hear so poor an

account of yourself; and the more so as, if the Coroner calls me in, I shall be for bringing it in *felo-de-se*."

Mr Bull was naturally anxious about the support of the Academy, and the matter preyed very much upon his spirits. He felt himself, or thought he was, unequal to the demand it made upon his time and his strength. From the real pressure of this burden he was relieved by the singular providence of God. His friend Mr Thornton, towards the close of this year, resolved to take the whole expense of the Institution upon himself; and, still further to relieve Mr Bull's mind, Mr Thornton also determined that, in case of his death, arrangements should be made for its continuance so long as its present tutor should live. This generous purpose was carried out; and, so far as the support of the Academy was concerned, there was no care in that matter for the next twenty-seven years; and then other means were found for its continuance.

In reference to this new arrangement Mr Bull says, in a letter from London, when Mr Thornton had informed him of his purpose,—"It has taken a great burden off my spirits; you cannot imagine what ease of mind I feel. This is far better than if I had quite thrown up the Academy." In a subsequent letter he adds,—"Last night we had a long talk about the Academy, and everything is to be settled according to my wishes; and when Greatheed goes away Tommy is to have his place."

Mr Thornton was very anxious to obtain a living for his friend's relative, Mr Thomas Bull; and through Mr Maitland he was presented to the vicarage of Renhold, in Bedfordshire, Mr Thornton supplementing the small income of that benefice by a liberal addition,—a practice by no means uncommon with this generous man. The Rev. Thomas Bull was subsequently presented to the living of Eldon, in Norfolk, which was in Mr Thornton's gift. I find, by one of Mr Thornton's letters, that, as the winter approached, he sent my grandfather twenty pairs of blankets for distribution amongst his necessitous poor; and this in addition to twenty guineas which he put into his hand every Christmas for a like benevolent object.

Early in the following year (1788) a great effort was made to get an evangelical clergyman into the church at Newport. "I am sorry," says Mr Thornton, "that we have lost Newport. However, the Lord's will be done. He orders all things well, though not as we would foolishly have it."

In February Mrs Wilberforce writes:—

"MY DEAR AND KIND FRIEND,—If I take up my pen to anybody, I am sure you demand it." After speaking of her sufferings she adds,—"My kind and tender Physician gives me the support I need. Sometimes I think I can lay my hand in his hand. Continue to pray that patience may have its perfect work."

The letter is written in a very feeble hand, but breathes throughout the same Christian spirit.

In March Mr Bull received the following flattering letter from a clergyman:—

"MY DEAR BROTHER,—If you had, for any particular reason, sought and wished to gain my heart and affections, you could not have taken a more effectual method than you have done, by your kind, precious, and most profitable letter. But I will tell you a secret with all plain sim-

plicity. Your excellent sermon in my house in the month
of July had gone before, and had completely won my
heart. The heart of man is a fortress, and a strong one
too. You had, however, so ably planted and so skilfully
directed your evangelical and spiritual battery as entirely
to win that fortress. There needed no more. But you are
resolved to take possession also. And in doing this, that
you might not leave your work unfinished, you have dis-
played equal skill; and, like a wise, mild, and generous
prince, have in the very act manifested the most tender
and amiable disposition of your spirit. You have clearly
shewn, in a sense most favourable and highly honourable,
of what spirit you are. But, to drop figurative expressions
and natural allusions, to which your uncommon and original manner has given rise, I observe, with peculiar pleasure, that your letter, like your sermon, is admirably full
of Jesus, of grace, and of covenant mercy and love. It is
now high time that I return you the most sincere and
grateful thanks of myself and my most dear Mrs Furly
for it. It reached her feeling heart, and I trust has had
its gracious and salutary effect. Nor were the younger
branches of the family without their sensibility, nor without their admiration." . . .

In the same month Mr Bull was asked to preach at the
opening of a Baptist Chapel at Thrapston, in Northamptonshire; and there were some interesting circumstances
worthy of record in connexion with that visit. The well-
known and highly-gifted Mr Robinson of Cambridge was
engaged to take part in the same service. He had already
become very latitudinarian in his views, but still minis-

tered amongst the professedly orthodox. This extraordinary man was remarkable, amongst other things, for a very musical voice. He had also wonderful self-possession. He took the morning service. The hymn which he gave out from Dr Watts' collection, though familiar to his audience, seemed to them, when Robinson read it, as something entirely new. He then took up a miniature Bible, and read the fourth chapter of John in a way that riveted the attention of the congregation. When he came to the verse, " Go, call thy husband, and come hither," there was a general movement, as if every one felt he must obey the injunction. Then changing his tone, in a tremulous voice he uttered the woman's reply,—" I have no husband ;" and so through the whole narrative. His text was from the same chapter,—" God is a Spirit, and they who worship him must worship him in spirit and in truth." It was remarkable for its eloquence, and as remarkable for its utter deficiency of all gospel truth. Amongst its many striking thoughts, there occurred a statement somewhat to the following effect :—He was contrasting the works of man with the works of God. An artist, he said, may represent upon his canvas a field of corn in all the ripe beauty of autumn. The picture may be perfectly true to nature ; but it is the great God alone who can make the gentle breeze to pass over that field of golden grain, and cause it to wave and glisten beneath the noonday light. Mr Greatheed, who was present, and who in his early days had been a great admirer of Garrick, said how much the exhibition of Robinson's powers reminded him of that celebrated actor.

In the afternoon Mr Bull "preached Christ" to the people. With the impression of the defects of the morning sermon upon his mind, he was more than usually full and earnest in the exhibition of gospel truth. His text was, Zech. vi. 13, "Even he shall build the temple of the Lord." Mr Robinson sat in the vestry with a handkerchief on his head, complaining that he had a cold, and probably heard little of the sermon. But after the service was over, a very old man, whose head was silvered with the frost of ninety winters, came up to my grandfather, saying to him, "Mr Bull, you don't know me, but I thank you heartily for your good gospel sermon; it has refreshed my spirit." "Yes, I do know you," said Mr Bull, "I heard you preach fifty years ago at Irthlingborough, when I was a very little boy. I behaved ill during the service, and you ordered me to be turned out." The good man was no other than the Mr Twelvetrees who so strangely divided the text, "Write, Blessed are the dead that die in the Lord," and which excited the smile of his little hearer.*

The ministers spent the evening of the day together, for there were no railways then to break up such gatherings, and to carry visitors at once to their homes. Mr Robinson, who was possessed of great conversational powers, was very free in the utterance of the rationalistic views he had imbibed,—filling his brethren with admiration of his talents, and with grief at their sad perversion.

Such is a very imperfect account of these circumstances as I have often heard them from the lips of my father, who was present on that occasion.

* See page 7.

"I hope," says Mr Thornton, writing to Newport immediately afterwards, "I hope my dear Bull has borne a faithful testimony at Thrapston to the ever-blessed Jesus." And again he says, a little later, "Alas! soon Robinson's eloquence will be at an end. He has the reward he seeks after. May Jesus vouchsafe to us ours; and when we rejoice evermore, he shall have cause for lamentation."

Mr Bull was in London in April; and there were two or three days of glorious sunshine, succeeding less genial weather. The spirits of my grandfather were cheered, and his thoughts at once went heavenward. He writes to Mrs Bull,—". . . But in heaven the sun for ever shines, the air is for ever still. It is eternal spring there, and you and I shall be for ever free from pain. Oh, how pleasant, how delightful, will that habitation be! Jesus, the dear, adorable Jesus, is the glorious sun of that upper and better world. Oh, how bright, how clear, how constantly He shines, and cheers, and warms, every one that beholds Him! His Holy Spirit is the vital air we shall for ever breathe. God—the great, invisible, eternal God—will be our Father, our Saviour, and our Comforter for ever. I am certain we should wish, and pant, and pray to be gone directly—not to live one hour longer—if dark, abominable unbelief did not interfere, and make us doubt whether we should ever come there at all; but if Jesus dwells in us now, we must, we shall dwell in Him for ever and ever. O glorious event!"

About the same time he writes a very earnest and judicious letter to his son on the welfare of his soul. In a letter a few days after he says, "Yesterday, I dined at

Omicron's, [Mr Newton's.] They were very kind and friendly; but as to academics and students, and all such matters, he was evidently and studiously reserved. Well, every one must have their way; and if they please themselves, I am sure I ought to be pleased. My duty is to please Jesus, and when He smiles everything smiles with me."

Generous as Mr Thornton's conduct was in undertaking the whole charge of the Academy, it is not to be wondered at that the committee, and Mr Newton in particular, as its originator, might feel that this circumstance was something like a reflection upon them, or, at least, taking the work completely out of their hands.

In September of this year, Mr Bull visited France with Mr Thornton. My father was also one of the party. They went by way of Ostend, Ghent, Antwerp, Brussels, and Lisle, to Paris. The records of this journey are very brief.

Writing from Ostend, Mr Bull says,—"The churches are large, and as full of images as possible. If a person wants to have an idea of heathen idolatry, he need only travel through Flanders. We enter a large church, and see nothing but altars, pictures, and images, and these often of the most paltry and rubbishy character. At the corners of the streets, in a hole in the wall, are frequently seen representations of the Virgin and Child, the Virgin being little better than a sixpenny doll; and along the road a rude cross, with a great wooden image nailed to it;—and the people worship all this trumpery; but they know no better. They have no knowledge, they have no reading, they have no teaching. I have been to the principal book-

sellers in this great town, and could not find a book in it
worth looking at,—only a few novels and tales.   Oh, what
a mercy to know the Bible,—what a mercy to be born in
England,—what a mercy to believe in Jesus!"

And so, writing from Antwerp, he says,—"There is a
very grand bookseller's shop here, but without books of
any worth.   Not a Bible or Prayer-book can we find in
this city."   They were at Antwerp on Sunday; and, speaking of the superstition of the people, he says,—"My soul
abhors lying vanities; but in the words of the living God
will I put my trust.   How precious does that word appear
to my soul!   Its price is above rubies.   We have," Mr
Bull adds, "prayer and exposition morning and evening,
and a sermon to-day at noon, and another at four o'clock."

At Douay they visited the English College, and proceeded thence to Cambray, where my grandfather was
greatly delighted by the sight of the memorials of the
celebrated Fénelon—a great favourite with him.   Over his
remains was an altar of solid silver.

In Paris, of course, there was much to awaken interest;
and visits were made to the Louvre, the Tuileries, the
Palais Royal, the Hotel des Invalides, the library of the
Sorbonne, and other places, with several convents and
monasteries.   At Versailles they saw the King and Monsieur at mass.   In the former case it was entirely a
musical performance, and lasted nearly an hour.

"To-day," (the Sabbath,) Mr Bull says, " I have preached
twice, and have also been to the church of St Sulpice, and
heard a sermon in French an hour long, and then stayed to
see a farce performed by forty actors in white smocks.   It

is called chanting vespers. Two men in red, with a great deal of gold lace, go up and down all the time chanting. Coming out of the church, I saw a mountebank doctor, to the full as earnest as the man in the pulpit; but he was playing tricks of legerdemain, and selling powders and pills. This completed the farce, and sent us laughing home." He says elsewhere, "There are no Sabbaths in France;" and, under the impression of the many splendid sights upon which he had gazed, he says, "Jesus is my gold, my pearls, my diamonds—my riches, my honour, my glory; Jesus in my heart, my life, my soul—my joy, my crown of rejoicing."

The party returned home by way of Dover and Ramsgate, at which latter place Mr Bull preached in Lady Huntingdon's chapel.

At the end of the year Mr Bull was in London, and preached at Surrey. "Yours of the 7th," says Mr Thornton, "I communicated to Rowland, [Hill,] who was not a little pleased at having you once more in Surrey Chapel. We hope the journey may rather improve than increase your complaint."

In December, Mr Newton wrote to his friend, giving a touching account of the serious and distressing illness of his niece, Miss Catlett. Her life was in great peril, and her mind was overwhelmed with the most fearful gloom.

Mr Bull immediately addressed Mr Newton as follows :—

"MY DEAR SIR,—When the subject of a correspondence is merely speculative, to be negligent is a duty I owe to

my infirmities ; but when the peace and comfort of a whole
family are at stake, if there is a grain of sincere friendship,
it ought, it will shew itself.

"The things which you mention as the ground of your
hope in Miss Catlett, have always struck me so much as
to make me love her; and I have not a moment's doubt,
if she departs, of her going into glory; but your information shocks and grieves me. I hope you will give me a
better account soon. I am troubled for you both, especially
for Mrs Newton, because I fear she will be less able (from
her own infirmities) to bear this trial than you will. Alas!
what can we—any of us—bear when put to the trial? Nothing—any further than Jesus is pleased to stand by and
support us; but his arm is strong and his word omnipotent. If He speaks, an infant shall sustain a mountain;
without Him, a straw can sink a giant into the grave.
Look to Him, lean upon Him, trust in Him, and He can
and will make thy strength equal to thy day. But what
shall I say to this poor benighted feeble child? Bid her
leave herself in the hands of Jesus. He will order everything just right and as it should be; and I hope He will
see fit to bring her out of this affliction. If He does not,
He will certainly be guided by a regard to his own glory,
which is all in all; and his conduct will be directed by the
tenderest love. Help her to look to Jesus, by gently re-
minding her of Him. You do not leave her for a moment
alone ; indeed, you ought not, as then the enemy will be
most busy and active. Pray tell me when there is any
alteration this way or that. A few lines will not cost you

much time. I will daily pray for you, and when you can give me better news, shall return thanks for it.

"Alas, what is our life, and through what false mediums do we estimate it! Surely we dishonour the Lord by overrating the life that now is, and greatly undervaluing that which is to come. Do, sir, let us look to Jesus, and try to say, 'Thy will be done.' The words are few, and to realize them is not an easy thing. I believe they are the language of your heart; but still there is a conflict between nature and grace, and I doubt not but one at your elbow feels it in all its extent. Speculation and fact are two things, and so are talking and feeling. I sympathize with Mrs Newton, and earnestly wish her all the support and comfort which a firm faith in a precious Jesus can afford, and pray that she may this moment enjoy that consolation.

"We unite in love to you, and shall impatiently wait for a better account from you. May the Lord Jesus be with you!—So wishes and prays, dear sir, your faithful, affectionate friend and servant,

"W. BULL."

In November, Mrs Wilberforce wrote to Mr Bull a brief and touching letter from her dying-bed, referring to the removal of the Rev. Mr Symonds of Bedford—a most godly man, and much respected by her. "Happy," she says, "is the dear man who has gone to glory; now in the presence of Jesus, whom unseen he loved. My heart seemed to jump for joy. Things have an awful appearance, and such as you can be ill spared. Myself better and worse—Jesus as good as ever."   Written in a very feeble and indistinct hand. This excellent woman died a few weeks after, having lived a long, devout, and useful life, a lover of good men, and ever anxious to promote the cause of Christ.

CHAPTER IX.

Visit to Scotland—Edinburgh—Melville— Balgonie—Glasgow—Dr Moyes—
Helmsley—George III. at St Paul's—Brighton—Bogatzky's "Golden
Treasury"—Mr Bull's health—Visit to Cambridge—Rev. Mr Simeon—
Letters from Mr Newton and Mr Hill—Brighton—Captain Jamison and
his son—Mr Thornton's illness—Mr Bull's last interview with him—Mr
Thornton's death—His great affection for Mr Bull—Character—Mrs
Newton's death.

Mr THORNTON's only daughter was married to Lord Balgonie, the eldest son of the Earl of Leven. He determined
to visit Scotland in the month of January, and wished Mr
Bull to accompany him. My grandfather was naturally a
little reluctant to undertake such a journey at such a season,
but Mr Thornton was bent both upon it and upon taking
his friend and " chaplain" with him. He had travelled, he
said, in Russia, and it was the best season for going to the
north. The truth was, when this good man's mind was set
upon anything, he was not to be diverted from his purpose.
He had had, moreover, some premonitions of declining
health, and probably thought any delay would prevent the
accomplishment of a visit he greatly wished to make; and
so it proved, for he was never afterwards equal to such an
effort. Mr Bull's scruples were overcome, and in the cold

and snows of January, he visited the north. It was a formidable journey in those days, but a postchaise and four greatly relieved the difficulty.

Mr Bull writes from Edinburgh,—"We expect the Balgonies every minute. I pray the Lord to be with you and bless you. I beg of you to keep near to Him; then you and I shall be together to all eternity. To Jesus I commit you, and am your loving devoted husband, W. Bull.— My best love to Tommy. May Jesus make him wise, dutiful, good." Again, January 25, Sabbath-day :—". . . Yesterday we went to dine with Sir John Belsher, who married one of Lord Leven's daughters. I liked my visit very well. After that, we called and spent an hour with Dr Erskine. This morning we went to his kirk and heard him pray and expound, and a young man preached a poor sermon. We went to dine with the doctor. After dinner we went to another kirk, and spent the evening at home. To-morrow morning we breakfast at Sir J. Belsher's, and leave Edinburgh at noon."

From Melville, Tuesday, January 22, he writes thus :— ". . . Just out of bed, with a charming fire, and a pipe in my mouth. Yesterday morning, after breakfast, we rode about the town. Edinburgh is a fine city; the Square of St Andrews is as fine as any square in London. We saw the college, which is large, but as mean as any parish workhouse in England. We then rode two miles down to the water-side, and got on board at Leith exactly at twelve o'clock. We sat in the carriage. The passage is about eight miles, and we got over by about half-past two; dined, and set off again at half-past three. It rained and snowed very fast; and night soon came on, and it was exceedingly dark. We had eighteen miles to go; and though we had four horses, could hardly get along. The roads were very bad, and the chaise often set fast. The postboys were obliged frequently to alight, and to search for the track. We were four hours and a half travelling these eighteen miles, and feared we might have to sit all night in the chaise: but patience did great things for us, and we got safe here by eight o'clock. The house we are in is truly a royal palace, for I think there are forty or fifty rooms on a floor, and exceedingly good rooms. Here we were introduced to the good old Earl of Leven and his lady. Lord Ruthven, his son-in-law, lives in the house; and Lord and Lady Balgonie were here to receive us. The dressing-table of my room was furnished with a dozen pipes when I came into it. Our supper consisted of ten dishes, all covered. A great bell rang for prayers just before supper, and I was called upon to be chaplain. And now, being in a hurry, I shall add little more. In everything I think the ever-blessed Jesus has been with us, and made our journey safe and very comfortable; so that I must desire you to bless and praise his great and dear name for all his goodness and mercy to me. It will give me unspeakable comfort to hear that you both are well. I pray that the good Spirit may be at work in the heart of Tommy, and that he may be every day more earnestly seeking after Jesus," &c.

Again he writes to Mrs Bull:—" Though I wrote a long letter to-day, I cannot please myself better, or fill up my leisure time better, than by writing to you for the great love I have to you. My obligations to you on a thousand occasions make writing both a duty and a delight.

"I never had a journey with Mr Thornton which I liked better than this, or, on the whole, more comfortable. And what makes it so is that I think the Lord is with us, though I have not yet had any opportunity of proclaiming his great and dear name in public. But because the Lord orders it so, and it seems to be his will that it should be so, therefore I think it a mercy that I have not, for all that is from Him is in mercy. I was a little fluttered at first coming into the company of great people, and still am in a degree; yet I remember they are but men, and I must soon come into the presence of the great God, who is the fountain of all greatness, and in comparison with whom all the inhabitants of the earth are as grasshoppers.

"There is much here to indulge curiosity—several paintings, &c , and a curious place in the grounds, which was one of the summer residences of Cardinal Beaton. But, O my love, how vain, how mean are all the palaces of the great compared with those blessed mansions above, which Jesus is gone to prepare for all who are humbly and earnestly seeking his favour! Oh, may that be your case and mine! Don't entertain fearful and awful ideas of Jesus, but come to Him cheerfully. If we have but a heart to pray, He has always got an ear to hear. The longer I live, the more beauty and excellency I see in Him, and the more evil in myself. How happy will it be for you and me, if, after a life of mutual affection and love, we should part in death with a comfortable assurance of meeting in glory to part no more! Let it be our daily prayer that this may be the case. Grace is as free for mine as it is for me. Oh that we may all three feel its power, and live under its sanctifying influence! Tell Tommy earnestly to seek the knowledge and love of Christ. This, and this only, will make him comfortable, honourable, and useful in life, and happy in death. I commit you both to the free grace and love of the Lord Jesus Christ," &c.

He writes from Balgonie, January 29 :—" I came from Melville this morning to this place with Mr Thornton and Lady Balgonie. The roads were very bad, full of ice and snow; and the country has a very dreary look—mountains covered with snow, and valleys streaming with floods—barren heaths and moors for miles together. But all this is compensated by the kindness and generosity of our hosts, who treat us like what they are—right generous, old-fashioned nobility. The good Earl and his Countess are both kind and excellent people. We return there on Saturday, and I am to preach on the Sabbath. I am in hopes we shall return by Glasgow, as I am anxious to see that city. There is great hospitality, and abundance of everything that is good; but the common people get neither meat nor butter nor honey, but boiled oatmeal, with some small beer poured over it. This is one dish we always see on the table. I tasted it, and found it very much like the bran and water that is stirred together to fatten chickens or to feed hogs; but the great folks seem to like it exceedingly well."

Mr Bull preached in the parish church at Melville, and the next day left for Glasgow. " We left Melville," he says, " this morning after the kindest and most friendly entertainment, and came safely to Glasgow, through Kinross, near Lochleven, and through Stirling, sixty-eight miles." At Glasgow he saw Dr Gillies, who wrote the Life of White-field, and he says, referring to that interview and his visit to Dr Erskine, "The sight of an old holy man of God always does my heart good. As for young Christians, though I tenderly love them, yet real wisdom and substantial good-ness is only to be expected with gray hairs. Life is too short to be wise before we grow old. It will be well for us if we are so then. You know that Jesus is the fountain of all wisdom and goodness. Consequently, they only are truly wise who live nearest to Him. It is not the largest understanding that constitutes true wisdom and goodness, but a humble and contrite heart, and a firm faith in Christ.

"Our road yesterday was most of the way along the mountains which divide Perth from Fife and Clackmannan-shires. They are wild and singular, and pleased me much; but there are hills of devotion, and mountains of salvation, that are infinitely more delectable, and to the contem-plation of which all these lower works of God should lead us."

In Glasgow, Mr Bull met with a Dr Moyes, a very extraordinary man. "Though blind from two years of age, he is," says Mr Bull, "a great linguist, philosopher, and mathematician, and an incomparable musician. He gives lectures in philosophy, and is one of the most com-municative, agreeable men in company I ever met with."

Leaving Glasgow, they saw the Carron Ironworks, which Mr Bull describes in a letter to his son, and travelled by Haddington and Dunbar, crossed the Tweed, and came once more into "Old England." They turned off the road at Thirsk, to visit a place called Helmsley—the scene of the successful labours of Mr Thornton's brother-in-law, the Rev. Dr Conyers. "So delighted," says Mr Bull, "are the people of Helmsley at Mr Thornton's being here, that the bells have been ringing most of the afternoon—a loud-speaking mark of respect to the most deserving man in the world."

My grandfather preached twice at this place on the following day, the Sabbath, he says, "with peculiar comfort, and, I hope, with the blessing of God, to very large and attentive congregations."

Soon after his return, Lady Balgonie says in a letter to him, "Your discourses in this country were most acceptable. The farmers at Melville are wishing for a lease of you; and Dr Goodsir, I hear, gave his congregation nearly the same discourse he heard from you at Balgonie."

Mr Bull happened to be in London when, on the 23d of April, George III. went to St Paul's to return thanks to God for his recovery. It was a very magnificent sight, and Mr B. saw as much as could be witnessed outside the Cathedral from the house of Mr Neale. The Commons and the Peers preceded the royal family, and the King and Queen were met at Temple Bar by the Lord Mayor and the city authorities. Their Majesties entered the church amidst the peal of organs and the voices of five thousand children singing the hundredth Psalm.

In July, Mr Bull went to Brighton to supply Lady Huntingdon's chapel for a month. Staying at Clapham on his way, he speaks of the tidings of the Revolution in

France—the taking of the Bastile—and of some of those fearful atrocities which had even then commenced, and of the number of refugees already arrived in England. My grandfather had a very pleasant visit to Brighton, and was kindly entertained by Mr Scutt, and preached with great acceptance to crowded congregations. He visited the scene of his former ministrations at Rottingdean, and preached there in a barn. He speaks of a young man, a Mr Jay, coming from Surrey Chapel, to preach at Brighton on a week evening. While at Brighton, Mr Bull heard of the death of his old friend Mr Barham. Lady Hill had died a few days before. "This news," he says, "affected me much, and called forth a tear or two."

About this time Mr Thornton was engaged in publishing a new edition of Bogatzky's "Golden Treasury." He wished to enrich and improve it with the contributions of some of his friends, and he sought Mr Bull's aid. "Send me a pearl," he says, "for the 'Golden Treasury' for January 31, on Matt. xiii. 5, 6;" again, "I get slowly on, as you did not mark the pages you remarked on;" and subsequently, "I thank you for 31st January pearl, and annotations accompanying it, and I shall hope, by a convenient opportunity, you will proceed to February 16, 'Let not sin reign,' &c., Rom. vi. 12. Berridge I will as little spare as Watts, when I think him not more edifying. One may find blots on the sun. What we are most used to we like best. Now let a Churchman (I don't mean a nominal one) have all the candour you can wish him, yet the Church will be uppermost; and so some degree of jealousy (I should better like a softer, prettier name) will arise when he peruses what comes from those of any other persuasion, and this is equally the case with Methodists, Dissenters, Moravians, &c., &c.   We all discern it in others, but it is our blind side that is rarely perceived by ourselves." Mr Thornton writes again three days afterwards, " I think I could not have better help than a Newport Bull and an Everton Ass, [Mr Berridge,] as he is pleased at times to entitle himself, and with their help I have got through three months, but it takes up more time than I expected, to be accurate."

From a marked copy I find that four original papers were written by my grandfather, and some others amended by him.   Mr Thornton himself is author of seven; and other contributions are from Mr Newton, Mr Bentley, and others.   Mr Bull's papers are to be found under the dates, January 18, February 10 and 16, and December 1.

Mr Thornton frequently warns his friend to take care of his health.   " You must have some mercy on your miserable carcass.   Let your moderation be known unto all men."   Again, " I return Mr Neale's letter.   I can only say, if it is too much for you to preach at Surrey Chapel, you ought not to do it; and if you do, you have no right to complain.   Did you stand as myself,—a single pin,—it would matter little; but if you involve a loving wife and a desirable son, and overset a hopeful academy thereby, it is not the Spirit of Jesus that acts so cruelly; but yet that, like many indiscretions, may be overlooked by a merciful Saviour, who, I hope, will direct you in this and every important business of life, and not suffer Satan, when appearing as an angel of light, to lead to your dissolution."

Once more he writes, " I am persuaded I am much nearer the end of the journey of life than you, with all your roaring, as your complaints are mostly brought on by your intemperance, whereas I can find no person to grind me young; however, I trust it will shortly be well with both of us. My dear friend, have some compassion on yourself, and proceed with more moderation, and don't wholly incapacitate yourself for usefulness, lest you rue it too late."

In the same letter Mr Thornton says, " I don't know whether I am to rejoice or lament that you have concluded the Psalms. May you be directed to something equally profitable."

In November, Mr Bull went to Cambridge, to the ordination of one of his students, Mr Gardiner. " I hope," says Mr Thornton, " a blessing will attend you at the University. I shall expect from you or your son a full account of the business you are on."

Mr Bull writes thus from Cambridge to Mrs Bull :—
" . . . Came here to dinner, and received very kindly by Mr Audley, a man diligently engaged in business, but a dear lover of Jesus. At night we went to the Meeting, a large old wooden building, which looks as if it would tumble on one's head. There were four or five hundred hearers, and I preached on John viii. 31, 32, ' If ye continue in my word, then are ye my disciples indeed; and ye shall know the truth, and the truth shall make you free.' I felt the love of Jesus glowing at my heart, and as it were the light of his countenance shining about me. He helped me to speak with great liberty, and I trust with holy delight in his dear name; and notwithstanding my

hoarseness, I think it was a blessed opportunity; however, it is with the Lord Jesus to give a blessing.

"Mr Simeon came to sup with us, a very dear and precious servant of Jesus. His company delighted me very much. He is exceedingly humble, holy, and heavenly. It is a wonderful thing in the divine conduct of the Master to raise up such a man in such a place as this. It must be intended for great good, and rejoices my heart exceedingly to see so glorious an instance of the grace and love of Jesus here. At half-past seven Mr Audley called us down to prayer. He read a chapter, sang a hymn, and I prayed. Then we went to King's College, to breakfast with Mr Simeon. I prated away for an hour with him, till I was quite fatigued. I prayed with him, and then he took us to see colleges, chapels, libraries, &c., till just now, and I am come in weary enough. We expect this afternoon Mr Smith of Bedford, and Dr Gordon of St Neots, who will perform most part of the ordination—only the charge, which you know who is to deliver.

"Tommy is gone out again to stare about him, but I have done for to-day. My hoarseness is better. I hope it will be quite well to-morrow. I fear I shall find Dr Gordon and Smith dry chips, but would hope the best. I will let you know to-morrow evening, if I can get time to be alone. The Lord Jesus be with you, and bless you . . . .'"

In January 1790, Mr Bull was with Mr Thornton at Clapham. He preached there several times, and at Surrey Chapel. In February, Mr Newton writes :—

"REV. AND DEAR TAUREAU,—The nice half pig (not the

half nice pig) which you sent arrived safely. Coming from you, it was sure of a welcome. Thank you for pig and letter, and for every token and expression of your love to old friends. My dear thanks you for your kind concern about her, and so do I. I have already written more than the three lines you asked for, but when writing to you, would time permit, I could send three sides or three sheets. I will at least keep on till the barber or the breakfast stops me." He speaks of his past life, his union with Mrs Newton, and what a blessing it had been to him, and adds, " The greater part of our journey is accomplished. How much further we have to go He knows—we know not. But I humbly hope He will be our guide and guard even unto death. The shadows of evening are lengthening upon us—the night cometh. I hope it will be but a momentary night, ushering in an everlasting day. Pray for us; I will try to pay you in kind. Mrs Newton and Catty join with me in love to you, Mrs Bull, and Tommy. The Lord bless you and yours abundantly !—I am your truly affectionate,

" JOHN NEWTON."

The following letter from Mr Hill to Mr Bull, written just before Easter, is amusing and characteristic :—

" MY DEAR BROTHER BULL,—At last the famous publication is out— Cowper, Bull, Hill, & Co.—*Parturiunt montes, nascitur,* &c.; and now the paper is so paltry, the printing so bad, and the typographical blunders so capital, that I have not ventured to advertise them. My printer is a poor man, and it is a charity to employ him, but the biggest blunderer in all the world, myself not excepted. I intend, if I can, not to advertise till the next edition, and that shall be more correct. Mr Cowper will find almost all his judicious amendments strictly attended to. The omissions are so small, that I think he himself would judge them scarcely worth an apology. I think you know them all. I have mentioned the corrector's name in the preface, just as you have directed. I mean to defer the other publication for a few months longer, till I see how this takes with the public. But, as I hope again to see you soon in town, I shall be able to judge better about the business, and have things in sufficient forwardness for your kind correction. The hymn-books you receive with this you have already more than paid for by your friendly assistance. The half-dozen more decently bound are for Mr Cowper. Will you send them to him the first opportunity? Madam Wallis's Travels in the same bundle. When you have had enough of her you will not forget to return her;—too good to be parted with for a trifle. Charming poetess! the best in her way that ever wrote!

"You are to come to London on Good Friday. This intelligence I received at Clapham, and I told Mr Thornton that I should ask you to come to our house on Good Thursday, and that if you preached a good sermon I would send you on the Good Friday afternoon to good Mr Thornton's, with a good number of thanks for your good services. My good wife also promises you a good supper, and a good pipe, and a good bed, provided you give us a little notice that we are to expect your good company. So, wishing you a good night, as it is a good while past eleven o'clock, I remain, though after a poor rate, your good friend and servant,   R. HILL.

"Friday Evening."

Mr Bull again visited Brighton in the summer of this year, supplying Lady Huntingdon's chapel during part of his vacation. A remarkable circumstance was connected with the journey to Brighton. The coach took up Mr Bull at Clapham. There was but one other inside passenger,— a man of gentlemanly bearing, and who had seen much of the world. He was an East India captain, named Jamison, but was about going out to Calcutta to hold a high office in the civil service. Though in other respects a very pleasant companion, his conversation was very profane. When Mr Bull had somewhat gained his confidence, he took an opportunity of telling him that his frequent and familiar mention of the name of God gave him great pain, and prevented the pleasure he should otherwise have in his company, and he hoped he would endeavour to restrain himself. He thanked my grandfather for his reproof, and promised to do his best, and hoped that if he made a mistake he might be reminded of it. The coach stopped to dine at Lewes. Mr Bull was much indisposed, and nothing could equal the attentions of his fellow-traveller. He said the coach should not start till my grandfather had finished his pipe; and, being accustomed to command, his authority was felt. He told Mr Bull that he had intended to stop at Lewes, but he should go on to Brighton. There they parted in a most friendly way, the Captain saying he should see Mr Bull the next day.

Nothing was, however, heard of him till about a month afterwards, when my grandfather was at Mr Neale's, at St Paul's Churchyard, intending to go the next day to Newport. In company with a Mr Cox, a friend of Mr Bull's, he entered, exclaiming, "I have found you at last, and I was determined to do so, if I had gone to the ends of the earth." And then the dialogue continued thus :—" Well, Sir, I am glad to see you; but what is your object?" " I am going, as I told you, to the East Indies. I have a son, and I am determined to put him under your care, for I found by your conversation that you keep an Academy." " Yes; but I only receive young men who are training up for the Christian ministry among Dissenters." "That's no objection. He is deaf and dumb, and I can leave him in no person's hands but yours." " I cannot receive him. What can I do with him?" " He is at Paris. I shall fetch him from thence, and bring him down to you in a few weeks, and will give you any sum you may please to ask." He then abruptly left the room, determined to take no denial.

Several circumstances occurred to delay the carrying out of this extraordinary purpose; but in May of the following year this youth actually arrived at Newport. He was about fourteen years of age, remarkable for the beauty of his person and the amiableness of his temper. His manner was peculiarly pleasing, but he was totally deaf. He had spent some time at Paris, at the institution founded by the Abbé L'Epée, and had learned his system of signs. By the study of this book, my father, to whose care he was committed, was soon able to converse with him. He had also been taught to speak by Mr Braidwood of Hackney ; but his tones were very harsh, and could only be understood by those who were always with him. He spent a great deal of time in reading, but he continually wanted to know the meaning of words he did not understand; and it was no easy matter to give him this information. But he evinced so much gratitude for the trouble thus taken with him, that it became a pleasure to help him through his difficulties.

Mrs Jamison, his mother, was a daughter of Sir Charles G——g. She had seen much of the gay world, and had taken her share in its dissipations. She was possessed of great talent and singular energy of character. She and her husband were not on good terms. There was a mutual dislike, but both were strongly attached to their amiable but unfortunate son. The Captain was determined that his wife should have as little as possible to do with their son. On one occasion he requested a friend to bring the youth to the East Indies. This was done without Mrs Jamison's consent; and as soon as she found the boy had sailed, she took her passage in another Indiaman, and followed the ship to the Cape of Good Hope, and from thence to Calcutta. Her vessel anchored so near that on which her son still was, that she saw him walking on the deck. She said to some of the sailors, "You see that youth : he is my son ; and if you will bring him to me I will give you the contents of this purse." The men boarded the vessel and carried off their prize, and the next day the mother sailed back to England with her son. This circumstance

Mrs Jamison herself related to my father,—it may be, with some little exaggeration.

She took a house in the neighbourhood of Newport, and seemed more than satisfied with the arrangement about her son, though after about two years she formed a plan to get him away, being desirous, as circumstances seemed to indicate, to have at her own disposal the money paid by the Captain on the youth's account. She informed Mr Bull that her husband had expressed a wish that their son should reside with her. Several circumstances led to the supposition that this statement was a fabrication; and, unfortunately for the success of the scheme, there came a letter in a few days from Captain Jamison, written in his usual style of affectionate regard, and full of expressions of gratitude and confidence, and saying that he had sent half a pipe of Madeira, which he had directed to his son, that he might have the pleasure of presenting it to my grandfather. Mr Bull at once appealed to the agents of the Captain, and refused to give up his charge till he had instructions directly from the father. Not many days, however, elapsed, before another letter arrived from the East Indies, announcing the death of Mr Jamison. Of course the young man left Newport, and the wine never reached its destination. During the residence of young Jamison at Newport he made very great improvement. His understanding was naturally good, and he had a great thirst for knowledge. I find from Mrs Jamison's letters that my father took very great pains with him. She says, in a letter to my grandfather,—"My brother was perfectly delighted with the progress Charles had made in propriety of speaking. I gave the merit where it is so justly due—viz., to Mr T. Bull's indefatigable care and attention." And again, in a letter to my grandfather,—"I have spoken of the obligations we are under to your son's zeal and ability." The disposition of this youth was very amiable, and he manifested at times a great deal of religious feeling.

His mother removed to Worthing, where she engaged in building speculations, and was soon involved in pecuniary difficulties, and eventually went to France. I have heard my father say, they never afterwards could learn what became of the son.

Writing from Clapham on his return, Mr Bull says of his Brighton journey :—"We left Brighton yesterday, in the morning, and arrived here by half-past three. I have seldom had a more pleasant vacation, because always well, and always in the way of usefulness. We came away with regret; we met with so much love and affection from the people. I hope we have left a blessing behind us."

Mr Bull spent a Sabbath with Mr Thornton, and called on Lady Huntingdon on his way through London.

A letter from Mr Hill, through some mischance, was unanswered, and under date Sept. 10, he writes again :—

"MY DEAR BROTHER BULL,—My last letter you did not answer. The engagements of the great are great. I hope, however, you will answer this, and answer it according to my liking. Surrey Chapel is under repair. The congregation have been turned adrift two Sabbaths already, and I fear will be for two more. I only now ask the favour of your assistance to preach one end of the day a charity

sermon for us; not the first, but the second Sabbath after
it is opened, and, at least, to stop one Sunday after that.
Modesty says, Ask but little of the great, and they will
grant the more. Now, I have some very peculiar distant
calls to attend to through the month of October, and I
cannot dare to leave the chapel without a minister that
the congregation highly approve. They love your ministry exceedingly. If ever Jesus blessed you in your life,
He has blessed you at Surrey Chapel. May you come,
and be blessed again!—In much haste, yours affectionately,   R. HILL.

"LONDON, *Sept.* 10."

About the middle of September, Mr Thornton wrote to
Mr Bull and complained of not feeling well, and Mr
Samuel Thornton wrote about the same time, requesting Mr Bull, if his engagements would allow, to pay his
father a visit. Accordingly, my grandfather visited him
early in October. Mr Hill thus writes in connexion with
this journey :—" As gray.as a badger the chapel shall be
before it is decorated again with my consent; but the
people called for it, and, indeed, not before the place
needed it. Besides this, my attendance on the business
has made me feel so very worldly, that I scarce know
where I am. I have, however, just sufficient sense left
me to recollect that you say you cannot come on the first
Sabbath I mentioned, but proffered your assistance for a
morning's sermon on the second Sabbath. . . . You say
you cannot stay longer than one Sabbath; I am afraid,
however, that the declining state of our dear old friend

Mr Thornton's health may make you alter your purpose. If so, however sorry for the cause, we shall be happy to avail ourselves of your services."

Mr Bull accordingly preached at Surrey in the morning of the 10th of October, at the little chapel at Clapham in the afternoon, and expounded the 145th Psalm at Mr Thornton's in the evening. Mr Bull, speaking of this visit, says:—"I came to Clapham with Mr Henry Thornton, from his banking house. Mr Thornton came down to prayers, but his nerves are so weak, that he spoke very few words to me. He stayed down about an hour." Again Mr Bull writes on Monday the 11th:—"I spent Saturday in solitude, very low-spirited and gloomy. Only saw Mr Thornton half an hour at night, but did not speak to him, he is so low in his spirits. Yesterday morning, he sent the coach with me to Surrey. The chapel was uncommonly full; the text, 2 Cor. iv. 6. In the afternoon I preached at the little meeting (at Clapham) on Exod. xxxiii. 14, and at night I spoke at Mr Thornton's. He was present, and seemed much revived and pleased to hear me. He came down again after supper and sat half an hour." He adds in a postscript:—"Mr Thornton has just been down, and we have dined together; but he is extremely weak, and spoke but a few words;" and again, " I have just taken leave of Mr Thornton, and I think I shall never see him again. I am exceedingly affected, and I can add no more."

On the 16th, Mr Thornton writes two or three lines to Mr Bull, simply saying that he was somewhat better, and going to Bath. Thither he went, and Mr H. Thornton wrote on the 28th that all hope of his recovery was at an end, and on the 7th of November this excellent man died.

The death of Mr Thornton greatly affected Mr Bull, and he preached a funeral sermon for him, at Newport, on the appropriate text, Matt. xxv. 21, " Well done, thou good and faithful servant." Mr Thornton's attachment to my grandfather, and to my father also, young as the latter then was, was very strong, and marked by many and unusual expressions of its reality. In writing to my grandfather,—and for several years he did so twice a-week, sometimes more frequently,—he sought his advice in all his efforts to promote the kingdom of Christ, and unbosomed all his religious experiences as to one in whom he could most fully confide, and from whom he looked for instruction and sympathy. He addresses him in the most affectionate manner, and often in terms of playful familiarity, as his " dear friendly Bull," his " dear Bully," " dear friend William." He says in one of his letters,—" I trust no love will be lost between us, and that we shall continue, while in the flesh, mindful of one another." Elsewhere :—" I had rather hear you set forth Jesus than any man I know." On one occasion he subscribes himself " your own faithful loving friend in a precious Jesus."

I never heard my father speak of Mr Thornton but with the deepest feeling of veneration and love. To the last the good man continued to apply to him his baby name of Tot. It is almost needless to say that Mr Thornton's was not a friendship of mere words. It was rich in the abundant fruits of kind and generous attention to all who shared it.

Most justly does Sir James Stephen say of Mr Thornton,
" He was renowned in his generation for a munificence more
than princely—one of those rare men in whom the desire
to relieve distress assumes the form of a master-passion."
But it was in the promotion of the gospel, and in the substantial aid he afforded in various ways to its ministers,
that he made himself so deservedly conspicuous. He was
constantly seeking, by purchase or otherwise, to get pre-
sentations to livings, into which the gospel might thus
be introduced : and when, as was often the case, the income
was inadequate, supplementing it from his own resources.
" You know something," says Mr Newton, writing of the
death of their intimate friend, " of my peculiar obligations
to him.   To him, under the Lord, I owe all my consideration and comfort as a minister."   Mr Newton's stipend at
Olney was insignificant, and Mr Thornton allowed him
£200 a-year that he might be enabled to shew " hospitality
to the saints," and be otherwise useful, and this was in
addition to a regular contribution for the poor of his flock.
To my grandfather he says in one of his letters, " When
you want money, remember I am your banker, and draw
freely;" again, " I am glad you are beginning on Sunday
Schools. When you want assistance, you know where to
come for it." There are very many such indications of his
exceeding liberality, in addition to others which the above
narrative supplies. Most justly does the poet say of him :—

> " Thou hadst an industry in doing good
> Keen as the peasant's toiling for his food."

Mr Thornton's liberality of sentiment was very marked.
A Churchman in principle, yet were Dissenters amongst

his chosen friends; in fact, the truth was dear to him wherever he found it, and though no man was ever farther removed from mere churchism, yet was he most tenacious of the great fundamental principles of the gospel, and knew nothing of that spurious liberality which is but a disguised unconcern about truth. His letters to Mr Bull abound with the most enlarged and liberal views.

In those letters, too, his *piety* shines forth very conspicuously. Religious exercises and religious services were his delight, and he often speaks of the obstacles which worldly occupations presented to the cultivation of piety. "I think it probable," says Mr Newton, "that no one man in Europe in private life will be so much missed."

Lord Balgonie, in writing to Mr Bull from Bath, suggested to him, to request Mr Cowper to write an elegy on the death of Mr Thornton. Mr Bull did so, and the poet gladly complied, and hence the lines commencing—

"Poets attempt the noblest task they can," &c.,

the MS. of which being sent to my grandfather is now in my possession.

Referring to an interview with Mr Bull in London, on occasion of this last visit to Mr Thornton, Mr Newton says, —"Our meeting last night was short and not over-joyous. Had you found me alone, I would have kept you a little longer, or accompanied you to Mr Neale's. I shall be with you in spirit to-day, and to-morrow hope to wait upon you in the shape of a letter. Perhaps we both need a cordial. If writing should prove one to me, and reading what I write should comfort you, I shall be glad. Well, then, to begin, if possible, at the right end, I will tell you, though you know it, that the Lord reigns, and that the Lord is our Lord." Then, after speaking of the goodness and the wisdom of God, he adds, " Mr Thornton has been long a burning and shining light. He is eclipsed by his present decline, but death will not extinguish him, for He who has the residue of the Spirit will never want instruments to promote his own cause, and to comfort his own people. You know something of my peculiar obligations to him. I hope my respect and affection were in some degree proportionable. It was a pleasure to me if I only saw him passing by."

In this letter, Mr Newton speaks of the illness of his wife, and about a fortnight afterwards he writes again " that there is little hope."

Another letter, dated Dec. 18, announces Mrs Newton's death, and the good man's abounding consolation under this heavy stroke. " I hope," he says, " the receipt of this will not cause your spirits to droop, or your head to hang down, when I, who am most nearly interested, can begin with telling you, all is well. I am supported, I am comforted, I am satisfied."

I find no letter from my grandfather to Mr Newton on this sad occasion, though it is impossible but he should have written to him.

Thus, this year closed under a dark shadow.

CHAPTER X.

Surrey Chapel—Brighton—Remarkable Incident—Birmingham Riots—Letter from Mr Cowper—Mr Bull's Letter to his Son when he commenced Preaching—Visit to Mr Newton—Letters to and from Mr Newton—Surrey Chapel and the King's Organist—Threatening aspect of the Times—Mr Bull's Popularity at Surrey Chapel—Politics of Dissenters.

IN the beginning of the year 1791, Mr Bull supplied at Surrey Chapel. " I meet," he says, " with respect and kindness from all quarters. I was never so popular." He received marked attention from the family of Mr Thornton, and preached once more on Sabbath evening in the drawing-room of the old house at Clapham. He was during this visit the guest of Mr Neale of St Paul's Churchyard, where he was daily engaged in what he terms " parlour expositions."

Mr Hill was very anxious that Mr Bull should come up to Surrey again at Easter, which he did for one Sabbath.

He also supplied Lady Huntingdon's chapel at Brighton, in July and August; and here again, as in the former year, his journey thither was fruitful in an interesting and important event. His companions in the coach were Mr and Mrs Davis. The former was a bigoted Churchman. His wife had been brought up under the gospel, but was prevented from ever attending it in consequence of the opposition of her husband. Mr Davis was a great coach and wagon proprietor, and had made a great deal of money, but was a purse-proud, narrow-minded man. Mrs Davis was sister to Mr Scutt, a banker at Brighton, and one of the principal managers of the chapel, and at his house Mr Bull was to make his home. Mr Davis was much pleased with the conversation of his fellow-traveller, but did not know his object in visiting Brighton, or whither he was going. He pressed my grandfather to call upon him. The next morning Mr Bull mentioned his intention to Mr Scutt. He said, " If you do, he will turn you out of his house. He says he will have no Methodist parsons come near him." Mr Bull told Mr Scutt he had been asked to call, and had promised to do so. " Well, then, go by all means, and I shall be curious to know the result of your visit." Mr Bull was not only kindly received, but repeated his visits, endeavouring to drop such hints as might be useful, especially as it was evident Mr Davis was going fast to his grave. Before Mr Bull left Brighton, Mrs Davis suggested to him to write to her husband, inquiring after his health, as it would afford an opportunity of saying what might be useful. This was accordingly done, the truths of the gospel, and the necessity of a personal interest in them, being plainly set forth before the dying man. The letter was always by his side, was read again and again, and it is believed was the means of effecting a saving change in a heart hitherto opposed to God and his truth. He expressed his earnest hope that he might meet that good man, who had so kindly written to him, in heaven. Mrs

Davis, from that time, attended the ministry of the gospel, and became a woman of eminent piety. She was henceforth a devoted friend of Mr Bull, who frequently corresponded with her.

Amidst the political and religious excitements of the time, the present year was disgraced by the celebrated riots at Birmingham, where the meeting-house and dwelling of Dr Priestley, and the habitations of many Dissenters, were burned to the ground. In reference to these events, Mr Cowper wrote the following letter to his friend while he was at Brighton :—

"MY DEAR MR BULL,—Mindful of my promise, I take the pen, though fearing, and with reason enough, that the performance will hardly be worth the postage. Such as it is, however, here it comes; and if you like it not, you must thank yourself for it.

" I have blessed myself on your account that you are at Brighton and not at Birmingham, where, it seems, they are so loyal and so pious that they shew no mercy to Dissenters. How can you continue in a persuasion so offensive to the wise and good? Do you not yet perceive that the Bishops themselves hate you not more than the very blacksmiths of the Establishment? and will you not endeavour to get the better of your aversion to red-nosed singing-men and organs? Come, be received into the bosom of motherchurch; so shall you never want a jig for your amusement on Sundays, and shall save, perhaps, your Academy from a conflagration.

" As for me, I go on at the old rate, giving all my time

to Homer, who, I suppose, was a Presbyterian too, for I understand that the Church of England will by no means acknowledge him for one of hers. He, I say, has all my time, except a little that I give every day to no very cheering prospects of futurity. I would I were a Hottentot, or even a Dissenter, so that my views of a hereafter were more comfortable. But such as I am, Hope, if it please God, may visit even me; and should we ever meet again, possibly we may part no more. Then, if Presbyterians ever find the way to heaven, you and I may know each other in that better world, and rejoice in the recital of the terrible things that we endured in this. I will wager sixpence with you now, that when that day comes, you shall acknowledge my story a more wonderful one than yours. Only order your executors to put sixpence in your mouth when they bury you, that you may have wherewithal to pay me.

" I have received a long letter from an unknown somebody, filled with the highest eulogiums on my Homer. This has raised my spirits, and is the true cause of all the merriment with which I have greeted you this morning. 'Pardon me,' as Vellum says in the comedy, 'for being jocular.' Mrs Unwin joins me in love to yourself and your good son, and we both hope, and both sincerely wish, to hear of Mrs Bull's recovery.—Yours affectionately,

"WM. COWPER."

Never had a child been more tenderly reared and watched over, or more carefully trained, than was my father. He had never been from under the eye of his parents. Every indication of religious feeling had been gladly noted and encouraged; he had always looked on a bright and holy example; and all his associations were favourable to the development of piety. Prayer had been made for him without ceasing, and utterance often given to the most fervent appeals on his behalf. At length the result was manifest, not only in religious decision, but in consecration to the ministry of the gospel. I suppose it was about this time that my father began occasionally to preach. My grandfather thus writes to him from London in October:—

"... For my part, I only wish you may love the Lord Jesus Christ with supreme delight, and serve Him with infinite zeal and prudence. I hope you preached yesterday morning in the vestry, and that Christ was your subject; that you felt at liberty, and was comfortable in your work; and that it is only the beginning of a long life of faith, love, zeal, joy in the work and labour of the Lord's vineyard; that you may live to preach thousands of sermons to the conversion of more than ten thousand precious souls from the condemnation of hell, and to the everlasting glory of the grace of our dear Lord and Saviour Jesus Christ. This is my daily prayer to the Lord for you. However, I must beg you will study and pray to be very humble, very wise, very holy, and very zealous; for I do hate coxcombs in all places, but in the pulpit they are quite abominable. Read, think, pray, and remember to do everything as one that must give an account. Let your whole soul be swallowed up in the contemplation of God our Saviour, and the glorious mystery of his person, blood, and righteousness. O my dear child, breathe, pant, long, wrestle, strive every day to become a temple of the Holy Ghost, the first door of which must be humility, then prayer, which makes worms omnipotent, and transforms beasts into angels. Pray every day for the birth of souls, and first and principally for the birth of your own soul. Keep close to Christ, and be diligent in business, and all will be well with you. Be sure not to neglect the students every day. Give my hearty love to mamma. Love to every one about the grounds. I commit you to the grace of the Lord Jesus Christ; and am, dear son, your faithful, affectionate father,   W. BULL."

It appears that towards the end of the year my father was ill, and that my grandfather's anxieties were awakened on his account; for in a letter from Mr Newton dated Dec. 10, after referring to another topic, he adds :—

" But I sit down to write upon a more important subject. Mrs Neale told me, when I was there on Thursday evening, that Tommy was poorly. I entered plump into your feelings, and therefore now I must write. Whosoever waits, Mr Bull must be served. . . . . I hope and pray, with respect to Tommy, that his sickness may not be unto death, but to the glory of God, and his and your future comfort. Give my love to him, and assure him that I shall be often with him in spirit. My love to Mrs Bull. I sympathize with her likewise in her part of the trial, and in all her trials, so far as I know them.

"I heard with great pleasure that Mr C.'s son was respited. How different is his trial from yours! The

Lord has given you, or lent you, a dutiful, hopeful, and affectionate son; and if it is most for his good and yours, he shall be long continued to you.—Your affectionate and obliged friend and brother,   JOHN NEWTON."

Mr Bull now regularly supplied Surrey Chapel twice in the year, spending the latter part of his summer vacation at Brighton, Reading, and elsewhere. While in London, it was his custom to spend the Saturday with his friend Mr Newton, in company often with ministers of like spirit with themselves. Mr Foster and Mr Cecil were frequently of the party. Old memories were also revived at this and other times, by occasional visits to the members of Mr Thornton's family. Speaking of his visit to London in January 1792, Mr Bull writes to Mr Newton :—

"I recollect my late journey to town with pleasure; and my hearing you preach, and having frequent interviews with you, was very comfortable. I get very infirm, and so weak in my spirits that almost everything fatigues and afflicts me; but still it is pleasant to look upward, and to press forward to a state of light, life, holiness, love, and joy, that will be eternal in its duration. The time is not far off. I do not feel reluctant at its approach, because I shall then see the Lord in his glory, and, I hope, feel his image in my heart. There is something alluring and delightful in the prospect of perfect holiness, perfect love, and, consequently, perfect bliss; and this must and will be the lot of all who die in the Lord. That Jesus, whose blood is our atonement, and whose righteousness is also our life and salvation, we shall see as He is, and rejoice before Him for ever. Delightful prospect! It soothes the infirmities of age, and gives beauty to the countenance of dissolution. If the love of Jesus is but felt in our hearts, we may say, Welcome age! welcome infirmity! welcome death! Jesus is our greatest comfort now, and Jesus will be our ever-lasting portion. I love to think of Him, look to Him, and lean upon Him, because I feel and find that his presence is equal to everything, and without Him everything is worse than nothing. When you write this way, I shall be very glad to hear you are both well, and all about you. Through mercy Mrs Bull and Tommy are well, and unite with me in love to you and Miss Catlett.

"I called on Mr Cowper last week, and thought he looked very thin and poorly. Mrs Unwin was in good spirits; but I doubt if she is quite well. We were none of us intended to continue here always, and it is good to be told so; but with the saints in glory I hope we shall live for ever. I commit you to the grace and love of Jesus, and am your most affectionate   W. Bull."

In reply to this letter, after allusion to its principal topic, Mr Newton makes the following observations in reference to the efforts against the slave-trade:—"When I was as-sured that Mr Wilberforce would renew his motion in the House this session, I preached (as I did last year) about the slave-trade. I think myself bound in conscience to bear my testimony at least, and to wash my hands from the guilt which, if persisted in, now things have been so thoroughly investigated and brought to light, will, I think, constitute a national sin of a scarlet and crimson dye. A motion since made in the Common Council for a petition to Parliament on the subject has been negatived. If the city wanted a motto, I would furnish them with '*Virtus post nummos.*' If the business miscarries again, I shall fear not only for the poor slaves, but for ourselves." . . .

In another letter, written three days afterwards, Mr Newton says, "The abolition business comes on next Monday. Help us with your prayers, that He who has all hearts in his hand may give a happy issue. On one side humanity, conscience, and the sense of the nation are engaged against interest and influence on the other. But interest is blind, and mistakes its own cause. However, the battle is the Lord's."

There were two excellent women in town, once connected with the Court, Mrs Cavendish and Mrs Cartwright, to whom Mr Bull had been introduced by Mr Thornton. He often met them at Clapham, and visited them at their own house in St James's Place. There he frequently conducted "parlour-preaching," on which occasions Lady Mary Fitzgerald was often present. A friend, writing for them when their infirmities rendered the labour irksome, says to Mr Bull, "Your letters are a great source of refreshment to your friends and their small society." Again, —"They love your letters. Lady Mary Fitzgerald desires me to assure you how much she is obliged by them." Mr Bull continued his visits till the death of these excellent women, which occurred very nearly at the same time in the summer of this year, (1792.)

In October, Mr Bull went to London to preach a funeral

sermon at Surrey Chapel, for the daughter of an old friend connected with that place of worship, and who had married a gentleman then residing at Newport.

In a letter to Mrs Bull he says, "We are this moment arrived at Mr Cox's, after as safe and as pleasant a journey as our sorrowful errand would admit. . . . . I shall expect a letter from Tommy in a day or two. Pray inform him that my most reverend condescension permits him to preach in my pulpit on Thursday evening, in preference to any of my domestic chaplains. Tell his reverence I commit to him the care of my students, expecting from his duty and piety the greatest possible attention, and from his genius the most desirable success. . . . . I commit you all to the blessing of a precious Jesus."

In the latter part of this month Mr and Mrs Neale were on a visit to Newport, and Mr Newton writes :—

"My dear Sir and Brother,—I wished to wait upon you in the shape of a short letter, (I have less time than ever for long ones,) while Mr and Mrs Neale are with you, that I might meet you all together. If they stay their proposed time, I am not yet too late. I tried hard to smoke a pipe with you when in town; but you were not at leisure one time, and the next not at home. Had it been necessary without doubt we should have met. May we meet in glory! I trust we shall. He who has invited and inclined us to seek Him will not disappoint the hope Himself has raised, nor the taste to which only He could form such minds as ours. Such a state of happiness as the Word of God describes—a state of wonder, love, and praise, surrounding and admiring Him that sitteth on the throne—would not have pleased me once. I should have preferred a pigsty to it. Now I hope I can say, Nothing in earth or heaven in comparison of Thee! And you can say the same. . . . . Do you ask how I am employed? I am making extracts from love-letters, not to a sweetheart, but to a wife. I have quires of them by me, which I wrote when I used the sea, or at other intervals of absence from home. Perhaps I shall find enough to make a Cardiphonia volume, which may bear reading when I am gone hence. This job cannot be performed by a substitute. It will engross much of my little leisure from other business, and will therefore, I hope, be accepted as a plea, if I should be tardy in correspondence.

"This is a voluntary offering, for I do not owe you a letter; and yet I am a little mercenary, for I mean by it to draw a return from you.

"Our love to your guests, to Mrs Bull, Tommy, and all your family, not forgetting the silent young gentleman, (Charles Jamison,) with whom I was much pleased when I saw him at Newport. The Lord bless you all! Amen.—I am yours indeed,   "JOHN NEWTON.

"*October* 19, 1792."

When Mr Bull was supplying at Surrey Chapel the beginning of the following year, (1793,) it had been arranged for the King's organist, Dr Duprée, to be there, to perform on the new instrument. In reference to this circumstance, Mr Bull writes thus to his son:—"When I came to the chapel, instead of beginning at the proper time, (it was the

Tuesday evening service,) they waited a quarter of an hour for Dr Duprée, the King's organist, who at length with the organ-builder made his appearance. The chapel was very full indeed. The organ was played four times. All the serious people were exceedingly grieved and affronted; so much so, that Mr Neale said he had a great mind to send in the books, and throw up his charge. Indeed all were affronted except the carnal world, who came in great numbers to hear the music. I had ten minutes to pray in, and fifteen minutes for my sermon. To be sure the music was delightful, but everybody that belongs to the chapel was annoyed; and poor Mr Hill was in such a taking, and his wife too, that I thought he would have gone mad. We came home all in dudgeon with each other; but I don't think they need have been so very angry as they were."

In reference to this subject Mr Hill writes the following characteristic letter :—

"MY DEAR BROTHER BULL,—How you must think of my treatment last Tuesday evening, when his Majesty's tweedle-dee and tweedle-dum man interrupted our worship; and that after such a serious introduction of singing with our organ which we enjoyed the Sabbath before. Pride must have its fall, and for the future all the tweedledums that kings love they shall keep among themselves. Their fine airs will never do for a Methodist meeting-house. And so farewell to the first and the last of the business. Brother Bull, thanks, a thousand thanks, for your last visit. The people sucked it in very greedily. That proves they desired the sincere milk of the word, that they may grow thereby. . . .

" But I forget the design of my letter. After my Tuesday blunder, Mrs Hill and I came over to Mr Neale's, in hopes of an interview with you at his house; but, like a nimble Jack, we found you gone, and so we did our very best to patch up our bad behaviour. I rejoice with you that your lovely son is as he is. Jesus gives you this joy. His great sacrifice procured all we ever had, now have, and ever shall have.

" Past ten o'clock; eyes half shut; mind marvellously stupid; spirit much exhausted; and candles burning to waste. I shall, therefore, save the best part of a halfpenny if I finish directly.—Yours very gratefully and affectionately,   R. HILL.

" Madam Hill's love to Madam Bull.

" LONDON, (some day, I know not what, in the month of February 1793, and here ends my present knowledge.)"

The following passages occur in a letter written to Mrs Bull from London in January :—" You may have heard that venerable and holy Mr Berridge of Everton died last Thursday of a severe fit of asthma. He was just coming to London when he was thus attacked. Yesterday, in reference to his death, I preached morning and evening on Phil. i. 23, ' Having a desire to depart, and to be with Christ.' The Lord Jesus Christ wonderfully strengthened me, helped me, and comforted me.* About five o'clock I was very much affected with thinking that I was going to preach, and Tommy also going to preach, in an hour's time.

* Mr Bull also preached at Tottenham in reference to the same event. His text there was, " An old disciple."

I retired, prayed, and shed some tears, that we might both be filled with the Holy Ghost."

In a subsequent part of the letter he adds :—" I very much fear we shall have persecuting times. Things every day look more and more alarming. As to France, one cannot think of it without horror, and indignation, and trembling. Their fine revolutionists are turned into a band of murderers, and I fear something of the kind is intended in England, under the pretence of a reformation. A Frenchman in London, who did not enter his name in the public books, has been taken up, and in his house were found 250 stand of arms, so that he is put in close confinement.

" There is a dreadful spirit against Dissenters in all companies, as if they had conspired against the Government. I fear some wish to stir up troublous times. But my heart's desire is to live and die in peace and quietness, if the Lord permit. I almost tremble for my dear child; he surely will see strange things. May the Lord Jesus Christ keep his heart close to the main thing, and enable him to abstain from whatever brings trouble. Ministers of Christ should mind nothing but the things of Christ, and avoid all political affairs whatsoever."

He speaks of hearing Mr Romaine with great pleasure, " though I think his doctrine was strong meat. He says very little about sanctification, but he is a most excellent man. I dine with him to-morrow." He afterwards expresses the gratification he felt in that interview, and adds, that Mr Romaine urged him to print his Comment on the Psalms.

In the same letter he refers again to the strong feeling awakened against Dissenters,—how they were all charged with being republicans. He again begs his son to have nothing to do with politics, and to give himself to meditation on the Word of God. "Say to your heart, 'Come, my soul, enter thou into thy chambers, and shut thy doors about thee, till the indignation be overpast.'" He speaks of the great acceptance and popularity which the Lord gave him, and the many attentions he received, and yet at the same time he was frequently dissatisfied with his preaching. Thus, in the same letter, "This afternoon the chapel was well filled, but I preached very badly—quite loud, noisy, methodistical, ranting, and often made some of the people laugh. This grieved me exceedingly, and all night I was very uneasy. This morning I have been to Surrey to take leave. Some hundreds crowded around me to say farewell, and all begged me to come again as soon as I could."

In April, Mr Newton wrote to my grandfather to ask if he knew of a minister for the Dissenting congregation at Newport, in Essex. He speaks again of his new publication, "Letters to a Wife," and concludes as follows:—

"We return joint love to you and Mrs Bull and Tommy, who, I think, is now big enough to be Mr Thomas, or the Rev. Mr Thomas, in my mouth. However, go by what name he may, I pray the Lord to bless him, and to make him a comfort and a blessing to you and many.

"I trust you will likewise continue to pray for us. This mutual prayer is one valuable branch of the communion of saints. This clause, as it stands in our Creed, is repeated daily by many who know no more of the meaning than a goose does of algebra. Nor should we have been wiser than they, if the Lord had not condescended to be our teacher. May all the praise be ascribed to Him by you, and by your very affectionate friend and brother,

"JOHN NEWTON."

In August of this year Mr Bull visited Irthlingborough, his birthplace, in company with his son, pointing out to the latter, with deep and touching interest, the various scenes of his early history. It appears from his index that he preached there.

In a letter from London in September, when he was supplying at Surrey, he refers to a remarkable religious movement in Ireland. He says, "Yesterday I read in the pulpit a letter from Mr Hill, from Dublin, where he now is. The contents were to the effect that many students in the University and many of the fellows are awakened. They preach Christ. The churches are opened to them; and they go in crowds to hear Mr Hill, and have him to visit them in the college daily. All their time is taken up by the Bible and prayer. This is glorious news."

His next letter contains an amusing reference to Mr Newton. "I came home to dinner, [at Mr Neale's,] and Mr Newton came here to dine with me. He looks very old, and has got exceedingly fat since I saw him last, but he is full of piety, holiness, and heavenly-mindedness. I shall go to dine with him next Saturday. He says he has found out that both he and I have a great deal too much indulgence, and therefore he will not sleep after dinner any more."

Writing two days later to his son, he says, " I hope you will go to Bury on Saturday, and not on Sabbath morning—that I expressly forbid. Preach about Christ, extempore if you can, and be as warm and lively as possible. Don't come home till Monday morning. I hate Sabbath-breaking. The times are awful, and a day of persecution is not far off. Mr Newton says, all the Dissenters, even the orthodox not excepted, are republicans and enemies to Government, and he thinks it the duty of Government to watch over them all. Could you think so good a man could be so weak? In his late journey to Southampton he met with Mr Bogue of Gosport, who he thinks is a very pious man, but he says he is as bitter against Government as any Frenchman or republican in the world! The truth is, a party spirit runs very high, and I have no doubt that it will come to blows soon, and as the weakest goes to the wall, it is easy to see how it will fare with Dissenters. It seems a settled point with the authorities that all liberty of speech on politics shall be taken away, and I fear liberty of conscience will soon follow; but everything is in the hands of God."

Whatever Mr Newton's suspicions about Dissenters in general, or even about the politics of his friend in particular, it abated nothing of that cordial feeling which subsisted between them. Mr Bull had written to Mr N. in reference to his new work: the letter is, unfortunately, not to be found. He thanks him for it, and says, " I accept it as

a full compensation for any or all the censures I may meet
from snarling critics.   I cannot expect that my publication
will be approved by those who have not feeling to qualify
them for understanding it.   But yours is not the only encouragement I have received." After alluding to his preaching and his own personal experience, he goes on, " I hope
January will bring you to town, and therefore I content
myself with what, when writing to you, I deem a short
letter.   I am much engaged at present, and therefore I
chiefly write to prevent you from thinking me negligent or
ungrateful.   Dear Miss Catlett is well, and joins me in love
to Mrs Bull, my reverend friend Tommy, and all in your
house.   May the presence of the Lord dwell in it, fill your
heart, and crown your ministry with his blessing.—I am
truly and always your affectionate friend and brother,

" OMICRON.

" *December* 20, 1793."

CHAPTER XI.

THE LIFE OF THE REV. WILLIAM BULL,

1794—1796.

WHEN Mr Bull was in London at the beginning of the following year, Mr Romaine applied to him to take a young
man under his charge previous to his going to the university, telling him that Mr Clark, a clergyman who lived at
Chesham Bois, being dead, he was at a loss where to send
him. His name was Greigg. He was a very pious and
amiable young man, and afterwards settled in Leicestershire. My father became very much attached to him, but
his days were cut short.

My grandfather had a great aptitude in improving passing events. While he was preaching at Surrey, a melancholy accident occurred at the theatre in the Haymarket.
The announcement that the King and Queen were to be
there on a certain night caused a great concourse of people
to assemble. So soon as the doors were open, there was a
tremendous rush. Many were thrown down and trampled

upon; fifteen or sixteen persons lost their lives, and from forty to fifty received serious injuries, which in some instances afterwards proved fatal. "Such," says Mr Bull, "is the reward of serving the devil; but I think all who frequent the house of God may expect the blessing of God." He adds, "There were some cases of peculiar distress, particularly of a young woman who went against her will to oblige some country friends staying at her house. She told her maid before she went that she was sure she should never return alive, for she had dreamed the night before that she should die. Her mother also had a similar dream, and both proved true, for both were killed."

On the Sabbath evening following this catastrophe, Mr Bull made allusion to it in his sermon at Surrey Chapel. At that very time a dissipated young man was passing down Blackfriars Road, on his way to a place of infamous resort in that neighbourhood. While waiting for his companions, he turned into the chapel just when Mr Bull was alluding to the accident at the theatre, on which occasion he himself had been present. His attention was arrested, and he became so affected that he gave up his original purpose; and that sermon, there is every reason to believe, was made effectual to his salvation. That very night he wrote a letter to Mr Bull detailing these circumstances, and at the same time expressing his deep contrition for his past conduct, and his determination thenceforth to attend regularly at Surrey Chapel. The letter was anonymous.

About ten weeks later, another letter was sent to Mr Bull, of which the following is the substance:—The writer was a Mr Richard Jones, of the Strand. After a very ample apology for intruding himself on Mr Bull's attention, he refers to the letter of thanks addressed to him by a young man in February for the benefit received from a sermon he had heard at Surrey Chapel. "It is with pleasure I inform you," says the writer, "that a sudden change of temper and disposition in the young man was the happy issue of your endeavours. He who was an abandoned and profligate rake became virtuous and religious; and instead of a shame and a disgrace, he became the delight of his friends, and an honour and comfort to his parents." He then goes on to say that "the young man was seized with violent fever, issuing in a rapid decline, which baffled all medical skill, and he died at the age of twenty-two. His affliction," he states, "was borne with great patience; he was constantly in prayer, was filled with compunction for his past sins, and earnestly sought forgiveness of God. He sang with great emotion portions of various hymns. Mr K. Calford (such was the name of the young man) in his last moments desired me to acquaint you in particular with his death. He said he had, so long as his strength permitted, constantly attended the chapel where he saw you, and had received great consolation from a Mr Hill; but his soul, oppressed with gratitude, panted with anxious expectation to see the man to whom he was under so great obligations, by whom he had been led to conviction of sin, and to hope in the mercy of God." He concludes with the acknowledgment that, though he himself was what is called a stiff Churchman, "yet, if I see religion and good moral principles have been the result of your labours, I shall feel

P

myself happy to contribute all in my power to your protection, and not be so illiberal as to withhold the tribute of applause due to your merits, because you perchance may be (by name) of a different sect from myself."

When my grandfather was in London in the summer, he writes, "Yesterday I went to hear old Mr Winter in the morning, and liked his sermon tolerably well. I went into the vestry to speak to him. He was very cross, and seemed to wish to quarrel with me, for what I knew not; but, at length, it came out that I mentioned in the pulpit, at White Row, the names of Pitt and Fox. He said it savoured of levity and gave great offence; I suppose to some few bigots who watch for something to lay hold of."

Mr Bull refers to a prayer-meeting at Mr Neale's, "at which," he says, "I shall have to expound, or rather to preach extempore." Mr Jones, in his Life of Mr Hill, speaks of this meeting as established at Mr Neale's during the time of the French Revolution, and when ministers differing in minor points met together in peaceful harmony. Mr Neale was a party to its establishment.

When he was in London and elsewhere, Mr Bull spent much of his time in reading and study. There are frequent references in his letters home to the books that were at such times occupying his attention. July 8, he writes to his son, " I am reading over a second time the three sermons of Bradbury on the sufferings of Christ, at the beginning of the second volume of the Lime Street Lectures. They delight me very much. The style and manner is beautiful and scriptural, but they are wanting in spirituality. I am very glad you are pleased with Doddridge's sermons. They are very good ones for you, and will give you a good idea how a good sermon should be made. Read them over and over again. I wish he had a little more fire; but sometimes he is a little animated, and always clear, scriptural, and argumentative, and in his schemes I have always thought he exceeds all men. Alas! what are sermons good for without spirituality? Try in all your preaching to be as clear, as scriptural, as lively, and experimental as you can. Liveliness is the soul of popularity." In a letter written at a later part of the same year, he says, "The reading of Dr Crisp's Works has greatly comforted me, though I hope I shall never embrace his sentiments in all their unguarded extent without adding to them those equally important parts of truth which he seems to have too much overlooked. He certainly was a great and good man, who built upon the right foundation. and had the clearest views of the work of Christ of any writer I have ever read. I hope you will read them for yourself, adding to them those great essential branches of divinity which he in some measure omitted."

The 15th of July being my father's birthday, my grandfather wrote to him the following admirable and affectionate letter from London on that occasion :—

"LONDON, *July* 15, 1794, (my dear boy's birthday.)

"MY DEAR LOVE,—I have charged myself not to enter on this day without thinking of you and praying for you: and—

"1. My prayer has been that your portion may be the wisdom that is from above,—that the Holy Ghost may come upon you,—that you may be a burning and shining light, and faithful witness for a precious Jesus in this age of apostasy and spiritual declension,—that you may clearly see the great principles of the gospel, and be a warm and lively advocate for them,—and that every circumstance in your future life may be ordered of the Lord for his glory, and nothing left to your own wisdom or passion, but that everything may be with you as the Lord pleases.

"2. My prayer is that I may be very thankful for the comfort I have had in you, the blessing you have been to me, and the particular happiness I have in your being to me a son of consolation and not of bitter anguish and woe. It is very comforting, indeed, always to think of you as giving strength to my feeble powers, and I hope not a little contributing to my feeble exertions to be useful in my station. O my son, pray to the Lord that you may never be suffered so to act as to grieve me, and thereby hasten my end; but that you may have grace to meet my best wishes and expectations, and be, indeed, a very answer to all my prayers for you, and then we shall be great helps to each other.

"3. My prayer is that I may be truly willing to give you up to the Lord, if He should take you out of the world before me. I pray and long that if such a trial should be appointed for me I may bear it with holy joy, to think that whatever becomes of me, my child is gone to glory; and that we shall spend an eternity together in sweet and delightful fellowship in the presence of the Lord Jesus Christ.

"I cannot compliment you with a copy of verses on

your birthday, but I can do what is better. I offer to God for you the sacrifice of a tender, sincere, and affectionate heart for your comfort and welfare. I wish you may be clear in your judgment, sound in doctrine, warm and lively in your regard to Christ and his truth, savoury and experimental in your preaching, chaste and delicate in your style. May you be prudent and discreet in all your life and conversation. I wish and pray that your life may be a blessing to many, and that to the last day of it you may live beloved, esteemed, and honoured by those with whom you have to do.

" I consider myself as nothing, through infirmity of body and mind, and my life is like a shadow that will soon pass away ; but I hope to live in you and by you, and in this respect to be a more wise, prudent, and honourable character than I have ever yet been in my own person. If you enter into my views of things, you will give yourself unto prayer—study it—enter into its very soul and spirit—its beauties, comforts, and uses. Let your whole life be one constant prayer to a precious Jesus. This only will enable you, through the Spirit, to know the world in which you are to act your part in the short, various and ever-varying, and fitful drama of human life. Grow every day in grace, till self is nothing, nothing at all, and Christ is all in all; then will you, at the end of your days, attain the highest possible pitch of human greatness in character, in comfort, in usefulness. Oh, think of God's eternal, electing, and redeeming love, of Christ's justifying righteousness, and the sanctification of the Holy Spirit. Remember once for all that the death of self and the life of Christ in us is our salvation. To his tender love I incessantly commit you, and am, with the most cordial love to our dear mamma, your faithful, affectionate parent,

" W. BULL."

When in London at this time, Mr Bull had numerous invitations to preach at different places, many of which he was compelled to decline; but notwithstanding his feeble health, his lowness of spirits, and a constant asthma which troubled him, he yet laboured abundantly in serving that Master he so much loved.

At Brighton, in the latter part of the summer, his lodgings were open for morning and evening prayers, and many attended. He says, "I am very happy in them, and take up the best part of an hour." Writing on Sabbath-day, August 24, he says, "This morning I was up at four o'clock. At five we set off to walk to the camp, and at six I preached to the soldiers in a chalk pit; had about a hundred hearers, and on the whole a comfortable opportunity. . . . I very much long to see home again, and especially to see you, [Mrs Bull;] but my visit to Brighton has been very pleasant, and I hope very profitable. Many are much grieved at the thoughts of my going, and many at Newport, I trust, will rejoice to see me. I tenderly commit you to the Lord Jesus Christ."

It appears that, at this time, there was a Government order to open all letters received at Brighton, I suppose as a town on the coast. Mr Bull says, "I believe all letters addressed to me are opened before I receive them, which gives me no trouble, as they who read them may pick up something to do their souls good, if they would but mind it."

In February 1793, one of Mr Bull's students, a Mr James, a very amiable and pious young man, took cold while preaching in the neighbourhood, a fever ensued, and in a few days he was removed by death. Mr Bull preached a funeral sermon for this interesting youth, (he was only twenty,) and so much was he respected that a monument by Bacon was erected to his memory, and is still on the chapel walls.*

About the same time, Mr Bull's fears were very much called out in consequence of the perilous circumstances in which my father was placed in a journey from Bedford, where he had been to preach. He left that place in the afternoon of Monday. There was at the time a considerable flood, and the road in some places was very dangerous, and the more so, from the recent breaking up of the ice. I remember to have heard my father say that the stream at one place was so violent that his horse was carried off the road, and as he was swimming in the deep water, a mass of ice struck him on the hocks, it caused him to plunge, and making a great spring, he providentially regained the road. With no small difficulty, my father reached Sherington Bridge, within a mile of Newport. Several persons on horseback were by that time there, all hesitating whether they should proceed along the road, which was under water, and crossed by several distinct currents. They concluded that it was impracticable, and turned their horses' heads towards Olney. The road

* See *Evangelical Magazine* for 1795, p. 118.

between Emberton and Olney was found to be very dangerous, but at length they gained the well-known bridge—

<blockquote>
"That, with its wearisome but needful length,
Bestrides the wintry flood."
</blockquote>

As they passed the bridge, large masses of ice brought
down by the stream struck against it and violently shook
it. But a little time elapsed and the main arch was blown
up. Devoutly thankful for his escape, my father hastened
home the next morning by another road, to relieve the
anxious fears of his parents.

To both these events Mr Newton refers in the following
letter. The missive which contained the tidings is destroyed or mislaid, as are all my grandfather's letters of
this period to Mr Newton. The good man says, " I sympathized with you in the death of your student. But now
the Lord has declared his will by the event, I hope you
will think it rather a subject for joy than sorrow, that
your young plant is safely housed, where no storms or
changes can affect him.

" But when I came to your son's dangerous return from
Bedford, and the many circumstances which concurred to
heighten and lengthen your anxiety, I pitied you very
much. A state of suspense in a point where the heart is
much interested is very painful. I know, by repeated experience, how busy imagination is at such a time in contriving and foreboding the worst that can happen. I joined
with you in praising the Lord for his preservation, and I
congratulate him, Mrs Bull, and you on the event; I likewise join in your prayers, that a life so spared may be

wholly devoted to the Lord, and prolonged for a blessing to many.

"When the comfort we feared to lose is returned to us again, we feel it doubly; and we are likewise reminded of the precarious tenure by which we hold all earthly things. Blessed be the name of our Lord, it is not so with our spiritual concerns. Our best blessings are in safe and sure hands. Neither frosts, nor floods, nor flames, nor heights, nor depths, can separate us from the love of God which is in Christ Jesus our Lord."

While Mr Bull was in London in July, he was very deeply affected by the death of one of his principal people. He was so exceedingly sensitive and prone to depression, that such events almost overcame him. He speaks of it as the greatest trial that had befallen him for many years, and writes in the most feeling manner to the family.

In his letters at this time, he speaks again and again of the state of the country, which at this period was very alarming. The price of provisions, and especially of bread, was very high, and in the best families the allowance of the latter article was very limited. "Mr Neale," he says, "I found without powder."

In July of this year the Rev. Mr Romaine died. Mr Bull, who was well known to many of his hearers, preached a funeral sermon for him at Surrey Chapel to a very crowded audience, from the text John v. 35, "He was a burning and a shining light;" and again in the evening, from Jer. xxxi. 13, when he says, "I was very lively, very rambling, and very comfortable." Mr Bull was much pressed to print his sermon for Mr Romaine, but declined to do so. Indeed he seems to have had a morbid reluctance to anything of the kind. Doubtless, my grandfather's tendency to depression often led him to depreciate himself. He speaks of a person coming to him at the Tabernacle, and telling him how his sermon there had been blessed, and begging that he would come again. Yet he says, "My sermons are nothing, at best a sort of rant." In another letter to his son, after many good wishes on his behalf, he adds, "And may you avoid all those rocks I have split upon. You cannot be ignorant of my manifold weaknesses and infirmities both of body and mind, and I doubt not will always be ready to draw a veil over them. I could wish you only to remember them as beacons and waymarks for you to guard against."

Mr Newton writes in December of this year,—"Though your spirits are weak, I am glad to find that your faith and resignation are strong. Yes, all will be well in the end; and all is well by the way, if we can but think so, and be satisfied that the infinite wisdom and love to which we have committed ourselves, upon the warrant of his faithful promise, will assuredly take care of us and lead us in the right path. We are not to expect that the Lord will miraculously interpose to change our constitutions, or to overrule the connexion He has established between causes and effects; nor is it needful. If He is pleased to give strength according to the day, and to support us under our appointed trials, it is upon the whole better for us than if we were quite exempted from them."

Again, seven days after, he writes :—

"MY DEAR FRIEND,—I should not have been two letters in your debt, if I had not waited to send you the anniversaries. I must thank you for your kind, seasonable, and acceptable favour of the 14th, which gives me the opportunity of sending two more copies, one of which expressly belongs to my friend Thomas. If he locks it up, perhaps in the course of forty years (should he live so long) he may understand it better than he can at present."

And at the close of the letter, "I wish you much of that holy unction, that oil of joy, which is the best cordial of low spirits, and wonderfully strengthens weak nerves. The Lord bless you all—father, mother, son, nieces, tutors and students, and servants! May your house be a church, and your heart a well-watered garden for yourself and a spring of living water for your people! Amen.—I am always your affectionate and obliged

"JOHN NEWTON."

"*December* 21, 1795."

Mr Bull's spirits continued very low, but he pursued his work. His congregations at home were now crowded, and his services were abundantly blessed; indeed, as we shall presently see, the year 1796 proved to be a very eventful period in his ministry. In a letter written by Mrs Neale in February, she asks, "Pray is your meeting-house as full as ever? Do the people flock as doves to their windows? I trust good will be done, and the church built in these troublous times." And then, in reference to himself, she adds, "Whatever you have, I have not any doubts of Mr Bull dying a believer, and like one too. That time, I hope, is far off."

In a letter written in July from London, Mr Bull mentions the purchase, made by the Missionary Society, of the ship *Duff*. The first allusion to this great work occurs in a letter dated November of the previous year, in which his correspondent, Mrs Neale, says, " What a goodly number are in town about the missionary business! It was a sight which afforded me much pleasure." And again, in another letter, she says, " How much Mr Hill is engaged in it!" And yet it appears that there were some who complained to Mr Bull, and found fault and spoke of the whole thing as the offspring of Dr Haweis's pride, and wished they were out of the Society. So true it is that such movements will always at the outset find some to disapprove, and to be a drag upon them.

From London Mr Bull went to Brighton and returned by Reading, his son accompanying him. From the former place he thus concludes a letter to Mrs Bull :—" When one is abroad there are a hundred little hindrances that make it difficult to write letters; only I must drop one word for my great and dear Lord, beseeching you, my dear love, to keep near Him, be much in communion with Him, believe in Him, and live upon Him. Bless Him for his goodness and mercy to me and mine in this long absence from home. Oh, may the Lord bring us together in health, and peace, and love, that we may rejoice in Him together for many years yet to come, if it be his blessed will! To his grace and love I commit you," &c.

Again from Reading, in a somewhat less cheerful tone, " Mr Parsons, from Kineton, is here, which is a great addition to our comfort. Still I am but poorly, though not very much amiss. I grow old and feeble. I am ripening for glory." It was at the close of this year that the circumstances occurred to which reference has already been made.

A young man, named Richard Patch, a hairdresser, and who had for a long time attended Mr Bull in that capacity, became ill. He was an amiable person, of moral habits, and withal a very stanch Churchman. My grandfather, feeling an interest in him, frequently sent or called to inquire after his health. In speaking to Patch one day he found him very self-righteous, and ignorant of the way of salvation by Christ. He considered himself perfectly safe. He said "he had never read any bad books, but only New-week's Preparation and Pope's Homer."

" At length being fully persuaded," says Mr Bull, (in a journal which he kept of the progress of this interesting case, and from which I quote the following statement,) " that he was a total stranger to anything like heart religion, I plainly and faithfully told him that he was in the gall of bitterness and the bonds of iniquity; that he and I and all were by nature in a state of spiritual death, and must come into everlasting condemnation unless the Spirit of God should work a real change in our hearts, bringing us out of that darkness in which I perceived he was. I endeavoured to shew him the absolute necessity of a saving faith in the Lord Jesus Christ, wrought in him by his Holy Spirit, which would entirely change all his views of his state and condition."

These statements, as may be supposed, were not very favourably received, and Mr Bull was not asked as before to renew his visits. Indeed it appeared that Patch was highly offended by what had been said to him. The narrative proceeds, " A few days after this interview, Friday, November 25, sitting alone by the fireside, he was suddenly impressed with a strong conviction of sin. He burst into tears, and thought his heart would break if he could not weep. He began to fear that he had been deceiving himself, and that everything he had done was sinful. The next day he sent to request that I would call. I found him in deep distress, indeed in a state of almost absolute despair. And so he continued for three weeks, complaining that if he attempted to pray, Satan took the words out of his mouth, and the very thoughts out of his mind, and that he had no comfort, no hope. I visited him every day; he was very thankful, and wept when I prayed with him; but as yet there was no glimpse of hope.

" On Sunday, December 8, he was tempted to think that Christianity was a fable. He, however, turned to his Bible and read several chapters in Matthew. When he came to the twenty-seventh, describing the sufferings and death of the Saviour, the clouds of doubt and fear seemed at once to pass from his mind; he was filled with astonishment, and began to hope he might be saved.

" On Monday, relating this to me, he said, ' Oh, would to God I could say the Lord is my portion, but I can only say I hope He is so!' Still he had many fears, and he spent his time night and day in prayer, and in reading the Bible and Watts' Hymns.

" On Tuesday the 22d I found him much more comfortable. His conversation was marked by deep humility and the most childlike simplicity. He said these words were constantly in his mind, ' Fear thou not; for I am with thee : be not dismayed; for I am thy God: I will strengthen thee ; yea, I will help thee; yea, I will uphold thee with the right hand of my righteousness.' Another passage always followed that in his thoughts : ' Unto you that fear my name shall the Sun of righteousness arise with healing in his wings.' He wept, but said he was happy, and his tears were tears of joy. He was exceedingly thankful, he said, for my kind attentions to him. He longed to be gone, and to be with Christ. His sight had become so weak that he could not read, and this was a great trouble to him.

"*Friday, Dec.* 23.—I found on calling he had passed a very bad night. He could only speak in a whisper, but his conversation was spiritual, and expressive of a most happy frame of mind. He repeated several verses of the Hymn-book, particularly 'My God, my hope my love,' &c., and he said he wanted to be assured of the thing in his heart, that God was *his* God. ' At times,' he said, ' I seem as if I could see Jesus my God and Saviour sitting at the right hand of the Majesty on high, and holding out his arms to me and saying, Come up hither; but I can only say in my thoughts, Lord Jesus, come and take me away.' Then, looking earnestly at me, he said, ' Oh, I think the Lord is very long. The time is long. I wish to be gone. I would not come back again into this life for all the world. It is full of sin, and I have never done anything in it but sin. All my actions have been sinful. If I were to return back again into the world, I should sin again. I want to be with Jesus.' He blessed God for the comfort he derived from my visits. 'I am happy,' he said; 'I cannot express how happy I am, happy in my precious Jesus. But I think I shall not see you again in this world;' and then pressing my hand, he begged I would tell him some of those precious promises, because he knew they were true, and would all be fulfilled, every one of them; and, now he was unable to read them, he hoped I would repeat them to him. I did so. He was greatly affected, and said 'they were sweet, very sweet.' I then thought it right to leave him, he seemed so near the time of his departure.

"*Saturday, Dec. 24.*—Found him this morning still living, and in the same heavenly frame of mind, and cheerful in the approach of death. In the evening he sent for me again. He coughed but little, and said he thought it a peculiar mercy, as it enabled him to enjoy my discourse. He longed to be gone to his Lord and Saviour, to that world where there would be no sin and no sorrow; but he could truly say he was happy here. He had not the least doubt that he was going to glory. He was enabled to commit himself wholly to the Saviour. He could not express the peace and comfort he felt. I frequently desired to pray by him, being fearful he would injure himself by so much speaking, but he begged I would continue talking, as he feared when I prayed I should go away. He said that the devil had been very busy suggesting to him that all I had said about Christ was false.

"*Sunday, Dec. 25.*—He sent for me in the morning, and I found him increasingly serene and happy. He said he was in hopes he should have gone to his Saviour on the preceding night, but he was willing to wait the Lord's time. He told me of a vision he had had of a beautiful garden filled with the most exquisite flowers and shrubs, and that he had heard music as of angels beyond the skies. Upon my asking him how he had been, he said, so soon as his fit of coughing was over, he had fallen asleep with these words upon his mind, 'Fear not, I am with thee.' 'Oh,' he added, 'how sweet are they to my soul! in my fits of coughing they come to me, and when I pray they come with great force.' I prayed with him, and left him at ten o'clock. He pressed my hand, and said, 'May God bless you.' He was unwilling I should go, but said at last, 'We shall meet in glory.'

"*Monday, Dec. 26.*—He is still living; but, longing to be gone, says, 'I would not be impatient. Jesus knows the right time. I cannot be more easy than I am. His sweet promises are my comfort.' He said he felt more happy every hour. He took an affectionate leave of me, and said how much it refreshed him to see me enter the room. I prayed a few minutes, and left him.

"*Tuesday, Dec. 27.*—I find on inquiry that this dear child of God coughed the former part of the night very much, repeating between these attacks his favourite passages. At ten o'clock the cough left him, and he was serene and cheerful, conversed with his attendant, and said he was going to glory. Between eight and nine in the morning he seemed exceedingly cheerful, and sent for his mother. After she was gone, he said to the nurse, 'There, now, she will see I die happy.' He desired to be placed a little lower in his bed. 'That will do. I shall die now;

Q

this is the right place;' and so quietly expired about nine o'clock on Wednesday morning.

" On the whole," adds my grandfather, " this is as clear an instance of conversion, and of the sovereign and glorious grace of our Lord Jesus Christ, as ever I remember to have met with."

An event had not happened in Newport for some years which produced so great a sensation as the circumstances of this young man's death. He was well known and respected by every one. Bitter were the reproaches cast upon Mr Bull for having, as was said, driven him mad and made him miserable. The vicar, a violent Welshman, both in the pulpit and out of it, uttered the severest censures against the truths of the gospel, and particularly against Mr Bull for having visited this young man.

A funeral sermon was preached on the occasion by my grandfather to an immense crowd of people, when the substance of the above narrative was made known, shewing the signal mercy of God to this young man, and how happily he had died. There were not a few who had seen him, and heard from his own lips the expressions of his faith in Jesus, and who witnessed the holy serenity of his soul. The effect was very extraordinary. Some were brought to think seriously on the subject of religion who had been previously quite unconcerned about it. The medical attendant of Patch became interested in Mr Bull's ministry, and left the Church; and one of the churchwardens was induced to take the same course. The latter individual had been a hearer of Mr Romaine in London, and received impressions under his ministry; but returning to Newport, and engaging in business, he for a time forgot his religion; but what he saw and heard of Patch awakened all his old feelings, and led to this decided step. Others were influenced in a like manner; and several persons left the parish church and became devoted Christians.

Previous to this time there had been progress in the religious community with which Mr Bull was connected, but it had been gradual. At the close of the year 1787, the church did not consist of more than sixty members, and these chiefly of the poorer class. Few of the leading persons in the congregation made any profession of religion. For many years there were no prayer-meetings, and no vestry in which to hold them. About the time just mentioned, Mr Bull urged the building of a vestry, and gave ground for the purpose. It was accordingly erected, and prayer-meetings were at once held. A Sunday school was also formed, conducted at first by a paid teacher—an arrangement, I believe, not uncommon in the early history of these institutions. There was soon, however, an improvement in this matter, and Mr Bull's students took a lively interest in the work. Cottage prayer-meetings were also conducted in different parts of the town.

Such was the state of things when the conversion of Richard Patch took place, and it was instrumental in giving a still greater impulse to the religious movement of which we have spoken.

It will awaken no surprise to learn that these things did not happen without giving rise to much opposition on the part of the enemies of the truth. Those who had left the Church suffered for a time in their business, in one or two cases to a great extent. The churchwarden was threatened with the spiritual court, and received no small share of abuse from the vicar, which led his wife, till then strong in her attachment to the Church, to leave it for ever, for she declared she would not go to church to hear her husband abused. About the same time the party who had thus opposed the Dissenters burnt in effigy the author of "The Rights of Man." The figure was made as much as possible to resemble Mr Bull, and a label was attached to it, on which was written, "Tom Paine, Parson Bull, or the Devil." Insult was shewn in every possible way to the Dissenters, and they literally became the song of the drunkard. There was a drinking-club in the town, designated the Ninny-hammer Club, where certain would-be wits mimicked their religious services, parodying some of the most touching and pathetic of Dr Watts's hymns. But all these things were borne with meekness and joyfulness, and there was the felt blessedness of those who are persecuted for righteousness' sake; while the persecutors, in some instances, like Saul of Tarsus, became converts to the truth, and eminent for their piety and usefulness.

Such was this memorable era in the history of the Independent church at Newport.

CHAPTER XII.

Commercial Difficulties in London—Rev. R. Hill—Prejudice against Dissenters—Mr Bull at Farnham—Funeral Sermon for Rev. Mr Venn—Refusal to visit—His Son's Birthday—London Professors—Letter to his Son—Riccaltoun—Opposition to Village Preaching—Supplies the Tabernacle and Tottenham Court—Mrs Beaty—Bedford Union—Prayer-meetings—Village Preaching—Journal of Lavater—Mr Newton's Letter—Ordination of Mr Bull's Son.

IN February 1797, Mr Bull preached a funeral sermon for the Rev. John Carver of Wellingborough, a very estimable man, of whom some account, written by my grandfather, will be found in Coleman's "History of the Northamptonshire Churches," p. 240, &c.

In the same month he supplied Surrey Chapel for two Sabbaths, and from thence he went to Farnham, where one of his students was settled. In a letter from London he says, "Yesterday two *Gazettes* extraordinary were published. One of them states that fourteen hundred Frenchmen landed in Wales, and were all taken prisoners by the populace.* Again, yesterday morning an order of the Privy Council was published, forbidding the Bank to pay away any more cash. The bankers have all done the same. The confusion and uproar this has occasioned all

* See Pictorial History of England, vol. vii. p. 523.

over the city to-day is inconceivable. It was feared there would be a riot at the Bank; but I believe it will blow over. Mr Neale sent a draft on his bankers to-day for sixty-three guineas. The banker would only send the odd three guineas, and the rest in paper. Bank-bills are offered for sale at a discount. One man, Mr Neale says, offered eight guineas discount to get cash for a hundred pounds bank-bills, but could not get it. It is not in my power to describe the general alarm that exists."

In the same letter Mr Bull says, " I heard Mr Hill preach last night a long, comical, but impressive sermon. He seemed to have hard work to go on; but many things were very striking indeed. He is the most original character I ever heard in my life. His text was, 'If thou canst believe, all things are possible.' The whole hour and five minutes were taken up in going over the context. But he is so simple, so sincere, and so earnest and so holy, that everybody loves him dearly, and so do I."

He closes thus:—" I commit you to the Lord, with unspeakable tenderness, affection, and love. God grant you may live to a good old age, and come to the grave full of days and of honour. I fully expect we shall have persecuting times in a few years. The prejudice against Dissenters is strong, and gains ground every day. I made a long speech at Mr Newton's on Saturday evening, before some very good company, and it was well received I find. The subject, ' The evil of a party spirit in religion, and the necessity of Church people and Dissenters uniting hand and heart against the common enemy, Infidelity.' The company were—Messrs Foster, Searle, Bacon, (the sculptor,) Cuthbert, (who preaches in the afternoon at Blackfriars,) Latrobe, and Gunn, (Mr Newton's curate,) who came all the way home with me, to lead me to the door."

From Farnham he writes,—"I don't intend to take the least notice of the Fast, but to preach concerning the Lord Jesus Christ. I shall begin with a short apology, by saying there will be political sermons enough in the kingdom without my adding to their number, and that I cannot possibly serve my King and country more effectually than by praying for them; and then, by way of exhortation, preaching Christ to the people, as I am persuaded nothing goes further towards making a man a good subject than making him a good Christian. Now, this can only be done by bringing men to the knowledge of Jesus Christ—to faith in Him, love to Him, and conformity to his holy and blessed example."

In April, Mr Bull gave the charge to Mr Savage, on occasion of his ordination at Farnham. His son drove him across the country by way of Reading. The weather was very wet, and the roads exceedingly rough and heavy. From Reading, where they arrived the second day, Mr Bull writes home,—"I am very weary, but I doubt not shall be better to-morrow. We are to have a house full of friends to-night, to hear me expound. Help me to bless the Lord that we are both well."

My grandfather paid his annual visit to Surrey Chapel in July. At its commencement he complains of ill-health and low spirits. "The King of Prussia," he says, "is likely to die of a dropsy in the chest; and I don't know but that may be my case."

The excellent Mr Venn of Huddersfield died about this time. He was held in great esteem by all who knew him, and had often supplied the pulpit at Surrey Chapel. Mr Bull preached in connexion with this event. His text was from Matt. xxv. 21, "Well done, good and faithful servant." In the course of his sermon he stated the remarkable fact that in three years Mr Venn was blessed to the conversion of nine hundred persons in Huddersfield. "My author," he says, "Mr Newton, had it from Mr Venn's own mouth." Mr Bull then added, "I should never forgive myself if I did not mention that he was also instrumental in the conversion of a man who died November 17, 1790, who was one of the brightest, most useful, and honourable of private characters, and to me the dearest friend I ever had—John Thornton."

Exhausted, probably, with the excitement of the morning's sermon, Mr Bull says in the same letter of his evening's discourse :—"It was a very poor, broken sermon, and the devil tormented me all the time, telling me I ought never more to preach in that pulpit, for my strength was gone, my day was over, and the people could all see it very plainly. This distressed me all the time, but Mr Hodgkingson came into the vestry, and set all to rights by saying I never held out so well before, my strength had not failed me so little at any time."

In a letter dated July 5, he writes,—"I have met with several very striking instances of conversion in persons who have been awakened under my preaching, either the last time, or the time before, I was in London. On Tuesday evening there was a gentleman to hear me, a Welsh magistrate. He was very much affected indeed. One of the city marshals also came to Surrey, and took the pains to write to me."

A few days afterwards, he writes of the many and pressing invitations he had to drink tea and dine, " Hitherto I have kept clear of them, as I think they would be a snare to me. Thus far," he adds, " I have been comfortable every time I preached. A precious Jesus has constantly been my subject. The people say I am stronger and better in preaching than I used to be. There may be some truth in it, and I think it is chiefly owing to early rising, and spending two hours every morning before breakfast in my room in reading, and not going out visiting." He says again, " There is a certain kind of religious connexion not at all to be depended on. I could gain on the one hand and lose on the other twenty of them in a week, if I would give my mind and my precious time to idling, gossiping, canting, &c. I think there is no greater snare to ministers in London than visiting; but through mercy I keep clear of it. After all, I should not like to live in London, no, not at all." In another letter, " I hope I can add I have much of the Lord's presence with me in my closet. I spend the whole of the day in my room with very few exceptions, and I find it of great benefit to me in preaching."

He writes to his son on the 14th July, telling him how he should spend the following day—my father's birthday :—" This is my plan for keeping it. To bless the Lord for giving you to me and leaving you with me for twenty-four years. For putting it into my heart to pray

for you from the day you were born that the wisdom that
is from above may be your portion;—to bless and praise
Him for your present measure of health ;—to beg and pray
that you may live to a good old age, and that every day of
your life may be devoted to his glory ;—that you may be
preserved by Almighty grace from pride, lust, and im-
purity, covetousness which is idolatry, extravagance which
leads to beggary, and from all the snares of the world, the
flesh, and the devil;—that the Holy Ghost may dwell
in you as his temple;—that you may clearly understand, and most dearly love, and most faithfully preach the
doctrines of the gospel ;—that your heart may be inflamed
with love to a precious Jesus, and with incessant delight
in Him;—that you may be simple, artless, childlike in
your spirit and temper, and full of the spirit of love;—that
you may never be entangled with the cares and the affairs
of this world;—that you may be a living pattern of all
that is amiable and lovely in society ;—that you may
never be unmindful of the poor—visit them, pity them,
relieve them, pray for them ; and be in everything the
very pattern of the Lord Jesus Christ;—that you may
delight much in secret prayer, and live near the Lord in
your closet ;—that you may always reverence, delight in,
and love your mother, and most fervently pray for her, and
bear with her when she is afflicted;—that you may never
enter into any connexion or relation of life but what the
Lord approves of, and chooses for you ;—that you may be
divinely supported on a deathbed, and bear a dying testimony to the grace and love of the Lord Jesus Christ ;—
that the Lord may crown your ministry with ten thousand

blessings;—that we may spend an eternity together in glory, through the blood of the covenant. These are my prayers for you." . . .

During this visit to Surrey, Mr Bull's labours appear to have been greatly blessed. The congregations were very large, and there were many to whom he was made useful.

My grandfather visited Brighton before his return home, and preached there for two Sabbaths. On his way through London, he preached out of doors, in the garden of a Mr Wilmot, at Bethnal Green.

He speaks thus of London professors :—" The greater part of professors here believe in their preachers, not in the Lord Jesus Christ. It is profession, and nothing else, with too many of them. Alas, how little real love to Christ is manifested by a conformity to Him ! The Lord grant that I and mine may be more and more concerned to grow like Him."

In March 1798, Mr Bull writes to his son, who was then at Reading,—" I earnestly wish that you may have much of the Lord's presence on his day. Do all you can for a precious Saviour; He has done great things, indeed, for you. Oh, be jealous and zealous for his honour and glory ; the first of these you will promote by a watchful eye over yourself every moment of the day, and the latter by preaching his precious name and his great salvation as often as you may, and as earnestly as you can. Tell me whether you have any parlour preaching at Mr Bailey's or anywhere else. . . . Give my love to all my friends at Reading ; and be sure you preach Christ to them. It is the only thing to do good to souls ; and make it your constant care to live

Christ. Let them see, in your example, what manner of man Christ was amongst men, and how wonderfully holiness and love met together in Him.

"I have been reading Riccaltoun* every day with great pleasure and satisfaction. He has convinced me that neither I nor any other person has any real religion in us any further than we have Christ dwelling in us; and that I firmly believe, but I doubt not I have something of that Holy Spirit dwelling in me, and I earnestly desire to be guided by Him in everything."

Again, writing to my father in London, he says, "Don't cheapen your young and tender reputation, by being a burden to anybody. Remember you are young; and from a person's manner, and conversation, and conduct at the first setting off in life his public character and comfort are determined as long as he lives. . . . . Don't forget that you are on a journey to another world infinitely better than this, and the journey does not prove so long a one to many as our foolish nature fondly imagines."

Mr Newton writes to Mr Bull in April. "Something," he says, "whispers in my ear (I hope it is not the voice of vanity) that, as it is long since you heard from me, you will not be unwilling to pay postage for a letter." Writing to his son (who was still in London) a few days after, my grandfather says, "Pray don't forget to thank Mr Newton very much for his excellent letter last week.

* Works of the Rev. Robert Riccaltoun, Minister of the Gospel at Hobkirk, containing Essays on Human Nature, the Doctrines and Plan of Revelation, and a Treatise on the Epistle to the Galatians, 3 vols. 8vo. "The most original thinker and writer," says Mr Newton, "I have ever met with."

Indeed I think it worth many fivepences. It did me good, and it will do him good to know it."

The next day he writes thus :—

" My dear Love,—I wrote a pretty long letter this morning, but it is so very gloomy that mamma will not let me send it. Therefore I must begin again. Last night I suffered much, and have consequently been low all day. I have nothing to tell you, but I cannot help writing, because I find a peculiar pleasure in supposing that, while writing, I am talking with you, and consequently, if talking, I must be your companion; and you know that your company is amongst the very best of my social comforts. And writing in shorthand never fatigues me. I wish all my friends could read shorthand; I should write twenty letters where I now write one. Last night I preached with pleasure on Psalm xxxiii. 1–11. On the whole, I am comfortable in my own soul about my interest in a covenant-God, and in Christ as my Redeemer and Saviour; but I certainly have a very troublesome imagination, which greatly takes off from my comfort. Trapp [one of the students] seems very poorly to-day; but, oh, how good the Lord is, that my dear boy is so well! Oh, how much do I wish and pray that your life may be preserved from everything that may dishonour the gospel, or lessen your comfort and usefulness! You are young, and the path of human life is very slippery and dangerous, especially at first setting out. I hope your journey to town will both improve your understanding and afford you real pleasure. It would kill me in one day to run about as you do; but

I am old and you are young. Oh, may a covenant God be your guide in youth, and your guard unto old age; and may you every day do something for the honour and glory of the Lord Jesus Christ! You must be in many different companies in a day. Remember in them all your business is to get knowledge as well as to communicate it, and in all companies labour to give the conversation a useful turn. If you preach anywhere on the Sabbath, be sure you make Christ your subject, because it is in itself the most grand, the most sublime, and the most useful topic that can be. I always think, when a man is not preaching Christ, he is preaching himself. If he is not seeking the Lord's glory, he is seeking his own. It is to be feared there is too often a mixture of both. . . . To his grace and love we tenderly commit you," &c.

In a letter written the next day, Mr Bull complains of the opposition made to village-preaching:—" I have had this morning a very warm altercation with Mr M—— [a magistrate in the neighbourhood] about the conduct of Mr P——, W——, W——, and himself, in opposing our preaching in the villages. I told him of several things they have done to hinder it. He was very hot, and said if he was either of these gentlemen he would suffer no preaching in his parish, nor any tenant of his to go to meeting, or to harbour in their house persons that do go to meeting. He thought it was his duty as a magistrate to hinder people from leaving the Church. He was very severe against poor Scott and against the tailor that lived at Lathbury. I told him we were ready to fight and die for our King and for our country's laws and liberties, but we were equally zealous for our religion, and would be restrained in the exercise of it by nothing but violence. We would rather die than abate the exercise of our religious liberty. He went away in a violent hurry. He said our religion was nothing but a cloak for disloyalty. Thus it was with all the ancient persecutors; they first blackened the character of Christians, and then destroyed them under these false pretences."

In addition to his annual services at Surrey Chapel, Mr Bull undertook from the year 1799 to preach regularly at the Tabernacle and Tottenham Court for two months in the year. He was induced to do this from the very earnest solicitations of friends, and because God was pleased, in a special manner, to bless his efforts when preaching in London. These he regarded as providential intimations of duty. At the same time, he could now feel himself justified in leaving his congregation at home, and his students, under the competent superintendence of his son. So far, too, as he himself was concerned, such was his peculiar temperament, that probably without these changes he would have sunk into a morbid state, injurious alike to his own peace of mind and his usefulness. He had occasionally supplied these pulpits consecrated by the labours of the greatly honoured Whitefield; but in March of this year he commenced these more regular services. Many desired his company, but he declined all such invitations, saying of the Chapel House, " I do so enjoy this stillness and retirement. My levee," he adds, " is crowded every morning." Nothing could exceed the attention of

Messrs Wilson and Foyster (the managers) to him. " I am grieved," he says in another place, " to observe the present state of religion in London. There seems everywhere a strange leaning either to Antinomianism or Arminianism. Oh that men were wise to hit the happy medium, and unite them both ; *sed incidit in Scyllam qui vult vitare Charybdim !* " Again, " Indeed I am quite weary of London Christians. They are so very different from all my ideas of serious godly professors in the country. But I would not judge uncharitably." Yet at the close of his visit in October he says, " I cannot but bless the Lord that this journey to London has been to me the most pleasant, comfortable, and useful of any I have made since the death of dear Mr Thornton."

During this year Mr Bull had a somewhat remarkable interview with one of his members who was then in London, and I give his account of it as shewing the strong attachments which were felt towards him :—" I found Mrs Beaty astonished and delighted to see me. She blessed God that she once more saw the man who was more to her than all the men in the world. I told her, when I received her last note, and found how very ill she was, I resolved at once to come to see her. ' Ay,' she said, ' that 's right, that 's just as it should be.' She described the awful darkness of mind in which she said she had been for weeks ; but now she should be comforted, for God had sent her dear Mr Bull to see her, and that was all she desired in this world, and she believed, if he earnestly prayed for her, she should be better, and that God would give her light and comfort. ' They brought Mr Worthington to see me every day. He is exceedingly kind and good. He is a good man, but he is not Mr Bull—no, not my Mr Bull. Yes, thirty-four years is a long acquaintance." Mrs Beaty recovered so far as to return to Newport, and died at the end of the year.

Two years before this, Mr Bull became President of a Society called "The Bedfordshire Union of Christians." Its object was to bring together Christians of different names for the promotion of brotherly love, and the extension of the Redeemer's kingdom. This was one of the earliest institutions of its kind in the country, and the Rev. S. Greatheed was very active in its formation. There was a congregation of Moravians at Bedford, with some of whose members Mr Bull was on terms of close intimacy. They sympathized with the spirit and objects of the Union ; and probably this circumstance led to the adoption of a resolution to send an address to the ministers assembled in conference at Hernhutt, from the " Union of Christians formed at Bedford in England." Both the address and the reply to it, sent to my grandfather as President of the Union, are highly interesting, and marked by a most Christian and loving spirit. I have by me the reply in German, and the translation by Mr Latrobe.

Early in 1800, Mr Bull was in London supplying the pulpits of the Tabernacle and Tottenham Court. The congregations were unusually large, and all his friends seemed glad at his return. " I hope," he says, " my popularity will not turn me giddy." He tells Mrs Bull, he gave notice on Sunday that he should be present at the prayer-meeting to be held the next evening, and that he expected all who were alive and lively to meet him there. " I find their prayer-meetings are greatly fallen away. I told them all about the prayer-meetings at Newport, and how much they were alive there, and that I would not have come to London, only I hope to communicate a spark of fire to them all, for I was happy at home, beyond description, in my own study and my own pulpit,—and a thousand strange things I said, (just like myself,) but I believe they were well received."

His next letter speaks of a society formed for the suppression of village-preaching,—that a report was to be laid before Parliament on the subject. " Mr Henry Thornton sent for Mr Greatheed to talk the matter over, and to try to get information about the state of village-preaching. He could not have sent for a better man. He did not mean, he said, to vote against the village-preaching, but he wanted information to fit him for speaking on the subject. There is no doubt something will be done this very session about it. We must leave it. Prayer is the only thing to oppose to the spirit of persecution."

Mr Bull was at Surrey in July. He speaks of his interest in several books which he read, and seems still to have refused many invitations, though in one day he had no less than seven. Sometimes he was very low-spirited. He read, amongst other books, the Journal of the Rev. John Lavater, a book, he says, much in the strain of Rousseau. It evidently had a depressing effect on his mind. " I shall certainly die," he says, " in the manner of poor Mr Cowper. I greatly fear I shall lose my senses before I die." In the same letter, however, he mentions the following pleasing circumstance :—"Mrs Jones said in the vestry that Captain Applegarth was first awakened under my ministry in hearing me preach in Mrs Davis's parlour, [at Brighton,] a circumstance which I never heard before. Oh, what an honour to be made useful to others! But that will not save my own soul; yet I trust in the Lord, and am not afraid but I shall be found right at last."

Some days afterwards he says,—"Yesterday I dined at Mr Neale's, and sent a long letter to Mr Newton on his birthday." This was probably a reply to Mr Newton, for I find he had written to his friend from Southampton, where he was staying. It was addressed, "My dear old friend," and contains the following touching expressions:—"Though the flame of our affection is not much supported by the fruit of frequent letters and converse, I trust it still burns brightly, for it is fed from a secret, invisible, and inexhaustible source. If two needles are properly touched by a magnet, they will retain their sympathy for a long time. But if two hearts are properly united to the Heavenly Magnet, their mutual attraction will be permanent in time and to eternity. Blessed be the Lord for a good hope that it is thus betwixt you and me. I could not love you better if I saw you or heard from you every day. . . . The almanac tells me, that if I live till Monday next I shall enter my seventy-sixth year. I believe you will pray for me on that day. My eyes, years, and legs likewise admonish me that I grow older. My writing days seem almost over. I cannot well see to write, but I make an effort to send you one letter more, which may probably be the last you will receive." . . .

The latter part of this year was signalised by an event which was the realisation of Mr Bull's fondest wishes. On the 23d of October his son was ordained as co-pastor with himself over the church at Newport. "Many will never forget," (I quote from an allusion to this event in the *Evangelical Magazine* for April 1815,) "while any powers of memory remain, the grateful sensations and the ecstacy of mind which were discovered by the venerable father on the memorable day when his son was united with him in the pastoral office." The charge was of course delivered by my grandfather. As no specimen of Mr Bull's preaching occurs in this Memoir, and as this special occasion awakened all the depth of feeling for which his public addresses were so remarkable, it may not be uninteresting to give the principal part of the discourse. It is as follows :—

" A variety of circumstances concur to render this the most delightful, the most painful day I have ever seen. It is the blessing of God on the most diligent, the most unwearied exertions of nearly thirty years ; the gracious reward of the most delightful services ; the answer of a thousand prayers ; the gratification of my fondest wishes ; the crown of all my labours ; and the glory that gilds the evening of departing life.

"You have the motto to the present exercise in Gen. xliii. 29 : 'God be gracious unto thee, my son.' These words were spoken by the first man in the land of Egypt, to the youngest son of the best man in the land of Canaan. They are the language of great tenderness of spirit, of the warmest love, and the most sincere devotion. The great man's spirit was melted, and he gives us a delightful example of patriarchal benediction. Let us read the whole verse: 'And he lifted up his eyes, and saw his brother Benjamin, his mother's son, and said, Is this your younger brother, of whom ye spake unto me?' And, without waiting for a reply, he cries out, with all the dignity of a patriarch, and all the unction of a saint, 'God be gracious unto thee, my son.'

"He looked, he gazed, he traced in a moment the very features of his venerable, his holy father, Jacob, (whom he had not seen for twenty-three years.) He saw those very features combined—exquisitely combined—by Divine wisdom with the delicate lineaments of the lovely Rachel, his own dear mother. Both the parents appeared to him in the striking countenance of a lovely stripling, on the recollection of whose image his own imagination had often fed and feasted for twenty-three years, with painful, with delightful feelings. In a moment, a violent commotion is excited in his breast, glowed in his cheeks, and sparkled in the bursting tear. 'And Joseph made haste, for his bowels did yearn upon his brother, and he sought where to weep; and he entered into his chamber, and wept there.'

"I shall not take up your time by a farther recital of the narrative, nor enter minutely into the duties, the difficulties, and the work of the pastoral office, which you have repeatedly heard from me in another place. It will better become my age, my situation, and connexion, freely and faithfully to express the feelings of my heart for your comfort and usefulness in this life, and your happiness in the world to come. With these views before me, permit me to accommodate the text to the present solemnity.

" 1. I wish and pray that God may be gracious to thee, my son, *in all thy experience as a private Christian, and thy personal walk with God.* Without this, however judicious, however well conducted your future ministry be, it must soon become unprofitable to your hearers and a calamity to yourself. May He bless thee with a deep and ever-growing sense *of the evil of sin,*—the infinite evil there is in sin,—and give you to discern its malignity in the mirror of his own holiness, the groans of Calvary, and the plague of your own heart. May God be gracious to thee, my son, by giving thee to the last moment of life an *increasing admiration of the dignity and glory of the Lord Jesus Christ,* a rich experience of his saving grace in thine own heart, and a most unutterable delight in the joys and glories of his salvation. May He bless thee with a clear and scriptural experience of the *work of his Holy Spirit in your own soul.* May He give you a strong and lively view of the nature, beauty, and excellence of that holiness without which no man shall see the Lord; and to the end of your days may this divine capacity for the kingdom of heaven grow in you like the palm-tree, and flourish like the cedars of Lebanon. May God be gracious to thee, my son, and daily strengthen thy faith in Him, thy love to God, thy love to Christ, thy love to holiness. May you progressively advance in real holiness of heart and life; and then I have the authority of an apostle to say, that having your fruit unto holiness your end will be life everlasting.

" 2. May God be gracious to thee, my son, in *all your private devotions*. It is in the closet that you must lay the foundation for all your comfort and usefulness in the pulpit. It is here that you must seek to bring down the dew of heaven on your own spirit. In your retired moments, be first and principally concerned to have your fellowship with the Father, and with his Son Jesus Christ. Pour out your soul at the throne of grace,—humbly, frequently, and fervently; praying without ceasing; 'praying always with all prayer and supplication in the Spirit, and watching thereunto with all perseverance.' That minister will generally prosper most who most waters with secret prayer that seed he means to sow in the pulpit.

" 3. May God be gracious to thee, my son, in all thy *preparatory studies* for the pulpit. You will then be led to choose the most interesting and solemn subjects; you will study to preach Christ and Him crucified; you will vindicate the regenerating and sanctifying graces of the Holy Spirit; you will deeply consider the value of immortal souls; you will often reflect, ' I am now preparing to speak to men whose eternal welfare is at stake,—I am going to speak to men in the name of God, and to speak to God in the name of a whole congregation. This very sermon I am about to deliver may be my last,—I must soon give an account of my stewardship, and be steward no longer.' Look up to the Lord in secret prayer for his divine assistance and blessing on all your studies. You will find in the pulpit the happiest effects from such a course of previous study and devotion. In your private studies pursue the knowledge of divine truth with vigour,

diligence, and the keenest investigation. Be always open
to receive the truth wherever you find it; and leave it to
little minds to confine their studies to a sect or a party.
An enlarged understanding will always pursue the truth,
take in extensive views of objects, and as complete and
comprehensive views as can possibly be obtained. It will
lead you to be always candid and generous to those who
differ from you. Despise the dirty meanness of a narrow
sectarian spirit, and the brutal blindness of bigotry, which
never was, nor can be, anything but the demon of persecution in embryo. Be assured you never meet with a bigot
but you see a persecutor in disguise. But you, my dear
sir, 'have not so learned Christ.' May your private studies
be so sanctified that even the enemies of the truth may see
in the fruit of them what it is to have been with Christ.

"4. May God be gracious to thee, my son, whenever
you *come into the pulpit.* May you always be concerned
to keep the right object in view—the glory of God and the
eternal salvation of your hearers. Pursue that object with
faithfulness, diligence, and zeal. Instruct the ignorant,
reprove the careless, warn the disobedient of their guilt,
and danger of going down into hell with the sound of
salvation in their ears. 'Warn every man, teach every
man in all wisdom, that you may present every man perfect in Christ Jesus.' Strengthen the weak and fearful,
comfort them that are cast down; enforce the consolations
of the gospel, the security of an everlasting covenant, the
infinite merits of the blood and righteousness of Christ,
the unspeakable ,riches of divine grace, the unshaken
faithfulness of God to his promises, and the certain joys

and glories which are set before them in the world to come, warning the aged of their approaching change, and endeavouring to prepare them for it.

"May God be gracious to thee, my son, and enable thee —First, To be always plain and simple, that none may misunderstand you. Often think of the simplicity of your great and dear Lord. He invites you to learn of Him. He was meek and lowly. Let the same mind be in you that was also in Jesus Christ.

"Secondly, Let your strain be always evangelical. Let it be evident that you are not come to amuse your hearers with a moral essay, but to deliver the living truths of the living God. At the same time, preserve the most sacred regard to the moralities of the gospel. Let zeal for gospel truths glow in your heart, sparkle in your eyes, and shine in all your sermons; then shall you prove yourself a true evangelist, and it will be manifest that God is gracious to you of a truth.

"Thirdly, Let your strain be spiritual and experimental. Strongly mark the work of the Holy Spirit in the heart, from its first beginnings in regeneration to its complete perfection in bringing the soul to glory. Describe the duties, the trials, the spiritual conflicts of the people of God. Let your hearers learn from your lips the truth of what they feel in their own hearts, what they have to fear, what to hope for, and what to feed upon in the way to Canaan.

"Fourthly, Let your strain of preaching be practical. Let it evidently lead to that temper, that conversation and walk in life, which Jesus requires from all his true disciples, and which shall most effectually stop the mouths of gain-sayers, and shame into silence the cavils of ignorant and foolish men. Your Lord hath said, 'By their fruits ye shall know them.' Let your hearers never forget that 'the wisdom that is from above is first pure, then peaceable, gentle, and easy to be entreated, full of mercy and good fruits, without partiality, and without hypocrisy; and the fruit of righteousness is sown in peace of them that make peace,' (James iii. 17, 18.) If God be gracious to thee, thou wilt never bring controversy into the pulpit, but will often remind your hearers that 'the fruit of the Spirit is love, joy, peace, long-suffering, gentleness, goodness, faith, meekness, temperance; against such there is no law.'

"5. God be gracious to thee, my son, to *sanctify your life and conversation*, and that you may carry into all your social and relative connexions the sweet and blessed fruits of what you have been delivering from the pulpit. 'Be an example of the believers in word, in conversation, in charity, in faith, in purity.' Let it be evident that you pursue no other object than the glory of God and the salvation of men. Let your whole life be meek, gentle, humble, and affectionate. Let it be always kind, friendly, and generous. Let it be decent, dignified, and holy, for real holiness is the highest dignity of man. Let it be manifest that as you profess to live for God, you do actually live to Him. Be always humane and tender. Pity the poor, and do them all the good you possibly can. No money is so well laid out as that which is given to the poor, and when your own circumstances will go no farther, use your interest with others that they may assist you in this good work. Visit the afflicted, and help them to bear their burdens. Never think yourself above the meanest of your hearers in their afflictions. Your Master, who 'measured the waters in the hollow of his hand, and meted out the heavens with a span, and comprehended the dust of the earth in a measure, and weighed the mountains in scales, and the hills in a balance,' He condescends to 'feed his flock like a shepherd, to gather the lambs in his arms and to carry them in his bosom, and gently lead those that are with young.'

" Preserve in all your carriage an easy dignity, and an endearing tenderness and courtesy. Shun the company of all those who are given to contention and controversy. It never does good, but always mischief. As far as in you lies, 'live peaceably with all men.' As you pursue truth in your study with perfect candour, so carry the same generous spirit into your life and conversation. Love everybody who loves the Lord Jesus Christ.

" 6. May God be gracious to thee, my son, *to give a divine blessing to all your labours*, and afford you effectual support under all the trials you must expect in your ministry. Without his blessing, Paul may plant and Apollos water in vain. Without this, the watchman watcheth the city in vain. Earnestly pray for Divine assistance in your work in all its extent, and then look wholly to the Lord for a blessing. Oh, may your ministry be so honoured and blessed, that you may have many who shall be your joy and crown of rejoicing in the day of the Lord. For 'they that be wise shall shine as the brightness of the firmament ; and they that turn many to righteousness as the stars, for ever and ever.' . . .

(*Conclusion.*) "'I charge thee therefore, before God, and the Lord Jesus Christ, who shall judge the quick and the dead at his appearing and his kingdom; preach the word; be instant in season, out of season; reprove, rebuke, exhort with all long-suffering and doctrine. For the time will come when they will not endure sound doctrine; but after their own lusts shall they heap to themselves teachers, having itching ears; and they shall turn away their ears from the truth, and shall be turned unto fables. But watch thou in all things, endure afflictions, do the work of an evangelist, make full proof of thy ministry. For I am now ready to be offered, and the time of my departure is at hand.' 'And may God be gracious to thee, my son!' 'The God before whom thy fathers have walked, the God who hath fed me all my life long unto this day, the Angel which redeemed me from all evil, bless thee.'"

CHAPTER XIII.

Antinomianism—Texts—Rev. T. Adam—A Talkative Visitor—Mr Newton—
Preaching acceptable—Calvinism—Letter from Mr Hill—Depression of
Spirits—Happy in Jesus—Visit to Algerine Ambassador—Letter to one
of his People—Preaching in London—Case of Conversion—King's Speech
—A Hutchinsonian—Love to his Son—Remarkable Dream—Visit to an
Undertaker—True Glory—Qualifications for a Minister—Rev. T. Raban
—Nervousness—Macknight—Cases of Conversion—Saturday Visits to
Mr Newton—Arminianism—Comfort in Preaching—The Mile Walk.

THERE was a circumstance which, about this time, caused
Mr Bull some uneasiness. An Antinomian spirit discovered itself amongst some few of the members of his
church, and seven of them refused to sign my father's invitation. They happily before long withdrew of their own
accord, so rendering that church-discipline unnecessary
which, however difficult it might have been found to exercise in the treatment of their pride and self-conceit, would
have been simple enough in its application to the immo-
ralities of which some of the party were subsequently
guilty. Stiil, the matter was a trouble to my grandfather,
and he speaks of it in his letters from London at the close
of the year. In some of these letters he gives wise counsels to his son about preaching, and says, amongst other
things, " You were happy in the choice of your text, and

the sound of a text goes a great deal farther than people imagine. The acceptance of a sermon is generally influenced, sometimes wholly determined, by the sound of a text."

He spent much time alone while at Tabernacle House, and as usual rose early and read much. He says—"I find Adam [the Rev. Thomas Adam, author of "Private Thoughts," &c.] a very entertaining companion, though he is too laconic and full of antithesis for me to remember anything; but Macknight comes in to amuse me very much with his curious criticisms. It may be truly said of him, *Quando bene nemo melius, quando male nemo pejus.*" Mr Bull was not always in such good company. He says,— "Two ladies came in to prayers; one of them had such a tongue, I never heard anything like it before. She cannot stop a moment. She lives quite upon the mount, is a disciple of Mr Romaine, and is so full of assurance, comfort, and delight, that it's quite intolerable. By this means my whole morning is consumed. Mrs Parr (the housekeeper) says Mrs Owen will talk me to death. Oh for some kind angel to come and send this old lady home to her husband; but I think he must have a miserable life. The Lord have mercy on the poor man! The alarum is off, and I can't stop it!"

He spent his Saturdays as usual with Mr Newton. Speaking of one of these occasions, he says,—"Though our interview was very affectionate, tender, and pleasant, yet I was much grieved to sit and observe how fast, how evidently, this great and dear man is hastening to his grave."

Mr Bull complained much of his asthma during this visit, but he says, "They tell me I must come again in March, for none fill the chapels as I do."

Accordingly, in March following, we find him in London again, and he speaks of the liberty and comfort he had in preaching, and of his crowded congregations. "It is an honour the Lord puts upon me, and may I be kept humble! Mr Wilson and Mr Foyster expressed the highest gratification at my services. Ah, this is mighty pleasant, but, like a fine day, will soon blow over, and be forgot. But if the Lord Jesus Christ smiles in upon my soul, the light of his countenance endureth for ever, and I shall derive everlasting advantage from it!" During this visit, he again suffered very much from his asthma, and complained that his strength was hardly equal to the great demands made upon it; and, as before, he longed to be at home again. "I am not sorry," he says, "that I came; but my strength is much impaired by my visit, and I should rejoice to give up coming to London as a preacher any more."

In a letter to his son he says, "You are very charitable in your views of ——'s preaching. I shall be very glad to find he is more Calvinistic, because I consider that as the glorious fabric of divine revelation, and the want of it the great cause of the declension in religion. The clergy have somehow been led into a very Calvinistic strain. It is astonishing how they increase and prosper, and how visibly the Lord owns and blesses them. I think the time is coming when all men will be Calvinists or Deists."

In June my grandfather received the following letter
from Mr Hill :—

"MY DEAR BROTHER BULL,—When your letter came I
was from home, and returned late last night; and the contents of your letter are of such a nature as that, if I was
near to you, I should be tempted to give you as good a
drubbing as you have had these seven years. In answer
to your former letter I only observed that, as postponing
the time had rendered it inconvenient for you to visit this
year, for this year, I told you, for once we might have provided another supply; but now, in one of your low mopish
fits, it has come into your nobby that you are not fit at all.
Leave that for others to determine, if you please, reverend
sir; but you must leave me to determine that your latter
excuse for not coming is utterly inadmissible. As, therefore, you did not choose to be let off on the ground of inconvenience for one year, I must give you to understand,
upon the high ground of my archiepiscopal authority, on
the ground of incapability you shall not be let off at all.
So that, as you did not choose to accept the offer of one
year's absence on the first terms, I shall not accept the
offer of your total absence on your second terms. You
will therefore be expected to be at London by the 26th of
July, for four or five Sundays. Herein fail not at your
peril.

"Given under my hand and seal this 17th day of June,
in the year, &c., &c.   R. HILL."

Mr Bull obeyed these orders, and spent five weeks at

Surrey in July and August. At times his spirits were greatly depressed. " How miserable," he says, " to be always under the influence of so gloomy an imagination, and the pains of so infirm a body! But I am thankful that I do not feel any of those violent struggles for breath from which I suffered last week. Well, the Lord Jesus Christ is still the same; and my soul, I trust, is in loving union with Him. I frequently long to be gone out of this body. It has become an insufferable burden and weariness to me: and yet I fear my desire to be gone is more owing to the love of ease than from love to the Lord Jesus Christ. However, I dare trust his faithfulness to his promises. This morning I read part of Dorney on Salvation. He enters more clearly and deeply into my views than any Protestant divine I have ever read. I earnestly recommend it to you. It is not once nor ten times reading that will exhaust this precious volume."

The clouds often passed away and sunshine followed, for he says a few days afterwards, " How do I bless God that He has enabled me to choose Jesus for my portion, my life, my strength; and to seek all my comfort, my pleasure, and my enjoyment in Him! I have nearly done with the world, but when I am alone I am very happy. Jesus is my Friend, my faithful, all-powerful Friend. I have always his company; I want no other. I am very, very happy in Him, and I only enjoy his company when alone, so that I go out as little as possible. Oh that you, my dear child, may in this matter follow my steps! I find it very, very difficult to avoid going out to dinner; but I will be my own master, and I love to be alone more than ever."

Mr Bull's sympathies were very much awakened by the severe trial of his old friend, Mr Newton, whose niece, to whom the good man was greatly attached, was suffering from mental disease. "He is almost overwhelmed with this most awful affliction. My spirits are greatly affected by it. May the Lord Jesus bless, support, and comfort him! I never saw a man so cut up."

On the 11th August he writes, giving an account of a visit he paid to the Algerine ambassador's. "Yesterday morning," he says, "Dr Benamore, wishing to oblige me, drove me to the Algerine ambassador's. It was rather a bold venture. He got first out of the coach, and then asked me if I had not better get out and walk in. I did so, a Turkish servant shewing us in. I was introduced into a room where a great monster of a man was sitting on a sofa, cross-legged, without shoes or stockings. He was the Capitan Pasha. There was another great man at his right hand, and several more in the room. After a considerable time spent in the feeling of pulses, &c., the doctor prescribed. Then he walked up-stairs, and bid me follow him. He entered a room where his Excellency was sitting, a venerable, pleasing old man, about seventy. He was all beard in front—a fine white beard. A tall, large man sat at his side, and in a common chair, but cross-legged, looking very black and very savage. By him sat the mufti, the ambassador's chaplain. The doctor told his Excellency I was his priest, and the ambassador shewed great pleasure at seeing me, and immediately called for coffee. A fine muslin cloth was spread over the ambassador's lap, and a common napkin over the laps of the rest.

They drank their coffee almost boiling hot. We stayed nearly an hour. They were surprised I could not talk Greek or Arabic. I told them I could not *converse* in these languages. Could I *speak* Hebrew? No. When we came away the ambassador rose from his seat, came up to me, laid hold of my hand, and seemed very pleased with my visit. They all rose at the same moment, and came up to me. I gave them my hand and said, 'The Lord bless you,' made the best bow I could, and walked out. Dr Benamore says this ambassador is a very worthy man: that he has obtained the liberty of two hundred and thirty English slaves by his influence with the Dey. I asked the doctor how such a man could be safe under such a government. 'Oh,' he said, 'he don't think of it. When the Dey thinks he has money enough, he will send for his head and take all his money; but at present he is a great favourite.'"

In a letter to Mrs Bull at the end of this visit, he says,—"Through mercy I am brought to the close of my very hard task at Surrey Chapel." It is evident from many circumstances that his services on this occasion were very acceptable.

After my grandfather's return home, my father visited Brighton and London. About the time of his return Mr Bull says, "If you can speak a word in the coach on Saturday to remind the company that a servant of Jesus Christ is present, it may do good. And if you can preach all the way, so much the better."

In September, Mr Bull writes as follows to one of his friends, a member of his church, then from home on account of his wife's health, and who himself had passed through very severe trials, which had thoroughly awakened his pastor's sympathy :—

"MY DEAR SIR,—Your letter gave me a great deal of pleasure, and I acknowledge it with no small thankfulness to our dear Lord, who lives and reigns, and does everything well. I am very glad you have found it out at last that *seeming disappointments are always distinguishing mercies to a child of God.* I wish the sentiment may sink deep into your heart, and be one step towards forming a holy habit of the will. This gracious principle, brought into habit, will sweeten all the bitters of life and give a general tincture of ease, comfort, and satisfaction to your whole experience. Remember, in everything, the Lord reigns. 'Acknowledge Him' (own Him, submit to Him, love Him) ' in all thy ways, and He shall' and will ' direct thy paths.' In all thy ways acknowledge Him. Why, then, are you not always happy? Because you are prone to acknowledge Him when the sun shines rather than when it is cloudy, dark, quite dark as pitch; and yet the latter is often more expressive of covenant love than the former. We forget that it is quite the fashion and taste of heaven for our dear Lord to veil Himself in clouds and darkness all about his throne, and especially when He makes a visit of superlative love to his friends and favourites; but faithfulness and love are the pillars that support the throne of his government. I perceive your journey was very much to your liking. I thank the Lord for it. Pray, learn in future to let Him have his own way, and you shall certainly find that He will lead you forth by the right way, that you may come to a city of habitation, (Ps. cvii. 7.)   But read the whole psalm, it will do you good."

*   *   *   *   *

November and part of December were spent at the Tabernacle and Tottenham Court. His labours there were both a toil and a pleasure. "To go to and from Tottenham every other sermon I preach, is enough to kill a horse, if horses were to have a pulpit-sweat in the middle of the process. Such changes from heat to cold, from the pulpit to the fresh damp air, require the strength of an elephant." Yet, again,—"Preaching is my refreshment, my comfort, my delight; but breathing is so hard a labour and so great a terror, that I think it will soon wear me out. I am not the first person who has had asthma; but I never knew what the word meant till now." Again,—"Last night I preached on Heb. xii. 2, 'Looking unto Jesus,' &c. It was the most wild ranting sermon I ever yet preached; but I hear to-day it was greatly blessed to several people. I don't know what to say to these things." Three days afterwards he writes,—"At half-past nine my room was full of the good old women. One of them, whom I had never seen before, affected me so much with her tale that I could scarcely contain myself. She came a long way, is very old, and has a cancer in her breast. She had one son, a very son of Belial. Some years since he was going the high road to hell in a very dreadful style indeed. The Lord called him by his grace under my ministry, and he is as

amiable and lovely as he was abominable and devil-like.
I cannot enter into the particulars."   In a letter just before
his return, he says,—" They have spoken to me to come
again.   How can I possibly do it?   I cannot even dress
and undress myself.   Last night Mr W—— did it for me.
My spirits are now greatly agitated; but the Lord Jesus is
infinitely good, and has carried me through with wonderful
assistance and blessing; I think on the whole never better,
excepting the asthma and low spirits.   These have been a
daily trial to me.   Yes, the Lord has been good to me—oh,
how good to me! since I came to this place.   But I am
worn out—and my latter end draws near."

While in London, he was earnestly requested to print
some of his sermons, but this he declined.

On the subject of politics, he writes,—" I have just read
the King's speech and the debate upon it; to me it is
inexpressibly loathsome, because every line contained a
lie or a misrepresentation.   There is no solid political
truth in what any one of them says, excepting this, they
inform me that peace is made.   In this I rejoice, but now
I will read no more.   I better like my Bible, and that is
full of curiosity and entertainment, and all of it true, and
all of it important, all interesting, and all is sealed with
the sanction of Divine authority.   O precious book !   How
pleasant, how profitable to my poor soul !   I am a dying
man, and my concerns lie in another world."

Elsewhere he says,—" We have in the congregation a
very curious old man, a grand-nephew of the great philosopher Hutchinson, and he is brimful of Hebrew and
Hutchinsonianism, and as great a bigot to it as you can

imagine. He thinks no man in the world should be suffered to preach who cannot read Hebrew, and that without the cursed human invention of vowel points. He has lent me Julius Bate's translation of the Pentateuch, and has shewn me some other books of Bate's and Hutchinson's which I have not before seen."

From home, while his son is out, he expresses the greatest love to him, and is always anxious. "I commit you," he says in one place, "to the Lord Jesus, with ten thousand wishes and prayers for your preservation. The Lord bless and keep you! Write as often as you can. May you be protected every hour of the day! I am full of anxiety for you. If you do not do all I wish, you do some things, and I make great allowances for youth. They are apt to be a little thoughtless and inattentive to old men. But I must say you are very, very good, and when you don't act quite to please me, I can soon forgive you, because I love you. Oh that the Lord would forgive me all my offences, and cleanse me from all my sins!"

In the course of this year a Mrs Davies, a member of Mr Bull's congregation, died, and made a very remarkable statement to him on her death-bed. Not long after my grandfather's settlement at Newport, Mrs Beaty, the lady of one of the principal persons in the congregation, was on a visit to Bath. While there she hired a female servant named Saunders. This young person had imbibed Socinian views; and understanding that Mrs Beaty's minister was a Calvinist, she requested that she might be allowed to go to church, or else she wished to decline her engagement altogether. Her mistress was unwilling to part with her, but told her that while she did not wish to control her in such a matter, she proposed that at all events she should first hear Mr Bull, and then, if she did not approve his sentiments, she might go to church. With this understanding she accompanied her mistress to Newport. But before she left Bath she had a remarkable dream. She thought she was walking in a meadow by the banks of a river. It suddenly overflowed; the waters rose higher and higher, and she was without power to escape. Her destruction seemed inevitable, when on a sudden a tall figure stood at her side having the appearance and wearing the dress of a minister; he directed her attention to certain stepping-stones she had not seen before, at the same time uttering these words, "When thou passest through the waters, I will be with thee; and through the rivers, they shall not overflow thee." The feeling of joy at her deliverance awoke her. She came to Newport, and as she had promised went to hear Mr Bull; and great was her astonishment when she looked towards the pulpit and saw the very person standing there who had appeared to her in her dream. Indeed she was so overcome that she was incapable of paying attention to the former part of the service. But, having somewhat recovered her composure of mind, she listened with a strange feeling of expectation for the text, and again she heard the words, "When thou passest through the waters, I will be with thee; and through the rivers, they shall not overflow thee." She no longer objected to go to the meeting-house, for that sermon, preached under circumstances to her so striking, was the means of her conversion to God. She joined Mr Bull's church, married a man named Davies, and after enduring many trials, became the victim of consumption. On her dying bed she related the above dream to my grandfather, telling him she never had found courage to mention it to him before. Surely, this is one amongst not a few other examples of the ὄναρ ἐκ Διός. No possible fancy on the part of the young woman, or any accidental coincidence between the circumstances of the dream and its remarkable fulfilment, can satisfy the exigencies of the case. Besides which, the great result—the conversion of a soul to God—may be looked upon as a sufficient reason for such an interposition.

Writing from London, in March 1802, to his son, about some alterations making in his premises at home, after calling his special attention to his directions, Mr Bull adds,—"*N.B.* This letter is not intended for the *Gospel Magazine*, nor for the *Evangelical*; nevertheless, it will deserve a great deal of attention and study from you."

The thoughts of my grandfather were very often busy on the subject of death. Sometimes they were of a melancholy caste, often were morbid, but sometimes quite the reverse. Here is an illustration of a rather quaint and business-like form which on one occasion they assumed. In the letter from which I have just quoted, he says,—" I have been at the undertaker's to know the expense of carrying my bones to Newport. The hearse and four horses would cost at least £20. The coffin, lined with the thinnest milled lead, will be about £10. He could make a coffin that would do without lead, but I think the lead would be better. It is Mr Wilkinson who says 'Amen' for me at the Tabernacle. I think it but right he should have the job. He thanked me, but I told him it would not (I hoped) be just at present. But I like to have things in readiness, and I would have ordered the coffin immediately, and sent it down, only it would be expensive carrying it backwards and forwards every time, or else I should like to have it ready. So much for visiting undertakers."

And now let me add to this another passage written a few weeks later. As Mr Bull was leaving London, great preparations were making to celebrate the peace with France, (the peace of Amiens,) and he speaks of the short-lived glory of all these rejoicings. "May God grant that I may live every day for eternity. I am almost dead to the world, and the world is almost dead to me; but Jesus lives and reigns, and I shall live and reign with Him for ever, when cities and kings and heroes and worlds shall be no more. 'They live too low who live below the skies!' I begin a little to think I may possibly live to see home, [he was on his way thither; the letter is written from Biggleswade.] Yes, I shall see my home, my everlasting home, and the poor play of human life will soon be over. The curtain is dropping, but the veil is also removing, and I shall see the King in his glory seated on the mercy-seat. I wish you well, well through an exceedingly dangerous pilgrimage to that land where Jesus will be all and in all." The same letter concludes,—"The Lord bless you, preserve you, quicken you, humble you, and sanctify you; so wishes and prays the tenderest of parents, W. BULL." In a similar strain of deep feeling he refers, in another letter, to Mrs Bull, and expresses his peculiar anxiety on her behalf.

While he speaks of his large audiences in London, he says,—"I could not please everybody. I believe I am strictly and properly a unique,—that is to say, *solus cum solo, unus sui generis.* I don't care a straw what they call me. I only want to live Christ—to Him, for Him, in Him, and always with Him." Again he says,—"He that would excel as a minister must unite the unction of the Mystic, the simplicity of the Moravian, and the deep, clear, sound judgment of the Calvinist. If either is wanting, the preacher is naught. Oh, my son, labour to unite sound judgment, divine unction, and all the simplicity of love!"

In June of this year Mr Bull preached a funeral sermon for Mr Raban, pastor of the Independent church at Yardley Hastings. The sermon was preached at Olney, the place of Mr Raban's residence. The crowd was so great that the congregation adjourned to the market-place, and a movable pulpit was brought out of the church, from which my grandfather preached. For an account of this sermon, and the character of Mr Raban, see Coleman's "History of the Northamptonshire Churches," p. 295, &c.

Mr Bull was often nervous and low before preaching, and at times trivial circumstances would disturb his composure. Being at Surrey in July, he says, "I am afraid the great Mr Mason will come to hear me to-night—Mason of New York. Well, and suppose even the great Tom of Bedlam should come, or any other great man, what is that to me? Shall I be afraid of a man that shall die? No, I hope I shall not." Mr Newton would often come to Surrey on Friday morning to hear his friend. On one occasion at this time, the good man said he could have sat two hours longer to hear my grandfather. Mr Bull's weak nerves were sometimes unequal to the singing after the exertion of the sermon, and so he writes,—"I made the following speech from the pulpit. I told them I liked their singing before prayer and before sermon; no one enjoyed it more than I did; but their singing after sermon split my head as if it was cleaved with an axe; and I desired, if they had any mercy on me, that they would no more sing after sermon while I was here, more at least than one or two verses. They promised to comply."

On my father's completing his thirtieth year, the day was, as usual, remembered, and he received a letter full of wise counsels and affectionate expressions of parental tenderness. "My first idea this morning was to think of you, my second care to pray for you, and now my third will be to write to you. . . . . I have spent this day in retirement, having been alone since morning prayer."

Writing about the same time, he expresses great indignation with Macknight, whose learning greatly pleased him, but whose unevangelical spirit roused his righteous indignation. "I read last night Macknight's Essay on Justification. It is the most artful, the most diabolical attack I ever saw on the doctrine of the atonement, and justification by the imputed righteousness of Christ. But this is the torrent of the day with all the unconverted doctors, both Presbyterian and Episcopalian. The great drift of mankind now is not to form their notions of divinity by the Bible, but to melt down and mould the Bible by their carnal, rational, and unconverted notions of religion, and so bring in a new gospel, or rather, as blessed Paul says, that which is no gospel at all. Oh, may the Lord preserve my child in the simplicity and wisdom of the good old way!"

In connexion with his visit to London at the end of the year, Mr Bull again refers to the case of the young man of whose conversion he had heard on the last occasion of his being at the Tabernacle. He came himself to thank my grandfather, who found he was going on well. The same day a gentleman from Jamaica, named Finlayson, called. He told Mr Bull he had led a very wicked life, and hearing him preach on the preceding Sabbath, became very uneasy indeed; but hearing him again on "Christ is all in all," he was somewhat comforted, "and came to talk to me about his soul." Again,—"Last night a gentleman came to ask me to dinner some day next week; a lady came with him, a relation, whom I was made useful to when last at Surrey Chapel."

My grandfather speaks once more of his Saturday visits to Mr Newton. On one occasion he gave a criticism on Gal. vi. 14. "Mr Newton," he says, "got up and thanked me; they all thanked me, and seemed much pleased. Well, Saturday last, as one criticism went down so well, I gave them another on Isa. v. 7, 'And the men of Judah his pleasant plant.' I told them that the word men was singular, and should be rendered, 'but the man of Judah is the plant of his delight.'" *

* Mr Newton used to say on these occasions, "Now let us find a nut to crack."

Speaking of another interview with Mr Newton at the house of a mutual friend,—" Before we parted, we made him speak, which he did for fifty minutes on ' I, if I be lifted up from the earth, will draw all men unto me.' But his understanding is in ruins. Yet its very ruins are precious, and the bits you pick up retain all their intrinsic value, beauty, and richness."

He tells Mr Gunn, as he accompanied him from Mr Newton's, that he thought gospel ministers in London all leaned toward Arminianism. He replied, " Yes, they did, and therefore the Lord raised up such men as Huntingdon, who went to the opposite extreme."

On the 8th of November he writes, " I had a glorious opportunity at Tottenham last night. My text was, ' The blood of Jesus Christ, his Son, cleanseth from all sin.' I never in my life had such a view of the evil of sin, and of the sole ability of the blood of Christ to cleanse from it, nor do I know that I ever spoke with more strength of reasoning and power of expression. This, I believe, was chiefly in consequence of reading since Friday morning six or eight sermons by one Catcott, a Hutchinsonian, but a spiritually blind man. I read all day on Friday, a good deal on Saturday, and one sermon yesterday morning. It is astonishing what an effect this reading has in quickening the powers of the mind." On another occasion he says, " I have not been sorry for coming to London this time, till to-night, when I thought I could not go on any longer. There is in all my sermons so strong a tincture of Bullisms, so many oddities; this grieves me very much, but I can't avoid it—especially when I feel weak and feeble."

During this visit, Mr Bull was earnestly requested to supply at Mulberry Gardens for a month, but this he at once declined.

My grandfather was very regular in his walks and rides. He had a circular walk in his garden, which was accurately measured that he might know how many times round it would make a mile. I well remember that a sundial stood at the gate, and at its side was a little ledge for holding bullets, which were moved from one hollow to another at every round. He received an account of the laying out of this garden-walk while in London; but he says, " I must have a string of beads like the Papists, and so move one every time I get round." I suppose the bullets were eventually fixed upon. It appears from letters written in after years, that his grandsons, then very young, were sometimes commended for quietly trotting at his side—*non passibus æquis*—for the whole mile.

CHAPTER XIV.

Letters to his Son on his Marriage—His own experience—Life, a tale told—
Baxter—What he expects in his Daughter-in-law—Duties of Husbands
and Wives—Pleasure in writing to his Son—Mr Newton performs the
Ceremony—Letter to Mr Newton—Providence—Thoughts of Death—
Preaching in London—Income-Tax—Doctrines of the Gospel—Armin-
ianism—On Letter-writing.

IN the year 1803 my father was married. It will readily
be supposed how deeply interested my grandfather was in
this event, what anxieties it awakened, and how many
earnest prayers it called forth. It was a sore trial to feel
that they should no longer dwell together beneath the
same roof. My father being in London some little time
before his marriage, he received from home a letter containing the following judicious hints :—" Your letter to-
day was a very good one, because it was very particular,
and informed me where you have been. I am glad Letty
went with you, and that you are happy together. I wish
you always may be. When two people come together as
you are likely to do, some things previous are necessary :
as (1.) That there should be a suitableness of outward circumstances. (2.) A suitableness of natural temper and disposition. (3.) A mutual agreement as to what objects are

to be pursued, and what is the best mode of pursuing
them.   (4.) A mutual forbearance with each other when
there happens to be any little difference in judgment, and
the less important the object is the more prompt the forbearance should be. Never let one strive for superiority
over the other; but let each give way. Remember that
an ounce of domestic peace is worth a hundred pounds of
superiority. Authority on the part of a man generally shews
the tyrant, on the part of a woman the termagant. (5.)
Whatever private comfort is to be enjoyed, remember
the old saying, *Nil nimium*,—except, indeed, spiritual
comfort. (6.) Never overrate the value of creature comforts, nor undervalue spiritual and eternal comforts. No
comfort is worth having that will not consist with a
good conscience, and can be enjoyed in union with the
favour and love of God. All other comforts are transient
and will soon pass away, which takes off greatly from their
value, but the favour and love of God endureth for ever.
(7.) To render the relation happy, there must be daily and
incessant prayer for the Divine blessing. Walk with God.
(8.) It may be a trial to meet with seeming opposition
from Providence; but unless you have the Lord's consent,
you had better never come together. (9.) When love is
mutual and sincere, you will not grudge to wait the Lord's
time. That must be a poor love, not worth having, which
is a stranger to patience. Wait for one another. While
you are contriving one plan, the Lord may be preparing
another. Be content to love each other, and pray for each
other, and be always willing to come together, as soon as
ever the way is quite clear. (10.) Never so overrate any

T

creature comfort as not to be able to part with it, without sinful pain and anguish. Life itself, with all its comforts, is very uncertain. Hold your comforts fast enough to make you thankful for them; but not so fast as to resist when the Lord inclines to take them from you.

"There is something peculiar in your circumstances, and what is the will of the Lord is not as yet discoverable; but sometimes those who wait longest for each other are the most happy when at last they are united. What at present appears impracticable, may by and by be very plain and easy. You know there is no difficulty on my part. Whatever pleases you I consent to. I am anxious only for your comfort; but I said before, there can be no solid comfort without the good-will of the Lord Jesus Christ. I think it possible that the present conduct of Providence may have some especial reference to the present awful aspect of the times. . . . The Lord bless you, and keep you in all wisdom and prudence. Farewell.

"W. BULL."

A few days afterwards my grandfather writes,—"I am glad to find you are so fond of Letty, and I hope it will continue as long as you live. But how you are to get through life when you are married I can't conceive, for I think the French will come and take all we have, or nearly so. However, you shall fare as well as I do, so long as I have anything to eat and drink." And then, in reference to his own experience, he adds, " I shall soon have done with a world where existence is become a burden to myself, and, I believe, to most others. But I am not affected with the thought of being separated from all around me as I ought to be. I am without that clear and solid prospect of a better world which I long for, and which is necessary to make the decline of life comfortable and easy. I feel a firm belief in the truth of revelation, and in the person and merits of the Lord Jesus Christ. I am firmly persuaded of his truth and faithfulness to his promises; and I am ready to say, if God's Word be true, I shall be saved, and I really believe I shall: and yet what seems inconsistent is, that if my faith were truly saving faith, it must and would be attended with certain effects which I do not perceive,—a deep humility, holiness in heart and life, a spirituality of conversation, and greater earnestness at the throne of grace, sorrow for sin, and greater anxiety in seeking fresh supplies of grace. Gifts are one thing, grace is quite another. Real religion does not consist in talking, but in walking. Oh that I could live and act more to the glory of God, and more like a child of God, and a faithful servant of the Lord Jesus Christ! It's one thing to be a real Christian, and a great thing too; but it's another thing, though not different, to be a real faithful minister of the Lord Jesus Christ; and it's an awful thing to see the time approaching when I must give up an account of my stewardship, and be steward no longer. Oh that I may give up that account with joy, and not with grief and shame! But I can't think I shall do it with joy. I can't say I have fought the fight, I have kept the faith." . . .

The next day the following striking letter was written:—
" The reflection was so just, so solemn, and so interesting, that it might equally suit a child, a philosopher, or a saint.

At four o'clock this morning it flitted on my imagination,
'We spend our years like a tale that is told.' In a moment, before my eyes were opened, it was followed by these
thoughts: It is a tale, an awful tale indeed—how idle a
tale—how trifling a tale—how unprofitable a tale; but, oh,
how infinitely important the tale; eternity hangs upon
it, an eternal state, unutterable happiness or tremendous
misery! And yet how carelessly is it told,—how little
attention to remember it. The tale is soon told, and as
soon forgotten by all who hear it—yea, even by our very
selves—till the great development of this awful tale bursts
upon us in death, and the great drama is for ever closed.
It will be everlasting sorrow or everlasting joy. I begin
to exist one day, the second day I existed, the third I die;
and the place that knows me shall know me no more. We
spend our years as a tale that is told. In this tale of life
how many different scenes are brought forward!—what
various, what continually interchanging appearances! 'Tis
chequer work!—'tis mosaic!—'tis enamel! How various
the colours,—how mysteriously interwoven,—how radiant,—
how striking. Sometimes all is beauty, then all is dejection.
Sometimes all is gay as the blushing rose, then all is sable
as a royal mourning. In all the variety of the tale there
are two threads always present, always visible, but not
always seen—good and evil; each discernible when sought
for, each but seldom seen. Two artists always performing
a part,—God and self. From the first comes nothing but
good; from the latter nothing but evil, guilt, and grief, and
woe. This long, this short tale, must in a sort be told
again. But, oh, what heart can feel, what imagination can

anticipate, the great, the dreadful or the delightful, of that vast event—call it the last judgment! Never let the sound be out of your ears. Let the preparation of it never depart from your heart. Your tale is nearly told. At sixty-five little remains to be related. The die is cast. The event is certain; and the tale will soon be over, and over for ever.—Thus I went on dreaming between sleep and awake. At length the clock struck six. I arose, and ventured into the world once more. My usual ablutions being duly performed, I lighted my pipe, and walked exactly a mile. I spoke to the Lord mentally—how broken, how wandering, how various!"

Again, in reference to his son's marriage, Mr Bull writes thus :—

". . . You have two aged parents. They have loved you, delighted in you, doted upon you, prayed a thousand times for you, and are never perfectly easy when you are out of their sight. Think how much you owe them, and don't go and overlook them or slight them, because you have got so many and so dear *new friends*;—no, no, but bundle up the new and the old ones together, and bless and praise Him who multiplied five barley loaves into a meal for five thousand people; yes, bless and praise and delight in Him—Him who has multiplied your two friends into ten or a dozen; and pray that the Lord will unite all their hearts, the old ones and the new ones, as one man, to wrestle in prayer for you. I wish, and my prayer is, that the Lord Jesus Christ may give you both but one heart, one spirit, one temper, one aim and end.

and that all your mutual comfort may flow from Christ
dwelling in you both, the life of your souls here and the
hope of glory hereafter. Be sure you come together determined never to cross each other, never to have two wills. . . .

"I read last night one hundred and fifty pages of
Baxter's 'Dying Thoughts.' His piety astonished me, his
free-will and self-righteousness disgusted me, so that I
fear I shall never get through the book; and yet it is a
good book, but it will not revolve in my orbit. His circle
and my circle will not move on the same axis.

". . . Remember to enjoy all your creature comforts in
Jesus. Oh, may your comfort in each other continue till
your head is as gray as a badger, and as serene as the
blue-eyed morning, beautiful and lovely through the grace,
the beauty, and the love a precious Jesus puts upon
you. . . .

"On your wedding-day be exceedingly careful of yourself,—your thoughts, your passions, your temper, your
conversation, your looks, your very attitudes, for though
there may not be many eyes upon you, yet those who do
look upon you will look with all their eyes. Let them see
only what it is to be a Christian, a gentleman, a scholar,
and a lover all at once. Manifest a dignified gravity,
united with a divine cheerfulness. Guard against a foolish
attention to your wife before company, on the one hand,
and on the other, guard against a manifest inattention to
her, as if you were meditating on the Penitential Psalms
the very first day; rather shew them how you hope to
behave to her to the last day of your life, with modest
endearment, and the most affectionate tenderness.

"Tell her she will have a hard task with respect to me; *because* I shall take it for granted that she possesses all the saving grace that can enrich the human heart, all the accomplishments that can brighten the understanding, or give a lustre to personal address; all the modesty that can adorn her sex, with all the tender amiabilities that can proclaim good breeding; that she will shew at once the piety of a Christian, the prudence and love of a wife, and the filial reverence that becomes my child.   Tell her I shall be prepared to put the best possible construction upon everything she says or does, and if she fails in her attempts, I shall make very large discount for prompt payments—that is, to overlook every defect when I see a desire to do right, though through human frailty she may often fail in her well-meant intentions."

After suitable remembrances to all his son's new connexions, my grandfather adds,—" I wish and pray that they may all be a blessing to you, and that you may be a blessing to them.   But prepare them all to meet with and bear with a good deal of weakness in me.   Remind them that I am a poor old man, who, I fear, will try their patience,—weak in body and mind, and withal peevish and afflicted, ' but the Lord thinketh on me.'

" I am very, very thankful for the Lord's dealings with you in this union.   Pardon, my dearest son, the prolixity of this letter.   My most tender feelings are all awake on this occasion.   I have but one child to give a wife to.   I am easy about you, I am cheerful, but every pore of my skin seems to have a tongue, and every tongue is employed in sending up fervent prayers for a blessing on you.   May the Lord Almighty bless you, and the goodwill of Him that dwelt in the bush be with you and your dear wife all the days of your life.—So wishes and prays your dear parent,   W. BULL."

On the day before my father's marriage my grandfather writes,—" Through mercy, I am not at all low-spirited to-day, nor do I think I shall be to-morrow, only a little thoughtful; and if I was not that, perhaps I should forget to pray for you, and that would be passing strange indeed. However, I am easy and comfortable, but shall be very thankful when it is over."

There seemed some little doubt about the wedding party going to Brighton. In reference to that matter Mr Bull says,—" Through grace I derive no small comfort from being ready always to give up my will to the leadings of Providence as things rise up before me. *N.B.*—Never lay a great stress on little things, either in human life or even in religion. One thing is needful, and if that be altogether right, nothing else can possibly be very wrong with you. Live in the Lord's will, and not your own. Whatever He appoints fall in with, though it were even to die a martyr; but let his will be your will, and then you will have your own will in everything; and he that has his will in every-thing has nothing to wish for, he is completely happy, because he can say, ' What the Lord appoints I approve; it is the Lord, and I am easy about the matter; even to the loss of goods, or estate, or life itself, it is the Lord.'

" Remember me affectionately to Letty and all the family. I wish you the gracious presence and blessing of

the Lord Jesus Christ. The effect of this event will be, I
hope, an addition to your comfort to the last day of your
life; but it will also be a certain addition to your cares,
trials, and afflictions. May all things work together for
you. Study and pray for a calm, serene, and tranquil
state of mind. Dismiss all anxiety. Look up to the Lord,
and cast all your care upon Him, for He careth for you.
Remember your are his and not your own. Let Him do
what seemeth Him good."

The next day the following letter was addressed to my
father at Brighton:—". . . This morning I was very
sensibly affected with the softness and warmth of the air—
thermometer at 62° in the shade. I over-persuaded
mamma to take a ride with me, that we might ride and
pray together for you on the road. The whole road of
human life should be paved with prayer. The weather
to-day is so delightful that I can't help hoping it may be
typical of the warming cheering sunbeams of the Sun of
Righteousness arising and shining upon you all the days of
your life long. Oh, may you be very happy! but all at
present is hoping, wishing, praying, and believing.
Whether in this case my faith is the substance of things
hoped for, and the evidence of things not *yet* seen, must be
left to your care, or rather to pray the Lord that He may
give me that blessing. I only wish you may be half as
happy in the affection of a wise, prudent, humble, and
heavenly-minded wife, as you have been in the highest
and warmest love and delight of two aged and worn-out
parents for above thirty years. Oh, may you be spared to

bless each other till you are more than sixty-five or sixty-seven! That also is with the Lord.

"I wonder how far you or your wife have studied the duties of husbands to their wives, and wives to their husbands. If you have had no lecture on the subject, you must be but imperfectly prepared for the discharge of these duties. But I know of no book in all the world so proper to instruct you both on the subject as the precious writings of blessed Paul. Search all his writings for precepts on this subject. How is it possible for a man and wife to be happy, when they come together, when they know nothing at all of their mutual duties? The want of this is the cause of infinite misery amongst mankind; but I know 'you have not so learned Christ.' Take care not to be a snare and temptation to each other. Never lose sight for one moment of your duty to take care of your health. Both of you take care of your health—the health of your bodies and the health and peace of your minds. Be afraid of your own spirits. Live in the spirit of the Lord Jesus Christ, and then Christ will live in your spirits; and then there will be a second marriage—a spiritual marriage, a marriage that shall never be dissolved, nor embittered by any crosses or afflictions attending it.

"Now, while I am writing this grave letter, you are perhaps dancing about the country, like the gossamer, light and airy and very cheerful. Well, well! be it so! This may never reach you, but the loss will not be great, and it always gives me pleasure to write to you—yes, it is a gratification that no one, not even yourself, can have any conception of. It is my greatest indulgence; but I don't know whether to call it a carnal, a mental, or a spiritual piece of self-indulgence. Perhaps it partakes partly of all these. I really think it does. 'Tis a social, 'tis a parental, 'tis a heartfelt gratification, growing out of thirty years' partiality, and I hope not an unsanctified production. Be it what it may, it always does me good—but enough of this. Where are you? at Brighton? Then I charge you give my sincere and hearty love to Mrs Davies, Miss Scutt, Mr and Mrs ————, opposite the chapel, and good Mr Smith, and tell me how they do, and how Letty does, and whether you like her the less for being married to her."

Speaking of the negligence of the workmen in getting his son's house ready, and of the anxiety and care of a friend who was hastening their preparations, he says :— " She is as full of business as the Secretray at War is, in preparing to meet Bonaparte when he comes, and I fear both the one and the other might spare themselves the trouble for the good they will either of them do. I wish that both you and his most sacred Majesty had better servants than you have. You both have a very warm interest in my prayers, but I must beg to pray for you first, and then for his Majesty, and then for his councillors, and his fleets, and armies, and the safety of his dominions. ' In the peace of the land we shall have peace.'

" It seems a long way to look forward to the end of next week before I shall see with my own eyes, and judge for myself. Tell her a tender father waits to receive her in the arms of his best affection." . . .

It was the wish of both families that good Mr Newton should conduct the wedding service, and my grandfather sent him a special letter on the occasion. The good man had become very infirm, and was really unequal to the work; but his great love to those who were so much interested in the matter induced him to consent. He sat all the time, and, as I have heard my father say, quite lost himself in the midst of the service, and exclaimed, " What do I here ?."

My grandfather felt gratified by this proof of his friendship, and wrote to him the following letter :—

" MY VERY DEAR SIR,—You are no stranger to the painful, anxious feeling of having one's life, as it were, wrapped up in a second person, and may easily guess what I must have felt about the marriage of my dear son. It was, and still is, a matter of peculiar feeling and comfort to me, that you, the dearest and oldest friend I have left, should perform the sacred ceremony on this occasion. Oh, may your mantle, may a double portion of your spirit, fall upon this dear youth! I write this to express my gratitude, and to return you my best thanks for this labour of love.

" You grow old, so do I. Your spirits fail you, so do mine. You have been a long voyage, and are now entering into port. I could wish your precious life might be spared a little longer for the sake of others, to be a comfort and a blessing to many. But if the voyage is nearly finishing, may you enter into port with swelling sails, and with the softest, sweetest gales; and

> ' May my little bark attendant sail,
> Pursue the triumph, and partake the gale.'

" The times grow stormy and tempestuous, but Jesus, a

precious Jesus, is still the same, and we shall ere long be
with Him where He is, and shall behold his glory, and be
changed into the same image from glory to glory, and so
shall we ever be with the Lord." . . .

Just before his son returned home, Mr Bull writes,—
". . . What a comfortable doctrine is Providence! How
satisfying to think that the Lord reigneth! Whatever for-
tuitous events lead the way to this or that situation and
circumstance in life, all things are in the hand of the Lord,
and He orders all things for the best. It is the glory of
faith to believe this, and to know it, and to meet every
event as coming from that Being who is too wise ever to
err, and too good not to act for the best on every occasion.
But, oh, how weak, how wicked, not to yield a humble conformity to his blessed will! We should meet the Lord's
will in every leading of his providence, and rejoice in his
salvation on every mention of his precious saving grace;
but we cannot do this if He does not prepare and enable
us thereunto by his Holy Spirit. And I beseech you, my
dear, remember you are launching out to sea on a wide
tempestuous ocean, where there are many dangers,—rough
winds, violent storms, many quicksands, and many rocks
which you may split upon; but remember your Heavenly
Father, your Lord and your God, sits at the helm, and will
steer the vessel. The voyage, though dangerous, is short,
and the Pilot infallible in skill, in knowledge, in wisdom,
and in love,—a most blessed and glorious companion. Keep
your eyes fixed on Him, and commit yourself to Him every
day. Soon, very soon, shall the earthly house of our taber-

nacle be dissolved. My time is short, and I must leave you, to enter into the world of separate spirits; but Jesus will be always with you, if you are careful to be with Him. Help each other all you can along the dubious path of human life. If you live near the Lord, and feed upon Him, your soul will be in health and prosper, and it shall be well and go well with you."

Writing from London in November, he speaks thus of his preaching:—". . . But I must preach to-night, and the Lord has not told me what I must preach from, and that will require thought and reflection and private prayer, and then it will go as the Lord would have it, and consequently it will go on very well. If the Lord is pleased, I shall be pleased. If it goes ill with me, that will humble me, and do me good; if well, then He shall have all the glory, and I shall be happy to think He condescends to make any use of me. Oh, we shall have charming living when we get out of this two-legged prison,—absent from the body, present with the Lord! And He has said, ' Be thou faithful unto death, and I will give thee a crown of life.' My dear love, take care of your health; devote yourself to the Lord; keep a constant eye on his mind and will in everything, and live to his glory. Give my love to dear mamma. I feel a great deal of pain when I think of her infirmities. Oh, may the Lord Jesus be her strength and consolation! Give my love to Letty as to your own self. I shall be always attentive to her comfort and happiness for your sake."

In another letter at this time, in allusion to the state of

things in the country, and with special reference to the Income-tax, he says he wishes to be equally careful neither to cheat the Government nor to cheat himself; but he says of the Act of Parliament, "that when our wise men were framing the bill, the angels in heaven were reading Gen. xi. 7, and immediately received a commission to put the text in force. *Quem Deus vult perdere, prius dementat.* To be sure, the sun shines very bright every day, but so it did when Lot entered Zoar. I hope the one is not typical of the other."

He speaks frequently at this time of the benefit and pleasure he derived from a reperusal of Dr Owen's Works. "Dr Owen," he says, "proves a very pleasant and agreeable companion to me. He gives more clear, consistent, and solid explanations of many things than I remember to have met with elsewhere. I do not always agree with him, but on the whole it afforded me a great deal of pleasure, and did me good."

On another occasion, in reference to the great doctrines of the gospel, Mr Bull says,—" According to my degree, I have a little knowledge of them. I have great love to them. I have always laboured to preach them, perhaps not so faithfully as I ought. However, the conclusion I draw from all this is, that now I am old, nearly approaching to the grave, and my approach to it attended with a general dejection of spirits, a degree of melancholy,—it may end in insanity;—but low as I am, or however it may end, at present I must say that I firmly believe these peculiar doctrines. I endeavour to preach them, I greatly love them, I delight in them; they are my strength, my support, my comfort; and at this moment I have no doubt, or very little indeed, of my eternal salvation through faith in these peculiarities of Christianity, and if they were not peculiarities of Christianity, I should disdain to call Christianity a divine revelation. But you know there are some men who flatly deny them; others believe them, or pretend to believe them, but want to interpret away their meaning; others preach them, but so muddily, that the gospel loses its power and beauty with them, but all this is for want of spiritual discernment of their power in the heart; others preach them with tolerable clearness, but in a dry, speculative way; others take only a part of these doctrines, and, by their free-will and self-righteousness, they transfer the glory of salvation from the Holy Ghost to themselves, smuggling it into their own free-will; and still some there are who, by a false interpretation of the doctrines of Christianity, make revelation an apology for the most abominable wickedness, — their god is their belly, they glory in their shame. Now, all these things trouble me. But it comforts me to think you believe and preach the peculiarities of divine revelation; and yet, through the natural deceitfulness of the heart and the insinuating address of some about you, I fear that my little flock will become Arminians before my death, and that you will scarcely be able to prevent it. This is a great trouble to me, because I observe that wherever free-will creeps into the pulpit it soon drives out the vitality, and spirituality, and life, and power, and all the consolations of the gospel. These peculiar doctrines of the gospel are the sole support and consolation and delight of me, a poor old man. May they be yours all your days, and then I know you will follow me to glory, and we shall meet in heaven."

In the two following quotations Mr Bull gives his views on letter-writing :—" I believe the great Lord Chesterfield made it one of the principal pleasures of his life to study and compose those letters which he wrote to his son ; but he was a man of the world, and all his views of happiness were confined to the pride of life and the carnal lusts of the flesh. He placed all his happiness in his son, especially in the latter part of his life ; but the scene of my happiness is laid in eternity,—the materials are made up of spiritual things. Thus far I resemble him, that my greatest earthly happiness centres in my son, and my greatest and most sensible delight is to write letters to him. Oh, how happy I should be, if by these letters I could speak to you from the grave !" . . . .

Some days later he expresses himself more fully on this subject, as follows :—" Those who write every day have need of some caution, that they do not degenerate into commonplace stuff or frivolity. The most ancient and celebrated letters in the world are the familiar epistles of Cicero. I remember reading them in four vols. 8vo. They pleased me, but I thought much of their merit consisted in the purity of the Latin, and the elegance of the style. The next great letter-writer in the order of time was Pliny the younger. His letters have an uncommon delicacy and beauty in the matter and the manner. His spirit is amiable, and his manner sweet. I like Pliny very much. But the most superlative letter in all the world is that of St Paul to Philemon. I never saw a letter to be compared with it. . . . Next to this, the blessed apostle's four short epistles to the Galatians, Ephesians, Philippians, and Colossians are the greatest masterpieces in the world in this way. But for dignity, sweetness, authority, beauty, and interest, there is nothing in the whole creation equal to the seven epistles of the Lord Jesus Christ, in the beginning of the Revelation. Compared with all this, what stuff your letters and mine are! but still they have their use in the small-talk way.

"He that would write good letters should take care of these things:—(1.) That the matter should be always new, and not the same thing over again. (2.) That his matter be always interesting, and especially interesting to the person to whom it is addressed, otherwise it will not so far affect his feelings as to prevent its being burdensome. (3.) The thoughts ought to be wisely arranged so as to meet the object in view, with as much possible ease as may be. (4.) Great care should be taken that the style be concise, clear, easy, and striking. It's always disgusting to see a great many words used to express what might be done at least in one-third of their number. I am soon tired in reading even a good book when it is loaded with verbosity; and it's a common snare to me, at the end of a paragraph, to stop and ask myself, how many words are there in this paragraph that might have been left out with great advantage? The writer's statement might and would have come with much greater weight upon the attention, and been thereby more improving to the understanding, gain more of our approbation, command more respect for the writer, and be more generally read. Compare these remarks with your letters and mine, and you may safely say our letters cannot, will not, be immortal. *We* must never say with the poet,—

> 'Non omnis moriar, multaque pars mei
> Vitabit Libitinam.'

How, I say, will these remarks apply to your letters and mine about hedges, ditches, haycocks, windows, grocery, weather, &c., &c.? Yes, they will thus far. Our letters are very interesting, to ourselves (but to nobody else.) They are concise, and cannot weary us in reading them. If they are very dull, they are very short. If they are not lively, they keep alive the spirit of an affectionate remembrance. They pay for the want, likewise, by occasionally breathing a spirit of devotion, and generally conclude with a prayer for a mutual blessing, and that is what neither Cicero nor Pliny ever thought of. And if we have no hope of their being immortal, they may remind us of a future, a glorious immortality, by discovering our own weakness, and leading us to the Lord Jesus Christ, from whom we have received the hope of a glorious immortality indeed."

CHAPTER XV.

Mr Bull to his daughter-in-law—Mrs Bull's illness and death—Mr Newton's
letter of sympathy—The Established Church—Letters to Mr Newton—
Spirituality of mind—Concern about his grandchild—About his son in
London—Preparation for the pulpit—The Rev. Mr Foster—Hutchinson—
Letter to Lady St John—In London—At Mr Newton's.

AT the beginning of the following year, Mr Bull writes to
his daughter-in-law who was alone in London, my father
having just left her :—

"MY DEAR LETTY,—Methinks you seem a little dull to-
day. It strikes me that a line from Newport may divert
your attention and somewhat cheer your spirits. Your
dear and mine is just now, perhaps, somewhere between St
Albans and Dunstable. The near and tender relation in
which you now stand to me will interest the finest feelings
of my heart in everything that attaches to your comfort or
trials. At present it cannot be expected that you should
enter into all the feelings of a child to a parent, like your
own natural parent. Such feelings must be the result of
time, and gradually grow up out of a mutual, confidential,
and endearing kindness, and after all may, perhaps, never
equalize what a child feels to a real parent ; but I shall

have an advocate in the person of him who, of all men, is most dear to you, and, perhaps, his example may have some weight in the argument ; at least, I can assure you it has with me very great weight, for I do love you very much for his sake, very, very much indeed, so that you stand on high ground in your attempts to gain my affections,—not only in being so nearly connected with the dearest object to me in all the world, next to my wife,— but also in your own just claims on the ground of your own good sense and personal merit. I must, therefore, beg you will give me full credit for all the tenderness, and anxiety, and love of a real parent, who will never for a moment let pass an opportunity of realising everything that you can wish from a father, or that I can say, on the subject of my most unwearied attention to your comfort. But the only true and solid foundation for comfort in this or any other connexion, *must and can only be laid in an experimental knowledge of the Lord Jesus Christ, a living faith* in Him, and a humble holy love to Him. On this ground, and on this alone, you and I may hope to promote each other's happiness in this life, and in a life to come, which shall endure to all eternity.

" It may seem strange for an old man to be courting the love and confidence of a young woman, and still more for him to invite the lady to court his affections. (*N.B.*—They will be easily gained.) The worst part of the argument is, that in the attempt you will have a rival who, if he cannot make me love him, will, at least, gain possession of my person, and put a stop to all offices of kindness, and affection, and love between you and me. *That* rival is Death, who seems every day to get nearer and nearer to me, and seems by his messengers—gout, asthma, &c.—to be really impatient for his prize. Well, be it so! the Lord reigns, and He will certainly act for the best. His wisdom, power, goodness, and love are equal to everything consistent with his holiness and justice, his covenant and his promise. Our duty and our greatest comfort must arise from communion with a precious Jesus and conformity to Him; and this is a sufficient reason why we should live much at the throne of grace. There is no blessing to be expected but in a way of free grace, and we ought not to enjoy a grain of comfort without giving glory to the Lord.

"My dear love, commit yourself and your husband to Him: leave yourself with Him, and in everything say, 'The Lord's will be done.'" . . . .

My grandmother's health had been long failing, and about this time her symptoms became alarming. My mother was still in London; my father at home. My grandfather, in a letter to my mother, after describing Mrs Bull's dangerous state, says,—"You know all things are of God, and He does all things according to the counsels of his own infinite wisdom. When we cannot rejoice in his dealings, let us be silent, or only say, 'It is the Lord!' I feel somewhat like a sentinel upon guard, and waiting daily and hourly to be relieved. Oh that I may have the sun shining very brightly upon me in that painful awful hour, when all things in this world shall be to me as if they had never been at all! Count not of enjoyments on this side the grave—they are all delusive.

Nothing gives solid comfort but Jesus. I daily commit
you to Him in prayer. Pray for me, my burden is heavy,
my strength is weakness; but Jesus says, ' My grace is sufficient,' and, blessed be God, I am enabled to believe what
Jesus says." . . .

Mrs Bull lingered a few weeks after this, and died at
the latter end of February, at the age of sixty-seven.
Her end was very peaceful. She was a godly woman,
and her especial delight was in the study of God's holy
Word. Her disposition was very retiring, and she was
emphatically "a keeper at home," and most diligent in
her discharge of its duties. To her husband she was
an invaluable comfort; to her son, a most affectionate
mother.

The last letter good Mr Newton ever wrote to my grandfather was on this painful occasion. It is as follows :—

" MY VERY DEAR BULL,—You will not expect me to
write much; but I must tell you that I have seen your
letter to Mrs Neale. It awakened my most tender sympathy for you and yours, and my concern was mingled
with joy to find the Lord so graciously supported you.
Faithful is He that hath promised.

" For want of eyes, I refer you to Matt. vii. 24–27,
which occurred in my reading this morning. How shall
the house upon the rock be proved to be upon a sure
foundation if it was not assaulted by the same rain, storms,
and floods, which swept away that which was built upon
the sand? I could fill the sheet if I could see, but I cannot. My dear Miss Catlett cordially joins in all that I

mean, when I subscribe myself, your affectionate and sympathizing friend and brother,

"JOHN NEWTON.

"9th March, 1804.

"Time, how short!　Eternity, how long!"

The time arriving for my grandfather's usual visit to London, he was prevailed upon by his friends to accept the invitation.　This he did with some reluctance, though for less than the usual period.　It was, however, in some respects a painful visit, for his bereavement was continually before his mind.　"I feel," he says, "like a mourning dove that has lost his mate.　I feel lonely indeed, and seem to forget that the Lord's presence is the best company; yet I am not alone, for the Father is with me.　God does not hide his face from me, but I hide mine from Him, and then come darkness, doubts, and fears.　Could I keep my mind upon Jesus Christ I should be always comfortable—always rejoicing.　But the Lord knows what is good for us.　Yet I don't feel as I used to do, when writing home, and addressing my dear love through you."

Again, in a spirit of quiet resignation, he says,—"I scarcely spend five minutes any day without thinking of dear mamma.　The recollection is painful and yet delightful, and as my time in this world is short, I feel quite reconciled.　I don't in the least complain.　I bless the Lord that I ever had her, and that she has been spared so many years, and I bless Him for the good hope I have of her present state."

"Behold," he says again, "what a long heap of chitchat I have indulged myself in. But my dear mamma is not alive to sit and hear you read my trifles."

Sometimes he felt unequal to the demand upon him in London. "I am almost become bankrupt in preaching, and have hard work to keep my head above water. I can barely have a going on. Well, I ought to be thankful for that, and I am thankful. The people do not seem generally to despise me. Alas! I quite forgot it was Monday, and I dare say I am Mondayish." Yet during this visit his ministry was more than ever acceptable in the pulpit, and in his parlour expositions he was happy in himself, and cheered the hearts of many.

Mr Bull expresses himself strongly in one of his letters on what he felt to be one of the great evils of an Established Church :—" All this morning I have been quarrelling with two ladies. I hate them both most cordially. There is old Madam Infallibility at Rome, and her Daughter, Establishment in England. The daughter is just like her mother, and imitates her in everything. And both of them judge persecution of others to be necessary to their own safety. She reasons thus :—' Surely it is the duty of the magistrate to establish a religion; and surely it is most natural, most just, most right, to establish his own religion; and surely, when he has done so, it is his duty to protect and defend it. But, on the same principle, he must think it his duty to afflict and persecute every man that does not conform to his establishment.' Hence, both the mother and the daughter must think it right, and even essential to their own safety, to distress all those who are not exactly like themselves. My soul abhors such harlotry.

It has not the shadow of authority to support it in all the New Testament, but is directly contrary to the religion of the meek and humble Jesus."

After his return home, Mr Bull wrote the following letter to Mr Newton :—

"MY VERY DEAR SIR,—Through mercy I got home from town as well as I expected, but am so low that I have had no spirits to write as yet, and I am so very weak in my feet and ankles that I have not yet walked out once to call on any of my friends. I can't walk at all, only across the room.

"It is otherwise in my mind. I seem calm and serene, and feel easy. All the Lord's dealings with us are wise, and holy, and gracious, but we have need of patience, that, after we have done and suffered the will of God, we may inherit the promises. You and I, dear sir, seem drawing to the close of our pilgrimage, but we are also drawing near to our crown, the great end of our faith, the eternal salvation of our souls. We must soon exchange a state of comparative darkness, dulness, and sorrow, for a state of light, life, love, and everlasting joy in the Lord—the Lord Jesus Christ, our God and our dear Saviour, Redeemer, and Justifier. Oh, how precious, as well as great and glorious in Himself! but I lament and mourn that He is not more precious to my soul.

"I think of you daily, with the most sincere affection and love. I feel much for the burden of age and infirmities you sustain; but I must and do rejoice in the great love of Jesus, which sustains you under them. Many pleasant interviews have we enjoyed in the house of our pilgrimage, but there is one interview yet to come, better than them all together. I trust through grace, rich, free, all-sufficient grace, we shall ere long meet to part no more—*for ever.* Oh, delightful interview indeed! Let us wait patiently for it, and endure as seeing Him that is invisible. The time and manner of our arrival are fixed by infinite wisdom and infinite love. Then, I doubt not, we shall know each other, and have sweet converse together about Jesus, to whom we owe it all. My dear sir, we shall see excellencies, glories, beauties in our dear Lord of which at present we have very feeble conceptions indeed; but these future views and prospects are agreeable to the Word of God, and to many sweet foretastes to which his dear children have testified; and I hope I may add that *we* know that their testimony is true. Experimental knowledge is the best knowledge.

"I must beg, my very dear sir, your acceptance of my best thanks for a thousand kindnesses bestowed on me all your days, and they are not less due to Miss Catlett, to whose favour and good-will I am greatly indebted. I shall always think of her with affection and love. Her tenderness to you, as well as her kindness to me, work powerfully on my heart. I pray the Lord to bless and reward her with a strong and lively sense of his distinguishing love to her soul. Give my respects to all under your roof. My breast aches with writing. I commit you both to the 'Rock of Ages.'— Your affectionate   W. BULL."

Again, at the end of the year 1804, when Mr Bull was

in London, he enjoyed the society of his friend, and on his return thus wrote to him :—

"MY VERY DEAR SIR,—The tender state of my health at my return home prevented my writing sooner; but through the Lord's goodness I am now tolerably well again, and am spared to the end of my sixty-sixth year,—a boy in comparison with you, but we both are children in comparison with what I trust we soon shall be. That Jesus, who, by his Spirit, has brought us into a spiritual childhood in this world, will soon bring us to a spiritual manhood in his kingdom above. There we shall not compute our mercies by months and years, but by an everlasting duration. And who is He that hath done all this for us? A covenant God and Father, a dear and precious Regenerator and Sanctifier, who has comforted us all the day long in the house of our pilgrimage, and 'who will never leave us nor forsake us.' Oh, how precious is that blood which cleanses from all sin, that redeems our souls from everlasting death! How bright and glorious that righteousness that justifies us, and gives us a right and title to everlasting life! How shall we enough admire the grace and love of that blessed Spirit who first called us by his grace, brought us to the knowledge of God our Saviour, and has been daily carrying on his design of grace and love in our souls, and is now working in us and upon us, to ripen and fit us for the full and perfect enjoyment of his love in a better world! How many blessed instruments does He make use of for this end—though very different in their nature! Sometimes He uses trials and afflictions; at another time, comforts and consolations; at all times, great and precious privileges,—at least you, my dear sir, and I, have great reason to say so. But soon all the means and instruments will be for ever laid aside, as being no longer needful for us. We now seek, and we shall soon find, everything in Jesus; for that event we look, and wait, and hope, and, at times, long. Jesus will then be to us 'all in all.' He will be everything we need, everything we wish, everything we can enjoy, and that without a change to all eternity. We shall behold his face in righteousness,—we shall be satisfied when we awake in his likeness. O blessed day! O glorious dawn! Sweet answer to all our prayers!—poor, and languid, and often very broken prayers; but having been perfumed with the sweet incense of a precious Jesus, making intercession for us, they will then be fully and most graciously answered beyond their utmost extent. Let these prospects daily cheer and exhilarate our spirits.

"But something says, 'Will it be so?' Leave that to Him, who says, 'It shall be so.' We have the word, and promise, and oath of our great and dear Lord, and He cannot, He will not deny his own word. Let us bless his name and daily rejoice in Him.

"I write this evening before my birthday, hoping that you will think of me, and lift up a prayer for me on that day. My son and his family are all well, and desire their love to you. . . . May the Lord be your strength and consolation every day! To his tender love I commit you, and remain your very affectionate and most obliged brother and servant, W. BELL."

My father was in London at the beginning of the year 1805; and the understanding was, that each was to write every other day, "for what," says my grandfather, "is three shillings a-week for two of the dearest friends in the world to hear of each other?"   "Oh," he says in this letter, "that I was more holy and heavenly-minded!   I lament the want of this very much.   To have our thoughts chiefly exercised on spiritual and heavenly objects, is the life of the soul, the greatest comfort in earth, and the surest evidence of heaven; where the treasure is, there will the heart be also.   I pray the Lord to dispose and incline your heart to be always as much as possible taken up with thoughts of God and things divine,—thinking of the Lord, and praying to Him when you are alone and when you are in company, when you are in the house, and when you are walking in the street.   Labour to bring your mind into a constant habit of prayer, and especially when you lie awake in bed.   There are no exercises more profitable than songs in the night.   Take pains to encourage your heart in this work.   Oh, how do I wish that the Lord may be always with you, and that you may be always sensible of it.   When you preach, seek earnestly to preach Christ, and not self.   Let Him be your Alpha and Omega in every sermon."

In another letter, after speaking of his continued sufferings of body, he adds,—"' In the world ye shall have tribulations,' but I trust at the end all will be well; and I doubt not that in life (with me) all things will work together for good.   Oh, how blessed a thing is it to have the heart always in union with Christ and to be always breathing after Him! I long for nothing but greater nearness to Him, and a more absolute surrender of my whole self to his will, and to live more to his glory. Oh, may He bless *you* every day!"

Again, two days later,—"I need not add how glad I shall be to see you all three* once more; and I hope your company and assistance will in some measure revive my spirits; but as to restoring strength to my body, I have little or no hope of anything of that kind. I only wish for spiritual strength, and that my faith may not fail me in my latter end. At present I am comfortable in that respect,—that is, I have no uneasiness about my salvation, or very little. I am the Lord's, and He is mine; and however dark and low He may suffer me to be in my latter end, it will finally go well with me. All will end well: because, if I know anything of spiritual and experimental religion, I do know that I have felt, and do feel, those things which none but a real Christian ever does. But, on the other hand, I must acknowledge that I see and feel many things that I often think no man could feel if he was a real Christian. There is therefore a degree of suspense."

Speaking of his grandchild, about whose health he felt very anxious, and of whom he feared he had not been told the whole truth,—"You see in me," he adds, "a lively picture of the infirmities of age, and the strong symptoms of approaching dissolution, by this, that every trifle agitates me, and my mind is liable to so many and so great anxieties, whether about great things or little things."

* My father and mother and their infant child.

Again, in reference to the ailments of the child, he says,—
" But our dear Lord is the God of infants as well as the
God of old men, and He can carry him through it, [his illness,] and crown it with a blessing,—only let us take care
to make it a matter of prayer, for without that all the
remedies in the world will do no good at all."

These letters were addressed to my father when attending the Religious Meetings held in London in the month
of May; and he thus warns him against religious dissipa-
tion :—" I much fear London will be a snare to you ; seeing so many ministers, and hearing so many sermons, will
rub off the dew or plumage from your spirit, what little
there is. A monk should be always in his cell; I think
he is best there. And a Christian should be always in his
closet, especially a minister; he is always best there. But
the world—the Christian world—is a sea of dangerous
navigation, because there are many storms, and many
quicksands, and great breakers; and he must be a very
happy sailor indeed who can make his voyage without any
loss or damage. But he that lives chiefly in his closet is
safest. Solitude with Jesus is safe, and comfortable, and
profitable; but company without this is a great snare.

" I must preach twice to-morrow. What a poor creature
shall I be this time to-morrow evening,—perhaps in Paradise! There are no poor creatures there. Well, I count of
it, come when it may, because I shall depart out of myself,
a body of sin and death,—and out of my own will, and be
swallowed up in the will of a precious Jesus."

In one communication, Mr Bull speaks thus on preparation for the pulpit, and on preaching :—" The more retire-

ment you have before you preach, the better, in general, will you preach. I like to read, before I preach, some good book, and the more spiritual it is the better. Then I like to preach my sermon over to myself for at least two hours. When I do this, I am sure to feel liberty. In all your praying and preaching, never lose sight of the Divine unction. Be as spiritual as you can, and as orthodox as may be. Remember, we are not heathen philosophers, nor philosophical moralists, but ministers of Christ, and are called to preach nothing but what is peculiar to the gospel of Christ,—either its doctrines, or its precepts, or its promises. The gospel—the peculiarities of the gospel—are the great duties of a faithful servant of Christ, and friend to the souls of men; but, perhaps, I had better learn how to preach myself than to be teaching you. I pray the Lord to be always with you. I wish you may be able to manage all your worldly affairs with judgment and discretion, and never lose sight of what is spiritual, for this is of the most importance."

Mr Bull had heard with pleasure that his old friend the Rev. Mr Foster had become the minister of Pentonville Chapel. "I think he will not live long to cultivate this large field of usefulness which the Lord has opened to him, but it may prove a great blessing while he does live, and may lay the foundation for the future choice of a gospel minister in the parish. I do bless the Lord that He is pleased to work so wonderfully in this half Babylonian Church of human authority and civil magistracy. But the Church of Christ can never possibly be a national Church while there is one unconverted man in

the nation,—that is, the Church of the Holy Ghost can
never be established by an Act of Parliament,—nor can
that be the Church of Christ which has the civil magistrate for the supreme head and ruler of it. But the Lord
Jesus Christ can, and does, plant his own Church within
that same national, civil, and magisterial Church as easily
as He can in a land of Pagan idolatry; and blessed be his
name that He does so.'

In several of his letters he refers to the perusal of
the works of Hutchinson. On one occasion, he says,—
" I have just finished the second volume — the most
fatiguing book, because the most difficult to understand,
I ever read in my life; but I have this reward, that I
have now a clear and perfect idea of his system of philosophy, and I do not repent, though I have paid dear
for it. I was determined to understand it, if possible;
as to believing in him, that is quite another matter. These
Hutchinsonians are strange people. Their philosophy I
admire, but their divinity I abominate. They are all
strangers to, and consequently silent upon, the great
change of heart in the new birth. It's awful to think
how a man can read the Bible with half the diligence
that Hutchinson did, and yet be blind to this *sine quâ
non* of salvation." Again,—" Of his typical and allegori-
cal interpretations of Moses, I have my doubts—I think
he carries it too far, though many of them are both natural and beautiful. .'. . . As a writer, I think him the most
obscure, the most prolix, ill-digested, and tedious of any
author in the world; still, I believe I shall read him
through in time if my life is spared. . . . Last night I

finished the seventh volume. I think he is half a madman, but a very surprising genius, if he had but sense enough to make his meaning intelligible. I afterwards read, in my little abridgment by Lord Forbes, the sense of this great 8vo in about thirty pages 12mo. Then, at supper, I began to read 'Forbes's Thoughts on Natural and Revealed Religion.'" He says of this latter book,—" It is the best defence of the divine authority of the Old Testament I think I ever read."

Mr Bull had become acquainted with Lady St John, the sister of Mr Whitbread. She lived near Bedford, where my grandfather had met with her, and had found her ladyship under much religious concern. I find a copy of the following letter, written September 5, 1805 :—

" DEAR MADAM,—If idolatry is the easily besetting sin of some, I know that indolence quite as easily besets others. When your ladyship's letter reached me, I looked it over, prayed over it, and said, 'Oh for a pen that would write without the trouble of guiding it. This letter must be answered,—shall be answered. Well, to-morrow; and then again—to-morrow.' Age and low spirits steal away my time, and all the little energy for exertion I have left. The grave must soon receive the rest.

" I read your ladyship's letter with great pleasure. Oh that thousands and tens of thousands had exactly your view of themselves—with what delight and joy could I then preach Christ to them! We cannot possibly have a worse opinion of ourselves than we deserve. Why is not a precious Jesus more sought after? Why not more beloved and delighted in? The reason is obvious. Because we think too well of ourselves. The more vile we are in our own eyes, the more precious will our dear Lord be to us; the more we see the need of the Physician, the more welcome will He be to us. Often am I bowed down and overwhelmed with a sense of the infinite evil of sin, and of the hidden plague of my own heart; and often do I write bitter things against myself, and for the moment believe my salvation is impossible, and then I feel the bitter anguish of despair. Then I look to Jesus, and behold the glory of his person, and the riches, the inexhaustible riches of his grace,—the infinite merits of his precious blood, his perfect righteousness, the sweet promises of his Holy Spirit, and the infinite and boundless heights and depths, the lengths and breadths of his distinguishing love to the vilest of sinners. I think of his unfailing faithfulness to his word; and behold I run away from self, quite away, as far as possible, and creep, and groan, and sigh after Christ; and behold I am set at liberty, and am full of comfort. The name of the Lord is a strong tower, and the poor guilty criminal runs into it, and is safe. Your sighs and groans, dear madam, are melody in the ears of a sin-pardoning and soul-saving Jesus. It may be disgusting to self, but it makes sweet melody in heaven. Angels look down upon it with delight, and Jesus says, ' These are the reward of my blood; I will perfume these groans and tears, and they shall come before the mercy-seat as a sweet-smelling incense.'

"In short, the worse, by divine grace, we are led to think of ourselves, the better we shall think of a most blessed Saviour. Jesus looks at a broken heart and a contrite spirit, and will assuredly accept those unutterable groans which his own Holy Spirit has produced in you. They will all end well; and He will have all the glory, and you shall have the rich consolation. Oh, what a mercy, what a mercy, to be brought through grace to know the worst of ourselves, and to know the best of Jesus! This is true wisdom and saving grace. May the Lord help you, madam, to believe and to rejoice in Him! To an awakened mind self is the parent of despair, and Christ the source, the only source, of life, consolation, and enjoyment.

"The Lord, I doubt not, has begun his great work in your heart. Do let Him carry it on in his own way, and in his own time He will make it perfect. But, remember what He has said, 'I have chosen you in the furnace of affliction:' be it so; if He has but chosen us at all, let it be at what time and in what circumstances He pleases; what He once begins, He will assuredly carry on, and complete in the manifestation of His own glory in your salvation. Believe in Him. He will save, He will rejoice in his love. Commit yourself to Him every hour in the day, and you shall find Him faithful. Blessed are all they that put their trust in Him.

"I rejoice that Mr Foster has been a spiritual father to you, and should he, in a relative capacity, become your son, I hope and pray that it may be a lasting source of domestic comfort and spiritual enjoyment. Whenever your ladyship talks of self, I expect the subject will savour of the dismal; but when you think and talk of Jesus, I hope

the theme will be cheerful, lively, and happy. I pray the
Lord, the Great Head of the Church, to be with you, and
bless you, and sanctify you and all yours.—To his tender
love I commit you, and remain, dear madam, your ladyship's faithful and affectionate servant,

"W. BULL."

My grandfather had been unable, in consequence of
bodily weakness, to visit London in the early part of the
year, but he was earnestly requested to supply Tabernacle
and Tottenham Court in September, even if he could take
but one service on the Sabbath. He had given up all
thought of renewing these services, but he was willing once
more to attempt the work. He, however, suffered very
much while in London; but he writes thus beautifully :—
" Since I came to town, I have been quite alone, or nearly
so." Then mentioning the names of some few friends who
had called, he adds,—" This is all the company I have had
since I came to London. Oh, may I be like to him of
Patmos, who was in the Spirit on the Lord's day, and enjoyed sweet visions of the Almighty ! When the Lord is
present, solitude is the best company." He was interrupted while writing by a visit from Mr Newton ; and con-
tinuing his letter, he says,—" Mr Newton is very feeble,—
had great difficulty to get out of the coach. I was obliged
to lift him with all my strength. He was most affectionate,
and said he would not have come so far for many people,
only for me. He wished me to come and dine with him
to-morrow, to be there at nine, and stay till seven."

Mr Bull accordingly spent the following day with Mr

Newton. It was, however, in some respects painful. The good man was strong in his opinion that he was as capable as ever of preaching, and defended his position with some warmth. But Mr Bull says, "Everybody else shakes his head, and laments that he preaches at all."

This was my grandfather's last interview with Mr Newton, as it was also the last time of his preaching regularly at the Tabernacle. He closed his services there, October 9, with a sermon from Acts xxvi. 22, "Having obtained help of the Lord, I continue to this day."

During this year the chapel at Newport was enlarged, and was re-opened in January 1806, when the Rev. Mr Hyatt of the Tabernacle preached.

CHAPTER XVI.

LIFE OF THE REV. WILLIAM BULL,
1806–1814.

DURING the years 1806 and 1807, Mr Bull went but little from home; and very few letters remain, if such were written, of this period. In December of the former year, he thus addresses his son in London. After speaking of his disturbed nights, and of the relief he obtained by sitting up in bed, which was a common practice with him, he proceeds to say,—" As a member of society at large I am dead, or like one dead and forgotten in the silent grave. My circle in the social compact is very much contracted. It is now quite confined to Newport, and about three miles round it. But this solitude I like. It suits my infirmities very much, for I now find I can nowhere enjoy any comfort but in the stillness of retirement and something like meditation, with now and then a thought lifted up to the Lord. However, I must say that this day I have felt very little of that dark dejection and painful unbelief which of late have been a heavy affliction to me. I began to read Boerhaave this morning on old age and the symptoms of disease. The dying words of the learned Salmasius have been much upon my mind early this morning and all day :— ' Oh,' said that great man with his last breath, ' if Providence would but spare my life one year longer, I would spend it wholly in reading the Psalms of David and the Epistles of St Paul.' I think much as he did, and will endeavour to put his wish into practice while I am spared. I believe nobody thinks it will be long; but that thought does not disturb me, not half so much as the fear of dying in the dark under the hidings of God's face. My dear child, while you live, live to the Lord,—to retirement, to meditation, to prayer. Live to Jesus, and be happy."

On another occasion, writing a little more cheerfully, he says,—" It is enough for me that I have a degree of hope, at times a very comfortable hope, of an interest in the love of God, and the blood and righteousness of Christ. This is all my salvation and all my desire. I am weary of the world, and the world is weary of me; but Christ is never weary of the sighs and groans of a convinced broken-hearted sinner,—no, never, never, but will hear and save unto the uttermost. I am often tempted to despair, and I live on the borders of it; but oh, what a mercy it is that I have the whole weight of the whole Word of God in my favour, and He is faithful!"

His affection for his grandchildren was exceedingly great, and he was always full of anxiety and interest about them. Of one of them (at that time between two and three years of age) he writes,—" I am not a little diverted with his intention to preach at Mr Buck's meeting-house. Could I be prophetically assured that he would one day really preach Christ and Him crucified, it would be the joy and rejoicing of my heart. But I think the mere disposition to it is a good sign, and I am very much pleased with it; but there is one preliminary which I hope he will not overlook—viz., that before he begins to preach he should learn to hear; that is, to sit still at meeting while he is hearing other people preach. If he learns this, and learns it well, by having been two months at London, it will be no small point gained in the education of so very volatile a pupil. Another point to be kept in view before he can preach with general acceptance,—he must learn to talk ; I mean to speak plainly, for at present I fear his vocabulary lies in a very small compass. I suppose ten, or at most fifteen, words would fill the book. When an old hen gets a brood of chickens, I daresay she can fancy music in their first attempts to chirp, and I have no doubt that even the chattering magpie has an ear for the same kind of music, though I think the first efforts of the young pies must be a very strange sort of unintelligible jargon, very much like my poor boy's preaching.

'Sed dulce est aliquando nugare.'

As for baby Thomas, I hope he is well, but I almost forget him. I don't in the least expect I shall live to hear him preach, but I can think of him and pray for him, and shall be delighted to see him."

Six months afterwards he writes,—" Baby Thomas has

made me a visit to-day. Lucy [the nursemaid] flatters herself that he can walk. I see no proof of it, or very little : but I think he is tolerably well, and let us bless the Lord for this mercy."

Mr Bull's health seems somewhat to have improved, and in the summer of 1808 he was once more induced to listen to a request to supply Surrey Chapel for a short time in August. Indeed, it appears that during this year he preached not only at Surrey, but occasionally at the Tabernacle, at Greenwich, and at Reading, besides in other pulpits in his own neighbourhood. He was, however, often compelled to sit in the pulpit, which he now constantly did at home.

He concludes a letter to his son from London thus : " Oh, my love, live near to the Lord, labour to give up yourself more and more to Him. Don't let the concerns of time rob you of your soul's interest. Labour to be useful to the soul of your dear wife. Pray that you may live for your children's sake. Oh, may you bring them up for Christ !"

He says of his preaching at the Tabernacle,—" The Tabernacle was very crowded. I was very feeble, but spoke loud, and was heard with attention; but this loud speaking prevents the right management of my voice, and disturbs my train of thought."

Towards the end of this year Mr Bull was visited by Lady St John, and soon afterwards he received the following letter from her brother, S. Whitbread, Esq. :—

" DEAR SIR,—I learned with great pleasure from my

sister, Lady St John, of the soundness of your health, and the continued cheerfulness of your spirits. Long may you be blessed with both, for your own enjoyment, and the happiness and edification of your friends and your numerous flock. Had circumstances permitted, I should have been gratified to have accompanied her to Newport, and to have paid my personal respects to you. Please God to spare us both, I shall assuredly never be in that neighbourhood without doing so. And it would make me very happy if I might be allowed to fetch you to a visit either to my sister or myself. Would you allow it?

" I have taken a great liberty with you, by ordering a hogshead of porter to be sent to you by the Newport wagon . . . .—Your obliged and obedient friend and servant,   " S. WHITBREAD.

  "SOUTHILL, *Nov.* 27, 1808."

In the next month, Mr Whitbread writes again. After expressing the hope that, when the days were longer and the weather warmer, he might receive a visit from Mr Bull, he continues,—" I have many reasons for wishing to keep up a correspondence with you; but you have thrown in my way an irresistible temptation to write to you thus early, by saying that you are in possession of the palinode of Cowper, in a copy of beautiful lines which have not been published, ['The Fragment.'] I pray you send them and let me see them. I will not even take a copy of them, if you do not give me permission. Do not, my dear sir, refuse this favour to a lover of poetry, and an admirer of your departed friend. I hope the porter turns out good, that your hearth blazes cheerfully, and that the hearts assembled round it are light and happy. Lady Elizabeth accepts your kind remembrance of her, and returns it to you with pleasure. . . . I shall impatiently expect your answer.—Your friend and servant,

"S. WHITBREAD.

"SOUTHILL, *Dec.* 21, 1808."

Eight days afterwards came the following, with its poetical enclosure :—

"DEAR SIR,—I fear you will find me a troublesome correspondent. I received your letter only this morning, and here I am again. For the rest, look at the enclosed. Set me not down as the most presumptuous fellow alive, for daring to attempt a poetical epistle upon the view of such a one as you have sent me from Cowper ; but I rhyme about once a-year, and to-day I was inevitably tempted. You are the victim. Tell me you pardon me, and believe me, dear sir, your obliged and faithful,

"S. WHITBREAD."

These are the lines :—

> "I thank you, Reverend Mr Bull,
> For your obliging letters, full
> Of every simple Christian grace—
> Your Cowper's pen did warmly trace
> When he your faithful portrait drew,
> In words, t' outlast both him and you.
> The lines enclosed one mite of fame
> Will add to their great author's name :
> And to the world once more impart
> How he esteem'd your head and heart.

Send me the precious bit of oak,
Which your own hand so fondly took
From off the consecrated tree !
A relic dear to you and me.
To many 't would a bauble prove,
Not worth the keeping.   Those who love
The teeming grand poetic mind,
(Which God thought fit in chains to bind,
Of dreadful dark despairing gloom,
Yet left within such ample room
For coruscations, strong and bright,
Such beams of everlasting light,
As make men envy, love, and dread
The structure of that wondrous head,)
Must prize a bit of Judith's stem
That brought to light that precious gem,
' The Fragment,' which, in verse sublime,
Records her honours to all time.
I 'll visit you, if so it please,
The great Director of our ways,
When Summer visits us again,
And frees me from the next campaign.
I 'll fetch you here, if you will come,
Pipe and tobacco box are welcome !
Your friends must always bless the art
That mends your health or cheers your heart ;
The box which Cowper gave to *you*,
Must surely meet with honour due ;
The pipe your contemplation aids,
More fragrant than enamell'd meads.
We 'll talk upon the Sacred Book,
Whence springs th' exalted living rock,
On which the Christian takes his stand,
By his Redeemer's great command ;
Whether spirits ebb or flow,
Sickly, faint, or healthy glow.
Nor time, nor accident can make
That solid footing ever shake.
I saw you once—your brother John
Just then entirely frantic run,

Goaded by devilish arts to evil,
He did the business of the devil.
Some fools there were who fear'd the Pope,
More knaves, full well, deserved a rope,
For sending through the troubled nation
False fears and dreadful execration.
You dared come forth, your ruddy face,
Free from all clerical grimace,
Shew'd the true picture of your soul,
Above all worldly mean control.
I shook your hand, and heard you say,
(In words enduring to the day
When memory shall fade away,)
' Hypocrisy I hate, nor fear
The Pope will gain a footing here.'
Farewell ! but don't forget the word,
By the first stage-coach, be so good
To send it, well directed hither,
And we will meet in better weather.

" S. WHITBREAD.

" SOUTHILL, *Dec.* 29, 1808."

Early in the following year, Lady St John wrote to my
mother expressing her thankfulness that Mr Whitbread
had the privilege of my grandfather's correspondence.
" Great will be the mercy should the Lord bestow a blessing upon it, by its proving a means of good to the soul of
my brother. Mr Bull has shewn him much kindness."

In consequence of the illness of one of the regular supplies at Surrey Chapel, Mr Bull was induced to visit
London again in the summer of 1809. He preached with
great comfort to himself, and evidently with great acceptance to others. The congregations were very large ; indeed, when he preached his farewell sermon on a week
evening, it was said there had never been so many people

in the chapel on such an occaion. He received many very pressing invitations to visit his friends, but he says, " The work at Surrey requires all my little strength, and time too; but it is not for want of a will. I have not one friend in London whom I would not gladly call upon, and testify my respect to them; but I must preach, and am very, very thankful for it, for it is my highest delight. *Non possumus omnes omnia.* The *vox populi*," he says, " is, ' Dear old man, what a pity he should grow old!' Sweet poison! I know its evil. It's time of high water with me. Perhaps before I leave, the tide will turn, ebb, and this frothy bubble subside. Let it. I value it not a groat."

He says of his farewell sermon,—" I gave out my text, ' Finally, brethren, farewell.' After this I altered my mind, and said I would take another. It was 1 Cor. i. 10, ' Christ made to us wisdom,' &c. The reason I gave for changing my text was, that on the first I should talk about myself and my hearers, but on the second I could talk about Jesus Christ; and great was the attention."

While in London, Mr Bull paid a visit to Lancaster's school, his system being then a novelty. As soon as he entered, Lancaster addressed my grandfather,—" Friend Bull, I am glad to see thee here. Thou art an old acquaintance of mine at Surrey Chapel. Thou wast the first man that ever opened my eyes to Christian liberality; and I am very glad to see thee." My grandfather gives a very interesting account of the mode of conducting the school. Lancaster returned with Mr Bull and his friends to tea, when the former gave them an account of his interviews with the King and the Royal Family.

While in London, Mr Bull dined with Mr Henry Thornton, where he met Mr Macaulay, Mr Babington, together with his friends Colonel Makelean and Major Handfield. There was a great deal of free conversation about Dissent; and Mr Bull found opportunity to speak to Mr Thornton respecting the continuance of the Academy. Subsequently, when at my grandfather's death the annuity left by the elder Mr Thornton ceased, and the institution was supported by public subscription, Mr H. Thornton became its treasurer and a subscriber of £20 per annum.

Before my grandfather returned home, Mr Bateman, my mother's uncle, prevailed upon him to go with him to Margate. He visited on this occasion one of his former students, who was settled at Sandwich. At these places he preached almost beyond his strength. He says,—" If I go on at this rate long, you will never see me again. Mr Tomlin wants me to preach here on Monday evening, but I will not, because I must preach amongst Lady Huntingdon's eagles on Tuesday. [The reference is to the supports of the pulpit and desks in the chapel at Margate.] The Baptist minister wants to publish me for the Sabbath after. I fear they will kill me before I can go away. I want to know how you are going on. I very much long to see the dear boys; but I also long to be instant in season and out of season. It's a pity to come a hundred and nineteen miles from home and do nothing when I am here." It appears that in sixteen days Mr Bull preached in public or in private not less than eighteen times, including a service at Chatham on his return to London.

Being at Ramsgate during this visit to the coast, Mr

Bull saw the transports which brought back the soldiers from the unfortunate Walcheren expedition. "They all looked weary, dejected, and, I think, ashamed."

He speaks in the strongest terms of the affection and respect he received on all hands, and especially of the very kind attention of Mr Bateman.

At the commencement of the year 1810, Mr Bull again felt the pressure of his infirmities, and speaks of his life as a burden. He was annoyed by the attempt of some parties to create a division in the congregation; but he says, "I leave it with the Lord; and I hope I shall outlive this most indecent and unchristian attempt to destroy my comfort at the close of my life."

My grandfather refers in the same letter, written from London, to the "alarming state of public credit amongst the merchants and bankers. . . . How glad I am," he adds, "that my lot is not cast in, but out of the world. I consider myself as not at all in the world, but I daily and hourly strive and pray to walk with God, and have my conversation in heaven; and so far as I look to the secret exercises of my mind from morning till night, it is so in a very comfortable degree. I bless the name of the Lord for what He has done for my soul. All my care, all my anxiety, is for you and your children. Oh that the Lord would answer prayer for you and for them! Give my cordial love to Letty and the boys. I wish she may every day grow more spiritual, more humble, and more heavenly-minded. Oh that I could see something like seriousness in the boys!"

In a subsequent letter he gives expression to an opinion

on religious biography in which many will concur:—" I have just been reading the Life of Mr Boswell. It has affected me very much. I have always found the lives and experiences of great and good men to do me more good than any other books, except the Bible. The lives of learned and holy men are the most profitable of all books to a minister."

In reference to this visit to Surrey, he says,—" I stand astonished to think how good the Lord has been to me, and how He has carried me through my work." Yet, at times, he was conscious of great feebleness. Speaking of one of his Sabbath exercises, he says,—" Yesterday morning I preached fifty-five minutes, with as much self-possession, and as loud, and every way as comfortably as I could wish. I soon found out the reason. They told me many, many prayers had been put up for me. All seemed pleased to see and to hear me." It was not without great difficulty that he fulfilled this engagement, and he felt—as it proved—that it must be the last time he attempted these services.

While in London, Mr Bull was invited by Mr W. Wilson to meet his son-in-law, the Rev. Daniel Wilson, afterwards Bishop of Calcutta.

Before he returned home, my grandfather went for a short time to Brighton. He says,—" Upon the whole, my visit to Brighton gives me more pleasure than pain. I am glad I am here, and I hope it will be useful to others; but I long to be home again." The chapel was crowded when he preached, and amongst his hearers was the widow of the Rve. Charles Wesley. Mr Bull's likeness was exhibited in the shops, and many told him they should weep when he left. Speaking of all this, he says,—"I hope a blessing has attended my visit; that is all I want."

Immediately after his return, he thus writes from London:—"The sea-air very much disordered me, but I worked hard every morning and evening for an hour. The Lord was with me, and I was comfortable, very comfortable in my soul, nor less so in my external accommodations. Every possible attention was shewn me, and a sedan-chair constantly attended me to and from the chapel. Still, I felt I could not live a fortnight in that situation. At length, however, I got away, to the no small grief of many. We had forty or fifty every morning and evening. Most of them came from town, and all of them knew me very well. Mr Pellatt did not miss one opportunity. However, at length, we got away. Mrs Johnson and her servant, Mr Pellatt and myself, had the whole coach. We set off yesterday morning exactly at nine o'clock, dined at Reigate at two, and had a very good dinner; stayed an hour to smoke my pipe. I prayed, and preached a sermon in the coach, and spent the day in holy and heavenly contemplation. It was much like a Sabbath day. We got to Mr Bateman's about nine o'clock. Mr Pellatt would pay all my expenses."

In a subsequent part of the letter, referring to a marriage of some of his friends, he says,—"I believe it will be kept at Richmond. I also am daily counting on a marriage, but it will be the marriage of the Lamb. If I live to come home, I shall be willing to get ready and be gone. My wedding clothes are already made, and Jesus is waiting to put them on me. It is an object of daily attention with me, and of earnest expectation."

On another occasion, when he was in some trouble, he writes thus:—"If I were to wish for death from a principle of love to the Lord Jesus Christ, and pray for it on that ground from a desire to be with Christ, this would be commendable and praiseworthy; but if I wish for death merely to get out of trouble, and because I am uneasy, this is wicked,—to want to die merely to get out of trouble, and therefore I do not wish it. I will not pray for death because troubles are come. I will rather say, 'Most gladly therefore will I rather glory in my infirmities, that the power of Christ may rest on me.' And if my troubles will add to his glory, let them come and welcome."

In a letter written to his son, when in London at the beginning of 1811, he says,—"I am to dine to-day at ——'s, to baptize his child. I shall have a little discourse on Christ being carried to the temple to be dedicated to the Lord, as this dedication contains all that I believe about baptism. I shall note the shameful abuses of this ordinance—(1.) by making it a saving ordinance, as containing a regeneration, as the Church does; and, (2.) by making one particular mode of it a term of Christian fellowship and communion amongst believers, as the Baptists do; and both parties making an idol of it, at the expense of everything else that relates to the new birth, a change of heart and life, and the whole work of the Spirit."

In the same letter, he speaks of his bodily weakness :—

" But as to my mind, I am calm, resigned, and easy, waiting for my change, but in no way uncomfortable. I know whom I have believed, and He is faithful and cannot deny Himself. My soul pants hard after Him. I have just walked a mile in the garden, and am wonderfully fatigued by it."

Mr Bull soon afterwards was attacked by a violent fit of the gout. It was, however, subsiding, and he tells his son that his medical friend speaks favourably of it. "As to the rheumatism, which seems to me as if it would for the present take away the use of my limbs, he made no remark; so let that stand in the account-current with old age, &c. 'Tis my mercy that I am not alarmed, I am not cast down. I know from whom it all comes, and I hope I love Him for all his ways, and can be thankful to see Him, though He hides Himself in the gout and rheumatics. I think I love Him, and can in the main approve Him in all things." He adds,—" Remember my tobacco, my tobacco-stopper, and almanac, and any other pretty plaything you can think of for me. But give yourself as little trouble about me as possible, for you give yourself quite enough for other people, much more than I would do; but that's your infirmity."

Again writing to my father in London, in the month of May, he says,—" Pray don't run about after the Missionary rout to endanger your health, about which you are never as careful as you should be. I pray the Lord Jesus Christ to look upon you, and be with you by his Holy Spirit. Keep close to the Lord in secret prayer. Oh, how do I wish you both to get safely, comfortably, honourably, and usefully, through this miserable world! You see daily much of the wickedness and folly of the world about you, and even in the religious world how much is there to lament and mourn over! May you and yours be preserved from its evil influences, and be brought safe to glory!"

Mr Bull was asked again to visit Surrey. "I fear," he says, "you did not speak with sufficient firmness to Mr Hill about my incapacity to go to Surrey. I cannot at present think for a moment of leaving home any more, unless I should recover a larger portion of strength than I now possess."

Towards the summer, my grandfather's spirits at least seemed to have revived, and at the earnest request of a very old friend, he visited Portsmouth, and returned home by way of Reading and London, preaching wherever he went, sometimes in the pulpit, and sometimes in the parlour, and delighting all his friends by his holy and interesting conversation.

He was very much pleased with his intercourse with Dr (then Mr) Bogue. "Mrs Bogue, a most excellent woman, told me she had heard some of my letters to Lady St John. She sent for all her children for me to see them."

Again,—"Last night I preached for Mr Bogue, but my mind was in no state of preparation for this blessed work. It was a poor broken piece of business, so far as I was concerned; but you know the Lord Jesus Christ can turn dust into gold, and make something out of nothing. I committed it to Him by fervent prayer. As for self, let that be sacrificed; let men say, 'This poor old man, far-fetched and dear-bought, was not worth having.' Be it so,—if Jesus is but glorified, I am satisfied."

My grandfather seemed to feel his long distance from home:—"The awful question, whether I shall ever reach home, hangs upon my mind with a dark gloom. I strive to put it away. The thought of dying from home fills me with horror. Still, I hope I am willing to die when and where the Lord sees fit. If my life is spared to see home again, I shall exceedingly rejoice for many things, and most of all to see and embrace you and all yours, whom I love to my very heart."

In a different mood he writes from Reading :—"I am now fallen into the very lap of love and indulgence; there are so many friends here that seem to love me, that I shall be very much taken up. I must preach to-night, but how I know not." Mr Bull visited an old friend, Mr French, at Midgham Hall, near Reading, and addressed his men at their harvest-home. He returned to Reading to preach the following evening, and next morning he had a large company of ladies and gentlemen to hear him expound. He had, he says, "a sharp battle to fight with invitations to dine with one, to drink tea with another; but I fought hard and got the day, so that I shall go nowhere. The people will kill me with kindness."

Spite of all his nervous fears, Mr Bull reached home in safety early in October. In some of the letters written during this journey, are many most wise and pious counsels about "the godly upbringing" of "the poor dear boys," as he fondly calls his grandchildren.

The year 1812 was of importance from the steps which

were then taken to continue the Theological Institution at Newport. Mr Thornton's legacy terminated with the life of my grandfather. He was manifestly drawing near his end. An effort was accordingly made to give the Institution a more permanent character. This was attended with success; and it was continued, first under the presidency of my father, assisted by myself, till the year 1842, when the Rev. John Watson, (afterwards of Hackney,) and subsequently the Rev. Wm. Froggat, undertook its charge. At length a very peculiar concurrence of circumstances, which it seemed impossible at the time to overrule, led to its virtual dissolution—a great loss, as many have thought, to the Church, and certainly to this neighbourhood. This Institution was the means, during its continuance, of sending forth about a hundred men into the Christian ministry.

It may be supposed that it was no small comfort to my grandfather to know that an Institution, in which he had felt so great an interest, would be continued after his removal.

In writing to his son in London, in January 1813, Mr Bull says,—"Tell me every day where you go, what you do, and how you manage to keep religion alive in your soul amidst all the whirligigism of your situation,—I might have said the teetotumism, for I think your brains must very much resemble a teetotum or a whirligig. The Lord help you! Do try to think, to read, to pray. Think of God, of Christ, of death, of the vast uncertainty of life, and think of vast unchangeable eternity." Again, —"I want to have my son perfect, quite perfect in wisdom, prudence, discretion, and everything that is good; but, alas! that you never will be, unless you turn Methodist. It is, after all, much better to be like Jesus Christ, because in Him dwelleth all possible perfection, and He is the only perfect character in the universe. Oh, pray incessantly to be more and more like Christ, and then I'll tell you how far you will be perfect—viz., just so far as Christ dwelleth in you, and no further. But He never did, I think He never will, dwell in any mere man to such a degree as to amount to *sinless perfection*, because that which is bred in the bone will never be out of the flesh. To be perfect, you must put off your earthly tabernacle. But, as excellent Mr Newton used to tell his hearers, you need not be afraid, for you may go a great way further in following Christ before you will be in any danger of breaking your head against the wall of sinless perfection."

Speaking of himself in another letter,—"My spirits are so weak that I find it difficult to fill up my paper. I am chin-deep (not in the Slough of Despond, but) in a second childhood, both of body and mind. . . . Last night, with the help of Watts and Doddridge, I got through, with the Divine blessing, I may say tolerably well for seventy-four."

It was my grandfather's habit, during his latter years, to read very much in the night, to relieve his long hours of wakefulness, and on one of these occasions, having gone to sleep, the candle fell on the table and burnt a large hole in it, but providentially no further evil resulted.

We quote the following passage from a letter of this period. It is addressed to my father:—" I am always with you in thought, and often pray for you; but I wish my spirits were not quite so low. I think it is owing in great part to my being so much alone, and reading what does not suit me just at this time, [from another letter he seems to refer to one of Dr Watts' Works.] I cannot walk much, and I cannot go out to see anybody. How are these things to be amended? I can think of nothing but flannel and patience. This wandering gout, as Cullen calls it, is very discouraging. But what says my great Lord and Master to it all? I know any change in my bodily circumstances makes no change in his love, nor in his wisdom, nor in his faithfulness, nor in his covenant. Sin is the parent of affliction, but affliction of itself is not sin. It's no sin to be afflicted. And whom the Lord loves, He loves to the end. He is the same unchangeable Jehovah. I see Him behind the cloud, and all is well, all will be well with me, quite to my own liking when I once get out of this body. I feel no anxiety about my departure. The Lord's time is the best time, and though I cannot rejoice, (for want of natural spirits,) yet I can believe, and trust, and rely upon Him; and I really do bless Him every evening and every morning for his dealings with me. Every pain is a mercy, my dejection is a mercy. I cannot trace the Lord Jesus, but I can trust Him. 'I am my Beloved's, and my Beloved is mine.' Josiah is very well, and very good after his kind. I wish he was always to be with me as he is now. Do William and Thomas [they were in London with my father and mother] discover any symptoms of seriousness? Give my love to them. Tell them I think of them, and pray for them every day." . . .

The year 1814 opened with very severe weather. An increase of infirmity was evident in my grandfather. Neither fires nor clothing could prevent his suffering from the cold. As if feeling a premonition that his end drew near, he desires his son to give his love to his friends in London, as he should never be able to see them again, unless they came to see him :—" Give my special remembrances and thanks to Mrs —— for a present of oysters. I would write, but I cannot write long hand. I have not ability to write common sense to anybody but you."

Speaking of some things that troubled him, he says,— " But the time is come when my energies are quite worn out. *Passivity* is now all that I am capable of; and my only work is to glorify God, either by doing or suffering the will of the Lord. ' Your strength is to sit still.' . . . Sin is the only thing that really grieves me, the plague of my own heart, the corruption of my own nature ; delivered from that, I should be the happiest man in the world."

No man was more diligent than Mr Bull in the right use of his time,—even to the last he felt he must be doing something for God. He writes thus to my father in London :—" It is very pleasant to me to know you are doing something in the service of Christ. If this is not attended to, you are awfully throwing away that precious talent which must soon be accounted for. Time is a great talent, of short duration, and it would be a sad thing to trifle it away. May you give up your account with joy, and not with shame, which latter, I often fear, will be my case another day, for I can make no apology for my indolent course of life. Age and bodily weakness are my only excuses."

It had always been the earnest wish and the oft-repeated prayer of my grandfather that his usefulness might be continued to the end of his life, and that prayer was answered. On Sunday morning, July 10, he entered his pulpit for the last time, preaching from Ps. xxvii. 9, " Hide not thy face far from me; put not thy servant away in anger: thou hast been my help; leave me not, neither forsake me, O God of my salvation!" A meeting of the friends of the Evangelical Institution was held on the Wednesday following. Mr Bull was present, and appeared very much to enjoy the services, expressing his great satisfaction at the prospects of its continuance. On the following day he dined at the very house, and with some members of the same family, where he had been entertained on the day of his arrival at Newport, just fifty years before. It was on the Saturday of this week that he was attacked with very alarming symptoms of a complaint from which he had never been long free, and which in a few days terminated his valuable life. From his knowledge of its character, he said if he could not get relief he should not be likely to continue above seven or eight days.

During the time of his illness his mind was remarkably calm and tranquil. " I am neither elevated by any lively transports, nor depressed by discouraging fears." " I am upon the Rock, I am upon the Rock!" was his repeated exclamation. " Death is but stepping out of the kitchen into the parlour."

Once, on the last day of his life, he complained of darkness; but, presently, when asked if he felt his mind composed, he replied, with great emphasis, " Yes; I am perfectly satisfied with the Lord's dealings." He suffered great bodily weakness, but his mental powers still retained all their vigour. Yet he found it difficult at times to fix his thoughts on any subject for more than a few moments, and observed on the folly of those who put off attention to their eternal interests to a dying hour. He said, " I can now only offer ejaculatory prayers;" but soon after he prayed aloud for some minutes, with great fervour, and expressed a desire, " that if the Lord was not pleased to answer those who at a prayer-meeting had been requesting his recovery, He would return a blessing on their own heads, and that he might be fitted for his change; but if his life should be continued, he begged that it might be for the Divine glory."

When his medical attendant was feeling his pulse, he said, " I shall not long continue in this state. My hours appear to be days. I understand better than ever the *tedium vitæ* of Horace. Time moves slowly; I wait for its hastier flight to bear me to my rest." When very near his end, he regretted the irregularities there had sometimes been in his preaching :—" I have occasionally tickled people's ears, when my sole aim should have been to affect the heart; yet," he added, " I hope I have been faithful to Christ and souls. I now find comfort in the doctrines I have preached."

He referred to several hymns which were a source of

comfort to him, especially to two of Dr Watts's, which he said were his princes,—

> "Dearest of all the names above," &c.;
> "Not all the blood of beasts," &c.

He repeated the whole of the hymn,—

> "With joy we meditate the grace," &c.

On the last day of his life he said, "Glory, glory, this Saturday."

To his eldest grandson, William, he said the same day, "The Lord bless you, and give you his Holy Spirit, and then you will want no good thing."

About half-past six (I can well remember it) he desired that his three grandchildren might be brought into the room. When we entered, he sent for three Bibles, and desired that one might be given to each of us as his dying bequest. But he had no strength to speak to us.

Around that bed of death, watching with mingled feelings,—feelings of sorrow for so great a loss, of gratitude to God for the wondrous peace of the dying saint,—stood his son, with his family, and some few others, who counted it an honour to minister to him. And as one friend was kindly fanning his fevered cheek, and another (one of his students, the Rev. G. Slade of Corsham, who still lives) supported his head, he was heard faintly to utter the words, "Bless the Lord," and then, sinking on the pillow, he breathed his last, without a groan. Thus calmly, like the setting of a summer sun, on the 23d of July, in his 77th year, did this most useful and holy man depart to his rest. It was, said one who stood by, more like a translation than a death. It is somewhat remarkable that the time of Mr Bull's departure was seven o'clock—which he used to call his canonical hour, or time of evening prayer.

My grandfather had often expressed a fear of death, lest he should die in despair, or under the influence of delirium, or in some way or other dishonour the gospel. But all these fears (and how often has it been the case?) were mercifully disappointed; for never, perhaps, did any one descend more serenely to the grave.

Great was the lamentation made for one so beloved and revered as my grandfather. The day of unrighteous persecution had to a great extent passed away, and all classes sought to do him honour. His people erected a very handsome tablet to his memory, which justly records his ability, his piety, and his long period of service to the Church of God.

CHAPTER XVII.

CONCLUSION.

IT is not my purpose in this chapter to attempt any formal analysis of my grandfather's character, or to deduce any of those conclusions of which the foregoing narrative is so suggestive : for many reasons this is unnecessary. There are, however, some things which could not be well embodied in the preceding pages which have yet to be mentioned, and without which this portraiture would be less complete than it may be made. These statements will, perhaps, be best introduced in connexion with a very general summary of the more salient points for which Mr Bull's character and life were conspicuous ; that is, so far as circumstances will allow, at a period so remote from the time of his death.

That Mr Bull was possessed of great intellectual powers is abundantly evident, and also that he was most assiduous in their cultivation. There is every reason to suppose that my grandfather was more than usually well-informed on almost every subject of human thought and inquiry. He was a very diligent student of the ancient classics, while he unquestionably excelled as a Hebrew scholar. Theology, however, in all its departments was the study of his life, and occupied his best and most profound thoughts. Few men, perhaps, read more extensively and more carefully than he did. Amongst other books, he perused the whole of the Fathers, and, I think, went through Augustine more than once. Night and day, at home and abroad, he read, always making notes in his own books. His library was large and rich especially in books of Biblical criticism and general theology.

His conversational powers were very remarkable, and his vivacity and humour scarcely ever forsook him, even to the last. His extensive knowledge, his brilliant imagination and ready wit, and, above all, his deep piety, rendered his society always attractive, and the delight of those who were favoured with it.

Whether the poet Cowper had any reference to his friend Mr Bull, I know not, but his lines in "Conversation" most aptly describe the characteristics of which I have just spoken :—

> " Who, when occasion justified its use,
> Had wit as bright as ready to produce,
> Could fetch from records of an earlier age,
> Or from philosophy's enlighten'd page,
> His rich materials, and regale your ear
> With strains it was a privilege to hear :
> Yet above all his luxury supreme,
> And his chief glory, was the gospel theme."

Some of my grandfather's sallies of wit have been preserved, and one of them, which I have often heard, may be given as a specimen. There was a person in the town who was rather given to say things which he, at all events, thought smart. Carrying his gun one morning, he passed Mr Bull as he stood at his door, and said to him, "I am going to shoot a greater fool than myself, if I can find him." "Then," said my grandfather, "you had better go home, Mr Knibb, and have your breakfast first."

Mr Bull partook of the eccentricity of the times in which he lived, and sometimes he said and did rather strange things in the pulpit—things which in some instances were afterwards a source of grief to him. Thus, on one occasion, just as he was concluding his sermon in the afternoon, and in the midst of an eloquent appeal which commanded the silent attention of his congregation, a female servant, regardless of everything else but getting her mistress's tea ready immediately upon her return home, rose up from her seat to pass through the length of the crowded gallery. My grandfather was annoyed at the unseemly disturbance thus created, and said to her, in a tone of authority, "Sit down, my good woman, sit down. It's no matter if Mrs Arthur's tea-kettle does not boil. I have not done yet." Mrs Arthur sat just beneath. She was a short-tempered woman, and, probably, not a little offended.

His illustrations were sometimes rather homely, but their design was to impress the truth he wished to convey. Thus, in speaking of that passage in Isaiah of those who draw sin as with a cart-rope, "Ay," said he, "a cable rope. But many of you don't know what a cable rope is. Why," pointing to one of his hearers, " it's a rope as thick as ——'s thigh." He would speak of people whose knees became as hard as horn by kneeling to pray.

He was once preaching at Surrey Chapel on 1 Cor. iii. 11, "Other foundation can no man lay than that is laid, which is Jesus Christ;" when, after proceeding in a strain of powerful eloquence, he suddenly paused, and said, in very familiar tones, "The people of Newport are erecting a new bridge there, and have had to go deeper than was intended, that the foundation might rest upon a rock. But that must yield at last; time will destroy it. But my text speaks of a foundation eternally secure. The Rock of Ages never moves."

Mr Bull was very notable for his punctuality, and especially particular in not exceeding his time in preaching. During one of his last visits to the Tabernacle, and thinking, I suppose, that "old age was garrulous," he desired the clerk, when he had been preaching forty-five minutes, to come up to the pulpit and let him know. He did so, and my grandfather thanked him aloud, and said he would conclude immediately. He used to say, it was of no use to talk to people about their souls when they began to think about their dinner. On one occasion he, however, purposely exceeded his time, and he saw some of the people stealing a glance at the clock. "Ah," he said, "I see you looking at the clock; but some of you have got into the habit of coming late, and I am resolved you shall not cheat God Almighty out of his time, and so I shall go on a few minutes longer, and make up at the end of the service what has been lost at the beginning,"—a reproof not without its effect. He was in the habit of walking in his garden early on the Sabbath morning, and if he saw any behind the time at the seven o'clock prayer-meeting, he would say, " I hate laziness in the service of God."

In my grandfather's days, afternoon congregations were always large; and in summer time not unfrequently drowsiness would overcome the hearers. Observing this to be the case, on one occasion Mr Bull said, in a loud tone, " My chest aches very much, and I will sit down and rest till you are all awake, and then I will proceed." Another time, under similar circumstances, he paused, took up a Greek Testament, and began to read. The sleepers were at once aroused, and all looked on with wonder, and some thought " the old gentleman was struck." But, looking up from his book, he said, " Well, I thought you could understand Greek as well as English when you were asleep. Now I will put this aside, and go on with my sermon." Here is another story about sleepy hearers. My grandfather had a servant very subject to this infirmity, and he was resolved, if possible, to cure him of it. Towards the close of his sermon on one occasion, he saw the man very soundly asleep in the gallery. He told the congregation that he wished the usual hymn after the sermon to be omitted, and begged they would leave the chapel as quietly as possible, " because," he said, " I see my servant asleep, and I don't want you to awake him." The people did as they were requested, and the man was left to awake in an empty chapel. He was greatly annoyed, and dreaded to meet his master. But he never said a word to him, then or afterwards. This person told my informant, his nephew, who, within the last twenty years, inquired of him as to the accuracy of the story, that he never slept again during divine service, a positive dread coming over him whenever he was inclined to do so.

I may just add, that there are many tales of this class still current which are wholly without foundation. They may be true, perhaps, of others, but do not belong to the subject of our Memoir.

Apart from these eccentricities, my grandfather's preaching was characterised by most of those elements which give power to a sermon. The impression produced by his efforts was sometimes very extraordinary. His addresses were often very original, sometimes very elaborate and well-reasoned, always more or less eloquent, and characterised by a remarkable depth and earnestness of feeling. His quaint touches of thought and occasional familiarity of illustration added to their impression. Closely did he follow the example of the apostle in preaching Christ and Him crucified. His love to the Saviour—as is evident from his letters—was most ardent. Once in the pulpit, he quoted the words, "About the ninth hour, Jesus cried with a loud voice, saying, Eli, Eli, lama sabacthani," he covered his face with his hands, and burst into tears. Unable to conclude the sentence, he said, "You know the rest." Often he would speak of the blessedness of the heavenly world in the most glowing terms. It is only a few weeks since I was told by a very old lady, who distinctly remembered his preaching, that "when he spoke of heaven it was as if he carried you there. His imagination was wonderful."

My grandfather excelled very much in exposition, and the Psalms was a favourite book with him in this exercise.

His accurate critical acquaintance with the Scriptures, and his eminently devotional spirit, especially qualified him for this work. These expositions constituted a large part of his "parlour-preaching," with which his friends were so much edified.

One word about Mr Bull's manner in the pulpit. It was aided, no doubt, by the peculiar dignity of his appearance; but there was a solemnity and impressiveness about it, especially in his devotional exercises, that could not fail to arrest attention. There is a remarkable illustration of this, with which I have been furnished by my friend the Rev. W. Spencer, to whom I am indebted for some of the other incidents of this chapter. He says,—"After my settlement in the ministry at Holloway, a female, somewhat advanced in life, sought admission to church-fellowship. Conversing with her as to the means employed to awaken serious impressions, she told me she was in the habit of frequently worshipping at Surrey Chapel. 'On one occasion,' she said, 'the Rev. William Bull was the preacher, and I was so much struck with the manner in which he repeated that petition of the Lord's Prayer, " Forgive us our debts, as we forgive our debtors," that the impression never left me, and from that time I date my conversion to God.'"

It is scarcely necessary to add, that Mr Bull was exceedingly popular as a preacher, and continued to be so to the very last. Wherever he was known, his ministrations especially in the neighbouring towns, were attended by persons of all denominations of Christians. Abundant evidence has already appeared in proof of his great usefulnesss.

Not only his preaching but his administration of the ordinances of Baptism and the Lord's Supper was very impressive and edifying. "I have," says one of his old students "at this distant period, a very lively recollection of his ' sacred solemnity and fervent devotion,' when baptizing an infant. We all felt it was no unmeaning ceremony, but an ordinance which, by him administered, had a holy, elevating, and instructive influence." He baptized his three grandchildren in public, and preached an appropriate sermon on each occasion.

Little more need be said of the character of Mr Bull's piety. It may unquestionably be described as eminent. Much religious thought, much reading of a devotional character, and much prayer, with the subduing influence of almost constant affliction, seem to have contributed to this blessed result. He never drove out, which at one period was his daily habit, without imploring the Divine blessing. "By his earnest request," says Mr Slade, (one of his students,) "I was his constant companion during the vacation in which he died. It was my daily custom to lead him round the garden, and frequently to drive him round Buryfield. At such times he invariably lifted up his soul to God, and prayed aloud for the Divine blessing upon his son, his son's family, his church and students, especially that the latter might become able and devoted ministers of the Cross."

Of the great affection and tenderness of feeling ever manifested by my grandfather, many proofs have been already given. His heart was truly bound up in the life and the welfare of his son, and that love descended upon his son's sons. I have myself personally but a faint remembrance of it, I was so very young when he died; but I know from other sources how great that affection was, how happy he was to have us with him, and how deeply concerned he was for our temporal and spiritual welfare. I am told, too, what kind words and loving acts he had for all the young people about him, and what a gratification even a word from the venerable man was to them, and how he would not unfrequently have a party of them to tea with him, entertain them with his pleasant talk, and let them romp as they pleased; so, no wonder they grew up to love and to venerate him.

One touching instance of the tenderness of his heart has been communicated to me. Not long after the death of Mrs Bull, my grandfather was applied to to baptize the child of one of his members. He asked, " Is the boy ill, and likely to die ?" " No, sir, he seems a very healthy child." " Then, how can you ask me to baptize him just now, and dear Mrs Bull so lately dead ? Why, if I were to go into that table pew, with her remains beneath my feet, I should swoon away. It must be left till I get a little better."

My grandfather's external appearance, like that of several members of his family, was very striking. He was above the ordinary height, his figure well proportioned, and his whole manner and bearing dignified and commanding. His countenance beamed with intelligence and kindness, and his bright and penetrating eye often sparkled with wit and humour. Mr Bull's dress was, of course, clerical. He wore a full-bottomed white wig, a sort of bishop's frock, and his whole attire, down to the broad silver buckles of his shoes, was characteristic of the times, —a truly English and manly costume. On two occasions he was mistaken for an Episcopal dignitary. In Dublin, a poor Catholic kneeled before him in the street, and besought his blessing. A most worthy man in London, whose manner was sometimes rather brusque, had treated my grandfather on one occasion somewhat curtly, on which a friend of Mr Bull's remarked to him, "Why, there is that in your very appearance (to say nothing of your past acquaintance) which should produce as much reverence in his behaviour towards you, as was manifest in Alexander upon his seeing the high priest at Jerusalem."

Great was the affection and esteem in which Mr Bull was universally held. The foregoing pages give ample testimony to this fact. The attachment of many of his students was most ardent. The late Rev. R. Elliott of Devizes, having heard that my grandfather was at Newbury, (it was the last time he went from home,) writes to my father, "Had I known he was within five hours' ride of me, I should have gone to see him. Boswell never felt a greater pleasure at the sight of Johnson than I do at the sight of your father. What a venerable pile it is! how majestic!"

At home, and all round the neighbourhood, the few who remember him, or have heard him spoken of in their homes, say he was almost worshipped. I feel it a great honour to have sprung from such a man, and a great pleasure and privilege to be permitted even thus feebly to portray his character, and to speak of the scenes in which he mingled. Yet, whatever my grandfather was, no man was more ready than he to ascribe it all to the grace of God. Humility was one of the leading features of his character; and in bringing this work to an end, I trust I can say, that my great aim has been to glorify God in him.

THE END.

was, no man was more ready than he to ascribe it all to the grace of God. Humility was one of the leading features of his character; and in bringing this work to an end, I trust I can say, that my great aim has been to glorify God in him.